THE KEEPER'S SHADOW

DENNIS FOON

 annick press
toronto + new york + vancouver

Text © 2006 Dennis Foon

Annick Press Ltd.

We acknowledge the support of the Canada Council for the Arts, the Ontario Arts Council, and the Government of Canada through the Book Publishing Industry Development Program (BPIDP) for our publishing activities.

Edited by Pam Robertson
Copy edited by Elizabeth McLean
Cover and interior design by Irvin Cheung/iCheung Design
Cover illustration by Susan Madsen

Cataloging in Publication
Foon, Dennis, 1951 –
    The keeper's shadow / by Dennis Foon.

(The Longlight legacy)
ISBN-13: 978-1-55451-028-3 (bound)
ISBN-10: 1-55451-028-7 (bound)
ISBN-13: 978-1-55451-027-6 (pbk.)
ISBN-10: 1-55451-027-9 (pbk.)

    I. Title. II. Series: Foon, Dennis, 1951 – Longlight legacy; 3

PS8561.O62K43 2006   jC813'.54   C2006-901780-8

Printed and bound in Canada

Published in the U.S.A. by   Distributed in Canada by   Distributed in the U.S.A. by
Annick Press (U.S.) ltd.   Firefly Books Ltd.   Firefly Books (U.S.) Inc.
                             66 Leek Crescent   P.O. Box 1338
                             Richmond Hill, ON   Ellicott Station
                             L4B 1H1   Buffalo, NY 14205

Visit our website at **www.annickpress.com**

This book is dedicated to
A. Von Brutical a.k.a. Ken Foon

IN THE SHROUDED VALLEY, THE PEOPLE OF LONGLIGHT
EVADED DESTRUCTION. FOR SEVENTY-FIVE YEARS THEY
QUIETLY THRIVED, ISOLATED FROM THE WORLD, NURTURING
A SMALL FLAME OF HOPE. IT TOOK LESS THAN ONE HOUR
FOR THEM TO BE ANNIHILATED.

—THE BOOK OF LONGLIGHT

The Keeper's Shadow is the third and final volume of *The Longlight Legacy*.

The first volume, *The Dirt Eaters*, tells the story of Roan—who, after failing to stop a raider from capturing his younger sister, Stowe, wakes to find his village destroyed and its inhabitants slaughtered.

Roan is soon discovered by Saint, the leader of a sect of warrior-Brothers devoted to a god known as the Friend. Under Brother Wolf's tutelage, Roan begins training in the art of war, determined to wreak revenge on those who massacred his people. During this time, he has experiences on a separate plane of reality—the Dreamfield—where mysterious beings, Dirt Eaters, advise him and lead him to discover the dark truth Saint is concealing.

Roan flees into the uninhabitable lands of the Devastation, where he meets Lumpy, a young man disfigured by Mor-Tick scars. Attacked by the Brothers, the two escape to the subterranean community of Oasis, where they forge friendships with Kamyar the Storyteller, Orin the Librarian, and Lelbit. But stirred by a new vision, Roan and Lumpy leave Oasis and journey to the village of Fairview.

There a healer (and Dirt Eater) named Alandra enlists

their help in saving fourteen special children from certain death. After a final battle that ends in Saint's demise, Roan, Lumpy, Alandra, and their precious cargo reach a safe haven, Newlight.

Freewalker, volume two, begins in Newlight, where Alandra has fed Dirt to the children. But after she takes them into the Dreamfield, they mysteriously fall into a deep coma. Roan, angry with Alandra and the Dirt Eaters, departs with Lumpy for the City in search of a cure for their young charges...and to find his sister, Stowe.

Stowe has been adopted by the Keeper of the City, Darius, and made an icon, worshipped by the masses—a role invented for her by Master Querin, the City's propaganda minister. Although her beloved mentor, Willum, does his best to nurture and protect her, Stowe's consciousness is invaded by a Dirt Eater named Ferrell in a Dreamfield battle, and she becomes increasingly unstable.

Meanwhile Roan and Lumpy meet a young shaman, Mabatan. A fellow Dreamwalker who also does not eat Dirt, she shows Roan how the Masters and the Dirt Eaters have partitioned the Dreamfield and built structures that have caused a huge rift in the Dreamfield itself. The fissure is tenuously held together by none other than the fourteen children. And the only way to save them is to stop the Masters' and Dirt Eaters' manipulations.

Determined to contact his sister and enlist her help, Roan and his friends travel to the City. But the meeting between the siblings is a disaster—in an explosion of emotion, Stowe wreaks havoc and escapes from the City. Captured by a treacherous Brother named Raven, she is taken to Governor Brack in Fairview. But before Brack and Raven can exploit her, Stowe slays them both and collapses.

Since Roan must continue his quest to heal the rift, he entrusts Willum and Mabatan with finding his sister. Sailing off on wings manufactured by the Gunthers, the techno-slaves of the City, Roan and Lumpy reach the secret mountaintop home of the Apsara, where Saint's life partner, Kira, now lives. There, Roan journeys deep into the Dreamfield to a place where Saint himself is bound in torment. Revealing Darius's Throne, he urges Roan to accept his fate and lead the battle against the Masters of the City.

In *The Keeper's Shadow*, Roan struggles to unite disparate peoples against the City, and discovers that in the face of unimaginable evil, it's necessary to question everything you believe in order to hold out hope for a future.

Characters of the Longlight Legacy

THE FARLANDS

Roan: He and his little sister, Stowe, were the only survivors when raiders annihilated their peaceful village of Longlight. Befriended by Saint, leader of the Brothers, Roan violently broke with them when he found out that they were responsible for the destruction of Longlight. The mysterious Rat and the Dirt Eaters introduced him to the alternate reality called the Dreamfield, but after rescuing fourteen special children—the Novakin—Roan ceases to trust them also. He balks at prophecies that single him out as a leader, but now the war against the City approaches, and Roan has to choose.

Lumpy: A survivor of the Mor-Ticks, voracious insects that left him hideously scarred and reviled by people who assume he is a carrier of this plague. Roan was close to death in the Devastation when Lumpy saved him, and they've been fast friends since.

The Novakin: Fourteen children who were saved from Darius by Roan, Alandra, and Lumpy, only to fall into a deep coma. While their physical bodies are maintained in the settlement of Newlight, their Dreamforms of rusting iron are bridged across the abyss, holding the Dreamfield together.

THE WAZYA

Also known as Those Who Wander, the Wazya are keepers of the earth and the Dreamfield. A very ancient race, they mostly travel alone, are well hidden, and are believed to be mythical. Their special relationship with the white crickets is also the stuff of legend.

Khutumi (*dreamform: Rat*): In his human form, he is rarely seen and lives in a very isolated spot only known to Mabatan. In his Dreamfield form, he is well known to Roan and the Dirt Eaters.

Mabatan (*dreamform: blue rabbit*): Friend to Roan and Lumpy. She knows and speaks the language of the Hhroxhi, and has explored much of this world and the Dreamfield. Like all Wazya, she does not require Dirt to travel. And having seen what has been done to both worlds as a result of its use, she has learned to despise it.

THE BROTHERS

Saint: Prophet of the Brothers and founder of the cult of the Friend. He hoped to join forces with Roan and topple the City, but he could never gain Roan's trust, and died in a last-ditch effort to win him as an ally.

Brother Wolf: Acting chief of the Brothers since Saint's demise, he is their instructor of martial arts. It was Wolf who gave Roan his hook-sword; made by Wolf's father, it is a twin of his own.

Brother Asp: The healer. During Roan's sojourn with the Brothers, Asp took him under his wing.

Brother Stinger: Spiritual leader of the Brothers, he teaches sand-painting, a form of deep focus and meditation.

Brother Raven: Sporting a bird mask and feathered cloak, he "negotiated" with towns for their children. Although he was in Saint's inner circle, Raven was Darius's spy, and ultimately betrayed the Brothers.

Feeder: The Brothers' cook, a failed novitiate.

THE HHROXHI (pronounced Ha-row-she)

Also known as the "Blood Drinkers," the Hhroxhi dwell beneath the earth through a network of polished tunnels (thrusalls) that provide quick transport. They are blood-drinking albinos, who file their teeth into fangs and sever their ears in order to separate themselves from those they detest: surface-living humanity. They revere the white cricket and preserve the prophecies, although many have doubts.

Mhyzah (*Ma-hi-zeh*): Friends with Lumpy, she taught him her language and enlisted him to be a Gyoxhip (*zho-ship*). Many Blood Drinkers are offended by her openness to humanity and violently resist her desire to assist Roan in the war against the City.

Xxisos (*She-soss*): Leader of the Hhroxhi, he knows the myths about Roan and Stowe and the Novakin, and has lent his support to Roan's cause.

Qrixxis (*Kree-shuss*): The most vehement of the human-haters, he spearheads the opposition to helping with the war against the City.

THE APSARA

Descendents of one of the original four rebel armies, the Apsara were believed to have been exterminated by Darius. In fact, only the men were killed. The surviving women went into hiding, creating a secret warrior army and infiltrating key political positions through strategic marriages. Their children, both male and female, are raised covertly in their true home, the Caldera.

Ende: Leader of the Apsara, sworn enemy of the City, she is a highly skilled warrior and teacher of martial arts and meditation to not only the Apsara but any warrior committed to bringing down the City.

Kira: Second-in-command of the Apsara, for years she lived in a Farlands village as the chosen mate of Saint, Prophet of the Brothers.

THE DIRT EATERS

One of the four original rebel armies, most Dirt Eaters dwell in Oasis, hidden caves that give them and the other residents perpetual youth.

Alandra (*dreamform: goat-woman*): A young healer, raised by the Dirt Eaters and placed by them in the town of Fairview to await the coming of Roan and the Novakin, she was instrumental in their escape and helped establish their safe haven, Newlight. But following the instructions of the Dirt Eaters, she fed the Novakin dirt, and lost Roan's trust.

Sari (*dreamform: mountain lion*): Spokesperson for the Dirt Eaters of Oasis.

Haron (*dreamform: wolverine*): Leader of one rebel army that fought Darius, he brought his people to Oasis.

Ferrell (*dreamform: lizard*): The Dirt Eaters' greatest architect, he is responsible for building both the Foresight Academy and Dreamfield construction known as the Wall. He invaded Stowe's Dreamfield form in an attempt to control her.

Orin: Historian and librarian at Oasis.

THE STORYTELLERS

Although based in Oasis, they mainly travel the Farlands, undermining the authority of the Masters through their tales and plays. Book lovers, they adore the library of Oasis, but do not trust the Dirt Eaters.

Kamyar: Leader of the Storytellers, he travels with a small group.
Talia: The most hot-tempered of the band, she loves a fight.
Mejan: The actress, spy, and diplomat.
Dobbs: Gentle, large, and warm-hearted.

THE GOVERNORS

Governor Brack: Ruler of the eastern Farlands. Lived in Fairview until he was killed by Stowe.

Governor Selig: Ruler of the southern Farlands. Does not know his beloved wife is an Apsara.

THE PHYSICIANS

Othard and **Imin:** Former Dirt Eaters, they now tend to the residents of the Farlands.

THE CITY

Stowe: After the fall of Longlight, Stowe was taken to the City, where she became the adopted daughter of Darius, the Keeper of the City, and a beloved icon for all. Fed excessive amounts of Dirt, Stowe's powers—and instability—grew fast. In a Dreamfield encounter with the Dirt Eaters, she was possessed by the Dirt Eater Ferrell. Fighting for her sanity, Stowe escaped from the City only to be abducted by the insidious Brother Raven and Governor Brack.

Willum: After a spiritual search in the Devastation, he went to the City, where he worked his way up, slowly gaining the Masters' trust until he achieved the position he was destined for: to become Stowe's Primary—her protector and teacher.

THE MASTERS OF THE CITY
Also known as the "Turned," the Masters are very old, kept alive by transplanted body parts obtained from the children of the Farlands. After the wars, they came to power in Year I A.C. with the formation of the Conurbation, and it is now Year III A.C. The Masters' Dreamforms are raptors, carnivorous birds of prey.

Darius, also known as Keeper of the City, Archbishop of the Conurbation, the Eldest: Together with Roan's great-grandfather and namesake, Roan of the Parting, he rebuilt a city destroyed by wars and an asteroid impact. After Roan of the Parting discovered the Dirt, they had a violent disagreement on its use that led to a civil war. Darius ruthlessly destroyed the four armies that rebelled under Roan of the Parting's influence and has ever since been intent on megalomaniacal control of both the earth and the Dreamfield.

Kordan: Stowe's former tutor and Darius's most devoted henchman. Frustrated by Kordan's failures, Darius maimed him in the Dreamfield, resulting in the paralysis of half his face.

Master Fortin: Head of COOPERATION UNLIMITED, the Enabler Factory. Enablers are a kind of mind control device developed by Darius to be used extensively on the Clerics, but lately more and more on the public at large.

Master Querin: Master of Inculcation, he oversees the City's propaganda and created the cult of Our Stowe as a means to control the population. Believed by many to be equal in power to Darius, Querin is deeply feared by all, including the Keeper himself.

Clerics: The City's police force/army.

THE GUNTHERS
Their ancestors were the survivors of one of the four rebel armies defeated by Darius. They went into hiding in the City, becoming the bespectacled drudges who maintain its power grid. Unbeknownst to the Masters, they have secretly established a great underground library and research facility.

Gunther Number Six: A leader of the Gunthers, he is short, balding, and rumpled, and a great friend to both Kamyar and Willum.

Gunther Number Seventy-Nine: Inordinately curious, she is a bit of a silent rebel and studies white crickets.

Gunther Number Fifty-One: An ill-tempered traditionalist.

Number One Hundred Twenty-Six, also known as Algernon: A multitalented and long-missing Gunther, he has committed the major offense of taking a name.

contents

the Living and the Dead

BEND EVERY SENSE TO THE KNOWING of WHAT HAS PASSED
AND WHAT IS ABOUT TO COME. READ THE LINES of ENERGY
THAT TRAVEL BENEATH YOUR feet for ALL THE TRUTHS
THEY ARE ABLE TO REVEAL. THEN YOU WILL fIND WHAT YOU
SEARCH for.

—THE way of THE wazya

HUNGER SNAPS AT THE EDGE of Willum's consciousness. Unwilling to allow anything to distract him from his search, he has not eaten since before the last full moon. Watching it waver now at the edge of the western horizon, the curve of the earth's shadow almost slicing it in half, he hopes he has not arrived too late.

He feels Mabatan slip silently beside him. He could not have accomplished the journey so quickly without her. It had taken her only a day to track him and since then it is she who has kept watch, steering him clear of any danger, so that he might chase, without interruption, the clouded stream of energy Stowe has left behind.

In the cold night air, a fetid stench wafts up from the lake. Here the trail ends. Standing hidden amongst the red stick trees of this forest, he assesses the gates of Fairview.

"There, on the south side, the guard sleeps," he whispers. And without hesitation he slinks across the open field to scale the wall spiderlike, trusting Mabatan to follow close behind.

The town slumbers and under the steady hum of its street lamps they easily navigate Fairview's web of streets unheard. As they approach the small cottage Willum has been seeking, he sees that its door has been left ajar. He stops, signals—two dead, two alive—and Mabatan takes out her knife.

The door is jammed against two dead men sprawled across the entryway behind it. Squeezing through the narrow gap, Willum silently maneuvers past the first of the bodies, but the second stops him. A feathered robe, a beaked mask: Raven. Acting on Darius's orders? Dried blood trails from the men's ears: Stowe's work.

Someone in the room has sensed him. A woman, crouched over Stowe. Before she can so much as turn her head, Willum leaps past a fallen table and seizes her by the waist. He hurls her toward Mabatan, who instantly pins her to the wall, dagger at her throat. The young woman, terrified, does not speak.

Willum holds the palm of his hand just above Stowe's forehead. Neither she nor Ferrell are awake but both are alive. Alive. Steadying himself, he opens his mind to the room and to the girl who only seconds ago occupied the space he crouches in now. Her scent and that of the house are similar…she lived here once.

"Hello, Alandra," Willum says, rising to face her. "Why have the Dirt Eaters sent you here when you are so needed elsewhere?"

The girl's terror hardens to a glare. "I don't know what you're talking about."

"You stink of Dirt," Mabatan grumbles as she reaches into a hidden pocket on the girl's sleeve. Pulling out a small satchel, she opens it.

"No!" the Dirt Eater cries, as Mabatan leans out the open door and scatters the satchel's contents into the wind. She watches coldly as Alandra desperately falls, wedging herself in the blocked door, frantic to scoop up what few particles remain.

A light goes on in the house opposite. Before curious eyes can spot them, Willum pulls Alandra back inside.

The Dirt Eater whirls on him. There is still the possibility that the girl may fight. "You don't know what you've done, how hard it is to get, how precious. Who are you people?"

Willum considers the situation pragmatically: time is of the essence. The bodies of the men must be disposed of. No trace of them or the method of death must remain. Stowe cannot travel in the state that she is in. She needs a healer's attention. Alandra must be persuaded to help them.

Softening his gaze, he pitches his voice to touch the Dirt Eater's heart. "We are here at Roan's request."

"I don't believe you."

"You don't believe that he would send someone to retrieve his sister?"

"I don't believe that he sent you. He would have come himself."

"If he could have come, then he would be standing here. Alandra. Look about you. At dawn this room must be clean and empty. No one must even guess at what transpired here. We must reach an agreement now or we will not get Stowe out of here alive. Would you be the cause of Roan's sister's death?"

"And what did transpire here, do you think?"

Willum takes a deep breath. The girl's tone betrays bitterness and confusion. He must tread gently. "Stowe is possessed by another life-force. He is compromising her sanity in his attempts to control her mind. Look at this room, the bruises on her body. The nature of the damage indicates her struggle was not with the dead men but within herself."

"But she was cooperating with them. Why would the Turned—"

"Not the Turned. She is possessed by a Dirt Eater."

Alandra shifts from one foot to the other. There it is. The hesitation he was waiting for. "That's not possible."

"I have heard of your abilities as a healer, Alandra. Stowe sleeps deeply; if you awaken her body, you will find the Dirt Eater I speak of. You will see the proof for yourself."

"What you're saying...it just can't be."

"If what I say is true, will you agree to help us get her out of here alive?"

The healer's gaze is steady, calm. "Yes."

"Good. I will attend to the disposal of the bodies." Seeing Mabatan about to protest, he signals that she is not to take her eyes off the Eater.

As his friend glides past him to stand vigil over the healer, his eyes fall again to the colorful feathers at his feet. Beautiful but ominously identifiable—people will know Raven was here. Still...that very thing might serve them well.

tHReSHOLD

WOLf, ASP, RAVEN, AND STINGER WERE THE PILLARS UPON WHICH SAINT CHOSE TO BALANCE HIS FAITH. RAVEN'S BETRAYAL WAS NOT UNEXPECTED BUT WHEN ASP WAS REVEALED A SPY, IT PROVED THE HARBINGER OF A NEW AGE FOR THE BROTHERS OF THE FRIEND.

—ORIN'S HISTORY OF THE FRIEND

THE SWORD THRUST NEARLY DISEMBOWELS ROAN. He spins back to avoid it, and in one fluid move brings his hook-sword down hard on the assailant's blade. A whip kick to the neck and the warrior clatters to the ground. But eight heavily armed attackers are still standing. He leaps forward, trying to break the gauntlet, but they're ready, swords held low, about to skewer him.

He circles, fanning the razor-sharp hook-sword around him, forcing them back. But as he whirls, the vision replays in his mind. *His sister consumed by fire.* What does it mean?

Cold metal whisks by his face. He lurches back, striking out, but he loses his balance and he's down, rolling back and forth to avoid the eight swords plunging at him.

Roan twists, jumps back on his feet, and feints to the left. He elbows one fighter in the neck, gets another attacker with a back kick. Only six warriors left but he's already panting. Not good.

His sister consumed by fire. Since the vision came to him late this morning he's been trying to decipher its meaning.

He remembers Stowe's voice cutting down the panicked crowd like a scythe at harvest. In that state, how could she avoid being detected by the Dirt Eaters? Would Willum and Mabatan be able to find her before someone from Oasis got to her? And even if they did, Stowe was so out of control, she might not be able to distinguish between friend and foe. Then there were the Clerics. They were sure to be out searching for her. He'd almost rather see her captured by the Dirt Eaters than back in Darius's claws.

Reaching deep within, he leaps and with a flurry of kicks and a swipe of his hook-sword, he finishes off two more warriors. Four left.

His sister consumed by fire. On their way to the Caldera, he could perceive her, feel her state of mind; but something in the rock here cloaks the sanctuary and he can sense nothing outside it. He grimaces in pain as a whip lashes him across the back. They've changed weapons. He steps forward, trying to get out of range, but another whip sings out, wrapping itself around his leg. He trips and feels the sting of another lash. Now they have his attention. He bolts up. Spinning, he twists the whips from his opponents and cuts them off before they can reach their swords. Chest heaving, sweat pouring off him, Roan stares at the eight Apsara warriors he's just defeated.

"Phew, that was almost embarrassing," says Kira, shaking her head. She holds out her hand, helping one of her clan to her feet. "You really are out of shape."

Roan offers his hand to another Apsara. "I won, didn't I?"

Kira pokes him in the gut with an iron-hard index finger. "Against a bunch of striplings! And they would have eviscerated you if you hadn't woken up. You've got to clear your mind. You should join the meditation tonight."

"If I survive the afternoon," says Roan ruefully.

"You will." Kira signals, releasing Roan's sparring partners. "Grandmother tells me your diplomatic skills are improving, so I doubt our guests will put your combat abilities to the test."

Roan laughs, embarrassed. "I think Ende has more faith in me than I deserve."

"Hope you're wrong, or Wolf and Stinger'll be eating you for supper."

"And Brother Asp?"

"He's receiving extremely detailed instructions in the set-up and maintenance of our hydroponic gardens and will be unable to attend. Between you and me, he seemed relieved, can't imagine why."

Kira winks, then smacks Roan hard on the back and leaves him toweling off his face, more than a little miserable. Earlier that day, when Brothers Wolf and Asp had appeared over the lip of the Caldera, he'd been so preoccupied with the dilemma of having to deal with them that he'd forgotten all about Lumpy's suggestion that Asp might be one of the Dirt Eaters. But the moment he'd smelled the Dirt, he knew his friend was right.

Roan had understood that if he accused Asp then and there, Wolf would cut the Dirt Eater down, no questions asked—and Roan had questions, lots of them. While he'd been considering his options, Brother Stinger had descended after a meditation at the summit of the Caldera and Roan had briefly considered seeking him as an ally. But putting his trust in one of the Brethren didn't seem wise, so he'd waited until they were whisked away to be fed, then had gone to talk with Ende. He wanted to make sure that if Asp was kept without Dirt, the Caldera's dark stone would cloak his presence from the Dirt Eaters, eliminating any immediate threat.

Roan was quietly relieved to find he had the Apsara leader's support, but that didn't mean the next few hours would be easy—in fact, quite the opposite.

The morning's mist is now high above the Caldera, the sun a golden haze. The brightly painted rock face is vibrant in this light and children are out playing—it's difficult not to be happy in the presence of so much color and life, but nothing could cheer Roan in the face of having to come to an agreement with the killers of his family.

Walking from the training field, he passes a stand of tall bamboo. Here, carved into black stone, is the cavern-like room housing the elegant mechanical wings that brought him and Lumpy to this dormant volcano. Seeing his glider glistening in the half-light, he's thrown back into the pure exhilaration of that flight.

The cry of a child momentarily stops his breath, but he quickly realizes the distant scream is one of laughter, not of fear or pain. He's jumpy. Ende's probably right when she claims that an ally doesn't need to be loved, that in times of war it is enough to be on the same side. But no matter how many times he goes over the reasons and justifications, an alliance with the destroyers of Longlight rankles. All the coaching in diplomacy doesn't make it any easier. Ende says "formality helps opposing parties reach agreement," but to him, using this new language of compromise feels a lot like lying, and he's not altogether sure that he'll fool the Brothers with it.

Edging closer, Roan glides his fingers over the translucent wings. Crafted to respond to his neural impulses, they were like an extension of himself...

"Don't even think about it." Lumpy, his arms crossed, is blocking the entrance of the cavern.

"I'm not," says Roan, stepping away from the wings. "Though I admit I don't like the idea of talking to those murderers."

"Yup, they're scary, alright," says Lumpy. "On the other hand, you did learn a lot from them."

"I don't know how I should take that."

"It's just...what they taught you could come in handy for what's ahead...maybe." Roan joins Lumpy out in the emerging sunlight. His friend's ravaged skin so resembles the lava-pocked rock that he almost looks carved from the Caldera. But the impression fades as soon as Lumpy speaks. "Remember that amazing general you told me about, the one who was the same age as you? You said that even though his bloodthirsty father had taught him how to fight, he still was able to listen to the sense his philosopher-teacher kept talking to him. Well, who says you can't fight alongside the Brothers, but use all you learned in Longlight to help you make the right decisions?"

"Alexander the Great was four years older than me when he started leading armies. His father was a conqueror. It was in his blood. Still, all that killing made him crazy in the end. And he was really young when he died."

"Well, maybe he wasn't such a good example."

"A fever paralyzed him so they thought he was dead. Some people believe his embalmers killed him."

"Yuck. But he did conquer a guy named Darius, didn't he—before they...stuffed him?"

"Let's hope we're as lucky with the first part...By the way, you were right about Asp."

"So I've heard. How're you planning to break the news to Wolf and Stinger?"

Roan stares out at the thick mist that cloaks this peak, wishing he were lost in it. He worries about what's expected of him. The shades of his parents told him his loathing of violence was his strength. Maybe they're right, but at the moment, he feels it's making him indecisive and weak.

"Guess you haven't figured that part out yet."

"All I know is I'm not going to open the discussions with it."

"You're not alone in this. You have powerful friends, like Ende—she wants to see you, by the way."

"Did she say why?"

"There's someone she wants you to talk to." Before Roan can form the question, Lumpy shakes his head. "That's all I know."

the awakening

WHEN THE DIRT EATERS BETRAYED ROAN OF THE PARTING,
WE WITHHELD OUR KNOWLEDGE FROM THEM. WHEN
FERRELL BUILT THEIR GREAT WALL, WE OPENLY CON-
DEMNED THEM. BUT WHEN THEY THREATENED ROAN OF
LONGLIGHT AND THE NOVAKIN, WE BECAME THEIR ENEMY.
                                        —THE WAY OF THE WAZYA

THE BLACK METAL IS COLD BESIDE MABATAN'S CALLOUSED FINGERS. She has made a silent promise to Willum and will plunge the knife through the Dirt Eater's heart if she must; but though she has imagined a moment like this many times, never once in these imaginings did her heart beat so fast or sweat slide over her skin like rain or her mind feel so angry and sad.

Last year her father had been injured in a Dirt Eater trap; he would never again be able to wander freely. This was why the call from Roan had come to her and not him. It was why she was here, weapon in hand, ready to kill if she must. Perhaps too ready.

Roan had believed this girl, barely older than Mabatan herself, would defend the Novakin's safety. But she betrayed Roan and deserted the children. Unable to contain her feelings, Mabatan finds herself blurting out, "You're a fool."

The healer twists awkwardly to look at her. "What?"

"You left the children in the hands of their enemies."

The girl's face becomes a stony white, ghostly like her

cave-living Dirt-eating friends. "Terre would never allow the children to be harmed."

"She may not be the one who is called to kill them."

"All the people in Newlight love those children. You don't know what you're talking about."

The Dirt Eater's voice is light, dismissive, but Mabatan can read the anger in the flush at her neck. "Not only a fool, but blind too," she whispers.

"I've got work to do," the healer snaps and reaches for her bag of medicines. Mabatan's grip on her dagger tightens. The Dirt Eater shifts to ensure Mabatan can observe her every movement. "The herbs aren't working. I have to try something else." There is an urgency in the healer's flicking fingers and the fear that rises in her shoulders, but Mabatan's father has often warned her of the Dirt Eaters' powers of persuasion; so she steadies her breath, alert for any evidence of deception.

Carefully unfolding the bundle she's taken from her bag, the healer thumbs through hundreds of shining needles before lifting one out and pushing it into Stowe's palm. The Dirt Eater inserts needles, one after the other, into the girl's feet, stomach, and chest. "This is the last one, the crossing point," she says, pushing it under the skin between Stowe's eyes. "Soon you will see that you are wrong. Dirt Eaters are not parasites."

As the needles begin to wave like grass licked by a summer's breeze, Mabatan wonders at the healer's arrogant certainty—she seems completely unaware of the malicious power she is facing. Mabatan, however, is not. She moves into the shadows, so that she will be well out of view when Stowe begins to stir.

Bruised and battered, Roan's sister groans; then, after taking a deep breath, her eyelids flutter, slowly lifting to reveal eyes that burn so bright it's as if the sun shines behind them. "Alandra," the girl sighs, but her voice is hoarse and strange.

A hint of confusion creases the Dirt Eater's brow. "How do you know my name? We've never met before."

"Of course we have," Stowe replies, "many, many times, in Oasis. Who was the one who taught you mathematics? Who took you to the Dreamfield for the first time?"

There is no doubt the healer's shock is genuine.

"August Ferrell? But I was told you were near death, in a coma, at Oasis."

"True. That is where my body lies. When I agreed to carry this burden, I knew I would never be able to return. My body will die. But thanks to you, my mission still has some hope of success."

"Mission?"

"Didn't they tell you, Alandra? Why else would you have come?"

"I was only told to find Roan's sister. To bring her to Oasis where she'd be safe."

"Well, at the moment she sleeps." Ferrell laughs. "Her last escapade wore her out, I'm afraid. Sorry about the mess we've made of your former home. Stowe and I were having some...control issues."

The eyes dart around the room. But Mabatan knows how to hide and is sure he will not see her.

"What did you do with Brack and Raven?"

"Their bodies were removed."

"They were just a tad too greedy and stupid to survive Our Stowe," Ferrell says. "Would you kindly take out these infernal needles, Alandra? You and I should be on our way before my charming little hostess wakes. She can be a handful."

"If we move her too soon, she could die and you along with her. The bruises in the body are deep. The needles are helping with the damage but she needs to rest awhile longer. I'll give her something to make sure she does."

"That would be wise."

Reaching back into her bag, Alandra chooses some powders to mix into the cup of water at her side. Mabatan struggles to pick up the scent of the medicines, to detect their intent, but the blend of flowers and earths is too complex.

Just then she hears, barely discernible, the near silent padding of a man's footsteps outside the door. Willum. Reaching out to her, radiating calm.

Slowly Mabatan raises the knife close to her ear. One step, one leap, and she can sink the blade straight into the healer's heart. If things go wrong, Willum must have the precious seconds he'll need to save Roan's sister.

With one hand gently behind the battered girl's back, the Dirt Eater supports Stowe so that she may drink the elixir.

"Vile stuff," winces Ferrell, coughing.

"Drink it all," the healer insists, keeping the cup at Stowe's lips.

"If I do, will you please take out those pins?"

"Soon." As Ferrell gulps back the drink, the healer smiles.

"What did you give me?" The apprehension of the creature inside Stowe is plain.

Mabatan's knuckles whiten around the dagger, but the child's breath is steady.

"Something to make sure Stowe keeps sleeping."

"Then why is it making *me* drowsy?"

Ferrell tries to shift out of the healer's arms, but she merely tightens her hold and peers deeply into Stowe's oddly luminescent eyes. "What you have done to this child is monstrous."

"You...you...betrayed me," whispers Ferrell, grabbing the healer's wrist. But he is obviously weakening and his grip slackens almost instantly.

As Mabatan watches Ferrell succumb to the drug, she hears the healer sadly murmur, "No. No, I am the one who's been betrayed."

For a moment all is held in suspension, as if none of them is able to believe the tonic has done its work. But Ferrell has been subdued, and as Mabatan sheathes her dagger the door opens.

"I didn't believe you," says the Dirt Eater, turning to Willum, her eyes brimming with tears. "I couldn't believe you. What was done to Stowe, invading her like a virus, is contrary to everything I was taught, everything we believe in." The healer's voice shakes with grief and anger as she deftly removes the needles from the sleeping Stowe. "Everything I've done, everything I am, is because of the Dirt Eaters, the result of their care. How could they do something like this, defile another human being in such a horrible way..."

Moving closer, Willum bends to gently stroke Stowe's hair. "In extreme times, people make extreme choices. Choices that push all they hold sacred into shadow."

The Dirt Eater lifts her head, her eyes swollen. "Roan warned me. I lost his faith because I could not believe him, lost fourteen children who trusted me, whom I loved completely. I have tried everything I know; nothing has worked. They lie still, close to death. I was told if I brought Stowe to Oasis, I would be able to help them. Is there no truth in that?"

Mabatan cannot believe the healer still harbors such false hopes. Willum's answer is direct and uncompromising. "Their plans for Stowe do not include freeing the children."

"How can you know that?" the Dirt Eater demands, staring helplessly at him.

"Do you not now know this yourself? Please. You have your answer. We made an agreement. Time is short. We must remove all evidence of a struggle."

"And how do you intend to get us out of here? It's not as if we can just walk through the front gates."

"But that is exactly my plan."

The gatekeeper addresses the Bird Man with great respect and not a little fear. "Is Your Worship leaving so soon?"

"Ah, my dear friend," Willum replies, his cloying voice, Mabatan guesses, mimicking Raven's. "It always pains me to leave Fairview; however, when the City calls, one has no choice but to answer."

His eyes fixed on the robe's brilliant feathers, the gatekeeper waves Willum and Stowe past, barely noticing the healer and assistant following closely behind.

As the gates swing shut, a foul wind rises from the lake. "People here must be used to the smell of death," Mabatan mutters. She has heard of Governor Brack and his justice, of all the people thrown in that acidic stew and dissolved in a day.

The healer's lips are tight, her whisper strained. "The people of Fairview live in comfort. They have electricity, imported food, fine clothes, and the best things the City can offer. They ignore the smell. You might too."

Mabatan snorts contemptuously. This Dirt Eater presumes much and understands nothing.

A strained silence takes them well past the edge of the red stick forest. Once safely concealed in its shadows, Willum lifts Stowe off the horse, removes its saddle and sends it galloping off in the opposite direction from Fairview.

"What are you doing?" gasps the Dirt Eater.

Willum almost appears amused. "The horse would not like where we are going."

"You look every bit like a Master of the City, or someone close to them," the healer accuses. Then looking over Mabatan, she sputters, "You could be anything. Boy, girl, man, woman. What are you?"

"I am a woman. The same age as you. We Wazya are different than most."

The confusion of emotions that play over the Dirt Eater's face is almost comic. Mischievously content, Mabatan turns and taps out an arrhythmic beat on a fallen log.

"People of the Earth? They're a myth. No one's ever seen them. Wazya! That's too easy a lie to tell."

Mabatan raises an eyebrow and at Willum's nod, tilts her head toward the Dirt Eater, grinning. "My father is a brown speckled rat. I believe you have met him. In your fenced-in Dreamfield."

"It's not possible." The healer sighs, slumping down on the log.

"If you wouldn't mind," Willum asks, indicating she might want to move.

As her seat begins to roll beneath her, she bolts up again

like a startled frog. When a fanged figure emerges from the exposed ground, the Dirt Eater stumbles back, gasping, "Blood Drinker!"

Mabatan scowls at the terrified healer. "This is Mhyzah. She's Hhroxhi. We'll be traveling with her now. And you will want to keep your ignorance to yourself."

Willum gently carries Stowe over to Mhyzah, who takes the sleeping girl and disappears into the hole. Then, with a firm grip on the Dirt Eater's arm, he murmurs, "After you."

the rat

THE EARTH'S FORESTS WERE REPLENISHED. ABUNDANT
WILDLIFE ROAMED THE LUSH UNDERGROWTH AND THE
WIDE GOLDEN VALLEYS. BUT THE EYES OF THE PEOPLE
SHOWED NO INTELLIGENCE. THEY PERISHED BEFORE THE
BEASTS DEFENSELESS. ALL THEIR DREAMS HAD BEEN TAKEN
FROM THEM.

> ——ROAN,
> VISION #117, YEAR 7 A.C.
> DREAMFIELD JOURNALS OF THE
> FIRST INNER CIRCLE

ROAN WALKS ALONG THE VOLCANIC ROCK, to where a dozen younger Apsara perfect their swordplay. The women dodge one another's blows in a mesmerizing dance. The blades never touch, though the sharp whirr of the steel leaves no doubt what would happen if they came into contact with skin and bone.

Inside the temple, several dozen more of Kira and Ende's people are seated cross-legged on the floor in deep meditation. Here the only sound is their perfectly coordinated breathing, the exhale and inhale so exact that it slits the air with the precision of a calligrapher's brush. The Apsara's discipline dwarfs that of the Brothers: it's no wonder they're such formidable fighters.

Standing before a heavy stone door, Roan waits. He knows that Ende will feel his presence and the door will open when she's ready. He doesn't wait long.

The room is so gracefully appointed it exudes serenity. At its center is a simple table, perfectly proportioned, the wood grain curved into a vibrant spiral. Two cups are set on it; made of fine white clay, they appear strong yet delicate. Even the bamboo mat Roan sits on is woven in a way that soothes the eye. The woman herself embodies the room's perfection: lithe, long limbs rippling with muscle, her aging face both beautiful and wise, her smile an invitation but also a warning.

"You have lost the clarity you experienced after your last ordeal," she says, pouring Roan some tea. The scent of spearmint rising from it calms him.

"I realize it's important to put the past to rest, but seeing Wolf and Asp and Stinger, hearing their voices...I just don't know if I can do it. They came to the Caldera with the intention of serving me but now, with the added problem of Asp—"

"You overestimate your obstacles. Keep in mind, Roan, that you are not being asked to forgive the Brothers or even to understand them, but to lead them. Accomplish this and you may also be able to guide them, in thought as well as action, and prevent the anguish you experienced from becoming another's."

Roan shudders.

"It may be distasteful to you, Roan of Longlight, but it is not an unworthy endeavor."

"I had a vision—"

Ende holds up her hand, stopping him. "I am not the one to interpret your visions but I do know to whom you must speak."

Roan extends his awareness beyond the room, hoping to get a sense of what awaits him.

"No, no," the ancient warrior sighs as she takes a sip of tea. "You cannot meet him here. Rat awaits you in the Dreamfield."

At the mention of the creature, Roan's stomach flips. "Large, with brown speckles?"

Ende puts down her cup. "Ah, you remember him. He thought you would."

How could he forget? And Rat was in his vision too. Their first encounter in over a year. This can be no coincidence. But what is the creature's connection to Ende? "I was under the impression that Rat was a Dirt Eater. They took orders from him."

"Think back on your meetings with him."

"The first time he came to me by himself. I was at my house, after Longlight was destroyed. He warned me to leave. He was right."

Without looking up, Ende pours herself another cup of tea. "Has he given you any other good advice?"

"Several times. But I'm telling you, he was also with the Dirt Eaters. I'm sure he was one of them."

"This is all you know of him?"

Roan remembers what Haron of Oasis told him. "During the Wars, when my great-grandfather decided to put a stop to the fighting and divide up the rebels, he said the instructions came to him in a dream, from a rat."

Ende touches her fingertips together. "The rat comes to those in need, and to those who share a common interest."

"Like what?"

"The preservation of the Dreamfield, for one. The Dirt

Eaters have only met a small part of the rat. They fear and therefore respect him, thinking him some kind of guardian animus, an aspect of the Dreamfield that can divine the future. Dirt Eater nonsense."

Studying Ende's face, every nuance of her body and voice, Roan can detect nothing but openness and truth. "Once he told me he was many and few. What does that mean?"

"That, you will have to ask him."

Roan is hesitant. "How? How do I move freely in the Dreamfield, without risking being found by the Turned or the Dirt Eaters?"

"You have the ring. The Badger is a protective spirit. When you breathe yourself into the Dreamfield, put a picture of it squarely in your mind. It will lead you to a safe place. Rat will find you there."

Roan considers Ende's instructions. Why does he see traps everywhere? Why has it become impossible to trust even those who seek to help him? As if sensing his doubts, his white cricket leaps onto his knee and begins to sing. "I see you've already made up your mind," Roan says. Closing his eyes, he slowly sips the air. His thumb passes over the ring Saint gave him and a picture of the enigmatic badger takes shape.

ROAN DUCKS DEFENSIVELY AS AN AVALANCHE OF BLAZING ROCK CRASHES AROUND HIM. BUT ALMOST IMMEDIATELY HE REALIZES HE IS SOMEHOW PROTECTED FROM THE INFERNO. REACHING OUT TO EXAMINE THE TRANSPARENT PERIMETER, HE GASPS IN AWE AS HIS HAND PRESSES AGAINST ITS FLEXIBLE SURFACE. GLOWING COALS EVAPORATE INTO DUST OPPOSITE HIS FINGERTIPS. AWARE THAT HE IS NO LONGER ALONE, ROAN DROPS HIS ARM. HE CANNOT KEEP THE SUSPICION FROM HIS VOICE AS

HE TWISTS TO SEE RAT LICKING HIS PAWS ON THE GRANITE FLOOR. "HOW DID YOU KNOW I WOULD COME?"

"I DID NOT KNOW. YOU ARE NOT THE ONLY ONE UNDER SEIGE, ROAN OF LONGLIGHT. THOUGH DARIUS CANNOT EXTEND HIMSELF PAST HIS BORDERS, STILL HE SENSES THE SHADOWS BEYOND HIS REACH. HIS CONSTRUCTIONS RIP AT THE FABRIC OF THE DREAMFIELD. NO ONE CAN WALK FREELY NOW. THIS IS ONE OF THE FEW PLACES THAT CAN BE SAFELY APPROACHED." RAT'S EYES ARE OPENLY CURIOUS. "DESPITE THE BADGER'S PROTECTION, YOU COME AT GREAT RISK. WHY?"

"ENDE ADVISED ME TO CONSULT YOU."

"TELL ENDE TIMES HAVE CHANGED AND SHE MUST NOT PUT SO MUCH STORE IN MY CUNNING. BUT SINCE WE ARE BOTH SAFELY HERE... "

"I HAD A...VISION."

RAT CLOSES HIS EYES. "TELL ME WHAT YOU SAW."

"STOWE WAS A TREE THAT BURNED TO GOLDEN ASH. I KILLED A BULL WITH MY HOOK-SWORD. BLOOD RAN DOWN IT AND FELL ON THE CHILDREN, THE FOURTEEN NOVAKIN. IT EASED THEIR PAIN. BUT THEN MY SWORD MELDED TO MY HAND. WILLUM GATHERED THE ASH THAT WAS STOWE AND SCATTERED IT OVER THE NOVAKIN. DO YOU KNOW WILLUM? YOU WERE ON HIS KNEE."

WITHOUT OPENING HIS EYES, RAT NODS ONCE. "PLEASE, CONTINUE."

"IN THE VISION, WILLUM TOLD ME WE HAVE ONLY UNTIL THE BULL RISES IN THE EAST. THEN, IF WE FAIL, ALL ENDS."

RAT'S EYES OPEN. "ROAN OF THE PARTING DIPPED HIS FINGERS IN THE RIVER OF TIME AND SAW VISIONS OF WHAT WAS TO COME, THINGS FOR WHICH HE FELT RESPONSIBLE. HE DECIDED TO TRY TO CHANGE THAT FUTURE. YOU MIGHT THINK

THIS PURE ARROGANCE BUT WHEN HE SOUGHT OUT MY ANCESTOR, AITHUNA, HE WAS ACCOMPANIED BY CRICKETS. THIS CONVINCED HER TO HELP HIM CARVE OUT THE PATH HE THOUGHT MIGHT SAVE US. BUT THERE ARE NO CERTAINTIES AND REALITY LAYS A CIRCUITOUS TRACK AROUND OUR CHOSEN COURSE.

"WHILE IT IS CLEAR FROM YOUR VISION THAT THE NOVAKIN MIGHT STILL BE SAVED, IT IS ALSO EVIDENT THAT YOUR SISTER'S SURVIVAL IS IN PERIL. FIRE IS THE ELEMENT OF THE SPIRIT. STOWE'S BURNS BRIGHTLY, ROAN, BUT WHEN SHE CAME UNDER DARIUS'S THRALL, HE LEVELED A GREAT VIOLENCE AGAINST HER. WILLUM WAS ABLE TO CONTAIN THE WORST OF HIS ATTACKS, BUT WE NEGLECTED TO ANTICIPATE THE DANGER POSED BY THE DIRT EATERS. WE UNDERESTIMATED THEIR MALIGNITY AND IT HAS COST US ALMOST EVERYTHING.

"THERE IS NO ONE WHO REGRETS OUR ERRORS MORE THAN WILLUM. HE KNOWS OUR MISTAKES HAVE COST YOUR SISTER A VITAL PART OF HER SPIRIT."

"WHAT DO YOU MEAN—HOW?"

"STOWE'S POSSESSION BY A DIRT EATER HAS TAKEN FROM HER WHAT SHE MIGHT HAVE SALVAGED HAD SHE ESCAPED DARIUS WHOLE."

"ISN'T THERE ANYTHING THAT CAN BE DONE FOR HER?"

"WE ARE DOING ALL THAT CAN BE DONE. BUT, ROAN, YOUR SISTER MUST BE ALLOWED TO WALK TOWARD HER OWN FATE AS SURELY AS YOU MUST HAVE THE FREEDOM TO WALK TOWARD YOURS."

THAT MAY BE, ROAN THINKS, BUT IF THERE'S A WAY TO PROTECT HIS SISTER, HE'S NOT GOING TO STAND BY AND DO NOTHING. HE CAN'T.

RAT FASTIDIOUSLY SMOOTHS HIS TAIL AS IF SEEKING ANSWERS ON ITS FLESHY PINK SURFACE. "YOUR VISION OUTLINES YOUR

DILEMMA. THE SWORD IS LEADERSHIP, THE BLOOD ON IT IS THE BLOOD OF THE BULL. THIS IMPLIES THE INVOLVEMENT OF THE BROTHERS OR THE FRIEND, OR BOTH, I CANNOT SAY. YOU KNOW THIS BUT FEAR IT BECAUSE YOU DESIRE A SOLUTION WITHOUT VIOLENCE. BUT ROAN, BLOOD IS ALSO A SYMBOL OF HOPE, OF LIFE. IN YOUR DREAM IT AIDS THE CHILDREN. VIOLENCE COMES WHETHER WE WILL IT OR NO. THE SWORD MELDS WITH YOUR HAND BECAUSE YOU KNOW YOU CANNOT TURN YOUR BACK ON THE RESPONSIBILITY BEFORE YOU. IF YOU DO, ALL WILL BE LOST."

"I HAVE SO MANY QUESTIONS."

RAT'S NOSE TWITCHES. "REMEMBER THE WORDS OF YOUR PARENTS: TO WIN WAR YOU MUST ENVISION PEACE. TO DO OTHERWISE CLOSES THE WAY." RAT CROUCHES BACK IN PREPARATION TO LEAP.

"WAIT!" CRIES ROAN. "TELL ME: HOW CAN YOU BE MANY AND FEW?"

"OBSERVE." THE RAT'S BODY MELTS ONTO THE STONE, BECOMING A SWIRLING MASS ON THE SMOOTH ROCK. IT CONGEALS FIRST INTO THE FACE OF AN OLD MAN, THEN A YOUNG WOMAN, SOON REPLACED BY A MIDDLE-AGED MAN. DOZENS OF FACES CHANGING IN SHAPE AND AGE, THE LAST OF A MAN WHOSE DARK EYES AND BROW SEEM ODDLY FAMILIAR.

"YOU RESEMBLE MY FRIEND, MABATAN."

"I AM HER FATHER." A SHADOW PASSES OVER THE MAN'S SMILING FACE. "THE PEOPLE OF LONGLIGHT LIVE WITHIN YOU, ROAN. FEEL THEM IN YOUR BLOOD, HEAR THEM IN YOUR MIND. YOU WILL NEED THEIR WISDOM IN THE DAYS TO COME." THEN IN THE BLINK OF AN EYE, THE FACE OF RAT VANISHES.

You desire a solution without violence but...violence will come whether we will it or no—Rat's words resound in Roan's skull like a bell tolling in a watchtower.

When he opens his eyes, Ende is still across from him. "Drink," she says, gesturing to his cup.

Roan takes a gulp of steaming tea, hoping it will steady him. "No matter what I do, people will be hurt, they will die. How do I accept that?"

Ende smiles sympathetically. "All life exacts a price, Roan, and there is no denying the unfairness of mortality."

"If it was only me..."

"I know well the burden of leadership, and the only relief I have found from it is in action.

"Consider the distracted child who looks carelessly behind her. She does not see the edge of the cliff. In the plunge to her death, there is no forethought, no hand of evil. Yet with this single unconscious act, she tragically alters the lives of her entire family. Goodness, innocence, they do not exempt us from grief. We weep over the fate of the distracted child and her family but it is beyond our reckoning. There are other fates, though, that we can change. As leaders we must recognize that they are more needful of our attention."

Kira, her long red hair severely tied back, appears at the door. She bows her head respectfully to her grandmother.

"Rise, Roan of Longlight," Ende commands, and taking his arm she effortlessly pulls him to his feet. "Our guests await you."

Plan for war, envision peace, Roan tells himself as he follows Kira and Ende out of the tranquil chamber. He knows the caution behind Ende's tale. In their world, the children aren't carelessly tumbling off a cliff, they're being pushed, and it's up to him to cut off the hand that's pushing them.

Homecoming

MABATAN INTERVIEW 1.3.

MOR-TICKS SPREAD LIKE PLAGUE AND WE WERE ALMOST
OVERCOME BY THEM. BUT THE WHITE CRICKETS HEALED
US AND SHARED THE POWER IN THEIR SONG. WE HAVE
WALKED WITH THEM EVER SINCE.

—GWENDOLEN'S CRICKET FILE

HISS, CLICK. HISS, CLICK. Insect-like and menacing, the sound forces an unwilling Stowe out of her comfortable dreams and into a low-ceilinged room illuminated by noxious blue gas. The light is so eerie, she thinks she might not be awake at all, but in some unknown corner of the Dreamfield. She identifies the source of the sound: two albinos, in a mad frenzy, fangs bared, fighting over...a meal? Could the meal be her?

But there is Willum; clever Willum, he found her. He seems concerned, though not for his life. Stowe does not recognize the fair-haired woman behind him—*she* is terrified out of her wits. The boy, though—or is it a girl—those dark eyes, Stowe's seen them before, but she can't place where. Willum and the boy-girl are listening with such keen interest, she's sure they can actually understand what those monsters are saying.

Suddenly, one of the albinos pulls out a short but very sharp-looking knife and waves it threateningly. The other takes a step back, but its hand shoots out and the knife goes clattering on the hard clay floor. That was good. That albino radiates a brilliant crimson. What could it be? The glowing red wisps spiral into deep violet as they bend and twist in the blue light. Beautiful.

Willum's picking up the knife and smiling grimly at the growling monster. Stowe watches it consider for a second, then lean back and vanish. Smart monster to have recognized Willum's power. Smarter than that other monster, Darius. Darius. How is she going to kill him now? She must find a way. She must...but it hurts her head to think of Darius, so she focuses on the walls instead. She sees holes, several of them. Where do they all go?

"Willum?" Stowe says weakly. Her throat is raw; it hurts. Willum is at her side in an instant, his hand enclosing hers.

"Do not worry, we are safe. But the Hhroxhi are divided, and we will have to go another way."

"Hhroxhi?"

Willum points. The color around the remaining albino is muted now, steadily fading. "Mhyzah here is Hhroxhi. I will explain the situation later. You must rest."

Suddenly her body spasms and she begins to shake with rage and fear. Brack. Raven. They were going to hurt her. And Ferrell—"Ferrell? Ferrell!"

Raising his hand to her brow, with a gentle pressure Willum relaxes the tension that's seized Stowe. "Stowe," he whispers. "Look at me."

Stowe breathes deeply. Willum's here. Willum will keep her safe.

"Stowe, for the moment, Ferrell sleeps."

"Asleep—for how long?"

"You must rest. Rest."

Stowe's about to protest but her eyes are heavy, and as Willum gathers her up in his arms, his breath's steady pulse drags her back into sleep.

Stowe hurts everywhere. Fingers poke at her neck and she bats them away angrily.

"Be careful, the wound needs tending."

It's the fair-haired woman who'd been cowering behind Willum. Her tone is imperious, her touch invasive, and Stowe dislikes her instantly.

"This is Alandra," Willum says, towering over the woman at her neck. "She gave you the tonic that has temporarily immobilized Ferrell."

And she should be grateful? Well, at least they're out of that horrid tunnel—Stowe can feel fresh air on her face. Peering past the people around her, she sees light and smells the forest beyond it. This must be the mouth of a cave.

Alandra...the name is so familiar. Alandra! An Eater, no less!

"Alandra," Stowe says sweetly. "Raven told me about you. You knew my brother."

"Yes."

The Eater's startled. Good. But just then a third face hovers into view, distracting her. Irritated, Stowe blurts, "And who exactly are *you*?"

"I am Mabatan."

Looking at the dark-skinned imp's dancing eyes, Stowe instantly remembers. "You were the young girl in that theatre troupe. With the drum."

"The day you saw your brother. I promised him I would help find you."

Stowe raises an eyebrow—as if Willum needed a waif to guide him! But Willum nods with such seriousness that Stowe forces a smile and squeezes out a very quiet thank you.

"This looks like a knife cut. Is it?" asks the Eater.

Stowe stares unabashedly at Alandra. She doesn't understand why an Eater would be helping them, but if Willum doesn't consider her a threat, Stowe can't see much harm in recounting the facts. "Raven was trying to perform a little operation on me. The gift of an enabler. They were going to make me their slave so they could use me as a weapon. I think I may have hurt them." She looks from one set of downcast eyes to another. "Are they dead?" she says innocently, but she already knows the answer, she knew it the moment she screamed.

Willum looks back at her, obviously unconvinced by her guileless act, but before he can speak, Stowe shifts her attention back to the healer and asks, "Eater, do you know Ferrell?"

"He was one of my teachers," Alandra replies.

"Oh?" Stowe's lips curve into a knowing smile. "Aren't you finished?" she says, careful to inject as much menace in her words as possible. She wants this healer's hands off her now—a student of Ferrell's will have to earn her trust.

"We must go," Mabatan urges, and striding to the mouth of the cave she climbs onto the biggest black steed Stowe has ever seen. Shadowed against a haze of light, she extends her hand to the Eater.

After one last look at Stowe, the healer closes her bag and rises to take the elf's proffered hand. Mabatan's revulsion at her touch is palpable. So she does not trust Alandra either.

Stowe cries out as Willum lifts her. Her battle with Ferrell has left her so bruised and battered, there is barely an inch of her that does not scream with pain. He raises her onto a chestnut stallion and winds straps from the saddle around her legs and over her hips. "You are not strong enough to sit on your own. I will hold you but you need to be secured, in case there are any...events."

"Where did we get the horses?" she asks. There certainly were no large animals in that dark cramped chamber with those fanged ghosts.

"The Hhroxhi have loaned them to us," Willum says, settling himself on the horse behind Stowe. "The tunnels would be safer but our friend, Mhyzah, was unable to secure our passage."

"The fight we witnessed."

"Yes. All the Hhroxhi once believed in the prophecies, the ones that told of a boy and his sister, and how they would open the way. But now they are divided. Many do not believe. They see themselves as separate and want nothing to do with humans and this human story."

Joining Mabatan and Alandra, they ride into a forest of serpentine trees. The slow canter of the horses and the lilt of Willum's voice take Stowe back to the comfort of her childhood, her father rocking her, telling her stories. Perhaps traveling in dank tunnels with fanged albinos seems to carry less risk to Willum, but from Stowe's perspective it's much nicer to be rocked by a horse's steady gait, nestled against a warm body, and have a heartbeat, strong and steady in her ear, to reassure her. Nothing can disturb her now that Willum is here. Even the tree trunks, winding around each other like crazed vipers, do not discomfit her. But they remind her. Yes.

They remind her of the Keeper of the City, his reptilian eyes peering out of that translucent face, so like a living skull… no, better not to think about Darius.

"Where are we going?" she asks Willum, hopeful that his answer will distract her.

"To your brother."

"Is he angry with me for running away?"

"Roan loves you and wants you well. We will see that he gets his wish."

With a gasp, Stowe stiffens, her body racked by spasm after spasm. Ferrell is scratching and grating his way up from her stomach into her throat. "You can't hold me!" he screeches. Against her will, Stowe's arms reach out and grab the reins from Willum. But the bindings he's placed on her constrict her movements and Willum's arm swiftly draws her back.

"Hello, Ferrell," Willum says calmly.

Ferrell wraps his mind around Stowe's, smothering her, suffocating her. "I'll make her scream. I'll kill you all."

"Stowe, resist him. Breathe."

As Stowe struggles against the murderous cry rising in her, a creaking, whistling music slides over Ferrell like liquid. It's as if the entire world is whispering, and that whisper is putting up a wall between her and Ferrell, separating his consciousness from hers. It drags him down into the darkest corner of her being and there he is still. Perfectly still.

Dozens of white crickets perch on her shoulders, her arms, her heart. The largest of the crickets, nearly the size of her thumb, climbs up her chest. Its multi-faceted eyes lock on hers, commanding her to rest, to sleep. They spin, iridescent like jewels, the entire world whispering it loves her, and finally she feels secure.

Stowe's jarred awake. They're galloping. Through bleary eyes she sees a fast-running stream before them. The horse, gathering speed, is about to leap over it.

With a suddenness that winds her, Willum pushes her forward, the side of her face hugging the horse's neck as it lands heavily on the other bank. An arrow passes a finger's width from her scalp.

"Fandor riders," Willum whispers. "Keep your body close to the horse."

Stowe does not need to move to see half a dozen riders, brandishing swords and bows, the stream behind them. She burns with a desire to strike at them with her voice. "Let me."

"No."

But she can see Alandra and Mabatan's horse is already starting to tire, its mouth foaming from exertion.

"Do not move. Do not speak." Willum stops the horse and swings to the ground. Without taking his eyes off the Fandor, he presses his palms to the earth.

Stowe senses a power, potent like nothing she's ever felt from him before. The Fandor's horses sense it too, and slow to a canter despite being brutally whipped across their flanks by their riders. The Fandor, however, seem immune. When they come to a halt only a few paces from Willum, they spring from their horses' backs, swords ready to slash him to pieces.

Do not move, do not speak—that is what Willum said. She has to trust him. She has to. She will not; she will not scream. But how can she stop herself? She so wants to make them sprawl on the ground, blood bursting from their ears. Willum must not die. Stowe feels...tears? Tears! How can she bear this helplessness?

His movement is so swift she does not see exactly how he gets close enough to touch them. But deftly evading their slashes and jabs, he makes contact with each Fandor. His hand covers each face like a claw until they all stand looking benignly at him, like simpletons.

"Sleep," Willum orders.

And without hesitation, every Fandor lies down on the ground and sleeps.

This display of Willum's has aroused the Eater's suspicions. Like a bony scavenger, she scurries over to examine the snoring men. "What did you do to them?" she demands.

How dare she! If Stowe could stop crying, she would hurt her. From a corner of her consciousness, she hears Willum respond calmly, "I've simplified their minds. Tomorrow they will wake up feeling entirely refreshed, with no memory of today's event. Perhaps you would like to forget it also?"

Stowe laughs at the sight of the Eater's stunned expression. She laughs and laughs, gulping for air, unable to stop. Willum's mind, ever so gently, touches hers. *A time of grieving will come but it is not now. Now you must rest.* And then there is nothing but the sound of his voice repeating over and over, *Soon, though. Soon you will be home.*

Willum gently nudges Stowe awake, then points to a village gate in the distance. The purple haze of sunset glints across its surface as if off a mottled gem. "This is where I spent the summers of my youth," Willum says, "with my sister. Some of her people, my people, are still there. We will be welcomed."

"You never told me you had a sister."

"There were moments I feared you might never learn

anything about me." Willum's eyes sparkle and he's smiling broadly. Why is he so happy? It's unsettling. "It's good to return here," Willum says, as if reading her thoughts. "It's been almost fifteen years."

As they draw closer, Stowe can see that the town's walls are fortified with scrap metal—rusting car fenders, steel barrels squashed flat, angular pieces of iron plate. From a battery of watchtowers, helmeted warriors aim crossbows at them. But when Willum looks up, they lower their weapons. One whistles loudly. The gate slowly opens and the four dusty travelers ride in from the plain.

Several of the tower guards leap from their posts and rush toward Willum. Tugging off their helmets, Stowe sees that the soldiers are tall, muscular women. And they all know her guardian well. Very well.

"Willi Boy!" A broad-shouldered woman with plaited hair is giving Willum a good-natured poke in the ribs.

Boy?

"Torin! It's been too long." Willum's poking her back while his other arm wraps around yet another brawny warrior. "Resa!"

This one hugs him so tightly, Willum groans in pain. "Whoa, Resa, you don't know your own strength!" he says and as soon as she releases him, he punches her hard in .the arm.

They're giggling. Like silly schoolchildren. Appalling.

"Let's get you and your friends cleaned up and fed," Torin says, giving him a good pound on the back. "We have a lot of catching up to do."

As Willum lifts Stowe from their horse, she asks as casually as she can, "Those women...are your 'people'?"

"Yes," he answers with a wide grin.

"They seem quite strong," Stowe comments wryly.

"They are Apsara," says Willum, his eyes penetrating hers. "They are the descendants of the rebels Darius set the plague upon."

"Only the women survived it," adds Mabatan, as she moves past Stowe. "Rage and sorrow and necessity forced them onto the path of the warrior."

If these are his people, Willum is Apsara. That means Willum is descended from the rebels who escaped Darius's clutches. What is she to him, then? Simply a means to attack his enemy? Stowe's breath catches in her chest; her heart beats wildly.

Gently placing Stowe on the ground, Willum bends to look inquiringly at her. "There is no need for anger."

"I am not angry!" shouts Stowe, desperately trying to remain standing as Willum meets her glare with a smile. "Smile all you want, Willum, I am not a child and I will not be charmed. If you have betrayed me, if your Apsara are using me, I'll…I'll…" But her head spins wildly and as dozens of Willums reach out for her the world fades to black.

an uneasy alliance

MANY THREADS BOUND ROAN TO THE BROTHERS: HIS
PAST BOUND HIM TO SAINT; HIS SWORD BOUND HIM TO
WOLF; HIS SCAR BOUND HIM TO STINGER; AND HIS DESTINY
BOUND HIM TO THE FRIEND.

—ORIN'S HISTORY OF THE FRIEND

ROAN HAS TO ADMIT, Kira's quarters in the Caldera were the sensible choice. Saint had been her mate, and she'd kept many of his things, mementos the Brothers revered. Feeling their Prophet's presence will make Wolf and Stinger more comfortable. If they are at ease, the meeting will have a better chance of going smoothly.

Or so the theory goes.

Inside the black stone walls, Wolf, acting head of the brethren, and Stinger, their authority in matters of the spirit, are seated under a mural of the Friend, god of the Brothers. Both are studying the map Lumpy and the Apsara draftswomen have been laboring over these last few days.

"The northern territory provides the City with coal, iron, and wood," says Lumpy, proud of his research. "The south focuses on agriculture; that's where the City's food is coming from. The west: sulfur and salt and what little oil they can produce. East is where the Masters go for the children they..." Lumpy sighs. Gathering his composure, he continues, "We need to drive a wedge between the Governors and the City. Interfere with their production, interrupt their transport. If we can control—"

Lumpy stops abruptly. Brother Wolf is no longer looking at the map. His eyes are riveted on Roan, who stands stock-still at the threshold, with Ende and Kira equally solid at his side.

Wolf rises from his seat. He looks more fearsome than ever, his shaved head gleaming, his hand falling almost lazily over his hook-sword. That sword had taken part in the annihilation of Longlight. It had been used to train Roan in combat. Once, Roan had even battled it for his life.

In a silence that quivers with tension, Lumpy clears his throat and grins nervously. "Roan, welcome!"

Kira and Ende smile at this effort but Roan cannot allow himself to acknowledge his friend with more than a brief nod. Wolf would interpret breaking his gaze as weakness, and Roan's instincts warn against anything but a show of strength.

It is Brother Stinger, rising to stand beside Wolf, who breaks the impasse. Pressing his dusky palms together, he waits patiently until Brother Wolf also adopts the ritual posture. Observing the cost of this action on Wolf, the effort of control in body and voice, tells Roan a great deal about the predicament the Brothers have found themselves in—much more than the words that follow.

"In the name of the Friend, in the name of the Prophet, we swear our fealty to you, Roan of Longlight. We will follow you into battle. Give our blood. We will serve you as we serve the Friend, Brother Roan."

The title cuts into Roan like broken glass. Words blurt

from his mouth before he can stop them. "I will never be a Brother."

Ende sighs, all too audibly. Kira grips Roan's arm, as if to hold him back.

Wolf's hands clench. "If you will not be a Brother," he snarls, "why have we been summoned?"

"To join us in bringing an end to the City's rule."

"We do not join," hisses Wolf. "We lead. And you were born to lead us, *Brother* Roan."

Again it is Stinger who intervenes. "You have many reasons to feel hatred toward the Brothers—"

"The Brothers will always have my people's blood on their hands." Roan finds himself rubbing the starlike scar he'd received from the Hhroxhi. From the moment he came into the room it has tingled uncomfortably.

"We do," agrees Stinger. "Our actions caused you and your people great harm. But these deeds were fulfillment of a prophecy. The fall of Longlight—and its willing sacrifice." Staring pointedly at Roan's chest, he adds, "We are not the only ones who have been scarred by spilling innocent blood."

Has Stinger read his unconscious worrying of an old wound as guilt? Or does he know the Hhroxhi? Mhyzah? Has he heard of the justice she and her kin exact for the murder of one of their own?

As Stinger's eyes meet his, Roan drops his hand to his side, embarrassed that he cannot deny the Brother's challenge.

"We adopted you. We trained you. We baptized you. You successfully completed every trial of your initiation. Whether you wish to avow it or not, you *are* a Brother."

Roan looks bitterly at Stinger. "I did not complete the final trial. I refused."

But Stinger has anticipated this response. Roan can see the satisfaction in his eyes, his sardonic grin. "You refused to put to sacrifice two Fandor. But you took the blood of the Prophet, and that action assured your ascendance as leader. After that moment, Saint began preparations for your rule. The Prophet's last instructions were that we should set about the liberation of the Farlands, first and foremost by keeping its innocents out of the City's clutches. This purpose, he said, would be one with your own."

"You've seen the children here, Roan," confirms Kira. "There are two sanctuaries in the north. We save all we can. Many more this past year with the Brothers' support."

Though Brother Wolf is still bristling from Roan's affront, he bows his head and holds his hook-sword out to Roan. "In the absence of our Prophet, I have been leading the Brothers. I now cede my place to you."

"I do not accept your place," insists Roan. "I would not be as able a Captain to the Brothers. It is best that you lead our efforts in the Farlands."

"Me? You mistake my abilities for those of Saint's. He had the confidence of the Governors, gave their shipments safe passage through the Farlands to the City, protected their towns, resolved their petty rivalries. Now that we are no longer aligned with the City, I cannot defuse their panic. They are as afraid of us as they are of Darius and his henchmen." Wolf pauses to snort in disgust. "They deal with smugglers. They bribe marauders. I cannot stomach them and I am no diplomat."

"That may be, but to win this war we must put aside our personal antipathies and look to the goals we share. And if Governors deal with smugglers, so much the better. We'll need one to help us get into the City." Wolf glares at Roan stubbornly. Shifting his attention to Stinger, Roan asks pointedly, "Are there no Governors who might be sympathetic to our cause?"

Brother Stinger lets out a weary sigh. "There may be one. Selig."

Wolf's hand wraps around the handle of his sword. "The Brothers need no allies. The prophecy says we will fall upon the City in a Visitation like a cleansing wind."

Roan raises his voice, to make sure Wolf understands the stakes. "Seventy-five Brothers? You would be slaughtered before you passed the gates. There will be no 'cleansing wind.' We will fight, Brother Wolf, but only when we have found a way to win with as little bloodshed as possible. And I need you to lead that attack because there is a second battlefield that must be won, where you cannot walk. If I lose that battle, all our efforts will be wasted. I cannot go there unprepared and there are precious few who can help me."

"Are you saying you seek an alliance with those who eat Dirt?" The edge in Wolf's voice is as threatening as his sword's.

Lumpy steps bravely forward. "I would look to my own house before leveling accusations."

Wolf, eyes flashing, glares at Lumpy. "You dare insult our Brotherhood?"

"We have reason to believe," says Lumpy, standing his ground, "that Brother Asp was sent by the Dirt Eaters of Oasis to spy on Saint and Roan."

"Impossible," whispers Wolf.

"My warriors are with him now." Ende's voice is quiet, reasoning. "He is a Brother under your leadership and so, in deference, I ask your permission to search him and his quarters for Dirt. When we find it, you will know."

"*If* you find it, he is dead," Wolf hisses.

"No," Roan interjects. "I want him alive. I do not mistake the Dirt Eaters for allies, Brother Wolf, but Asp may have useful information."

Wolf, bristling, glances at Brother Stinger, who locks eyes with him and nods. Turning away, Wolf silently mulls over Roan's order. After a moment, he shrugs his assent and Kira strides from the room.

Wolf squints, examining Roan with what seems a grudging respect. "You knew this when we arrived. That is why Asp is not here. How? How did you know?"

"Dirt has a scent which it leaves on those who eat it."

"It is possible to smell a Dirt Eater?"

"Would that we all had Roan's talent." Ende catches Wolf's eye and Roan observes the silent understanding between them. "But the Dirt Eaters have many spies who do not eat the Dirt; they will not be so easily detected. *You* will need to keep a watchful eye."

Wolf bows as Kira arrives followed by four Apsara forming a circle around Asp. For a moment the air is electric with the possibility of violence. Dealing with Wolf will be like wrangling a wild horse.

Opening her hand, Kira loosens the ties on the pouch she's holding and reveals the Dirt. Wolf snorts, angrily turning his head away. Stinger and the Apsara remain impassive, while Lumpy leans forward trying to get a better view.

Roan considers what he knows of Brother Asp. This was the man who healed any who came to him, who used Roan's knowledge to detoxify large tracts of land, so hundreds, even thousands of people could grow healthy crops. And all the time he was a Dirt Eater, spying; spying and probably making sure the Brothers didn't kill Roan. All the time lying. How is he going to distinguish Asp's truth from his lies? He couldn't then. I've grown, Roan thinks, I've changed. But will it be enough?

Ende steps forward. Cinching the pouch shut, she takes it from Kira. "I will destroy the Dirt so that no trace of it remains. Will you require my warriors for your interrogation, Roan of Longlight?"

Roan declines, as he knows he was meant to, and one by one the Apsara gracefully exit, leaving Asp standing alert but calm.

"I am sorry for this, Brother Asp. I wish it were not necessary. You were a trusted friend. But that was pretense, wasn't it? All along you were a spy. A Dirt Eater spy."

Before Asp can respond, Wolf has put a blade to his neck. "You betrayed your Brothers, your Prophet, and the Friend. My only wish is to see you burned alive."

In an instant Roan is at Wolf's side. "Please put down your sword, Brother Wolf."

Wolf looks down at the blade point of Roan's hooksword, poised to pierce his heart, and slowly backs away. "As you wish."

Meeting the man's barely disguised rage with utter calm, Roan continues, "Perhaps it would be best if you left me and my...Lieutenant alone with the prisoner."

Without discernible hesitation, Wolf pivots and, with a bow, Stinger follows. Roan might have had Stinger stay, but as the door closes behind the Brothers, he knows it is best this way. Facing back into the room, he almost smiles at his friend's startled expression. He'd just blurted it out, but he likes the idea of Lumpy having a title the Brothers can understand—after all, Lumpy is the only person he really trusts.

Asp lets out a long, weary sigh. "I always knew that you would be the one to expose me."

Standing across from the Dirt Eater, Roan introduces Lumpy, then explains, "I could never understand how a man as kind as you could live with the Brothers and abide their violence. It was my Lieutenant who pointed out that you might not be one of them."

"You are the Mor-Tick survivor I was told traveled with Roan," Asp says, looking curiously at Lumpy. "As a man of healing, I've seen many die of your scourge but never met one who lived. If I survive this interrogation, I hope you will tell me your story."

"Didn't you know Lelbit?" asks Lumpy.

Roan looks at him, surprised. Lelbit had died saving Roan's life. That was many months ago, but the sorrow in Lumpy's voice is raw, as if he'd lost her only yesterday.

"I've heard of her, of course," Asp answers, "but I was with the Brothers long before she came to Oasis. I know though, that she was greatly loved."

"Yes," says Lumpy. "She was."

Asp's mention of Oasis is all the confession Roan needs. "How did the Dirt Eaters know I would end up with the Brothers?"

Asp looks directly at Roan. What had been lost between them has come at last to this. The interrogation has begun. "A simple question with many answers."

"Some more relevant than others," Roan says pointedly.

"Then I will begin with the prophecy. It foretold that a rain of fire would descend on Longlight…"

Shouts. Explosions. Crazed skull-masked invaders on horseback, waving torches, slashing, burning.

"...Once the City had abandoned its policy of toxic bombardment, we had to discover what alternate tool of destruction it would choose. Saint, prophet of the Friend, had emerged. It was our belief that he would be chosen to rain fire on Longlight and find you. So, I was sent to join the brethren and await your coming."

"Why didn't the Dirt Eaters try to find Longlight themselves?"

"They did. But your mother was shielding you. She was probably shielding the entire village."

"How would you know that? Couldn't it have been anyone?"

"All attempts to locate you were deflected by an impenetrable barrier. It had a specific protective quality that was recognized."

It's the prophecy. His father's voice had woken him. *That's only a myth.* Only a myth, his mother had said. *We have to leave. We have to leave now.*

"She was very powerful, Roan."

"She didn't believe in the prophecies."

Asp is startled by the statement. "She said that?"

Roan remembers his father's voice, desperate, trying to convince his mother. *You know the truth. We always knew this time would come.* Then she, strong, determined: *Wake them. Go, go, go!* "It's possible, isn't it, to know something but not want to believe it? Not until you have no other choice."

Asp considers Roan's question, then nods once, sadly. "Saint had conceived of the Visitations as a purifying wind of fire; it took your arrival for him to realize they were really genocide, performed under the orders of Darius. Saint did see the madness of it, in the end.

"In fact, all the Brothers were haunted by the destruction of Longlight. Your people sang as they were led to their deaths, Roan. An eerie humming. It was obvious the entire community had come to an agreement. They did not fight. They allowed themselves to be sacrificed. Why? Simply to fulfill a prophecy?"

All will not be lost. That was what Roan's father had promised his mother that terrible night.

Asp stares at Roan, hungry for his answer, but Roan says nothing. The Dirt Eater digs his fingernails into his palms so hard he draws blood. "I've had much opportunity to consider this question. Originally, I assumed it would have been better for your parents to seek Dirt Eater protection. But now I realize they could not risk such an alliance. We had been underground too long, alive too long to remember the pain of death, the agony of individual suffering. For us the battle had ceased to be about the needs of ordinary people, the kind of people who trust me to mend their wounds, heal their sicknesses, detoxify their lands. The eldest among us had ceased to think of the earth and how it must be healed. They strove more and more against Darius, and less and less for humanity. They broke every taboo when they placed Ferrell inside your sister. I now understand that Longlight had no choice but to trust in the prophecy."

As he drives his fingers even more deeply into his palms, blood drips from Asp's clenched fists onto the stone floor. "I will never take Dirt again," he says vehemently. "Your great-grandfather was right to reject it. Dirt has been our ruin. Let Wolf kill me. I've seen more than I can bear."

Roan gently places his fingers over Asp's bloody hands. "If you really want to make amends, help us."

Asp's eyes clear. "You would trust me?"

"I want to trust you. I don't know if I can. But there's something I think you could help me with."

"Ask. I will tell you if I am able."

Roan hesitates, scrutinizing the former Dirt Eater's face, listening to his breath, the blood pumping through his veins. Asp is telling the truth.

"I need to map all the territory occupied by the Turned and the Dirt Eaters in the Dreamfield."

"My own knowledge is limited. Any map I might draw will be crude at best, certainly not precise enough for your purposes." Asp frowns, his gaze turning inward. When he looks back at Roan, his eyes flash with enthusiasm. "I have some friends, though, who might be able to help you."

"Dirt Eaters?" Lumpy asks.

"Once, but no more," Asp maintains. "Their names are Othard and Imin. They questioned the ban on City technology and were deemed criminal. Rather than recant, they broke with Oasis and became traveling physicians. Soon after, they were overcome with a devouring illness. Fearing for their lives, they asked for my help. I had seen symptoms like these before and recognized that they were going through a withdrawal. It awakened them—and me—to the Dirt's darker side. From then on, I used Dirt sparingly, anxious for the day I might also sever my ties with Oasis. That day has finally come."

"So exactly how might these two physicians help us?"

"Have you ever heard of the Foresight Academy?"

After an inquiring look at each other, Roan and Lumpy shake their heads.

"It was the architect Ferrell's school. The Dirt Eaters' most valuable records and books were kept there, including maps of the Dreamfield. Darius discovered its location so it had to be abandoned, but Ferrell and his pupils managed to conceal the library before barely escaping with their lives. We are certain the Clerics found nothing of value in the great cavern but Darius, no doubt suspecting treachery, ordered the entrance to the complex obliterated. The explosion was felt for miles around. The library was assumed lost and all records of its location were destroyed. But Othard and Imin are convinced it is still intact. If they are right, you may find the information you require there."

"If they know where it is, why haven't they gone there themselves?" Lumpy asks, voicing Roan's very thought.

Asp chuckles. "In the years after its destruction, forays were attempted from which no one returned. Othard and Imin are scientists, not warriors. It is not a journey to be taken by the defenseless."

Roan's unsure why but he feels driven to seek out these physicians, find this Academy.

Unwilling to completely trust his compulsion, he glances at Lumpy, who's studying Asp. "What do you think," Roan asks, "worth the risk?"

"Yes," says Lumpy with a certainty that echoes Roan's.

"Stay here with Asp and plan a route to these physicians. I'll try to wrap up with the Brothers so we can leave first thing in the morning."

But before Roan reaches the door, Asp calls out, "It might be easier if I was to join you."

Roan turns back and looks at the man sadly. "You must stay here, Brother Asp, under the Apsara's protection. There is no doubt in my mind that if you left here, Brother Wolf would find you and kill you."

"I will gladly stay, Roan of Longlight, but, all respect to Brother Wolf, my fellow Dirt Eaters would surely kill me first."

The clouds that encircle the lip of the Caldera obscure the path to the valley below. Though the promise of dawn hovers over the southeastern horizon, the humid chill of night settles in Roan's bones. In a month, ice and snow will make the descent from this mountain treacherous, so Ende is already organizing the placement of her warriors in various villages across the Farlands.

He'd presented his plan to seek out the Foresight Academy to Stinger and Wolf the previous evening. His only hope of convincing them, he knew, was to call on the memory of their Prophet. So he reminded them that Saint collected books, not because he enjoyed reading them—he didn't know how—but because he'd believed that books contained information that would help him fight the City.

To Roan's relief the Brothers had agreed that he should try to find the library; what he hadn't counted on was that they wanted to accompany him. He'd had to insist that if they were to attempt to contact a smuggler and a Governor and arrange a meeting, it needed to be before winter set in and storms became more frequent and unpredictable. In the end, they had reluctantly conceded that to accomplish all of their goals they would have to, at least briefly, go their separate ways.

Roan's startled at the tenderness with which the Brothers part from Ende. He'd become so used to the formality of their meetings that he was unprepared for the intimacy of their goodbye. But he's not alone. Lumpy's mouth hangs open as each hulking warrior bends to accept Ende's blessing. It makes Roan think of pictures he's seen of knights and their queens, except for the fact that this particular "queen" is small only in appearance and could undoubtedly thrash her former students without breaking a sweat.

Turning to Roan, Stinger asks, "When may we expect you, Roan of Longlight?"

"In two or three weeks. I'll be there by the new moon."

"Have you settled on the location of this meeting?" Wolf is irritable. No doubt at the thought of having to contact a smuggler and a Governor.

Roan knows what he's about to tell him will only make it worse; he just hopes Wolf will accept it without their hook-swords being drawn.

"The camp of the Brothers."

As Wolf opens his mouth to disagree, Roan raises his hand. "The camp is well fortified and easily defended. Our visitors will feel safe there."

But Wolf is adamant. "We cannot allow heathens to taint our sacred ground. It is against all our beliefs."

"The Friend is everywhere. He is here, in Kira's home. He was on the mountain with Saint. The time is coming when all ground will be sacred. It must be so if we are to survive."

As Roan watches Wolf consider, he catches Ende's eye. She had said invoking the Friend would get Wolf to listen. Still, doing it makes Roan feel like a hypocrite.

"Perhaps," Wolf spits out.

"Do not forget the words of the Prophet." Kira's command gets Wolf's attention; this reminder is for him and him alone. "You made a vow to Saint, a promise to prepare the way for Roan of Longlight."

"And I will."

Ende's eyes slowly meet those of everyone gathered in the early dawn's chill mist. "Much has been discussed. As I taught you early in your training, Brothers Wolf and Stinger, the green branch bends, it yields and thus survives. The Apsara will join you within three days of Roan's arrival, at moon's first crescent."

Accepting her dismissal, Wolf and Stinger promptly take their leave.

As their shadows melt into the morning haze, Lumpy lets out all the breath he's been holding for the last few minutes. "I'd say that went...pretty well."

"Yes," says Kira, "no one died."

"We can be thankful for that," Ende agrees wryly. "You have taken your first step, Roan. You began it tripping, but in the end, your foot landed firmly. I would urge you to continue to consider the value of the Friend. The Brothers are deeply religious men, with thousands of followers in the Farlands. They have transformed their faith to accommodate you. This is no small gift to a leader. It must not be scorned."

"But it's dishonest for me to accept this gift. I don't believe in the Friend. He's not real."

"That is a harsh judgment," Ende says. "Roan of Longlight, you know there is more to this world than what most men see. You should not be so quick to deny another's truth before you have even attempted to meet it."

Kira whistles and within moments a young Apsara warrior joins them, a mare and stallion in tow. "Hope you like a fast horse." Kira grins wickedly at Lumpy.

Lumpy strokes the young mare's flank. "When I'm up that high I kind of keep my eyes half closed anyway."

Placing one hand over Roan's heart, Ende smiles. "There is so much that we must share and we have had so little time. If we all arrive at the Brothers' camp safely, I should like to convene a small council of my own—to tell you at least some of what I know of your great-grandfather." Joining Kira at the crest of the path that heads back down into their Caldera home, she calls back to Roan, "May you find what you seek, Roan of Longlight."

After they disappear from view, Roan looks helplessly at his best friend. "I think I made a mess of it."

"What do you mean? You accomplished everything you needed to."

"Didn't impress Ende."

Lumpy's unconcerned. "I have a feeling that's pretty much impossible."

Roan groans, putting his face in his hands. "What does she mean, meet the Friend? It's not just her either, even Rat said saving the children might involve the Friend. But I just can't see how. He's a figment Saint pieced together from pictures he saw in a book."

Lumpy taps him on the head. "When we get to your old stomping ground, maybe you can show me? The book. I mean, as your...Lieutenant, I should see it, shouldn't I?"

Roan raises an eyebrow at Lumpy and the proud smile lighting up his face.

"Well, it'd be a start, wouldn't it? I mean if there's anything to it. The Friend being...a friend...in some way."

Not knowing how to respond to Lumpy's openness to an alliance with a bloodthirsty god, Roan feels the impossibility of what he's attempting settle over him like a cloud. He barely remembers anything he said in yesterday's meetings. The future's tugging him forward, but he's not sure he's ready to embrace it. Everything seems so unreal, so unlike anything he's imagined. "How am I going to do this?"

Lumpy shrugs. "Just keep taking good advice and you'll be alright."

"And how do I tell good advice from bad?"

"If it's bad, and you take it, I'll kick you in the butt—or stamp on your toe…or something. Okay?"

Lumpy at least seems real. Real and surprisingly unafraid. Real and a friend.

"Okay."

the price of dirt

WHEN ROAN OF THE PARTING CAME TO US, AITHUNA COULD
SMELL THE DEATH IN HIM. LITTLE WAS KNOWN THEN OF
THE DIRT, BUT IT WAS CLEAR THAT IT WAS THE CAUSE OF HIS
ILLNESS. AND AS AITHUNA CLEANSED ROAN AND THE MANY
OTHERS WHO FOLLOWED, IT BECAME KNOWN TO HER THAT
JUST AS ITS USERS RAVAGED THE DREAMFIELD AND MADE IT
BARREN, SO THE DIRT DID UNTO THEM.

—THE WAY OF THE WAZYA

THE EARTH ERUPTS. Snakes of light furrow up out of the cracked, bleeding ground, shrieking. A great needled mouth splits open the sky. The gyrating light-serpents tear into Stowe's body.

"Stowe. Stowe!"

Someone's come to help her. "Here!" she screams. "I'm here!"

"Stowe!"

But no one comes, maybe they didn't hear her. Before she can call out again, the snakes whip around her. Lacerating her flesh, they pull her closer and closer to two unblinking eyes swimming in mottled green gore. Each pupil rolls with nauseating independence in an opposite direction, penetrating her thoughts, insinuating itself into her mind.

Stowe!

Willum. Willum! The monster's shaking her so hard she feels as if her head is about to explode.

Stowe! The voice wraps around her and she floats in a cool bubble that expands and contracts with her breath, slowing it, calming her.

Opening her eyes, she sees Willum's worried face above her. "Was it Ferrell?"

White crickets are all around her, on her blankets, her pillow, clinging to the bedposts. "No. Not Ferrell. The nightmare. A mouth swallowing…calling out my name, and the eyes, the eyes…"

Gently propping up Stowe's head, Willum holds a glass to her lips. "Drink it all, you've lost a lot of fluid."

Her pillows and sheets are soaked with sweat, even though one or another of Willum's Apsara friends comes in regularly to change them. Realizing how thirsty she is, she downs the water in one long swallow.

Willum places the flat of his palm on her forehead and a soothing warmth spreads through her, relaxing her. But the instant he draws his hand away, she feels as if every fiber of her being is moaning with discomfort.

"What's wrong with me, Willum? Why am I still so sick?"

Willum weighs his words carefully. "The crickets are containing Ferrell, but he draws what life he has from your spirit. It drains you and makes healing impossible. I've been doing my best to mask your presence, but he has weakened you to such a degree that something got through. Something powerful and…evil."

Stowe cannot seem to prevent her body from trembling. "You think Darius has found me?"

"No. Not Darius himself…but it is connected to him somehow. I cannot keep you safe here. You need to be at the Apsara's true home; there the rock can shield you."

"I thought we were going to Roan."

"He is there, but the journey is long. I had hoped you could regain some of your strength before we continued but you're too vulnerable here to stay. We will leave. Today. Rest while I make preparations."

Unable to bear his sadness, she turns away. Still, she can't help hear the heaviness of heart in his every step as he leaves her.

Willum says her brother is with the Apsara; if Roan is there, then surely that is the safest place to be. Does Roan have dreams like hers, she wonders? Visions of a monster constantly seeking him out, wanting to consume him?

"No," Mabatan snaps. She knew Willum would be proposing something unpleasant when he'd led her to the outskirts of the village's busy market. "What you are asking is dangerous. It's beyond my abilities."

"Very little is beyond your abilities, Mabatan."

"She is a Dirt Eater, Willum."

"That door is no longer open to her."

"I do not trust Dirt Eaters. I cannot."

"Perhaps not. But you trust in the path. You must open yourself to what it offers, Mabatan." Willum pauses to glance at a stand displaying stacks of antique photos and picture postcards. Mabatan knows he's waiting for her to agree. But she cannot guide the healer through the cleansing on her own. It is not possible.

Willum holds up a picture of a man and a woman posing in front of a gigantic tree. "These trees may return one day. We might stand before them like these two…if we defeat Darius."

Mabatan takes the picture from his hand and gives it back to the vendor. "And what has our succeeding to do with the Dirt Eater?"

"Her name is Alandra. She is not evil, Mabatan. She was only a child when the Dirt Eaters found her. She was sick, alone, and afraid."

"That is the past. Roan warned her, Willum; still she remained with them. And right now, there is so much Dirt in her system, it will be easy for the Dirt Eaters to walk in her dreams. What will she do then, Willum? What will she tell them?"

Turning to face her, Willum grips her shoulders. "That is what you need to discover. If you can find a way to trust her, Mabatan, then we can be sure she will work with us. She saved the Novakin once, gave up a great deal of her spirit to do it. She is linked to them, perhaps in ways we cannot understand. She is deep in her sickness, her behavior too erratic to make travel with her safe—and I must travel quickly if Stowe is to survive."

Mabatan's father had warned her that trusting the path and allowing it to lead her would often be difficult. Perhaps the future will reveal truths that she now finds impossible to imagine...and she can see that Willum will not be swayed. She slowly nods her head in agreement. "I pray you both reach your home safely."

Willum's smile is grim. "I have no choice. You too will accomplish your task, Mabatan. Because you must."

"What do I do if she cannot be trusted?"

Willum takes her hand, drawing her closer to him. "That you must put in the hands of the Apsara."

After he walks away, Mabatan picks up the picture of the

giant tree. There is writing on the back. And though she cannot read it, she knows what the smiles of the people in the photograph are saying. "Look at us," they say, "how can we be so small and this tree be so big? How can we be so young and it so old? Our flesh so weak, its wood so strong? And yet, despite all these things, we are its master."

The Wazya have planted the seeds. Some, even now, are being tended. Neither she nor Willum will live long enough to see them grow so tall. But perhaps if they all follow the path with open hearts, these giant trees will thrive once again, the Masters of today long gone into the earth that will feed them.

Mabatan returns to the house where she left Alandra under Resa's watchful eye. The warrior is standing outside, leaning on the door. "No real problems, but—" says Resa, pointing out the mess of overturned food and broken bowls that was once Alandra's dinner tray, "she's as testy as they come."

Shaking her head, Mabatan sighs. "I will need your help, Resa, over the coming days."

"Whatever you need, just ask. Why aren't you killing her, anyway?"

"She is to be cleansed."

"Ah," says Resa knowingly, and laughs. "A fate worse than death!"

With a wry smile, Mabatan opens the door, muttering, "Yes, but for who?" And stopping just one step inside the room, she waits until the door locks behind her.

The room stinks of Dirt. Dirt and sweat. And fear. The healer's body is never still, never relaxed. She's been pacing so much she's worn a path on the hemp mat that covers the cellar floor. Kicking at the wall, the Dirt Eater cries out in frustration. "What do you want from me?"

Mabatan would much rather be anywhere else, in the company of man-eating Skree, for instance, than here beginning this, but she sits cross-legged on the floor, her ease a pointed contrast to the Dirt Eater's agitation. "I want you to be cleansed of Dirt," she answers simply.

"What do you mean?" the healer demands, every word rising in desperation. "You took my Dirt. Cast it into the wind. Locked me in this room. How am I not cleansed?"

"Perhaps in a week you will be cleansed. Perhaps, not for a month. How often and how much you have taken the Dirt will determine your recovery. Until then, the Dirt Eaters can find you. You know this." Mabatan notes the way the healer's left hand squeezes the fingers on the right, the way she looks down at the floor.

"They came into my dream." Although barely above a whisper, the healer's words are clear. "How did you know?"

"It is what they do. What is it that they want?"

"Stowe. The children. Me. To go back. Back to Oasis." Alandra slumps onto the floor. She seems exhausted, her tone defeated.

"What did you tell them?"

"That I don't have Stowe. That I have not discovered what happened to the children."

Mabatan listens carefully to the beating of the Dirt Eater's heart. It is fast but steady. She is not lying, but she is being as careful with Mabatan as she was with the Dirt Eaters in her dream.

Mabatan speaks slowly so that her words might be heard and understood. "Dirt owns those who use it. And it will fight the body that does not remain true to it. You are a healer. Tell me your symptoms."

The Dirt Eater puts her fingers to her neck and counts. "My heart rate—much faster than normal. And I feel weak, irritable, not myself. I thought it was just fear, but I'm not afraid now, and still my hands…" Holding them in front of her, the healer tries to steady their trembling. Mabatan can see the anxiety mount in her eyes when her effort fails.

Mabatan rises and takes the Dirt Eater's hands in her own. They are so ghostly pale and fragile. They could so easily be broken. "Did your friends ever tell you why they have no children?"

The healer looks at Mabatan, surprised. "There is a chemical in the caves of Oasis. As long as they stay inside, they age slowly but they can't reproduce."

"So the Masters of the City," says Mabatan, carefully picking her words, "battle old age, because they do not live in the Caves?"

"That's right."

"But the Masters also have no offspring."

Alandra shrugs. "That could be their choice."

Mabatan focuses squarely on the healer. "It is because they eat Dirt."

The Dirt Eater's eyes shut tight. When they finally open, they're blazing with fury.

Squeezing the healer's hands tightly, Mabatan pulls her even closer. There is so much this girl does not understand and so little time to explain. "The area of the Dreamfield that you, the Dirt Eaters, and the Masters of the City know is only one small country among millions. But what you have done in this small space has caused a rift that is destroying all. The children hold this rift together. They will do it for as long as they can, but time is short and we must act quickly. Willum believes you are needed. And so you must be cleansed. I will bring herbs to help with the discomfort."

"Discomfort?"

"You will see."

The healer's eyes still harbor suspicion. Mabatan understands her doubt; the task will be a test for them both. Not everyone survives the cleansing.

It is already dusk and the journey so far has been gloomy, exceedingly gloomy. Though Stowe is immensely grateful to the white crickets, it is difficult to get used to having...well... bugs, perched on her head and shoulders; plus she is surrounded by four Apsara. They talk incessantly with Willum, like old cronies, drowning her in idiotic banter.

"Unhappy, Stowe?"

Why does Willum have to sound so caring, so concerned? She hates that tone. That insistent, persistent, I-have-the-patience-of-mountains voice Willum so likes to use on her. "You neglected to mention a crowd would be accompanying us," she says, her voice dripping with sweetness.

"This territory is plagued by Fandor, so I asked for an escort."

Stowe can feel Willum's inward sigh. Now he's patronizing her! "We do not need the Apsara. You and I have more than enough power to defeat an attack."

"Demonstrations of our kind of power are extremely unwise. It takes only one hidden observer to report back to Darius."

She feels stupid suddenly. Why are her thoughts so muddy? Darius has spies everywhere. No one knows this as well as she. Darius, eyes sharp as daggers, hands like claws combing through her hair, Darius calling her. Daughter… daughter…daughter…

"Stowe. Stowe, listen to me. I am doing my best to block him, but it is exhausting us. It will be easier if you sleep. Sleep. When you wake, you will meet my family. My sister and my grandmother. We will be safe."

She feels Willum's mind touching hers, soothing her. *Soon*, it says. *Soon you will be free of Ferrell. Soon you will be home.*

As she drifts into sleep, she reaches to touch Willum's cheek. His face is wet with tears. Silly Willum. Whatever could he be crying for?

a story worth telling

the son and the daughter of Longlight will rise
against those who hoard the dirt. stand with them
and you will reap all the benefit of their victory.
turn your back and you will live forever in shame.
—the book of Longlight

Stowe is close. Roan can sense it. He can't reach her, though, because there's a wall around her, like the Dirt Eaters used when they were trying to hide him from the Turned. But unlike their engulfing sands, or obliterating threads, this barrier is fluid: it leads him straight to Stowe and then shifts her presence elsewhere. Could it be Willum? Protecting her? Maybe he'd been too hasty in his decision to go in search of Ferrell's library, maybe he should be more actively searching for Stowe. But despite his yearning to see his sister, he knows he's made the right decision. Something's drawing him to Ferrell's library, something other than the map he seeks.

The effort to stay warm and the strenuous ride down the mountain have made Roan ravenous and the aroma of Lumpy's cooking soon commandeers his attention. "Smells ready," he declares, greedily eyeing the stew.

Lumpy smiles broadly. "Dig in."

Roan plunders the pot that hangs over a small fire. Lumpy's improvised a meal with greens and grains cultivated in the Caldera and the heat of the bowl and the steam rising from it cause Roan to sigh with pleasure. In short order the stew has made its brief journey into Roan's stomach, and he proclaims his satisfaction with a loud, uncensored burp.

"Like the stew?" says Lumpy.

"Delicious," Roan replies. But detecting a glint of mischievousness in Lumpy's eye, he asks, "What kind of protein is this?"

"One guess!" Lumpy grins.

"Where did you find bugs?" Roan burps again, only this time it's not so complimentary.

Ignoring the comment, Lumpy is more than happy to disclose his source. "The Apsara. They make this great jerky from them—for traveling and as an emergency food supply in case of a siege or something. There was a ton of it. They sure do know their bugs!" After a deep breath, Lumpy sighs. "Isn't it great, being out here again?"

"Nothing better," says Roan. The Apsara's volcano may be secure, but its rising mist obscures the night sky and Roan had missed seeing the stars.

Lumpy pulls out the leather cord that hangs from his neck, puts the silver whistle strung on it to his lips and blows so hard his whole face contorts. No sound comes out, at least not any the two friends can hear. Their white crickets become agitated, though, so they're sure the whistle's working. Tucking it back beneath his shirt, Lumpy listens, looks, then frowns in frustration. "How many times have I tried now?"

"Five thousand," smiles Roan, but Lumpy's too frustrated to do anything but glare back.

"When Mhyzah gave me this thing, I was told if I blew, the Hhroxhi would come. So...where are they?"

"You'd be happy if any old Hhroxhi showed up, right?

…Or is it Mhyzah you're hoping for?" Roan grins, hoping to tease Lumpy out of his disappointment. But though Lumpy turns an interesting shade of red, he remains steadfastly sullen.

"Maybe they found a new—what was it they called you?" Roan asks.

"A Gyoxip," Lumpy snorts. "It's hard to prove yourself as an intermediary when even your one friend, at least someone you thought was your friend…"

But Roan's stopped listening. In an instant, hook-sword in hand, he's leapt to his feet and is taking a fighting stance. He nods toward a figure skulking over the hill.

"What have we here?" it booms. "Why it's the mythical savior of civilization, and his erstwhile friend and budding theatrical genius!"

Roan relaxes the grip on his hook-sword at the sound of the familiar, mocking voice.

"Kamyar!" Lumpy cries, his humor instantly lifted by the Storyteller's presence.

"Good to see you, young Lump," says the Storyteller. "I came as quick as I could. Any more of that scrumptious-smelling banquet left in the pot? Is it bugs?"

"What are you…what brings you…how did you—?" Roan hesitates, unable to frame a question that doesn't seem rude and disrespectful. Why should he be suspicious of a proven friend like Kamyar? Because he knows loyalties can change, and he's learned the hard way that people are often not exactly who they say they are.

"I sent for him," Lumpy says, a little sheepishly. "You said you couldn't wait to see Kamyar's face when you told him about the library. I sort of took that literally."

Embarrassed, Roan turns back toward the Storyteller. "Sorry, there's just so much going on."

"No offense taken, Roan of Longlight. I'm gratified to see that you've adopted the free advice I gave in Oasis: ask many questions, accept nothing at face value...Not a bad turn of phrase. Now, what's this about a library?"

Kamyar listens intently as Roan relates Asp's tale of the two doctors. Finding himself a comfortable spot by the fire, he unfurls his bedroll with a flourish. "They have quite a reputation at Oasis, those two. A bit dotty, as I recall. Brilliant, though, in their own peculiar way. I have to say I'm envious, if they've got it right. I've done quite a bit of snooping myself and never come up with any satisfactory answers. The Dirt Eaters are rather secretive about their...secret locations. I don't suppose you could delay a day or two? I'm meeting up with Talia and Dobbs..."

"Wish we could. But we have to get to the Brothers' camp by new moon and we've no idea how far we'll be taken out of our way."

"And what business, pray tell, do you have up on the Brothers' mountain?"

"We're hoping to meet with a smuggler. And then Ende's coming with some Apsara. And a Governor will be there," Lumpy says rather proudly. "Maybe. I've never even seen a Governor, never mind met one."

"Hah!" Kamyar crows jubilantly. "Sounds like a war council to me. Am I invited?"

"Yes," Roan blurts. "I mean. We'd like you to attend." Being caught between his friendship with Kamyar and his need of him as a political ally is making Roan feel more awkward than he would like. "Darius has a lot of enemies, but right now they aren't talking to each other. It's not much but I thought getting some of them together might be a start."

Kamyar, however, seems unconcerned with Roan's ineptitude. "Wouldn't miss it for the world," he announces. "And don't underestimate the power of communication, Roan. The City's controlled the Farlands by dividing its people and fomenting distrust, but I think the time is ripe to turn the tide." Then, procuring, with an almost magical sleight of hand, a generously proportioned bowl, he leans into the fire. "Don't mind if I do, thank you," he says as he fills it with Lumpy's fragrant stew. "I confess I am a little surprised to see you've left the Caldera just when your sister's about to arrive."

"Willum found Stowe! Is she alright?"

"How well she is, I don't know. But I've had word she's alive."

Roan throws his arms around Kamyar and hugs him, lifting him right off the ground. "Thank you. You don't know how much hearing that means to me."

With his full-to-the-brim bowl of steaming stew balanced precariously in one hand, Kamyar winces. "Actually, I think I do."

"Sorry," says Roan, carefully releasing the Storyteller. "I've been so worried. In the mountains, I couldn't sense her."

"Well, if anyone can help her, Willum can." Raising his bowl to his nose, Kamyar takes a theatrical sniff. "Umm. Now if you'll excuse me..." Settling himself against his voluminous pack, Kamyar attacks his meal with gusto.

Clearing his throat, Roan shifts uncomfortably. "So... does your being here mean we can count on the help of the Storytellers?"

Kamyar abruptly raises his head. "Now, there's the

question. Well." Squinting at Roan, he continues, "There are twenty-four Storytellers. Only three are from Oasis; the others found their way there as waifs from the Farlands. A few, like myself, maintain close ties smuggling in Dirt for the Eaters, but for most it's not much more than a rest stop. Its main attraction, as you know, is Orin's library. Ah. We come to that again. You're going to Othard and Imin's for the map?"

Roan can't help but grin at the Storyteller's persistence. "That's right."

"Suppose you left us some sign..."

Lumpy jumps in excitedly, "We could mark the trees, the way you etched the stone when we were caught in the labyrinth into Oasis."

"Inspired suggestion, Master Lump. What say you, Roan of Longlight?"

"Can't see why not. It'd have to be inconspicuous, though. And we'll be moving quickly."

"Quick I'm expert at and I'll let you in on a trade secret. Vertical line for north, horizontal for south. East is a diagonal, starting from the top, right to left, and west is its opposite. If you're traveling northeast you combine the appropriate symbols. Keeps the markings to a minimum, only be sure to indicate when you change directions—otherwise all is lost."

"Do they know these symbols in Oasis?" Roan asks carefully.

"I work for them, Roan. My secrets, I keep to myself and those I trust. History, legend, myth—it's true I've sweetened their medicine and made sure it was well distributed. But even in that I have veered dangerously from the proscribed path, almost from the very beginning."

"Why?" Roan asks.

"Ask many questions." Kamyar chuckles. "I ought to be more careful to exempt myself from my own sage advice. All right then. A story. Mine. I met a fellow, a good twenty years ago, who changed my life. I had just finished plying my newly acquired trade before a deeply appreciative audience when this slight, ageless-looking man came up to me. 'The only stories worth telling,' he said somewhat disapprovingly, 'are ones that can change the world.' Well, he burst my self-satisfied bubble, but, luckily for me, I was overcome with a feeling of momentousness. I knew somehow I should listen to him, and listen well. Turned out he was the greatest teller of tales I'd ever met. The Carrier of the Wazya bloodline. It's been three years or more since I last cast eyes on Khutumi, but his voice echoes in my mind as if we'd spoken yesterday."

Lumpy says the word slowly. "Wazya. I've heard about them, some kind of magical creatures."

"Not magical, at least not the way you mean it. Just hard to find. But tiny miracles do follow where they tread. The Wazya are one of the oldest of all the cultures of humankind. Solitary travelers, they seed and tend our ravaged earth. White crickets are said to appear in their wake. And from the beginning, they've traveled the Dreamfield without Dirt. There is one in each generation that carries the accumulation of all their stories. Khutumi is the carrier for this one."

With a flash of insight, Roan knows. "Rat. Khutumi is Rat. I saw it in the Dreamfield. One face melding into another. One and many. Khutumi and his ancestors are all contained in Rat."

"This meal is really sensational, Lumpy," says Kamyar, helping himself to another bowlful.

"Where does one find Khutumi outside the Dreamfield?" Roan wonders aloud.

Kamyar licks his spoon. "He was always an elusive fellow. Then, last year he suffered an injury, one grave enough to prevent him from traveling. Only his daughter knows where he can be found. My conduit to him is through her. She's fed me many a tale, many a myth, even a few about you."

"His daughter?" asks Lumpy.

Roan leans over to touch his friend's arm. "It's Mabatan. Rat told me but by the time I got down to see you, Wolf and Stinger were already there and..."

But Lumpy waves away Roan's apology, shaking his head in amazement. "That's how she travels without Dirt, and why she's connected to the crickets, and...and...she knows so much. She's Wazya."

Wazya. The word touches something buried deep within Roan's memory. A story his mother told him long ago. He was so young then, it's difficult to recollect it. Except for that word: Wazya. And...his mother, guiding his hand over rock and wood and leaf, asking, "Can you feel it?" She must have known about them. The Wazya and Longlight were connected somehow, he could feel it.

"Did Mabatan find Willum—is she with him?" Roan feels an urgent need to know.

"Last I heard she was in that village where Saint used to sometimes lay his head. The one with all those very...strong Apsara." Kamyar smiles broadly. "They can be friendly, if they like the story. So when I'm there, I'm always at my best. Anyway...apparently she has something to do in that village.

Whatever it is, I'm sure she'll join up with you again…when it's done."

Roan snorts, half out of frustration, half out of amusement. "If any of those myths of Khutumi's give some straight answers," says Roan, "I'd like to hear them."

"Truth be told, Roan of Longlight, the problem is often not in the answer but in how we hear it." Kamyar wipes off his face, and pats his well-fed belly.

"Now I'm wondering if I should have left the Caldera at all." Roan sighs. "This searching for a library that was probably destroyed…"

"You know," Kamyar says, leaning into the firelight, "one of the most useful things Khutumi told me was that we discover possibility for ourselves and for others in the stories that we are told. But possibility is useless unless you chase after it. Roan, you have to pursue the opportunities laid out before you. If you do, you can gain the power to reinvent not only yourself but the world. Trust the path and the way will open before you." And with a wide yawn, Kamyar diligently begins to make himself comfortable for a good long sleep.

But Roan's not ready to let the Storyteller drift off. Not yet. "Yes, well, you sort of told me that before. Create the future as you go. But there are already so many stories about me. It's like my life is one of your scripts, and there's nothing really left for me to do except act it out."

Kamyar props himself up on his elbow and eyes Roan sympathetically, if a little sternly. "Well, we all feel that way at times, my boy, if we bother to think about it. Truth be told, though, all those prophecies are pretty vague about *how* things will happen. It's a script, yes, but with a lot of room for improvisation. Which, make no mistake, is never easy, but

I'm sure you're up to the challenge." Kamyar's head drops on his blanket and as if in afterthought, he adds blearily, "Oh, yes. About your request earlier. Being a bit of a leader-type myself, I think I can safely speak for we Storytellers as a group. You can rely on us to assist in whatever way we can. I may even have a few ideas, if you care to..." And with a snore, Kamyar calls a halt to the evening's discussion.

Roan leans back to take in the waxing moon as Lumpy tucks in for the night. Their crickets sing, wings glowing in the firelight. "A story to change the world," Lumpy murmurs drowsily. "What a story that will be."

When Roan wakes, there's a thread of silver moonlight in the west, and a firelike glow announcing dawn in the east. Kamyar's already gone, no doubt hoping to be quick enough to head them off at Othard and Imin's.

At the crest of the hill silhouetted against dawn's corona are two figures. Moving closer, Roan can see that it's Lumpy in an animated conversation with the Blood Drinker, Mhyzah—that should make him happy. Roan joins them, bowing courteously to the young Hhroxhi. She bares her fangs and hisses. Though Roan can tell from her intonation it's only a greeting, he keeps his distance. The scar on his chest burns a little. Despite his attempt to make peace with Mhyzah and her people, Roan feels the blood of Mhyzah's father will always stand between them.

"Any chance of the Hhroxhi joining our cause?" Roan asks.

With a glance at his red-eyed friend, Lumpy shakes his head. "Her people are split. Some believe they should act in support of the prophecies about you and the Novakin and the downfall of the City but others are against it, violently against it. It's very close to erupting into civil war. Mhyzah still hopes some of them will be able to help. They're trying to establish a secret network." Lumpy's distress is obvious, his pocked brow creased with worry. "It's dangerous, Roan, what she's doing. I told her we'd be grateful but not at the expense of the lives of her own people."

Roan shares his friend's uneasiness. He certainly doesn't want more Hhroxhi blood on his hands.

Mhyzah touches Lumpy's arm and as she speaks, Lumpy translates. "She says Xxisos is working to persuade their people that this struggle belongs to both Hhroxhi and human. That we share a common enemy. She's sure she will have secured passage through enough of the tunnels by the time we need them. You are defender of the Novakin and she will not dishonor her people with failure."

Roan's eyes meet Mhyzah's in acknowledgment. He can detect nothing but friendship, trust, hope. She believes in him. He watches as Lumpy extends his thanks to her. When Mhyzah places her hands on his chest, Lumpy does not hesitate to cup his over hers affectionately. It's such an easy gesture, but so far from possible for Roan that it makes his heart ache. Roan's always admired Lumpy's ability to get close to people. He makes people feel comfortable—at least those who know enough to look beyond the Mor-Tick scars.

As quietly as Mhyzah appeared, she's gone.

"She seems to like you."

"It's the oozing Mor-Tick pits. She knows looking hideous and potentially fatal separates me from the rest of humanity. Sort of the way fangs and blood drinking set her apart." Lumpy grins. "Don't look so glum. Mhyzah knows how to take care of herself. What we're trying to do, it's just as important to her. She wants to help."

"Even though I killed her father?"

"Because you came forward and admitted to killing her father," Lumpy says emphatically. "If you hadn't, they would never have known who to fight with in the struggle ahead. That scar you were given, it's a bond. A bond between Mhyzah and you, a bond between you and the Hhroxhi."

Clear skies have made the morning's ride easy, but the landscape has cast a pall over Roan and Lumpy. Charred stumps spread before them like a sea of ancient tombstones. This is all that remains of a forest that grew here long ago, a bleak reminder of Darius's destructive capabilities. Still, Roan wonders why no one has settled in this part of the Farlands. Some of the land around Longlight had once looked like this, but seeds had been planted and it had been made fruitful again. He cannot feel the Wazya's presence in this place at all. How do they choose to reclaim one spot over another?

Interrupting Roan's thoughts, Lumpy says, "Don't like the look of that."

A massive bank of storm clouds is rapidly moving in from the northwest. "Will we get there before it hits us?" Roan asks gloomily.

With a disgruntled snort, Lumpy pulls out a makeshift map and examines it closely. "They live somewhere in those woods," he says, pointing to a wavering band of green on the horizon. "We should be there by mid-afternoon. But those clouds will be on top of us in an hour."

As lightning streaks across the barren landscape, Roan looks longingly at the forest ahead. The Apsara provided them with winter cloaks, but Roan knows they will be soaked through by the oncoming storm. As if simultaneously having the same thought, both he and Lumpy raise their hoods and urge their horses forward at greater speed.

By the time they reach the woodland, the rain has turned to sleet and the sky is so dark it's difficult to see. Signaling Lumpy, Roan slips under the cover of the tall conifers and dismounts. "Maybe we should walk the horses. Don't want to scare anyone off."

Shaking the ice from their cloaks, the friends set off through the trees with quiet precision. But after only a few moments in the lush forest, Lumpy stops, awestruck. "They've been here. The Wazya. You can feel it."

Roan's been so preoccupied with thoughts of Darius and his apparent omnipotence that he hadn't noticed the forest around him. Under the canopy of dense foliage, there's a rich verdant smell that makes him want to join Lumpy and breathe deeply. The only ones who seemed to be having any real success against Darius are the Wazya, growing forests like these, ensuring life still thrives under the Keeper's thumb. The contrast with the morning's landscape is startling.

Roan suddenly realizes that Darius never stopped waging his war. He had scattered the rebels and devastated the countryside but that hadn't been enough. He'd wanted the Farlands under his control. So he demoralized the people by stealing their children and taking the fruits of their labor. Or he tried to exterminate them—like the Apsara...like Longlight. A slow burning rage warms the pit of Roan's stomach. Even if it kills him, he's going to put an end to the war Darius began long ago.

Lumpy's cricket is perched on his shoulder and Roan

looks down to see his own leaping onto his hand. Soon their song is answered by dozens of unseen others. The friends stand mesmerized listening to this secret language until it quiets abruptly.

"That sounded a lot like talking."

"Well, at least it seemed friendly."

"Lumpy, can you understand why the Wazya reclaimed this land and not where we were this morning?"

"I've been thinking about that too. Remember how after we'd sailed about four days out on the lake at Fairview, it started to change? The life in the water was slowly detoxifying it. Maybe what the Wazya try to do is find the best spot to start from and then the renewal spreads from that place. They must have planted these trees right after the wars." As Lumpy scans the forest, he stops abruptly, pointing. "Look."

Following the direction of Lumpy's finger through the needle-leafed trees, Roan sees a pair of horses grazing in a small corral.

"This is the spot," Lumpy confirms, checking his map.

"But there's no sign of a dwelling."

With a grin, Lumpy casually points a finger up. Roan peers into the dense foliage. "Are you sure?"

Lumpy shrugs. "According to Asp."

"Give me a minute."

Leaning against a tree, Roan takes a few deep breaths and in a very short time, his ether body follows his exhalation up through the leaves. When he comes to a structure made of woven branches he knows his search is over. Past the cleverly camouflaged walls is a rustic laboratory. Two middle-aged men in shabby robes sit at a table intently pouring liquids from one vial into another. Roan inspects every shelf and container of the rough-hewn room. There's no sign of Dirt. Or weapons.

Satisfied, Roan falls back into his body. "Found it," he mouths to Lumpy with a grin, and locating the correct tree, begins his ascent.

"Don't forget this," Lumpy whispers, holding out Roan's hook-sword.

But Roan shakes his head. "Won't need it," he says, and reaching to the next branch, he pulls himself up and away.

Secure foot and handholds make the ascent as simple as climbing a ladder. Finding an opening at the base of the treehouse, he quietly lets himself in. The two men continue their work as Roan does something with his real body that his ether form cannot: to his relief, there is not the slightest scent of Dirt.

Roan clears his throat, but the men, utterly engrossed in their work, ignore him. "Excuse me," he says, quite loudly, worried they might be hard of hearing. "Would you happen to be Othard and Imin?"

Both are visibly startled, but only one peers over his test tube to acknowledge the visitor. "I am Othard. Who are you?"

"My name is Roan of Longlight."

Both physicians freeze as if confronted by some fantastic apparition.

"Roan? Of Longlight?" asks the other physician.

Roan nods. They stare at him quizzically, then at each other. Imin, presumably, stands up and pumps Roan's hand. "Forgive us. There is a virus in Farlands we are trying to defeat. It's become a rather absorbing obsession."

"Brother Asp told me you might know how to find a

place I'm looking for," Roan says, wanting to get straight to the point.

"And what might that be?" Othard asks.

"The Foresight Academy," Roan answers, almost causing Othard to tip his test tube over in its stand.

Imin leans against the table for support. "You planning on traveling there alone?"

"No," admits Roan, "I've a friend."

Othard and Imin share a worried look, before Imin asks: "Is he strong?"

"He's a Mor-Tick survivor."

"That'd do it."

Nodding in agreement, Othard bravely steps forward. "May we come along?"

The doctors wait, eyes wide, not breathing.

"I was hoping you'd ask," Roan replies.

"Oh, thank you, thank you!" they shout, embracing each other.

"You have no idea how long we've dreamed of going there," says Imin, taking Roan's hand in his.

"But our responsibilities were huge, and the dangers in going to the Academy great," Othard adds.

"We are not warriors like you..."

"...or as frightening in our countenance as a Mor-Tick survivor..."

"...so we dared not take the risk..."

"...but we did the calculations..."

"...and there's a good chance it's survived." Imin stops, suddenly unsure, and peers at Roan. "The library. That's why you're going, isn't it? For the library?"

As Roan nods an assent to Imin, Othard reaches inside

a cabinet and removes a false wall from the back. Inside is a rolled-up parchment. Withdrawing it, Othard explains, "It has taken years to piece this map together. Questioning the Dirt Eaters was not an option. It would have only increased their already growing suspicions of us. But there were clues. Clues in the library at Oasis, here and there."

"Here and there," Imin echoes, "in journals."

"And letters," Othard adds. "Duty rosters. Memorandum."

"Doctors," Roan interrupts. "The map?"

"This is it," says Othard, tapping the roll in his hand.

"Did we mention," interjects Imin, "the place is booby-trapped?"

"How do you know?" Roan asks.

"Rumors..."

"...Reports..."

"...Accounts..."

"...No one who's gone there has ever—"

"Yes! I understand. Thank you. Maybe you'd like to pack a few things for the trip?" says Roan, attempting to stem the tide.

"Oh! Are we going now?" asks Othard.

"Yes. Right now."

"This is a great day, Roan of Longlight," exclaims Imin, quickly throwing some clothes and notebooks into a pack.

As the two physicians charge toward the hatch and collide with each other, Roan can't help but wonder if he's made a mistake in inviting them along.

the exorcism

MABATAN INTERVIEW 2.4.

WE WALKED FOR MANY YEARS WITH THE WHITE CRICKETS BEFORE WE KNEW THE LANGUAGE OF THEIR SONG. THEN WE UNDERSTOOD THAT THE EARTH SPOKE TO THEM, AND THROUGH THEM, ITS MESSAGE CAME TO US.

—GWENDOLEN'S CRICKET FILE

THE ROOM IS TOO SMALL. The healer needs to writhe and scream and run—exhaustion might soothe and dampen her senses. Watching her claw the walls, Mabatan yearns for the quiet wetlands she called home. She can feel the paddle in her hand, the boat slipping through the current, smell the new growth all around her. Perhaps she will never see them again. The thought flits around her like a hungry fly, ready to land and bite the instant she weakens her guard.

The Dirt Eater's hair is limp with sweat; her eyes gleam with the rage that the craving brings. Mabatan dips a towel into a pail of cold water and offers it to the healer. "Keep chewing the leaf, it will help with the pangs."

The healer twists the towel in her hands, panting. "You say the children are in the Dreamfield. You say I am to help them. How? You lie to me, Wazya. You lie. How can I help them if you deprive me of Dirt?"

How the Dirt Eater is to aid the children is a mystery to Mabatan. Even in the best of conditions, years of training are required to travel to the Dreamfield on the needle's song.

So she ignores the question and holds a bowl to the healer's lips. "Drink as much as you are able. The water is infused with purgatives."

Mabatan waits as the Dirt Eater struggles between thirst and anger. For the moment thirst wins.

As the healer drinks, Mabatan's white cricket crawls out from her pocket and onto her arm. She smiles, listening to it. She has always lived in the company of crickets and enjoyed the aura of protection and friendship they bestow. After her mother had disappeared and her grandmother died, the crickets had soothed her to sleep, opening her eyes to the things her ancestors had loved and cared for. They had guided her *wichumin*, the journey each Wazya must take at the age of thirteen. Since that time, if her father needed her, the crickets had been the ones to let her know. Of all her teachers, friends, and family, they'd always been the most constant.

"I must go," she says, putting down the bowl. "I am needed."

But as she rises, the Dirt Eater kicks over the bowl and clutches at her arm. "You understand the crickets?"

Suppressing her urge to thrust the healer aside, Mabatan answers patiently, "They speak to me. I hear them."

"What do they say?"

"That I must go." Mabatan recognizes the desperation that colors the healer's voice, the fear of being alone in her pain and the feelings of self-destruction that are hidden in its wake. "I won't be far. Keep chewing the leaves, drinking the water. You are strong. Use your strength to fight your enemy." But the Dirt Eater will not let go of her arm.

"Who are you?"

"I am Mabatan."

"That is not an answer!"

The healer's grip on Mabatan's arm is tightening. "Release my arm."

"The Wazya are a myth. Who are you really? Are you from the City? Your friend, he looked like a Master. What do they want from me? Why don't you kill me and have it over with?"

Mabatan twists, bringing her free elbow down hard just above the Dirt Eater's heart. As the healer collapses forward, her grip slackens. Pulling herself free, Mabatan swings round to sit on her fallen charge.

"I do not blame you for distrusting me, but you must understand I will not allow myself to be harmed by you, Dirt Eater."

"My name is Alandra," the healer spits out defiantly.

"I know your name, Dirt Eater. I know the name of your old teacher as well. And, despite your protests, I have no reason to believe you are not also capable of his actions. You were thrust in my path and I help you because it seems that I must. But until you prove yourself otherwise, you are my enemy, and I will name you as such."

"Why do you hate the Dirt Eaters so much?"

Ah. Mabatan must not forget that this one is a healer. "Is it not enough that their actions are destroying the Dreamfield? That they think only to use the children you tried to save as weapons?"

The healer looks up at Mabatan defiantly. Her lips widen into a venomous smile and the air in the room becomes thick with her desire to hurt Mabatan. "Liar," she whispers.

Suddenly aware of the frantic pounding of her heart, Mabatan stands and knocks on the door, never taking her eyes off the Dirt Eater. The healer laughs contemptuously and Mabatan does not breathe easily until Resa shuts the door behind her.

"How's it going in there? Sounded a bit noisy," Resa comments knowingly.

Mabatan scowls, then looks urgently at the Apsara warrior. "Resa, there is something I must do. I will be in my room. I cannot be disturbed."

Resa nods. "I understand."

"Do not let her sleep."

The warrior shifts uneasily from foot to foot. "How strong will she become when the sickness leaves her?"

"You think her capable of overcoming you?" smiles Mabatan.

Lips pursing, Resa stands a little taller. "No one knows the limits of Dirt Eater power. Even the bravest warriors fear what they do not comprehend."

"Yes, you are wise to fear her," says Mabatan, the healer's dry laughter echoing in her mind. "Take appropriate precautions."

Willum gazes out at the shifting mist that masks the top of the volcano. The Caldera itself is still as he remembers it: black stone, warmth rising from deep inside the earth, green fields, swaying bamboo. But the Apsara community has grown: there are more children than when he last visited, many more buildings and paintings, swirling kaleidoscopes of color, pleasing to eye and heart. So much changes in fifteen years. And though Ende is still strong and fit, the lines in her face are deeper when she smiles, partly the ravages of age, partly those of worry. Willum feels her burden. Apsara are sure to perish in the battles to come, and she loves each as a mother loves a child.

Footsteps, almost silent. The right leg is favored, ever so slightly. No one else would notice, he is sure. Always ready to attack with the left. This is how their mother's death marked her. "Kira."

"Grandmother is ready."

"When is she not?" He never understood why Ende chose Kira to take on the challenge of Saint, but there is no doubt Kira is the stronger for it. She has grown into the warrior she was destined to become; the only residue of the terror she experienced as a child is the battle readiness she carries even in her most relaxed moments. "Did I tell you how good it is to see you again?"

Kira grins at him. "Yes, when you first arrived, then again at breakfast, and last night as well."

"The City has made me clumsy at sharing my heart."

"I'm teasing," Kira says dryly. "I'm sure I've told you just as many times how awfully good it is to have *you* back. I've missed you terribly." Then, putting her arm through his, she leads him toward Ende's quarters.

With her touch comes a surge, a vision: her face distorted in pain. How or why he cannot tell. Only that it will be death she faces, death. But as hard as he tries, he cannot reach further, cannot see the outcome.

"What is it? You sensed something, didn't you?"

"Yes." Willum knows better than to lie to his sister.

Kira elbows him in the ribs. "Fifteen years of fooling Darius and the Masters and you still couldn't try to pull the wool over my eyes?" she grins.

"Kira…"

"No. It's all right. I don't want to know. I have no illusions about what's to come, Willum. Darius is ancient, his power vast and insidious. I fight for the children. Whether or not I'm to be part of their future, only fate can decide."

Kira stops and, placing a hand on his cheek, she kisses Willum gently. "You think the girl will help us? She was pretty angry when we told her Roan had gone."

Touching his forehead to his sister's, Willum whispers, "If there is enough of her left, yes, she will."

Moving again toward Ende's threshold, they are greeted by the aromatic scent of burning herbs. Through the misty doorway, Willum can see Stowe lying eyes open, breath shallow.

"Come," Ende calls out.

Stowe reaches up a hand to Willum. "What took you so long?"

Squeezing her hand comfortingly, Willum observes with concern that Stowe's eyes are stained with blood. The strain of keeping Ferrell in control is rupturing her blood vessels.

Ende places a hand on Stowe's shoulder. "Stowe has many questions. Not the least of which concern our motives in this situation. I have striven to assure her that what she is about to undergo is in her best interests as well as ours. I have asked her to seek this truth within herself."

"This could kill me and you know it," Stowe snaps.

"*Could* is a great distance from *will*," Ende replies, her tone gracious. "The exorcism is not without danger, but if you allow Ferrell to continue to possess you he will terminate your life. This is certain."

"You are Apsara. I cannot trust you."

"Is there anyone you trust?"

As realization of this harsh truth hardens Stowe's delicate

features, Willum fights to retain his composure. She is his charge and he has failed her. He acted too slowly. Saw the truth too late. It is no wonder she has lost her confidence in him.

"I will not let you face this alone, Stowe. I will be with you," he says, gently encouraging her. Though she will not look at him, her small hand grips his more tightly.

"Remain still," Ende warns Stowe. "Find your breath." She stabs the floor with a long needle and flicks it with her finger. It emits a sound, soft yet penetrating, sweet but unyielding. Dozens of white crickets emerge from Willum's pockets, from under Stowe's blankets, from behind the candles, from the cracks in the walls.

"Ferrell," Stowe gasps.

"He must wake. We cannot purge him if he sleeps. I stand with you, Stowe. Can you feel the vibration of the needle? How the crickets sing with it? We must join their song. It will take us where we need to go. I will see to Ferrell." And as Stowe beings to sing, Willum gently crosses the threshold of her mind.

What are you up to, my little house?

You will stay back, Willum commands.

Dodging him, Ferrell seeps up Stowe's spine. **Trading one master for another, are we?**

But Willum quickly adds his song to Stowe's and, together with the tone of the needle and the singing of the crickets, their energy swells. It bursts out of their chests, a great sonic wave that sweeps Ferrell mercilessly in its wake.

Boulders of flaming rock crash into the protective barrier above them. A crimson lizard emerges from Stowe's right side and lunges at her throat. With a cry of

TERROR, STOWE SLASHES AT THE ATTACKING REPTILE. STUMBLING, SHE FALLS HARD ONTO THE UNYIELDING GRANITE FLOOR. THE LIZARD DIGS ITS TEETH INTO HER SHOULDER, AND THEY BOTH HOWL WITH PAIN——THEIR BODIES ARE FUSED, THEIR SENSES ONE.

WILLUM'S HAWK EYES GLEAM; THERE IS NOTHING HE WOULD LIKE MORE THAN AN OPPORTUNITY TO SNAP OFF THIS ONE'S HEAD, BUT HURTING FERRELL NOW MEANS HARMING STOWE.

"I THINK I WILL KILL YOU, MY LITTLE HOUSE," THE LIZARD HISSES. "BETTER THAT WE BOTH DIE NOW."

"IN THAT, FERRELL, YOU WILL FAIL." THE WARNING COMES FROM BEHIND THE LIZARD AND HE TWISTS TO IDENTIFY THE VOICE. WILLUM WATCHES, CONTENT TO SEE FERRELL FLINCH NOTICEABLY AT THE SIGHT OF RAT. NOW, AT LAST, THIS MONSTER CAN BE DISPENSED WITH.

"YOU CANNOT KILL ME," THE LIZARD SCREAMS, JAWS SNAPPING. "I HAVE A RIGHT TO BE HEARD!"

"YOU HAVE A RIGHT TO NOTHING." THE RAT'S LIPS PEEL BACK TO REVEAL ITS TEETH. "YOU GAVE UP THE HIGH GROUND WHEN YOU INVADED ANOTHER HUMAN."

"THE MASTERS MUST BE DEFEATED——"

"YOU DEFEAT NO ONE BUT YOURSELVES."

"WE FIGHT FOR THE SURVIVAL OF ALL."

"WE HAVE NOT COME TO LISTEN TO YOUR JUSTIFICATIONS, BUT TO SEPARATE YOU FROM THE ONE YOU HAVE DEFILED AND RETURN YOU TO THOSE WHO SHARE YOUR DELUSIONS."

"BUT YOU CAN'T——YOU'RE NOT A MURDERER AND I WILL SURELY DIE," FERRELL WHINES, TWISTING DESPERATELY IN STOWE'S SIDE.

HIS EFFORTS HAVE NO RESULT, HOWEVER; THE RAT ONLY CONTINUES TO STARE AT HIM UNBLINKING AND DELIVERS THE

SENTENCE FOR FERRELL'S CRIME. "THE PROCESS OF SEPARATION WILL ERASE YOUR MEMORY. YOU WILL BE AS A CHILD, EVERYTHING AND EVERYONE YOU ONCE KNEW YOU WILL MEET AS IF FOR THE FIRST TIME. PERHAPS THE ONES WHO SUPPORTED THIS ABOMINATION WILL FIND IT IN THEIR HEARTS TO ASSIST YOUR RECOVERY. PERHAPS NOT. AND, FERRELL, YOU WILL NEVER BE ABLE TO TREAD IN THE DREAMFIELD AGAIN."

AS THE LIZARD JERKS VIOLENTLY, RAT ASKS, "STOWE, WILL YOU HAVE THIS THING UNDONE?"

"YES." STOWE'S VOICE RISES BRAVELY OVER FERRELL'S PROTESTATIONS.

A BLUE RABBIT BOUNDS IN FROM THE SHADOWS TO JOIN THEM. MABATAN. AS SHE LETS OUT A LONG, PIERCING NOTE, A THUNDEROUS CACOPHONY ECHOES ALL AROUND THEM. DOZENS OF WHITE CRICKETS, EACH ONE AS LARGE AS A MAN, APPEAR IN THE SHELTER AND A CASCADE OF SOUND ENCLOSES THE GATHERING.

HUNDREDS OF REFLECTIONS STARE BACK AT STOWE FROM THE CRICKETS' MULTIFACETED EYES. THEY ARE ALL OF A PERSON SHE DOES NOT RECOGNIZE——LONG BLACK HAIR OVER A PALE, NARROW FACE——UNTIL THE EYES, GREEN AND COLD, MEET HERS: FERRELL. AS SOON AS SHE KNOWS IT IS HIM, THE IMAGES SHIFT TO A LIZARD, THEN A CLAY GIRL. AND AFTER THAT, HER-SELF, IN HUMAN FORM. THE CRICKETS' EYES SPIN FASTER AND FASTER, BREAKING THEIR LIKENESSES APART AND MIXING THEM UP: LIZARDS WITH CHILDLIKE HANDS, GIRLS WITH LIZARDS' HEADS. THOUSANDS OF DIFFERENT COMBINATIONS FLASH RELENTLESSLY BEFORE HER UNTIL THE PRESSURE IS UNBEAR-ABLE. AS IT CRUSHES HER AGAINST THE HARD GROUND, SHE IS RIPPED IN TWO. SHE TRIES TO SCREAM, BUT SHE HAS NO VOICE. HER HAND REACHES BUT THERE IS NOTHING, NOTHING ON HER

RIGHT SIDE. NOTHING. JUST A HOLE WHERE SHE ONCE HAD HALF HER BODY. HER EYES SEE ONLY RED, AS IF THE WORLD WERE SWIMMING IN BLOOD. BLOOD AND SILENCE. SHE CANNOT EVEN HEAR HER HEARTBEAT.

WILLUM STARES INTO STOWE'S VACANT, OPEN EYES. "I CANNOT REACH HER."

RAT SNIFFS AT THE TWO BODIES BETWEEN THEM, THEN LOOKS UP FROM THE LIZARD AND THE CLAY GIRL. "NO," HE AGREES. "BUT THERE IS STILL HOPE. TAKE HER NOW, WILLUM. HURRY. MABATAN WILL GUIDE YOU. I WILL RETURN FERRELL TO HIS PEOPLE."

THE RABBIT HOPS CLOSER AND AS THE HAWK SHIFTS TO ACCOMMODATE HER, HIS WING BRUSHES AGAINST RAT. WILLUM'S HURLED VIOLENTLY INTO A VISION OF FIRE AND TERROR: THE SHRILL CRIES OF CHILDREN DESPERATE TO ESCAPE THEIR BURNING VILLAGES; THE TERRIFIED BLOODIED FACES OF A MOB STAMPEDING AWAY FROM THE CITY'S SILVER TOWERS AS WHOLE SECTIONS OF THEM EXPLODE; DEEP IN THE UTTER DARKNESS OF THE PYRAMID'S DUNGEONS, MABATAN AND KIRA TRAPPED, BROKEN AND DYING. SPINNING UP THE SHAFT AT THE PYRAMID'S CENTER, WILLUM IS TOSSED OUT ONTO THE COLD GLASS TILES AT ITS APEX. DARIUS IS RAISING A KNIFE TO STAB STOWE. PICKING HIMSELF UP, WILLUM LUNGES. STOWE SCREAMS. THERE IS BLOOD. BLOOD EVERYWHERE. AND SCREAMS. HORRIFIED SCREAMS. AND AS WILLUM IS SUCKED BACK INTO DARKNESS, HE REALIZES THE SCREAMS ARE HIS OWN.

SHAKING HIS HAWK'S HEAD TO CLEAR HIS MIND OF THIS NUMBING VIEW OF THE FUTURE, HE NOTICES THE DEEP SADNESS IN RAT'S WATERY EYES AS HE SPEAKS TO HIS DAUGHTER. "MABATAN, I KNOW DEATH HOVERS OVER YOU. BUT IN THIS TIME, DEATH HOVERS OVER US ALL. ONLY REMEMBER, THE PATH SHIFTS DAILY

AND WE HAVE UNTIL THE BULL RISES IN THE EAST TO DO WHAT WE CAN TO EFFECT OUR FATE."

THE HAWK AND THE RABBIT SIGH AND SPEAK TOGETHER, "AFTER THAT COMES THE END OF ALL POSSIBILITY."

PLACING A PAW ON STOWE, THE RABBIT INCLINES HER HEAD TOWARD THE HAWK. WILLUM CLENCHES THE CLAY GIRL IN ONE OF HIS CLAWS AND RESTS HIS OTHER ON THE RABBIT. THE RABBIT BLINKS AND SUDDENLY ALL THREE ARE NOTHING BUT GLITTERING MOTES OF DUST TRAVELING THE WIND IN AN AZURE SKY.

WHEN THEY REACH THE SHORELINE OF THE ENDLESS SEA, THE HAWK GROWS STEADILY LARGER AND RELEASES THE RABBIT. WITH A BEAT OF HIS WINGS, HE GRASPS STOWE IN BOTH CLAWS AND SOARS. THE RABBIT, TAKING HUGE LEAPS, LEADS BELOW.

SHE WILL NOT DIE; SHE CANNOT DIE, WILLUM PRAYS, AS HE FOLLOWS MABATAN FROM ONE ICE FLOE TO THE NEXT. FINALLY SHE STOPS ON A ROCK CLEFT THAT JUTS UP FROM A WHIRLPOOL OF STEAMING, CHURNING WATER.

SHE WAITS AS WILLUM DIVES THROUGH THE VAPOROUS AIR, PLUMMETING INTO THE SWIRLING VORTEX. HE FEELS HER REACH OUT TO HIM IN ENCOURAGEMENT, UNTIL, WINDING DOWNWARD, HE'S OVERWHELMED BY THE ROAR OF RUSHING WATER. BUT SOON HE HEARS A SWEETER SOUND. HUMAN VOICES. THEIR SINGING DRAWS HIM THROUGH THE RAGING WATERS TO A TERRACE WHERE THE SHADES OF LONGLIGHT AWAIT.

SCORES OF OVERLAPPING WHISPERS RISE AND FALL TO GREET HIM. "WELCOME, WILLUM OF THE APSARA."

WILLUM GENTLY LAYS STOWE DOWN ON A BED OF THICK MOSS AND BOWS TO THEM. "FORGIVE ME."

"YOU HAVE SAVED HER MORE THAN ONCE, COUSIN," SAYS STOWE'S MOTHER. "AND NOW YOU BRING HER HOME TO ME. WHAT IS THERE TO FORGIVE?"

"She will not be whole again."

Stowe's mother leans over the motionless clay body, passing her hands over the barely beating heart. "Few of us have the privilege of living whole. What is important is that she will live. We cannot ask for more."

Willum's hawk eyes cannot cry, but his anguish makes them smart all the same.

"Do not abandon hope," the woman says, lifting one hand to gently caress his cheek. "You cannot stay, Cousin. This place is not for you."

Inclining his head to take one last look at Stowe, Willum steps away. Spreading his wings, he soars through the twisting sea. What will he do if Stowe does not heal in time to help them?

the foresight academy

ROAN OF THE PARTING foresaw that with DARIUS'S RISE,
knowledge would burn. And so when his followers
fled the city he ordered them to take all the books
they could carry. This is how foresight came into
being.

—the war chronicles

THOUGH ROAN IS EXHAUSTED, sleep is an unwilling companion. Whenever he closes his eyes he's catapulted into
a world of blinding pain. Everything is bathed in blood and
there's an intolerable pressure at the center of his being, as if
someone were splitting him in two.

Wrapping his bedroll tightly round his shoulders, Roan
slips past the snoring doctors. Finding a mossy hollow not
too far from the fire, he leans back against a frosty boulder
and gazes at a fragment of starry sky. Why is he having these
visions? Have Willum and Stowe made their way safely to Ende?
Could something terrible be happening to Mabatan in Kira's
village? Is he seeing what might one day happen to him?

"Worrying about what we're heading into?"

Roan turns to see Lumpy smugly tapping a roll of parchment against his chest.

"You snuck up on me!" Roan exclaims, surprised.

"I've been practicing some new tricks I picked up from the
Apsara, but I probably couldn't have done it if you weren't so
tired," Lumpy insists in mock apology.

Roan brings his fist smartly down on Lumpy's foot.

"Hey! What was that for?"

"Don't let it go to your head."

Laughing, Lumpy takes a seat beside him.

"So, what do you think of Othard and Imin?" Roan asks, casting a mischievous glance in Lumpy's direction.

Lumpy groans. "Having a Mor-Tick survivor at their mercy, you'd think they'd died and gone to heaven. I'm considering gags." Cheering up at the thought, Lumpy unrolls the parchment and inclines it to catch the light of the full moon. "I'm afraid our physician friends could cause us a lot of problems in a couple of days. We're going to have to travel across some open ground. With two chatterboxes like them, we might as well be shouting, 'Moving targets—come and take a shot!'"

"I'll talk to them."

"Thanks. It's a good map, Roan. Fills in a few blanks. People have tended to stay away from the area around the Academy. Apparently, it's believed there are ghosts there. The shades of Dirt Eaters killed when the Clerics blew the place up." Lumpy scrunches up his face comically. "Specters! Phantoms," he says, imitating the physicians.

Scratching his back with a stick, Roan yawns. "I thought all the Dirt Eaters got away."

"People don't know that. And to them the ghosts of dead Dirt Eaters are just as dangerous as the real thing. The fact that anyone who dares to venture into the area never returns doesn't help. You asleep yet?"

Roan opens his eyes a crack and sighs wearily "Almost." He watches Lumpy studying the map, his face haloed in the moonlight. Their crickets are perched silently on one corner of the parchment, but Roan doesn't need their song. His lids unbearably heavy, he drifts off into a dreamless slumber.

Someone grasps his arm firmly and places a finger across his lips urging silence. Lumpy. Roan opens his eyes but he can already hear them. Still a fair distance away. He signals Lumpy to return to the doctors but his friend shakes his head. He stretches both hands in front of Roan, pumping them twice. Twenty warriors. Too many for Roan to take alone. Pulling his friend toward him, Roan whispers, "I can do it, if I'm not worrying about those doctors. They need you more than I do. Go!"

Pressing Roan's hook-sword into his hand, Lumpy scrambles toward the fire. Roan sprints in the direction of the oncoming warriors. As he closes in, he recognizes their smell—Fandor. A knife glints to his right and Roan backhands it away. He kicks the Fandor wielding it hard in the stomach, toppling him backward. Lunging forward, his blade swings in a wide arc that takes down two more of the enemy. The Fandor pause—obviously he was not as easy a victim as they'd hoped.

Taking advantage of their momentary confusion, Roan advances stealthily. Positioning himself halfway between two of the marauders, he smashes his elbow into one Fandor's chin while he kicks the other backward. Then, twisting in slow circles and fanning his blade, he drives the attackers back. He hears the unmistakable snap of arrows being released and dives, pulling the nearest Fandor into their path. Swiping at another's feet, he avoids the slashing of a third. Roan's feinting and jabbing, every swing hitting true, but there are too many swords thrusting at his face, his chest, his legs. As he somersaults through the crowd of assailants, he hears an ear-piercing whistle. Are they calling for reinforcements?

Trusting Lumpy got the doctors to safety, Roan marshals his fears and studies his opponents. He targets the weak links. Spinning and twisting, he cuts a swath through his assailants.

When he turns to deliver a whip kick to a screaming Fandor, he's startled to see snarling, yellow-toothed dogs everywhere, leaping on the necks of the marauders, digging teeth into their legs. The Fandor next to him is fighting a large gray shape at his shoulder, jabbing his sword wildly, but the dog's massive jaws manage to snap on his arm. In an instant, two more mangy mastiffs are tearing at him and he's down. Eyes shining yellow in the predawn shadows, saliva dripping from their maws, the hounds resemble avenging demons. Terrified, the remaining Fandor flee, snarling predators snapping at their heels. Only one dog stays behind, its huge head swaying, glowing eyes fixed on Roan. But Lumpy's at his side whistling, and tail tucked between its legs, the beast skulks off, whining piteously.

The doctors scurry over to Roan. "Any wounds?" asks Othard.

"There's a scrape," Imin says, opening his bag.

"Thanks, Lumpy," Roan mutters, smiling at his friend.

"Oh yes, thank you," Othard adds.

"Yes. How did you know how to do that?" Imin asks, awestruck.

Othard, also impressed, says admiringly, "Uncanny..."

Imin nods. "...and precipitous."

"Before I met Roan, I wandered the Farlands alone for years. I had a choice—learn to understand the wild dogs or get eaten."

"That's how we met," explains Roan, "Lumpy saved me that time too." At a groan from one of the fallen Fandor, Roan turns back to his friend, "We better get out of here fast. They'll be coming back for their wounded. You take the doctors ahead; I'll cover our tracks."

For the next four days, their progress is slow. The overgrown trail they've been following is treacherous for the horses and so they've had to walk most of the way. Still, the path can be easily marked for Kamyar and it's kept them safely hidden from roving marauders on six occasions.

Despite the danger, the doctors are finding it more and more difficult to suppress their excitement as they draw closer to their destination: though they always begin with sign language, signs rapidly evolve into wild gesticulations that inevitably become agitated whispering and Roan is forced to silence them again. He's almost grateful this part of the Farlands is overrun with Clerics and Fandor—the terror of an imminent attack seems the only thing that keeps the chatty physicians in check for more than an hour at a time.

By the middle of the fifth day the lost library is within reach. Riding up as close as he can to Roan, Imin whispers, pointing across a vast wasteland, "There it is..."

"...Where the entrance used to be," Othard says, trying to nudge his way between them. "Between the second and third of those grassy hills."

"Looks like the explosion collapsed the entire structure," Lumpy mutters, drawing Roan's attention to a mass of huge broken stones.

"We won't know till we're closer," says Othard, initiating an avalanche of banter to urge Roan forward.

Roan can understand their exhilaration, they are at the brink of realizing a dream, and he feels almost sorry to be putting a damper on it—almost—but the terrain is too open to allow chatter. Letting his gaze fall witheringly on the two physicians, he whispers with as much menace as he can muster, "You two! Not a sound or..." and slowly draws a finger across his throat. Othard and Imin blanch but Lumpy's smiling behind them and Roan has to turn his mount away before his performance falters.

As he leads the way across the dry, cracked land and they are encircled by its eerie silence, Roan understands how the legends of Dirt Eater ghosts came to be. The tread of their horses seems so invasive in this place one could easily imagine the ground swallowing them up in annoyance, leaving no trace whatsoever of their passage.

Unfortunately, proximity to the rubble left by the explosion doesn't provide them with any answers. If there's a way in, no one can see it. Spotting a trickle of a stream, Roan turns to Lumpy. "We've been riding all day without a break. The horses need water. Let's take a rest."

After leading his own horse to drink, Roan relaxes against a great boulder and closes his eyes. With a few quick breaths, he's left his body and is soaring, searching for an opening. Between the two hills, he glides through dense underbrush and finds a fissure in the stone. Speeding through it, he discovers a narrow grotto that reaches as far back as his eye can see.

He notices a slab of rock that's fallen from the cave wall. Reaching out from it is a skeletal human hand. Someone was once crushed underneath it. A booby trap. Are there more? Advancing carefully, he finds two more fallen slabs. Around both lie skeletal remains. Roan scrutinizes the walls for an unsprung trap but can find none. I'm looking in the wrong place, he thinks. Casting his eyes down to the floor, he finds it—a loose stone. As you walk along here, you have to watch your feet, a difficult task in darkness and shadow. Proceeding along the narrow grotto, he finds seven more unsprung traps and commits them to memory.

Just when he thinks he's detected them all, he spots a different snare. As the cave opens up, a high ceiling is revealed. A dried-up corpse hangs from it, snagged in a net. Clutched in its mummified hands is a huge gold-embossed book, *Dante's Divine Comedy.* He wouldn't be the first person in the world to die for a book, but it must have been a long, hard death, starving up there in the gloom.

Beyond the cavern-like area, the path splits into two. Venturing left, Roan discovers a steep drop-off cleverly hidden by a wafer-thin floor. Corpses are piled in the pit, scraps of blue cloth clumped among their bones. Clerics. Here on Darius's orders? Or in pursuit of someone? Questions without answer.

Backtracking to the fork, Roan explores the other passageway. It also comes to a dead end but, remembering the extraordinary stonework of Oasis, Roan searches for and locates a locking mechanism. He examines it for booby traps but finds none. Whoever set the snares must have believed this door undetectable. Passing through the stone, Roan stares up in wonder. As in the caverns of Oasis, dozens of polished mirrors are strategically placed over the entire expanse of the ceiling to capture and amplify any natural light from the surface. Enough to brighten this large room filled with tables and chairs, most burned and broken, relics of Darius's attack on the Academy some fifty years before.

Roan glides through classrooms and sleeping quarters, dining room and kitchen. Though all are littered with the shattered remains of the assault, the Clerics never bothered to tear down the walls or drag up the floors in search of documents or books. Why? Thinking back, Roan doubts that Clerics would have found, never mind known, how to open the cleverly crafted entrance. The Dirt Eaters must have left it ajar, giving the impression that the place had been abandoned. The Clerics must have assumed everything of value had been taken away. If there's a library here, Roan can't see any trace of it.

Having learned all that he can, Roan returns to his body with the speed of a thought, and opens his eyes.

The doctors and Lumpy are standing close, engaged in a tense, muted conversation.

"I know Dreamwalking when I see it," Imin snaps irritably.

"He doesn't take Dirt. He's meditating," Lumpy says, sounding his most reasonable.

"He is not. We meditate. You can see he is not present. Look," Othard commands.

Lumpy barely suppresses a laugh as they both turn to see Roan smiling, open-eyed and Buddha-like. "This way," he announces as he pops up. Striding to the underbrush that camouflages the entrance, he draws out his hook-sword. With a few strokes, he makes short work of the vines and branches tangled there, exposing the fissure.

"How did you know this was here?" Imin asks suspiciously.

"I meditated on the problem," Roan says with a grin.

"We'll need torches," Othard grumbles, distrustful but obviously not enough to lose sight of their goal.

While Lumpy takes the task of concealing their mounts, the others gather dry brush into bundles to make serviceable torches. After Roan has finished his, he carves a warning in an open area on the way to the path, where Kamyar's sure to see it. When he looks up from his labor, he realizes with dismay that someone's missing. Anxiously finding Lumpy, he whispers, "Othard's gone."

Lighting a torch, Roan looks down the entrance of the narrow passageway. When he glances back at his friend, his expression is grim. "Don't go past the third corpse. Walk carefully. Don't touch anything and stay behind me."

Leaving Imin in Lumpy's capable hands, Roan rushes ahead. Othard is a few steps past the third sprung trap. He doesn't feel the loose stone beneath his foot, but Roan senses it instantly and dives forward. Pushing Othard out of the way, he's barely able to throw himself forward before the gigantic slab of rock slams against the floor.

Othard, shaken, mumbles almost inaudibly. "You have extraordinary reflexes."

Trying not to sound too angry, Roan addresses the doctor firmly. "I know you're excited, but as we agreed at the beginning of this trip, it really would be better if you follow my lead." Turning back to Lumpy, Roan cautions, "The triggers are on the ground, walk in my footsteps."

Squeezing past the new obstruction, Lumpy and Imin cautiously follow, their torches animating the passage with flickering light. When the narrow crevice opens up into the larger cavern, Imin gasps and pushes forward, reaching toward one of the few books scattered there.

Roan whirls, grabbing the physician's cloak. "You don't want to do that," he says, pointing at the ceiling.

The company follows his finger to the withered corpse swinging above them. "Pick up one of these books and it might be your last."

Appraising the corpse and then Roan, Imin grimaces skeptically but does not, thankfully, reach again for the book.

By the time Roan exposes all the other traps and leads them to the concealed door, both doctors are openly expressing their discontent. Ignoring their indignant grumblings, Roan runs his fingers up and around the end of the cave, feeling for a small protrusion. As he pushes on it, the door slides open.

"That was a little too easy," Imin comments testily.

"And don't say you came upon it meditating," insists Othard.

Roan gives Lumpy a weary look, not at all pleased to be divulging his methods. "I project a part of myself outside my body, not into the Dreamfield, but here in the world."

"Astral projection," Imin asserts, obviously relieved.

Othard nods his shaggy head beside him. "Why didn't you say so before?"

"Nothing mysterious in that!"

Roan stares at the doctors. "Can *you*. . .astral project?"

"No," says Imin. "Of course not."

"But we know about it."

"And, after all, you *are* Roan of Longlight..."

A bit taken aback, Roan looks at his friend, but Lumpy merely shrugs, obviously amused, as the physicians push their way into what must have once been an impressive foyer.

"We're looking for a clever hiding spot," Roan says,

studiously ignoring Lumpy's wide grin. "A concealed entrance, much like the door we just saw. When the clerics invaded this place, they missed it."

"We won't," Othard snaps.

"We know how the Dirt Eaters hide things..."

"...Their tricky little doors..."

"...False panels..."

"...Shifting walls."

Lumpy joins Roan to search the perimeter, their hands tracing over every inch of the stone surface. "Walking through that cave, seeing those bones, took me back," he shudders.

"The labyrinth at Oasis," remembers Roan.

"Yeah. Making company into corpses seems like a Dirt Eater specialty."

"Somehow I don't think the Dirt Eaters are responsible for these bones."

"Oh? Why's that?"

"Asp said the Dirt Eaters who came here trying to find a way in were never seen again. They'd know how to avoid their own traps. Besides, I have a feeling."

Lumpy snorts. "Well, then, say no more."

After hours of fruitless searching, the group gathers in the first chamber, weary and frustrated.

"There's nothing here," Imin laments.

"We were so sure," Othard adds dejectedly.

"We must have missed something," says Lumpy. "We'll just have to start again."

"If there was a door in here, we would have found it," Othard states emphatically.

Roan strides over to the entrance of the Academy, mumbling to himself. "The door was left open—not only so that it would appear nothing of value had been left...but also to divert the Clerics...from the real hiding place."

Stepping out of the chamber, Roan studies the cave wall across the threshold. After a moment, he sees the barely discernible bulge in the granite. Reaching up, he locates the locking mechanism. Searching with his fingers, he remembers what he learned in the tunnels of Oasis, and gently trips the lock. With a satisfied grin, he watches as the wall glides open.

"You've found it," gasps Imin.

Roan walks onto a platform overlooking a massive room forged out of rock. Transparent green tourmaline covers the walls, causing an unearthly light to be cast over the entire chamber. The doctors and Lumpy crowd behind him on the landing, gaping at the majesty of this gigantic atrium: its graceful pillars, wide marble tables, long couches. Hundreds of people must have studied and read and meditated here.

"Where are the books?" Othard moans, despairing.

"Let's have a look around," replies Roan, and with an encouraging glance at the physician, he steps down the narrow stairs. But when he reaches the bottom, he stops short and, raising an arm, captures the group's attention. Putting a finger to his lips, he motions them closer. "There's someone here."

Eyes darting everywhere, the doctors tiptoe alongside Roan and Lumpy as they proceed toward an archway on the opposite side of the atrium. There are gasps all around when they see that it opens onto another chamber containing a well-tended hydroponic garden.

"People are *living* here," whispers Imin.

"What did they do with all the books?" asks Othard, noticeably piqued.

Moving through the chamber, Roan pauses at a large wooden door, sword raised. Inhaling deeply, he opens it, sighs, then gestures the physician forward. "Othard, we've found the books."

The library is beyond anything Roan could have imagined. It dwarfs the huge collection at Oasis and the holdings of the Gunthers. Chamber reaches back onto chamber, and each, from ceiling to floor, is crammed with books. All saved from the burnings ordered by Darius.

Running along the stacks, Othard shouts, "Agriculture! Physiology! Astronomy! Psychology! Physics! Chemistry…"

Placing a hand none too gently over the physician's mouth, Lumpy whispers, "Shh."

Grabbing a fistful of each physician's cloak, Roan shepherds Othard and Imin amid the stacks. "Stay here and be quiet," he whispers. Chastened, the doctors remain perfectly still. Shaking his head wearily, Roan mutters, "You can *look* at the books, just don't get too rambunctious."

As one room opens onto another and then another in a seemingly endless collection of knowledge, Roan glances at Lumpy, awestruck. "There must be tens of thousands of books here. Maybe hundreds of thousands."

Lumpy nods, his face filled with the wonder and joy of discovering hidden treasure. "Before I met you, I'd never even seen a book. Now I'm surrounded by more books than I could ever read. It's—what?"

"He's over there," Roan says quietly. "Around that tower of books." The two friends cautiously round the stack, only to find yet another wooden door.

Roan shifts his hook-sword from hand to hand nervously. "Whoever's on the other side of that door must already know we're here."

Lumpy shrugs. "So I guess we storm in and hope for the best."

At Roan's signal, they burst through the doors. Books and papers lie scattered everywhere in the already cluttered room. Plates of half-eaten food sit moldering on the floor, clothes are flung over the chairs. And in the farthest corner, huddled over a desk, is an old man with scraggly white hair and beard. He scribbles something onto a scroll, then goes on reading the worn and tattered notebook he's hunched over. Roan approaches the old man slowly. As he moves closer, he sees that the man's face is wet with tears.

"Have you come to finish what was once started?" Though the old man's voice creaks and croaks as if rusty from disuse, it manages to convey a great sadness.

"No," Roan says gently. "We've come to read. To learn."

Blinking up at him, the old man asks, "Where did you learn to read?"

"Longlight," answers Roan.

The old man smiles, then squints curiously at Roan's companion. "Come forward, come." As Lumpy edges toward him, he laughs. "One of the Shunned!" Ignoring Lumpy's consternation, he turns back to Roan and shakes his head. "And you. You must be Roan of Longlight."

"How do you know this?" asks Roan a little coldly, upset at the insult to his friend.

"I've only deciphered the first chapter, but it's all here," the old man says, patting the notebook.

As Roan scans the arcane code, his heartbeat quickens,

his breath becomes shallow, he feels lightheaded. The room seems transparent, as if the present were a shimmering pliable substance he might grasp and remold with different possibilities, undamaged by war and greed, free of despair and pain. What he's feeling, he realizes, is the essence of this book. The hope of it. Eyes glued to its mysterious ciphers, he asks the old man, "What is this?"

"What I've spent the last forty years searching for. Your great-grandfather's notebook. The Journal of Roan of the Parting. He wrote it for you."

the curatrix

> the syzygy may be used to pool our strength in
> times of danger. but be warned: the sharing must be
> respectfully held in balance; anything less will cost
> you your mind.
>
> —the way of the wazya

T HE SMELL IS INTOLERABLE. Try as she might, Mabatan cannot get the healer to hand over her clothes, and the tiny chamber is redolent with the acid stench of Dirt-tainted sweat.

"I won't!" the healer cries petulantly, throwing her bowl across the room. Shattering against the wall, it joins the fragments of the two plates and pitcher she'd smashed that morning.

"Sit," Mabatan orders in her sternest tone, but Alandra continues pacing. Her eyes clouded with craving, she sees nothing, hears nothing. So Mabatan throws out a leg, tripping her.

Tumbling to the floor, Alandra snarls, then rolls her body upright inches away from Mabatan.

"You must focus your attention," Mabatan asserts coolly as she holds out another bowl of infused water.

Alandra takes it and squeezes her eyes together, as if debating whether or not to smash it in her tormentor's face. But in the end, she puts it calmly to her lips and whispers, "Tell me why you hate the Dirt so much and I'll do it."

Mabatan begins with only a hint of the fatigue she feels. "Like all Wazya, I have walked in many places and witnessed the results of the war between Darius and Roan of the Parting—"

"Deserts where once forests and cities flourished, the animals and men that live there now twisted and deformed. Yes. I understood that the last time you told me. That is what you think, but it is not what you feel. Why you *hate* is what interests me."

Returning the healer's furious gaze, Mabatan quiets her breath. What the girl wants is irrelevant. Mabatan is not here to share of herself, certainly not with a Dirt Eater. "You claim you love the children, feel their difference, their specialness. You say you can sense they are our only hope. If these words have any truth in them, then sit and focus. Do not waste time on useless questions."

"If I cannot understand why you are here, how can I trust what you say, what you do?"

Mabatan knows these questions are meant to keep her from her purpose. She will not be so easily distracted. "You do not need to trust me. Roan tried to warn you, you trusted him once. You know what Dirt has done to you. Believe in the truth of what *you* feel and know."

"And you, Mabatan, Wazya, what do you believe in?"

How long does she have to remain buried in this suffocating room with this bullheaded healer? Frustration burns in her throat and squeezes at her heart. Reaching forward, she takes the healer's hands into her own. "Alandra." The healer tries to twist from her grasp but Mabatan is the stronger. "I, Mabatan, Wazya, believe that Darius must be killed, the Dirt destroyed, and the children freed from the abyss. If Willum is wrong and there is no chance that you will agree to stand with us in this fight, then release me from my duty to you, Alandra. Release me and I will go and leave you to choose some other fate."

A shock courses from the healer's hands into Mabatan. White crickets emerge from cracks in the floor and ceiling. Dozens, hundreds, until the room quivers with them. What Dirt Eater power is this?

"What are you doing?" whispers Alandra. Her hushed voice and wide eyes make it clear to Mabatan that the healer is as shocked as she.

"I'm not sure," Mabatan says, trying to remain calm. But her chest feels about to explode and as the crickets begin to sing, her life force shoots out of it, binding her heart to Alandra's. Alandra's terrified eyes latch onto Mabatan's as the song becomes so powerful it creates a sonic vortex that encloses them. Drawn out of their flesh as one, they are swept up into a whirlwind, out of body, out of control, out of this world.

MABATAN FEELS STRANGE, SWOLLEN, HER EYES SEEING IN EVERY DIRECTION AT ONCE. THERE'S A POUNDING IN HER HEAD—DEAFENING AND FAST—SLUSHING IN AND OUT LIKE THE TIDE. CLOUDS CHURN ABOVE, THE GROUND RIPS BELOW, AND ALL AROUND A STORM RAGES. SHE SQUEEZES HER EYES TOGETHER, TRYING TO STOP ALL THE IMAGES.

SCREAMS BECOME A GREAT ROAR THAT TWISTS AND GRINDS ACROSS HER SKIN AS COLD, OILY FIRES TURN THE TEMPEST INTO A RANK STEAM, CHOKING HER. OPENING HER EYES, SHE SEES THE HEAD OF A GARGANTUAN VIPER, FANGS BARED. SHE TRIES TO DIVE AWAY FROM THE BEHEMOTH, BUT THE DIRECTION SHE IS MOVING IN IS THE OPPOSITE OF WHAT SHE INTENDS. HER ANXIETY MOUNTS AS SHE FINDS HERSELF LURCHING CLOSER TO A GREAT FISSURE.

In the distance, she sees the Novakin stretched across the crevice, rain lashing their rusting bodies. She cannot let the beast near them. Her panic and terror are instantly replaced with a wash of sadness and joy. These are not her feelings.

The children are here! Here! Mabatan told the truth!

The sound of the heart, the feeling of relief, the thoughts springing vividly into Mabatan's mind...they're Alandra's!

Her father spoke of this. In times of great need, beings could link, bridge in harmonious balance. The Syzygy. It must be the Syzygy.

The crickets often protected the people of the prophecies. They had saved Lumpy. Kept company with Roan. Watched over Willum in the Devastation. They had often spoken to Mabatan about the Novakin, their importance to the future of humankind. The children must need someone to care for them, someone who could be spared from the struggle ahead. So the crickets connected her life force with the healer's, making it possible to draw Alandra here. But now that that's been accomplished, Mabatan knows she should break the Syzygy at once, because balance is not possible between them.

Slowly collapsing the reach of her awareness, Mabatan allows the force of Alandra's presence to grow. Little more than a mote floating on a molecule of gas, Mabatan enters the lungs of the creature Alandra's become and is expelled violently into the storm with its breath. As the molecule drifts down to the ground, Mabatan allows her dreamfield form to expand and looks up.

NOT ONE HEAD, BUT NINE, BOB ON LONG NECKS, THEIR FORKED TONGUES FLICKING ACROSS SCALY MOUTHS. SHRIEKS OF AGONY SLASH THE AIR AS ONE LASHES OUT AT ANOTHER, TIPPING THE BEAST PRECARIOUSLY. CLAWING THE ROCKY SOIL TO RIGHT ITSELF, IT STUMBLES, CAUSING THE GROUND TO QUAKE BENEATH THE TINY BLUE RABBIT.

MABATAN CRIES OUT, "ALANDRA!" STARTLED BY THE SOUND OF THE NAME, ALL NINE HEADS SNAP AROUND WITH FRIGHTENING PRECISION TO OBSERVE THE AZURE RABBIT WITH THEIR BLACK, ALMOND-SHAPED EYES. IT WOULD BE EASY TO LOSE ONESELF IN THAT OVERWHELMING WELL OF POWER. BUT THE CRICKETS HAVE TAUGHT HER THAT IN THE DREAMFIELD, POWER IS NOT RELATIVE TO SIZE AND APPEARANCE.

PROJECTING CALM AND CONFIDENCE, SHE CALLS OUT, "ALANDRA! IT'S MABATAN! YOU KNOW MY VOICE. YOU HAVE BEEN GIVEN THE FORM OF THE HYDRA! YOU ARE THE BEAST YOU SEE. STOP FIGHTING YOURSELF."

ALL NINE HEADS WAVE AND SPIT FIRE.

"LISTEN TO ME, ALANDRA! THE HYDRA IS A POWERFUL GUARDIAN BUT TO HELP THE CHILDREN, YOU MUST MASTER IT."

BLACK EYES PULSATING, THE HYDRA'S NECKS WRITHE AS IF TRYING TO WRENCH THEMSELVES FROM THE BODY THEY SHARE. WORRIED THAT THE HEALER WILL TEAR HERSELF APART, MABATAN LETS OUT A HIGH, SHRILL WHISTLE. THE TWINING NECKS FREEZE, THE HEADS SLOWLY TURNING BACK TO THE RABBIT.

MABATAN HOLDS HER GROUND AS THE NINE HEADS STRETCH DANGEROUSLY CLOSE, MOUTHS WIDE, TEETH GLISTENING. "IT IS HARD TO SEE THROUGH NINE PAIRS OF EYES. BUT IF YOU GO TO YOUR CORE——THE PART THAT WAS YOU WHEN YOU USED TO ENTER THE DREAMFIELD——YOU WILL FIND THE STRENGTH TO GAIN CONTROL."

Nostrils flaring, the hydra's heads swerve to snap their jaws at Mabatan. The four taloned legs swipe the air and scratch the earth in front of her but the blue rabbit remains resolutely still and waits, surrounding herself with memory.

There was once a paradise in this spot where in times long past, the chosen Carrier of her people's traditions would be taught the way of the Dreamfield. Her great-grandmother, Aithuna, had watched it pass from what it was once into what it is now, a desolate and broken wasteland. The depth of that loss had been passed down through four generations and with it despair for the future. But Mabatan can feel the strength in the hearts of the Novakin and, awash with their unflagging hope, she allows possibility back into her being.

How long she has waited, she cannot tell. But the hydra is calmed and in its eyes she senses the one who calls herself Alandra.

"Go to the children, Alandra. Go!"

The hydra leaps to where the Novakin are bridged across the crevice, and wails. When the fourteen iron children see the ghastly creature, they are not frightened but smile in recognition. Their metal shells creak from the pressure; even this slight movement threatens to rend them apart.

Clinging to the edges of the ravine with corroded, cracking fingers, they slowly pivot their necks, calling out: "Alandra!" "We missed you!" "You're finally here!"

The hydra lowers her heads to nuzzle the beleaguered children, but then stops, as if fearing that any touch might break their tenuous hold. She roars

ANGRILY TO THE SKIES, SPITTING OUT FIRE. AS THE FLAMES CONDENSE INTO AN OILY SUBSTANCE, THE HYDRA EXTENDS HER MANY TONGUES TO LAP IT OUT OF THE SKY. CRANING THE GREAT NECKS FORWARD, SHE LOVINGLY SPREADS THE GREASE OVER THE CHILDREN'S STRAINING LIMBS.

THE RABBIT SHUDDERS BUT THE CHILDREN MOAN, CONTENTED: "THANK YOU, ALANDRA!" "MY TURN." "ME TOO!"

THE HEADS GYRATE IN EVERY DIRECTION, SPREADING THE BALM GENEROUSLY ONTO EVERY CHILD. THEIR SIGHS OF RELIEF ARE MATCHED BY A RUMBLING SOUND THAT VIBRATES DEEP IN THE BELLY OF THE HYDRA, A PURRING THAT SEEMS ALSO TO SOOTHE THE AILING NOVAKIN. THEN, REACHING ACROSS THE RAVINE, ALANDRA DIGS HER TALONS INTO EITHER SIDE, HER MUSCLES STRAINING FROM THE EFFORT.

"ALANDRA," MABATAN CALLS OUT SOFTLY. "I MUST GO."

ONE OF THE HEADS TURNS TO MABATAN AND NODS WITH CALM GRACE. THE CURATRIX OF THE NOVAKIN. THEIR HEALER. MABATAN ALMOST ENVIES HER. ALANDRA AT LEAST IS WHERE SHE WILL BE REQUIRED UNTIL ALL IS RESOLVED OR LOST. MABATAN, ON THE OTHER HAND, MUST MOVE ON TO THE NEXT TASK WITHOUT REALLY KNOWING WHAT WILL BE ASKED OF HER—OR EVEN WHY. STILL, ANY SACRIFICE THAT MIGHT RETURN THIS PLACE TO WHAT IT ONCE WAS IS WORTH MAKING.

AND SO, AFTER ONE LAST LOOK AT THE CHILDREN, MABATAN LEAPS AWAY, SKIRTING THE WIDENING CHASM, AND THE WHISTLE OF THE WIND DRAWS HER INEXORABLY BACK INTO THE WORLD.

ROAN of the PARTING's JOURNAL

MORE NIGHTMARE THAN VISION BUT VALERIA AND KRISPIN
SAW IT TOO: EYES SWIRLING IN OPPOSITE DIRECTIONS AND
WHEN ONE FIXED ON YOU, YOU WERE HELD SCREAMING
WHILE YOUR LIFE WAS SLOWLY TORN FROM YOU AND
DRAWN INTO AN EXCRUCIATING VACUUM BEYOND THE
RELIEF OF DEATH.

—BARTHOLD,
VISION #782, YEAR 38 A.C.
DREAMFIELD JOURNALS OF THE
FIRST INNER CIRCLE

"I am cursed for eternity," the old man reads.

"I have unleashed a great affliction upon the world. A scourge so malevolent that every action I have taken in this life to contain it has only led to more destruction. I have come to know that I alone cannot stand against it. It will take the combined efforts of three generations to undo what I have done.

"You, Roan of Longlight, along with your sister, are the vanguard because the sin is mine and you not only share my blood but bear the legacy of Longlight. So that you will not be alone to fight this cause, another has joined with me and has promised her descendants to it as well. The Shunned will also stand with you. They, more than anyone, will recognize you for who you truly are. One, the closest to you, will give you faith when you least expect and need it most.

"Great sacrifices have already been made; greater sacrifices are to come. And though the chances for success are small, we have done everything in our

power to ensure you will succeed where we have failed. This book is only one of our many efforts.

"Feel free to judge me as harshly as you wish; there is no forgiveness for my sins. But please trust that my mistakes were not intentionally evil. I believed I had discovered a miracle, an impossibly easy access into the Divine that anyone could obtain. I was wrong. I learned too late that my intentions were nothing before the desire for power. What I saw as gift, one I had called friend saw as weapon...and in the gap between us a shadow was born. Since that moment, I have striven to understand my enemy and have gathered all my knowledge here. For you. Use it well."

When the old man stops reading, Roan shudders. His feelings and thoughts are so confused he has to close his eyes to sort through them. Anger. Yes. He feels as angry at Roan of the Parting as he did at Saint and the Dirt Eaters. All of them defining him as if he were not a separate being, not himself, as if he did not have a choice. But there is hope too. "*Not alone.*"

Rat has been there, ever since he first began to see into the Dreamfield. Wazya. The one of his generation to keep their history, their stories. He must be the descendant of Aithuna, the one who joined Roan of the Parting in his cause. That means Mabatan is like Roan—she too must have been asked to shoulder this same burden. Who else? Willum, Ende, Kira? He'll have to ask when he sees them. But Roan does not want to accept that Stowe will be "the vanguard." That would mean her going back to the City and he can't let that happen. Not again.

Roan opens his eyes and sees Lumpy's smiling face, radiating a fierce pride. "*One, the closest to you, will give you faith when you least expect and need it most.*" Lumpy was plucked out of time too. Chosen...by the crickets? But he comes to this freely. These sins, borne over generations, do not rest on his shoulders. He's doing this because he believes it's the right thing to do. This, more than anything else, has helped to convince Roan to accept the responsibility that's been thrust upon him.

"How did he know who we were, that we'd be here?" asks Lumpy.

The old man looks up to the ceiling, as if he could read an answer to Lumpy's question there. "Visions of the future were recorded in the journals kept by the first Nine of the Inner Circle—visions they had had in the Dreamfield," he pauses, tapping the tip of his nose, "at a place one of the members described as 'a river that carried time.' You could dip your hands in it and experience the flow of time in its entirety. Roan of the Parting was the most powerful of that group. He's sure to have seen more than most. It was said the visions were what changed him."

He places the journal into a small cavity in the wall, and closes the stone facade that seamlessly covers it. "See this. I found it in there. Forty years I'd spent looking, and could have been for another forty." He stops, looking expectantly at Roan and Lumpy.

"Uh huh, good hiding place," says Lumpy.

"That's not it!" the man exclaims, then with a frown, he asks, "Did I not mention the cricket?"

As Roan and Lumpy shake their heads, the old man searches through the ink-stained papers on his desk. Finally finding the one he's looking for, he lifts it, revealing a white cricket comfortably ensconced in an empty inkwell. "I don't know how the insect got in here, but it did. And it perched right up on top of the release mechanism. Those stone masons of Oasis are tricky little toads, aren't they?"

"So you're from Oasis?" asks Roan, his heart sinking.

"Me? From Oasis? Not in your life! I'm from the City. I don't suppose it would do any harm to tell you...but perhaps it might be best to remain silent...of course, it's been forty years, they could all be dead now. They must be. Someone would have come to fetch me. Darius must have cottoned on and killed them all." He groans at the thought. "No. No. They're still alive. They must be. Too well hidden. Best to stay quiet." He gives Roan and Lumpy a stony look. "I'm sorry, I cannot say any more."

"Are you a Gunther?" guesses Lumpy.

The old man's mouth drops open, revealing a full set of yellow teeth. "You've heard of...Gunthers?"

"We met some not that long ago," says Roan.

"Oh?" The old man's face twitches, at once relieved, but then annoyed. "I suppose they thought it was too risky to come after me. Are they still playing at being idiot savants? Fixing electrical panels, talking in a monotone, wheeling around little carts, pretending to be invisible?"

After a quick smile at Roan, Lumpy says, attempting to maintain a serious air, "Yes. I guess you could say that."

The old man snorts derisively. "The minute this suicide mission was proposed I volunteered. Having to pretend all the time was infernal enough, but when Darius set me to work on his enablers and I was chastised for even expressing concern over drilling into people's brains—well!"

Roan is thunderstruck. "You worked on enablers?"

"I designed the prototype," he sniffs. "But when I saw how it was going to be used, I said no to serving that beast and gave myself over to books. Hundreds of thousands of books. The best company anyone could ask for. But perhaps I'm rationalizing again. Living here like a hermit's driven me half mad." He clucks his tongue. "Or at the very least a trifle eccentric. Still, what of it? Eating Dirt and building things in etherworlds. Now there's madness."

"The Constructions," Roan says. "That's exactly what we've come to find out about. This place is supposed to have maps of the Dreamfield."

"Oh yes, yes, we have those here too. All kinds of maps."

"May we see them?" asks Lumpy, barely containing his eagerness.

"Certainly. They're in the geography room," the old man says, smiling benignly but not moving.

"It would help if you could direct us to them," Roan prompts politely.

"I beg your pardon. Oh, my goodness. Not used to company. I'll take you there now." The Gunther freezes halfway up from his seat. "Ah...no. No. Shouldn't mention it. Might be considered presumptuous," he mutters. "Still, most human beings have at least one."

"If you tell me the problem, maybe I can help," Roan offers.

The old man looks up at him with a childlike expression. "Oh. This is rather embarrassing...it has to do with the matter of my...name."

"I thought Gunthers had numbers, not names," says Lumpy.

"Quite. But you see, after forty-some years, I seem to have misplaced my number. Forgotten it."

"We could give you a temporary number," suggests Roan.

"Out of the question!" the Gunther snaps. "It might be

someone else's. Impossible!" he insists, then with a shy smile, adds, "And...I've found such a lovely name."

"What is it?" Lumpy asks encouragingly.

An excited grin stretches across the old man's face. Pursing his lips, the Gunther slowly speaks, savoring each consonant. "...Algernon."

Roan and Lumpy nod approvingly.

"You like it! I read it in a play. By an Oscar Wilde. Clever man. Very funny. Made me laugh. Not the name, of course—the play. Oh yes, laugh. Not enough of that in the City. Laughter."

"It's a great name!" says Lumpy, holding out his hand. "Pleased to meet you, Alge—Alger—?"

"Oh. Oh!" the Gunther squeals. "It's a bit long, isn't it? But please, please, you can call me Algie for short, if that's easier for you."

"Sorry, Algie. My name is Lumpy."

Algernon takes Lumpy's hand, musing. "Lumpy. Could that be short for... Perlumpo?"

Lumpy shakes his head.

"No? Alumpelle, then? Not that either? Clumpington?"

"No," says Lumpy, chuckling. "Just Lumpy."

"Oh. Well, then, Lumpy, Roan, allow me to escort you to the maps." But as the Gunther slowly makes his way around his desk, a deafening alarm begins to peal. Raising his hook-sword, Roan rushes toward the door.

"Wait! Wait! No need for that, sir!" Algie shouts over the din. "The tintinnabulation is simply notification that one of my snares has been tripped."

"Intruders."

"Yes, I suppose."

"Don't you go check?" Lumpy yells at the top of his lungs just as the alarm abruptly stops. After looking sheepishly at Roan, he fixes Algie with a stern glare. "Well?"

"Well—" Algie frowns, clearly uncomfortable. "To tell the truth, no. I'm not in a position to deal with the sort of people who come nosing around here. That's why I installed the traps."

Lumpy's appalled. "You leave them to rot? There are all kinds of skeletons out there!"

"Yes, I suppose there must be," says Algie guiltily, "but not that many, I'm sure, when you consider how long I've been here and it was that or leave the library vulnerable to attack. They did try to destroy it, you know. I knew they'd be back. The slightest suspicion is good enough for them. And all these books. They had to be protected. But, if you feel so inclined, please, I would be most grateful if you could investigate. That particular bell signified one of the book traps, so the victim may be a book lover."

"Only one?" asks Roan.

"One snare, yes. Can't guarantee how many it's caught, though. There's a pulley system, just past the entrance to the left fork. If you want to get them down, that is."

"Algernon, two of our friends are waiting in the physiology stacks. Would you take them to the map room?" As the old Gunther nods, Roan turns back to Lumpy. "Let's go," he says, remembering the bones he saw in the net. "The intruders made their way past the first snares—not that easy—we should be prepared for the worst."

As Roan and Lumpy silently wind their way back toward the entrance, the music of three voices rises in perfect harmony to greet them.

"Mony a ane for him makes maen, But nane shall ken whaur he is gane. Over his banes when they are bare, The wind shall blaw for evermair."

Roan and Lumpy relax their stance. Moving into the high-ceilinged cave, they wave to the three captives swinging inside the net.

"Lovely view up here, you really ought to try it sometime," Kamyar's voice booms out. "You remember Talia and Dobbs?"

"Good to see you, Roan!" yells Dobbs.

While Lumpy locates the pulley and slowly lowers the trio, Roan calls up, "Didn't you see the warning?"

"Who could resist Chaucer!" Kamyar blusters. "Such a prize left to perish ignominiously in the dust! Please tell us there are still greater pleasures to come." Kamyar raises his arms and leans backward, stretching. "Ah. That's much better. As much as I love my cohorts, I prefer not being sausaged in with them."

"We hope you're not expecting anyone else," says Talia, giving Roan a hug. "We took the liberty of covering up the entrance and removing the warning."

"Are you sure it's not safe to rescue this copy of *Gulliver's Travels*?" As he clamps a huge arm round Roan's shoulder, Dobbs wistfully eyes a large illustrated book.

"When you see what we've found," smiles Roan, "you won't give it a second's thought."

Kamyar gasps. "The library's intact?" Roan doesn't think he's ever seen the Storyteller so impassioned.

Roan nods. "And, there was somebody already here when we arrived," he says, enjoying the rapt look on the Storytellers' faces. He realizes it's the first time he's the one with exciting information to convey. "A Gunther found it forty years ago. He's been here ever since."

After looking to his cohorts for confirmation, Kamyar nods. "It must be the legendary Number One Hundred Twenty-Six. Before he disappeared, that man spearheaded projects the Gunthers are still perfecting—everything from filo-armor to intuitive flying machines."

"He's got a name now," Lumpy says, leading his friends to the entranceway.

"That'll stir things up," laughs Talia.

"Well, don't keep us waiting, young Lump," Kamyar says with a sly smile. "What is it?"

"Algie. Short for…" Lumpy looks hopefully at Roan.

"Algernon!" blurts out Kamyar. "Wonderful," he sighs, but it is not the name he is reacting to. Stepping aside, Lumpy's allowed them their first view of the cavern. "But where are the books?"

Roan laughs. "That's what Othard said."

"He's here?" asks Dobbs over his shoulder as he scurries to follow Lumpy.

"Imin too?" inquires Talia.

Roan begins to explain, but Dobbs and Talia, like Kamyar, have reached the library entrance and are spellbound by the sight of its multitude of books.

"We are privileged to see this day," says Kamyar, savoring the moment.

Talia sniffs dramatically. "Those blasted Masters thought they'd burn all hope from the world. But knowledge finds its own way. Here is the proof."

"Nothing could have prepared me for this," says the good-hearted Dobbs. "Pinch me, please. Have I died and gone to heaven?" Seeing a head poking around the corner of a stall, he calls out, "Othard!" And rushing over to the doctor, he lifts him off the ground in a big bear hug.

"Oh my! Dobbs! Was that you? Well, thank goodness you weren't hurt," Othard says, attempting to pat the giant storyteller's back.

"Othard saved my life, oh, must be fifteen years back—Nethervine poisoning—I still have the scars," Dobbs says to Roan and Lumpy over the doctor's shoulder. Then, pulling back to look at Othard, he adds, "I was worried about you—five whole years without even a word!"

"Dobbs! Can't you see the man wants to tell us something? Come, come my good physician, spit it out!"

Othard, gaping at Kamyar, struggles for words. "It's...it's an honor...to be in your presence, learned one—"

Kamyar snorts. "Let's have none of that or we shall be here an hour exchanging 'worthies' and 'celebrateds' and 'distinguisheds' until we've put all the others to sleep."

"Here! Here!" Talia adds. "Where's Imin, by the way?"

"That's just it. I've come to fetch you all to the geography room. Algernon and Imin are waiting there." Gesturing for them to follow, Othard leads the way through dozens of rooms crowded with overflowing stacks, until they finally arrive at a large open area.

The Gunther and the doctor are sitting at a long table where a most unusual map is spread out. It's been folded and refolded to create a three-dimensional chart tracking the sky, surface and undersurface of the Dreamfield.

"Remarkable, isn't it?" says Algernon. "Hand drawn by the great architect August Ferrell. He was presiding over the Academy when it was abandoned."

"Well, at least he did something right," mumbles Kamyar. "Imin," he says with a friendly tap on the open-mouthed physician's arm. "And you must be Algernon," Kamyar moves forward to grasp the old man's hand. "A privilege and a pleasure. I'm Kamyar—and permit me to introduce my very rude fellow storytellers, Talia and Dobbs," he says as both storytellers lean inquisitively over the map, barely sparing the old man a smile.

Roan, too, is entranced by the drawing but try as he might, he can't recognize anything he's looking at. "None of it seems familiar."

"What you're seeing here is the mere fragment the Masters claimed for themselves," explains the Gunther. "This map's terribly outdated, I might add, based on notations that were made at the time of the wars. By now I'm sure there are many more Constructions."

Roan points at a long row of ebony pillars that bridge across all three layers. "Wait. I've seen those before."

Algernon nods. "The Ramparts. He built that to separate the Dirt Eaters' domain from his own."

"Would it be all right if I borrow this?" Roan looks around the table, not exactly sure who he should ask for permission.

"It is not the only one, if that is your concern," says the old man, gesturing at the stacks behind him. Hundreds of cylinders lie stacked in diagonal tiers above shelves of massive tomes. "There are quite a few more amongst all of those."

Dobbs sighs as he slides a huge atlas off a shelf. "I could stay here forever," he says to Kamyar, in a hushed and reverent tone.

"Be careful," says Algernon. "Time flies in this library."

"Ah. Time," groans Kamyar. "Yes, it would be easy to forget the outside world in such a place." Kamyar squints, one eyebrow raised at Roan. "I seem to recall that you have a previous commitment at new moon and that's less than a week away."

"This is what I came for," Roan says, coaxing the map back into its tube with some assistance from Lumpy. He pauses, looking at the Gunther. "But before I go I need to ask one more favor, a large one. I think...well, I would like your permission to use the Academy as a base of operations for our fight against the City. Everyone is scattered across the Farlands. We need a neutral place where we can all come together."

For a moment there is utter silence as all eyes shift between Roan and the Gunther.

"What an inspired idea," says Algie. "It is centrally located, well concealed and has a great many rooms and facilities in the school wing. As long as they don't smudge the books, having some people around might be...nice."

"If it's the same to you..." Othard says tentatively.

Imin nods enthusiastically. "... we'd be more than happy to stay..."

"...until you get back..."

"...and keep Algernon company..."

"...if that's alright with Algernon, of course."

Stepping forward, Talia and Dobbs look imploringly at Kamyar.

"Oh, all right," he says begrudgingly. "But I'll want a full report. Full."

Algie smiles. "Wonderful, nothing better than the society of readers. Thank you, Roan of Longlight, for your insightful suggestion. I'll try to have a few more sections of the journal decoded by the time you return. Maybe some of my new companions could be enticed to help," he says, looking meaningfully at the Storytellers behind him.

"Journal?!" says Kamyar. " Journal?" he repeats, turning to Roan. But he has only to look at him to know. "Where? Where!" he demands, following Roan. Just before leaving the map room, he doubles back for a moment. "Talia! Dobbs! Give Algernon all the help he needs. I expect results!"

Roan smiles as the old Gunther beams—whether from the prospect of help or at the sound of his proper name, Roan can only guess.

"Well, don't just stand there grinning like an idiot," Kamyar blusters. "Lead on, Roan of Longlight, lead on!"

Remembrance

> the apsara's fighting techniques combine the
> military knowledge their first leader, steppe,
> gained as a master with the meditative discipline
> her daughter ende acquired from the wazya.
> they are believed to be unparalleled.
>
> —orin's history of the apsara

GAZING ACROSS THE FROZEN VALLEY, Willum tries to shake off the cold from his limbs and the icy despair in his heart. Worry and frustration gnaw at his conviction: he wants to shield Stowe from suffering, protect her from pain, but he is helpless to do either, so he's become restless and uneasy. Only her true parents and time can heal her now; he must set aside his anxieties and clear his mind for the task ahead.

Kira sought him out late last night. There were reports of Clerics spotted uncomfortably close to the Caldera. Coincidence? Or part of Darius's continuing search for Roan and Stowe? Whatever it was, it was not good. So Willum and Kira began their journey down the steep and heavily camouflaged path at daybreak, hail and frozen rain slowly forcing its way through their heavy cloaks.

As they reach the foot of the path, Kira turns to him, her cheeks ruddy from the cold. "I smell a fight in the air," she says, voice brimming with joyful anticipation.

"And here I was hoping to avoid a confrontation," says

Willum, eyebrows cocked. But her instincts are keener than she knows. Pointing to a distant rise, he adds, "They're on the other side."

Kira laughs as she adjusts her horse's girth strap for the ride ahead. "Maybe you should hide here while I eliminate the problem."

"Not so fast." Willum's command snaps Kira to attention. "I know your abilities, you have no need to prove yourself to me," he says, hoping to check her rising indignation. "But there is boldness and there is carelessness. The latter, as you know, gets you unnecessarily dead."

The thoughts that play across Kira's face are so intense that Willum can easily read them: she knows he's had a vision of her death or something close to it. Knows he's speaking not just from the position of a protective older brother, but from one who has experienced her suffering.

Lowering her eyes, Kira nods. Her heart rate and breath slowly normalize. "How many?" she asks quietly.

"Two. Probably scouts. More will follow."

"We have to kill them, Willum. They can't be allowed to take back any information about the Caldera—"

"It may be possible to erase their memories, if we can—"

"Willum." Kira's tone makes it clear this is no longer his sister talking, but the head of the Apsara army, responsible for the safety of her people. "There are no other choices. Not in this. If Darius discovers who and where we are, he will, as he did before, come after us and try to wipe us out. He will take every child and use them in any way he can to further his life and his power. You have seen. You know. I will take no chances that this might happen, Willum. No risks. Do you understand me?"

"Kira," Willum says, reaching out to her.

"Don't," she snaps. "I have had to watch infants wrested out of the arms of their mothers, weeping children torn from their parents' sides. Do you think, for an instant, I would waste an opportunity to limit the number of Darius's henchmen? Reduce his power?"

"No," Willum says simply. There is no advantage in fighting her on this. Mounting his stallion, he nods. "Let's go."

In an instant, Kira is behind him. "A little faster, please," she cries with a devilish grin as she slaps her scabbard across the flank of Willum's horse. With a piercing whinny, it rears, nearly throwing Willum, then gallops wildly across the plain. Kira, close behind, howls with laughter.

Pounding the half-frozen ground, the clatter of the horse's hooves echoes through Willum's body, driving out his apprehensions. He flicks the reins, urging his mount to greater speed.

Races like this had been a daily event after they'd been reunited with their grandmother. Ende had insisted on play, every day, all day, long and hard, for almost three years. That was how long it had taken for them not to imagine their parents' deaths in every silence. Willum often wonders if Kira does not still hear her mother's screams whenever she faces an enemy or in the empty hours of the night.

As they near the rise, they slow their horses and dismount. Unsheathing their swords, they silently climb until they hug the slope's edge. The two Clerics, simultaneously reaching the same place from the other side, cry out at the sight of them. With a roar, Kira whirls, sword flashing, and with two quick thrusts the first Cleric falls. She pivots to avoid the second's blade, and with a huge swipe nearly cuts him in two.

An arrow whizzes by Willum's head. A dozen heavily armed Clerics are charging out from the tree line, straight for them. Too many to seize with his mind. Another arrow speeds toward Kira and he bats it away with a flick of his sword. At his sister's side, he plunges directly into the fray. Kira slashes and stabs and slices in a blood frenzy, her sword moving so quickly it seems an almost invisible force.

But the arrows continue to come—not from these warriors. Where?

Following their trajectory, Willum locates two crossbowmen poorly concealed just beyond the tree line and runs toward them. With the flat of his blade, he strikes their arrows, causing them to ricochet into the chests of Kira's attackers. Though volley after volley are fired, he deflects them all. When he is within several feet of them, the bowmen realize the futility of their endeavor. They throw down their crossbows and, with crazed battle cries, they leap at him, swords flailing.

Willum falls to one knee and lowers his head. Then, with a single stroke, he fells them both.

Moments later, Kira, chest heaving, slaps him on the back. "Well, that takes care of that," she says, glancing at the dozen fallen Clerics that litter the field behind her. "Nice trick with the sword, Will."

In that moment, one of the dying bowmen reaches out to Willum. "I know you," he rasps. The enabler in his neck is throbbing beneath his skin, and his eyes have the glassy look of impending death. "Our Stowe's Primary. Have you found her?"

"We search still," Willum says.

"Forgive us. We did not...know who you were," says the

Cleric, his breath rattling. "Thanks to the Archbishop...for his wisdom. We asked for the Apogee...but we were given only bows. And so...you live." The Cleric's body spasms, and he is still.

"Apogee?" Willum searches his mind for a clue as to what the bowman might be referring to.

"You don't know?" Kira asks. When Willum shakes his head, she gives him a grim look. "Sounds like one of Darius's deadly surprises."

Willum's about to respond, but a whirring sound coming from the dead bowman distracts him. The enabler in the Cleric's neck vibrates wildly. With a popping sound it stops abruptly, then melts, leaving a sickly green contusion in the man's neck.

Without comment, Kira leaps up and checks the necks of all the fallen. She returns to Willum ashen-faced. "The same for all of them. I've never seen this before. You?"

"No. New enablers. A new and apparently lethal weapon. Clerics this far afield. Darius is on the move."

As Willum takes a deep, troubled breath, Kira puts a hand on his shoulder. "I should ride ahead to the Brothers' camp. Warn Roan. Will you come?"

"I must wait for Stowe. If she wakes in time, we will travel with Ende. Then, we must return to the City."

STOWE CLIMBS, HAND OVER HAND, INSIDE THE TRUNK OF THE BIG EMPTY. SHE'S ALMOST AT THE TOP WHERE THE LIGHT STREAMS IN. IT'S A HARD CLIMB. HER HANDS ARE SMALL AND THE HANDHOLDS ARE BETTER FOR THE BIGGER KIDS.

FINALLY SHE REACHES HER SPOT ON THE LITTLE LEDGE, HER NAME CARVED IN HUGE LETTERS OVER IT. SHE PUTS HER FEET ON

Roan's rope seat and pokes her head out of the broken treetop. All around her are hundreds of giant hollow trees. Everything is surrounded by a preternatural glow, pale and iridescent, as if everything were made of light. The light of her childhood.

Hearing laughter, she looks down and sees Roan chasing Lem. They glow too: Roan is blue like the early morning sky, with orange wisps as if he were reflecting the sun. Lem, though, has little yellow flames darting all over, like gleeful fairies tickling him. Stowe stifles a laugh as she hears the little door open below. They're coming in! She feels in her pocket for the apple her mother gave her.

"Stowe? Are you up there?" She sees her brother's face and silently giggling, drops the apple. He moves just in time to avoid it and yells up at her, "Stowe, you're in for it now!" Unable to hold back any longer, she explodes with laughter.

"Stowe...Stowe?"

Stowe's terracotta eyes open. It's her father, tending her. "I was dreaming again."

"How old were you this time?"

"I don't know...six or seven. I was in the Hollow Forest, up in Big Empty. Roan was there." Stowe smiles. "I dropped an apple on his head!"

But her father doesn't laugh.

"What's wrong?"

"Nothing."

"Don't lie," she complains. "Is there something wrong with my dreams?"

"No. Of course not." He pauses as if struggling to

FIND THE CORRECT WORDS. "IT'S ONLY...WE'D HOPED YOU WOULD HAVE RECOVERED MORE... BEFORE..."

KNOWING NOW THE REASON FOR HER FATHER'S SADNESS, STOWE SHIVERS. THE MEMORIES, THE DREAMS, THIS TIME SHE'S SHARED WITH HER PARENTS—IT HAS ALL BEEN PARADISE. UNDER THEIR CARE AND THE PROTECTION OF THE SOULS OF LONGLIGHT, SHE'S HEALING, GROWING BACK WHAT WAS LOST WHEN—THE MERE THOUGHT OF IT FILLS HER WITH REVULSION.

"I DON'T WANT TO GO," SHE WHISPERS. "NOT YET."

HER MOTHER JOINS THEM, EYES DARK AND DEEP. "DARLING," SHE SAYS, THEN PAUSES, POSTPONING THE INEVITABLE, IF ONLY FOR ONE LAST MOMENT.

"MOMMA, I'M NOT READY," STOWE BEGS. "I'M STILL SICK. LOOK AT ME. I'M STILL BROKEN."

HER FATHER MOVES CLOSER TO HER, RAISES HIS HAND AND TOUCHES HER BROW. IN THAT INSTANT, HER CLAY EXTERIOR FALLS AWAY AND STOWE LOOKS WONDERING AT HER OWN BODY. SHE FEELS HERSELF, NOT QUITE BELIEVING THAT NOTHING'S MISSING.

"THE HOLE THAT FERRELL LEFT IS HERE," HER FATHER SAYS, HIS HAND OVER HER HEART. "YOU COULD STAY HERE AN ETERNITY, AND STILL IT MIGHT NEVER COMPLETELY HEAL."

STOWE FEELS THE AIR AROUND HER CHANGE. SICK WITH FEAR, SHE CRIES, "HOW CAN I BE STRONG ENOUGH TO FIGHT, TO SURVIVE DARIUS, WHEN I HAVE THIS GAPING NOTHINGNESS INSIDE?"

HER PARENTS DO NOT SPEAK BUT THEIR EYES ARE INFINITELY ELOQUENT. THERE IS NO QUESTION OF BARGAINING FOR TIME. NOTHING SHE SAYS WILL MAKE A DIFFERENCE. IT IS NOT THEIR DECISION.

"DARIUS WILL TORTURE ME," SHE SAYS, TEARS ROLLING DOWN HER CHEEKS. "HE'LL USE ME AND THEN, WHEN HE'S DONE, HE'LL KILL ME AND THROW MY BODY TO THE DOGS!"

"Stowe!" Her mother's voice slashes her like a slap, but moving closer, she puts her arms around Stowe, and stroking her hair, she sighs. "Darius will not kill you. He will not. You are too strong." Stowe feels her mother's tears blend with her own. Holding Stowe's head so that she can look deeply into her daughter's eyes, she adds, "Never, never forget that."

"Please, keep me with you!" Stowe whimpers. She clings to her parents desperately, but a great gust lifts her, and she flies up, fingers futilely reaching for her father's outstretched hand.

Willum hesitates outside the door but it opens instantly. Ende has always been especially sensitive to his presence and he has never been able to shield himself from her. She sits behind the one candle illuminating her chamber and its wavering light carves deep hollows in her aged face as she gestures for him to join her.

"Please, Willum. I would like to speak my mind with you, thoughts I cannot share with my warriors. You may refuse; you are not bound to this favor."

But of course he is bound. By blood. By the deep pain of wounds never healed, impossible to heal, and left to fester. By the legacy of Darius and the Dirt. And sitting across from her in the dim light he says only, "I will listen."

"Watching all the men of my family," she begins, her voice heavy with grief, "all the men of my people, suffer through Darius's plague, has left me with memories I have never been able to dispel and of late they afflict my every waking moment. Leading meditation and training, conducting council, preparing food, teaching the young ones, these activities have always sustained me, but now nothing keeps the images of the past at bay. They wash over me as if they had only happened yesterday and not fifty years ago—blood seeping from the eyes and ears of our men and boys, the desperate unceasing coughing that ripped them apart from the inside, the blisters pooled under their flesh that burst at our slightest touch. There was no relief that we could give. No herb, no balm, no soothing caress. I was eighteen when I watched them all die, all those fathers and husbands and sons. My rage would not quiet and so I left to wander the Devastation. The man who became your grandfather found me. Zoun trained me in the way of the Wazya. I learned control, but control is not a cure. And now I dream increasingly of the knife I might hold to that monster Darius's throat."

Though his grandmother holds her anguish at bay, Willum sees it in her blank stare, the way her fingers smooth the line of the wood grain on the table, the deep and even rhythm of her breath being strictly controlled.

"I am going to cede my position to Kira, Willum. The bloodlust is in me and it is strong. I will continue to advise, but only in consultation with Roan. That boy is determined that this be a bloodless conflict—impossible, of course, but it will keep my head clear and directed at the preservation of the individuals in my army, rather than the destruction of my enemy at any cost.

"Willum, I was always more skilled at soothing your sorrow than I was at helping Kira. I identified too strongly with her desperate anger and I did not prevent her from nurturing it. And so, Kira is a bit…impetuous—" at this, Willum could not help but smile, "as you know; so is Wolf. But again, we can be thankful that Roan considers everything before he acts, and so a balance is obtained."

Pausing, Ende leans forward and places her hand over his. *One of his grandmother's most trusted lieutenants, Petra, eyes wide and lifeless, dropping from Ende's arms. A cry so piercing, death rides on it as surely as it directs its instrument. Ende's sword so quick, its passage is only determined by the blood that suspends against the sky in its wake until—*

Willum pulls his hand from hers so abruptly, hope of concealment is impossible; besides, Ende's stern gaze does not permit him to look away.

"My fate is written by my history, Willum. I have awaited it a long time. But Kira…Willum, do I make the right choice?"

Willum wants to say nothing. To *see* is a curse. He may have been given this vision because he has a part in determining the fate he has witnessed. But what did it mean, really? And what could he possibly say? If he told her what he had *seen* of Petra's death or of Kira suffering in the dungeons of the City, would it save them, or simply ensure their fate?

Since Willum feels there is no viable alternative to what Ende intends, he says, "Yes." But he worries that this one word, this simple utterance spoken to relieve his grandmother's burden, might cost both Kira and Ende their lives.

a broTher reTurns

though roan of longlight was acknowledged as the
titular head of the brothers, his true acceptance
did not occur until he had received the touch of
fire and could be called prophet of the friend.

— orin's history of the friend

The last five days have been the worst Roan's experienced in all his travels. Their troubles began right after
he and Lumpy parted ways with Kamyar. As soon as the
storyteller announced that there was no need to overdo a
good thing by arriving at the Brothers' camp too early, the
rain started pelting down. And when darkness arrived—
hours before it should—the rain fell frozen, sticking to their
cloaks and assaulting their horses. The intense cold made it
especially difficult to stay awake, to keep watch, and the icy
ground made morning travel treacherous.

But, blissfully, today has dawned with sunlight and a
warm wind from the south. And, having spread their capes
over their horses' rumps to dry as they ride, the two friends
feel, if not comfortable, at least a little thawed.

The sun is high in the sky when they stop at a pebbled
trail Roan remembers all too well. He'd traveled it on Saint's
motorcycle, first as a prisoner, then as a friend. How easily
he'd trusted him. Saint's betrayal was the first of Roan's life
and it angers him that it has left such a scar. Not visible like
the one on his chest, but much deeper and more damaging.

Seeing his friend's enquiring face, he explains, "I feel like this is my last moment of freedom. Once we cross into that valley, everything changes."

"Well, the horses could use a rest," Lumpy offers, and without hesitation he dismounts from his piebald mare and leads her to water.

Giving me time, Roan thinks. A small moment of nothing but the warmth of the sun, the smell of the earth and the babble of water slowly smoothing pebbles in the stream. A brief respite, to be nothing but myself.

They linger at the edge of a long meadow that reaches down into the valley. Sheltered from the winds and icy rains, the last greens of autumn still thrive here. While the horses graze, Lumpy leans against an ancient gnarled tree still clinging to the gold-flecked crimson of its dying leaves, his nose in a small book he borrowed from the Apsara to practice his reading. Roan, for his part, spends the afternoon listening to the whisper of life all around him as if it were the most important activity in the world. But when the sunset casts its radiant hue over the mountain, he knows they can delay no longer. Still, Roan allows his horse a slow gait as they follow the stream that leads to the Brothers' camp.

Try as he might to extend this moment of serenity, it is not long before the gully of jagged rocks and tall trees at the camp's base comes into view and they are greeted by a deafening peal of bells.

"So much for downplaying our arrival!" yells Lumpy.

High in the trees Roan can see the platforms where Brothers armed with crossbows keep watch. Saint chose this place because the gully created a natural fortress. There's only one path into the Brothers' camp, and Roan and Lumpy urge their horses up it. Passing through a row of huge boulders, they reach the plateau and are confronted by some fifty armed warriors captained by Brothers Wolf and Stinger.

"Roan of Longlight!" shouts Stinger.

The Brothers raise their swords in salute. "Roan! Roan, Roan, Roan!" they cry, then stand at attention, silent.

Lumpy leans inconspicuously toward Roan. "I think they're waiting for you to say something," he whispers.

As Roan scans the men's faces, the bull from his vision appears in his mind's eye. Craning its neck so that its dark eyes burrow into his, it speaks with Rat's voice: *The blood of the bull, you know it.*

Roan's hand touches his hook-sword. He immediately grips it, and swings it over his head. "The Friend!" he calls out.

The men pump their swords in the air, replying, "The Friend! The Friend! The Friend!"

Turning to dismount, Roan notes Lumpy's incredulous grin and shrugs. Trying to maintain some composure, the two studiously apply themselves to unbinding their rucksacks.

"Welcome, Roan of Longlight," says Stinger, directing a novitiate toward their horses. But when the Brother-in-training sees Lumpy, he nervously backs away. By his third step, Wolf's grabbed him by the collar. "He is Roan of Longlight's Lieutenant! Take the horses and groom them well." Stepping toward Lumpy, Wolf lowers his voice. "They have been advised, but their fears are old ones, ones of survival, and are not so easily shed."

"As long as they don't start throwing stones," Lumpy replies lightly, but Roan can hear in the tightness of his tone all the old injuries flaring up.

The novitiate, face flushed, gingerly takes the reins from Lumpy and leads the horses away.

"Roan of Longlight," Wolf hesitates, looking uncomfortably at Stinger.

"Brother Wolf would like to conduct class before nightfall," Stinger quickly interjects.

"Forgive me, Brother Wolf," Roan apologizes. "Please, make no changes in your schedule on my account."

Accepting Roan's leave, Wolf strides toward the center of camp. The power and economy in his every step remind Roan how much he'd loved Wolf's classes. He remembers the day Wolf gave him his hook-sword, one of two identical ones his father had made. "One was for me," Wolf had said, "the other for my greatest pupil."

Roan and Lumpy follow Stinger past a sloped amphitheater. Roan tries not to look at it, but he can't resist scanning the tiered benches. It was here that he spent his last minutes with the brethren. Their mad chanting "Kill, kill, kill!" still echoes in his ears. "Kill, kill, kill!" urging him to behead the two Fandor warriors he'd been told led the assault on Longlight.

Roan had turned his blade on Saint instead. Stinger had told him that action had ensured his acceptance here today. Would he have done it, Roan wonders, if he'd known then what he knows now?

Coming upon several rows of small tents, Roan nudges Lumpy. "That tent on the end is where I used to sleep."

"Think they're putting us there now?"

"Certainly not," says Stinger. "You will have Saint's tent."

Roan stops dead in his tracks.

"You will no doubt wish to consult privately. Conduct

interrogations without fear of distraction. The smuggler, for instance, is quite keen to have his business with us concluded. It is the only appropriate place for such endeavors."

Lumpy sticks his elbow into Roan's ribs.

"Yes. Yes," Roan stammers, clearing his throat. "Thank you, Brother Stinger."

Bracing himself, Roan enters the home of his dead mentor. Stinger points out several rooms as they move through the narrow hallway, but Roan's no longer listening.

Lumpy lets out a low whistle when they reach the central tent. Smoke billows up to the high canvas ceiling from a blazing fire in the middle of the vast, richly carpeted room. Roan too had been impressed when he'd first seen it. As he smiles at Lumpy's awed expression, time seems to stop. In that moment, Roan sees an apparition of Saint sitting on the rug behind the fire. The serpents woven into the carpet seem to twist and writhe. Saint the Prophet, as he once was. But as Roan watches, a solitary leech crawls out of Saint's mouth and slowly crosses his cheek. Then, one after another, they erupt from his ears and abdomen until he is nothing but a mass of writhing bloodsuckers, his eyes screaming desperation: the Saint Roan witnessed in hell.

"Your supper is on its way. After breakfast tomorrow, we will bring you the smuggler." Brother Stinger pulls a pouch out of his pocket. "We found this in Asp's tent."

As Roan closes his hand over the pouch, he brushes against Stinger and becomes suddenly aware that the scar on his chest feels inflamed. Lifting his head to question the Brother, Roan finds Stinger already gone.

Lumpy, however, is eagerly nudging his hand. "Can I look?"

Opening the pouch, Roan holds it under a candle. The violet material inside glitters faintly in its light.

"I've never seen anything quite like it."

Roan lets the shimmering dust slowly spill into the fire. "You wouldn't have. It's not completely of this Earth. They quarry it where the great meteor fell."

"Why would something like that connect people to the Dreamfield?"

"I don't know. But however it does it, it's not good. Maybe the Dirt itself isn't destroying the Dreamfield, but the people who use it are and that says something."

They freeze at the sound of tapping. Roan reaches for his sword but stops at the sight of the slight young man standing in the entryway.

"Feeder?" Roan says, approaching him. "Is it really you?"

"Did you think I was a ghost?" Feeder holds out a tray of food. "I've brought your supper."

"Are you alright?" Roan asks, concerned.

Feeder's watery eyes swim in dark circles that discolor his face from brow to cheekbone. He looks emaciated even though he's bundled up in a huge wool scarf and has sand-painting furs on from top to toe.

Feeder grimaces. "What do you mean?"

"Just asking," Roan shrugs.

"Fine. I'm fine."

"Feeder was my first friend when I came here," Roan explains to Lumpy. "When I left—"

"I was to be the sacrifice to the Friend," Feeder finishes Roan's sentence as he puts some bowls on a low table near the fire. "But Roan flew the coop and things changed. Of course, we don't make those kind of sacrifices anymore, so I'm alive and still in the kitchen." Uncovering a tureen, he doles out large helpings of stew. "And now you've come back to lead us in victory over the City. I'm proud of you, Brother Roan."

Suddenly Feeder shakes convulsively, and the ladle flies out of his hand. "Sorry, sorry, my fingers, they..." Head bobbing, muttering apology after apology, he falls to his knees, using the end of his long scarf to mop up the spill. But when Roan touches his arm to help him to his feet, Feeder jerks violently away and the scarf slips from his neck exposing a fist-sized bump, red and raw, bulging behind his ear.

Every hair on Roan's back rises. Two years before, Raven had placed what could only have been an enabler in Feeder's neck. It was how they'd made him compliant and willing to be sacrificed. Now, who knew what influence the device was exerting on him. "Feeder..."

Hastily grabbing at the scarf, Feeder pulls it over the wound, explaining, "The Prophet told Brother Raven...to take it out. But he said he didn't know how. Brother Asp tried...he almost got it, I think, but he stopped because he was afraid of... killing me. He must have broke it, though, 'cause I...lost my good mood and I stopped saying yes to everything. The skin around it's itchy and swollen. And I get dizzy sometimes. But it doesn't hurt much. The Friend is looking after me." Roan and Lumpy stare speechless as Feeder, twitching uncontrollably, backs his way out of the tent. "Just leave the dishes out by the door. I'll come and fetch them later, Roan of Longlight." And bowing low, he trips out over the threshold.

"It comes at night, it has a bite, and leaves its stinger in you. You will not cry, you will not die, but one wrong word can kill you."

Roan looks quizzically at his friend. "What's that?"

"Storyteller lore. Never said the word enabler, but people knew what they were talking about. Still, I've never seen anything like that, not on Clerics—or their victims. Not in anybody we saw in the City."

"Raven used enablers but he was no doctor. Feeder was a sacrifice; he wasn't meant to survive."

"You think it's killing him?" Lumpy asks.

"It doesn't look good, does it?"

Saddened and weary, they silently pick at their meal. Throwing down his spoon, Roan mutters in disgust, "The Friend. He thinks the Friend will save him."

Lumpy looks up from his bowl. "Isn't that better than having no hope at all?"

"Hope?" Roan says in disbelief. "Saint made the Friend up. He borrowed an idea. What good is having hope in that?" Roan bolts up. "You want to see, come on, I'll show you!" He charges down the hallway to the bedroom that once belonged to Saint. It's exactly as Roan remembers, nothing in it but a woolen mattress and a few carpets. Lifting a rug beside the mattress, Roan bares the stone floor. He puts the point of his knife into a crack in the stone and pries it up, revealing a metal box. Opening the lid, he removes the book inside, and places it in Lumpy's eagerly awaiting hands.

"The Religions...of An...Ancient Rome," reads Lumpy.

Roan opens the book to the chapter on the cult of Mithras, and shows Lumpy the images: the god Mithras being born out of a rock, soldiers sacrificing a bull, two men holding lit torches, one pointing to the sky, the other to the ground. "This is the book that Saint used to create his religion. It all came from the ancient Romans. The Friend is Mithras."

Lumpy surveys the illustrations. "So they believed in the Friend way back then. That means the Friend is thousands of years old."

Roan stares at Lumpy. "Are you joking?"

"No. So what if Saint renamed him? What difference does it make that he made his discovery in a book? You've told me that's the whole point of books—to save and share important information. That's why I'm learning to read—so I can make discoveries, find out things I didn't know."

Trying to calm himself, Roan takes a deep, deep breath, then speaks very slowly. "Just because it's in a book doesn't mean the Friend is real."

Lumpy scans the chapter on the constellations. "I've never been to the Dreamfield, but you tell me that's real. You've seen dead people there, and animals that can speak to you. Things from there come to you in dreams. What if... ancient gods exist there too? Only you just haven't seen them yet."

Roan throws himself onto Saint's bed and presses his fingers into his temples.

"Roan? Okay. I'm just gonna say it. Don't be mad but—is this more about Saint having to be wrong and not about what's possible or impossible at all?"

Roan props himself up. *Knowledge is Power*. It was an old saying his father had often repeated when Roan's desire to be out and running overwhelmed his ability to study. He didn't understand it then, but looking into Lumpy's patiently waiting face, he can see it now. Lumpy's instincts have always been good, but since he's learned to read he's been able to use his insight more pointedly—there's no denying he's right on the mark now.

"Okay," Roan sighs. "Let's say the Friend is real, that all the mythical gods are real. That they exist, somewhere. What difference does it make?"

Lumpy's hand rests protectively on the book cover. "Maybe they can help us. You said you saw the bull in your vision, that its blood healed the—where are you going?"

"I'm sorry, I need to sleep," says Roan. "To forget about the Friend and Saint and the Brothers and…everything for awhile."

"Keep your sword close tonight," Lumpy cautions. "Just in case."

"I keep it close every night, Lumpy," Roan says sadly. "I can't remember the last time I didn't."

The walls seem to close in on Roan as he walks back to the central tent. He feels queasy bending for his pack, his hook-sword almost alive in his hand. He can taste blood, smell it. Every moment of pain and terror he'd experienced in this camp converges on him all at once.

Stumbling into one of the bedrooms, Roan tries to fall on the only piece of furniture there. The dense woolen mattress has not been slept on in awhile; everything has the musty odor of disuse. It seems as if nothing's lived here since Saint died except ghosts. Rat had said Roan's future was tied to the Brothers, or the Friend, or both. Is Roan really only rejecting the Friend's existence because of Saint?

Lumpy had to work hard to survive. He had to lose preconceptions and learn to use everything he could. If Lumpy could do that, then maybe, maybe Roan could overcome his assumptions about everything connected with Saint.

Survival. Of the world he knew and all the life on it. That's what was at stake. His problems with the Brothers and the Friend seem indulgent by comparison. Why has it taken him so long to understand that? Roan wonders, as he lays a hand over his hook-sword and drifts off to sleep.

Roan awakens only seconds before Brother Wolf arrives in the doorway, but he is up off the bed in an instant.

"Ah," says Wolf, openly appraising Roan. "I am happy to find you awake and alert." Stepping over to Roan's mattress, he lays out a thick black tunic. "It is time to raise the sun."

Roan is about to refuse but thinks better of it. "I'll meet you outside."

Wolf smiles, turns on his heel, and leaves.

Roan throws the tunic over his head, remembering Saint's silhouette, arm drawn back to release a flaming arrow into the predawn sky. It feels odd, running his hands over this coarse fabric, taking Saint's place.

The bells begin to toll, and as Roan snaps out of his reverie, Lumpy stumbles in, rubbing his eyes. "These Brothers are certainly early birds. The sun's not even up yet...hey, new clothes. Impressive."

"You can sleep some more, breakfast's not for an hour."

"Then why are we up?"

"Have to raise the sun."

Lumpy yawns. "Didn't know it needed your help." He starts to wander back to his room, then stops. "You taking your sword?"

"Not allowed."

"Then I'm coming."

"It's alright. All the Brothers will be there. If somebody's going to make a move against me, it'd be a pretty stupid place to do it. Go back to sleep."

"If you insist," Lumpy says sleepily, making a beeline for his bed.

Roan heads down the long canvas corridor. Brother Wolf is waiting in the near darkness and together they walk to the rise at the edge of the camp. As they reach the highest clearing, he senses Wolf leaving his side. The frigid air at the edge of the bluffs whips through his robes. Bracing himself against it, he has the illusion that he's growing larger. Large enough, maybe, to face seventy-four brethren, standing in perfect rows, exhaling and inhaling in unison, every eye upon him.

Roan participated in this ceremony every morning for over a year; he needs no script to deliver the words it requires, only resolve. The pressure of the Brothers' expectations, the rhythmic echo of their unified breaths, and the hint of light emerging from the horizon combine to unleash his voice.

"For us He raises the sun!" Roan calls out, holding his fist up to the sky. "For us He brings the dawn!"

Every man is silent. Brother Wolf hands Roan a crossbow, and like Saint before him, Roan fits a cloth-tipped arrow into its groove. Wolf puts a flame to the cloth and Roan releases the burning arrow into the sky. Soaring high over the valley, the blazing dart dips down and plummets out of view.

All watch the horizon in hushed anticipation. Then it comes. The first glimmer of sunlight. Rising where the arrow fell into darkness. Every Brother cheers, the emotion contagious. Finally, Roan raises his hand, commanding silence. He bows low to the sun, then leads the assembly back down to the camp.

Roan joins Lumpy at the breakfast table. Fearing contagion, the Brothers have avoided sitting near his friend, leaving a conspicuous space around him, but it's convenient for their whispered conversation. "I don't know how, but. . .I just raised the sun."

"I'm not surprised," Lumpy says, scarfing down a heaping spoonful of hot cereal. Smacking his lips, he pauses before delivering his judgment. "Good mush," he says heartily, and then brings his foot heavily down on Roan's.

"What was that for?" Roan whispers sharply.

"I don't want you to let all this sun-raising business go to your head." Lumpy winks, then nods to Stinger and Wolf, who are pushing back their plates. "Better eat up! They're coming to get you!"

But Roan's lost his appetite and watches, envious, as Lumpy devours his breakfast.

Arriving at his side, Wolf asks, "If you're ready, Roan of Longlight?"

"My Lieutenant's joining us," Roan tells him, "presuming he's finished with his porridge, of course."

He smiles as Lumpy reluctantly puts down his spoon and stands, mumbling, "I'm ready," through a mouthful of gruel.

With heavy brows furrowed over restless greedy eyes, the smuggler, at the best of times, would not be a man to inspire trust. But Lumpy's presence has made him downright twitchy. "There are rumors in the towns——"

"I have no interest in rumors," Roan says firmly. He can see the man's trying to assess him—a mere boy, sitting in what was once Saint's place—wondering how much he can draw Roan out and get information to fatten his purse.

Cocking his head, the smuggler throws up his arms. "Straight to business then, if that's the way you like it."

Roan stares at the man impassively. "You have skills I would like to purchase."

"What exactly is it that you want?"

"I need someone smuggled into the City."

"That's all well and fine," the smuggler blusters, his shaggy mustache twitching, "but since Master Querin's decided it's best to hang smugglers, the price will be high."

The question is not resources—the Brothers have adequate stockpiles accumulated from their years of marauding—but whether he really wants to trust this man with any information at all. Kira had said this would be their best hope of getting into the city, but sitting on Saint's rug, Roan can almost hear the Prophet's advice and it doesn't involve letting this man walk out of the tent alive. Maybe it shows in Roan's face because the smuggler begins to sweat.

Unable to endure the silence any longer, the man blurts, "Look, kid—" But seeing both Wolf and Stinger step forward, he stops, his gaze flitting from one to the other apprehensively. Wiping his brow, he assumes a harmless jocular air and shrugs. "Look, you won't say who you are, so what am I supposed to call you?"

At a signal from Roan, the Brothers step back. Breathing easily again, the smuggler continues: "All I'm saying is, smuggling anything into the City, I'm taking my life in my hands. They're killing my friends and my business and I've got three families to feed."

"You'll be adequately compensated for your services."

"If that means well paid, then we have a deal."

As they stand, a high-pitched bell rings out in a single staccato burst.

"We have guests," hisses Wolf.

Stinger points at the smuggler. "You. Come with me." Then quickly guides him away.

Hook-sword in hand, Roan follows Wolf out of the tent. "Clerics?" he asks as they sprint to the edge of camp.

"You forget the signal, Roan of Longlight. Single burst. Less than five riders. Clerics travel in larger packs these days."

Strategically poised at the only access point to the camp, a dozen Brothers tensely aim their crossbows at the trail below as Roan and Wolf reach the cliff overlooking the valley.

They scramble up the lookout tower to see what they're facing. Four cloaked figures. Roan sighs with relief when the lead rider lowers her hood. Kira.

As Wolf orders the men to stand down, Roan strides out to greet her and her fellow Apsara. "You're two days early—gave us a bit of a surprise." But Kira's gaze travels behind him so he turns.

Wolf's at the top of the trail, scowling. "You're lucky to be alive," he snaps.

"Apologies, Brother Wolf," Kira says, respectfully addressing the irascible Brother. "But I've information that couldn't wait."

As the Brothers gather closer around the visiting Apsara, Roan extends an arm to Kira, "We can talk in my tent."

Kira's sitting by the fire. She's been quiet since they've entered the huge room, no doubt sensing Saint's presence here, just as Roan had. He waits as she sweeps her hand back and forth across Saint's rug. When she finally looks up at him, her voice is barely above a whisper. "It's just as he described it. This is where you read to him, isn't it?"

"Yes." Though sorrow clouds her voice, it is easy to see

the unasked question behind Kira's eyes. "I'm alright. It's hard to get used to being here, that's all. I feel like I'm walking in the shadow of Saint's ghost and it's not a sensation I like."

"Maybe a live threat will give you the jolt you need. Willum and I had an encounter with some Clerics and made a couple of unwelcome discoveries. One of the Clerics recognized Willum. Told him Darius had a new weapon—the Apogee—that this particular group was denied. Lucky for us, because he hinted we'd not be alive otherwise. Then after the man died, there was this whirring sound, a pop, and his enabler…melted. I checked the rest of the Clerics—each of them had a putrid green pit at the base of their skulls. Willum thinks Darius is up to something. I thought I should come early, let you know to keep a lookout for it. The sooner we move, the better. Have you met with the smuggler?"

"Yes. Kira…I don't trust him."

"You sound worried. About me?" Kira laughs. "Well, you needn't be. I'm not foolish enough to trust a smuggler either. The question is, can he get me into the City?"

"He says yes, but he could smell a profit. I think we should wait, at least until after the Council, to make our final arrangements."

"Don't you think the sooner I move the better? If I leave now, I—"

"You wouldn't get very far."

Both Kira and Roan turn, shocked to have been taken unawares by the Storyteller.

"Don't look so surprised! I've other skills beside my bluster. Although it was my golden tongue that convinced an armed escort of Brothers to accompany me into camp. A little less dramatic than that entrance of yours, Kira, or so I hear."

Walking up to her, Kamyar offers his hand. Taking it, she pulls him toward her in a rollicking hug that the Storyteller returns with equal vigor.

Roan stares nonplussed and, as Kamyar winks mischievously at him over Kira's shoulder, he wonders if he's ever going to be able to have an uninterrupted meeting in this place.

"Word is the City's locked down. Hundreds of arrests a day. No one's safe. Seems Darius has been in a fury since Stowe's disappearance. Mejan's on the way with more specific information. Surely the possibility of some accurate reconnaissance is worth the wait." Kamyar smiles engagingly despite Kira's frown.

"And what do we do with the smuggler while we wait?" she asks indignantly. "I don't think we want the lout here when the guests arrive."

"Roan? If I may make a suggestion?"

Why not? Roan thinks and at his nod, Kamyar informs Kira about the library and Roan's plans to use it as a base of operations. Summing up, he says, "So you see, some Apsara warriors are exactly what's required to secure the place. With a few modifications, a guest room in the Academy should suitably contain our smuggler."

"But," Roan interjects, "the smuggler can't be taken there! He'd sell us out in a second!"

Kira gives him a wry grin. "Roan of Longlight, with a bit of scorpion brew in his belly, and a thickly woven cowl over his head—well cinched at the neck—he'll not know which way is up, I guarantee it."

Since the notion seems to have cooled Kira's heels, Roan reluctantly agrees.

The Storyteller rubs his hands together thoughtfully. "Now how do we get the Brothers to part with some of their precious brew?"

Roan laughs. Clearly this plan involves Kamyar's active participation. "Lumpy's at the main tent talking to Feeder, who, I'm sure, will be able to direct you to a source."

As he watches his friends wander toward the center of camp, a few brethren stop and bow, making Roan more than a little uncomfortable. Anxious to get as far away from his "followers" as he possibly can, he veers off in the opposite direction, heading toward the stream that leads up the mountain.

It is almost midday and, awash in memories, he ambles lazily up the slope. Eyes half-closed, he recalls how he carried a boulder along this trickling stream and then all the way up the distant mountain where he finally dropped it, exhausted and bleeding, beside a statue of the Friend. The Friend arose from stone, Saint had cried. Born from stone. Born from the stone, chanted the brothers. That had been his second trial. Stopping to let the noonday sun warm his face, he tries to clear his mind of the memory.

Roan hears the footsteps too late. A handful of stinging dust hits his face. His eyes are on fire. He wants to scratch the infernal toxin out, but through the burning haze he sees the shadow of a long knife held high. Jerking backward to avoid the blow, Roan falls twisting into the stream, splashing water into his eyes. It eases the pain a little and clears his vision enough to make out the shape charging toward him, blade poised to kill. Roan lurches away, back onto the bank, holding his arm out to block the knife. That gives him enough time to bare his sword as the assailant strikes again. Blindly waving it in front of him, he feels the percussive jolt of the knife careening off his blade. Sweeping his hook-sword around him in quick circles, Roan hopes for connection, but hits only air. He can't keep this dance up forever; between the fire in his eyes and the spinning, he's getting dizzy. He feels a stick between his feet, and trips.

Wherever he looks it's like a thick fog, so he shuts his eyes and listens. The assassin isn't moving, is waiting him out. Roan can hear his breath. He's standing just on the other side of the stream. Roan grimaces, lowers his sword and groans, buckling over as if in pain. He hears the footfalls, the quickened breaths of his attacker. Roan waits until he can smell the sweat of the man charging toward him, then shifts his weight and puts all his power into a kick. It connects, smashing his assailant in the chest, sending him flying. The assassin tumbles on the bank, hitting a rock with a sickening crack.

Roan dunks his face in the water, rinsing out more of the dust. When his eyes stop throbbing and his vision begins to clear, he steps over to his assailant.

Feeder, eyes glassy, murmurs, "Roan wins again."

"Why did you attack me, Feeder?"

The cook lets out a little laugh, his teeth red with blood. "You stole my immortality. You, the special one. Never me." His body convulses, but Feeder's hate-filled gaze stays riveted on Roan until the light fades from his eyes forever.

Roan studies the young man's face, recalling his awful life. Sold by his parents into slavery when he was ten, his greatest joy was becoming a novitiate with the Brothers. But he failed the trials and was delegated to cook. Feeder's hope for redemption was to be made a ritual sacrifice; a glory denied him by Roan and made unbearable by his return.

Roan's white cricket scrambles out of his pocket, then leaps onto the growth at Feeder's neck. Following the insect's lead, Roan touches the lump, reaching his mind into the tumor and the enabler beneath. He senses that the device is inert and has probably not functioned for a long time.

Shouts and footfalls splashing through the creek interrupt Roan's examination.

Brother Wolf, quickly assessing the situation, asks, "Any wounds?"

"No."

Wolf nods to the guards, who quickly take the body away. Then he holds out a hand to Roan. "You are not supposed to leave the perimeter without an escort."

"The sentries did their job. It didn't take you long to find me."

"Too long. Forgive me, Roan of Longlight. Ende warned me to look out for Dirt Eater spies, but this one—"

"Feeder wasn't a spy. He was acting on his own."

"But why? He couldn't ever hope to defeat you in battle."

"My escape from here deprived him of his only hope for redemption. He knew the tumor was killing him. He had nothing to lose."

"Raven and his stinking enablers!" Wolf curses. "Impure, vile, inhuman! There's no honor in that tainted City technology. Only Darius would want an army of puppets. Disgusting."

Roan is surprised by the intensity of Wolf's revulsion, but he understands it. He felt it too, in the City, the strange listlessness, the lack of feeling. An army of puppets...Darius's control over his army depends on enablers. If there was a way to——

"How should we dispose of the body, Roan of Longlight?"

"Like any other Brother who has fallen."

Wolf's jaw tightens. "He's not one of us. He was never made a Brother."

"He served the Brothers, and was destroyed by the act of a Brother. His only dream was acceptance. We will give him that in death at least."

At the summit of the mountain, where the statue of the Friend overlooks the camp, logs and sticks have been piled high, the final resting place of Feeder.

The Brothers stand in a circle around the pyre and Roan holds the torch over his head. "The Friend arose from the stone!" he calls out.

"Born from the stone!" chant the Brethren.

"And to the Friend we return!"

Roan sets the torch upon the wood and as the flames spread, they are reflected on the polished surface of the statue. The Friend's skin glows red, lifelike, his hand reaching out, as if to say: "Come to me. Come."

Roan watches the Brothers disperse and waits until all that remains of Feeder is ash. This was what he'd wanted. To be given over, placed in the hands of the Friend.

Friend—Mithras—does he really exist? And if he does, is he as old and powerful as Lumpy suspects? Would he help? Could he...if Roan were able to find him?

the mark of the hhroxhi

ONCE YOU HAVE ONE, FOR AS LONG AS YOU LIVE THEY WILL
SENSE IF YOU ARE IN DANGER AND COME TO YOUR AID. BUT
YOU TOO MUST ANSWER TO THEIR MARK—THE HHROXHI
BROOK NO BETRAYAL.

—THE WAY OF THE WAZYA

ICE FORMS ALONG THE EDGE OF HER WOOLEN HOOD, but the bracing cold suits Mabatan's mood. She's anxious about leaving the healer behind in Kira's village. It's defended by less than a dozen Apsara warriors. If it were attacked, the unconscious healer would be at the mercy of any marauder who breached the gate. But the Apsara had told Mabatan she was expected at the Brothers' camp and could not stay and stand guard with them. Her future lay elsewhere.

A series of horrible, haunting whispers cuts through her fears like a hot knife. Lives, dozens of them, perishing. The small scar above her elbow, the one given to her by Mhyzah, throbs wildly. The lives are Hhroxhi.

Mabatan sprints through the shimmering forest and as she runs, more heart-wrenching whispers echo through the frozen wood. An explosion shudders the air and falling icicles smash on the ground all around her. Bursting through the wood, she sees, through the pelting sleet, the smoldering remains of a Cleric truck. Dozens of pale, earless bodies are splayed across the clearing. All are covered in tiny silver shards, the apparent remains of what has exploded.

In the distance, more than twenty Clerics, brandishing swords, are closing in on a pair of Hhroxhi. Fangs bared, the two Blood Drinkers stave them off with daggers, but they have no hope against these odds. Running swiftly toward them, Mabatan reaches into her pack and pulls out three sections of burnished reed. The toxin of the Nethervine is not to be used lightly but right now it is the only way to help. Lowering herself behind a rock, she assembles the sections into one long tube, places a dart inside it, aims, and blows. A Cleric clutches his hand, screams, and falls, convulsing. She blows again and again, each dart finding its mark, but she may not be fast enough to save the Hhroxhi. There are still too many Clerics, and the Blood Drinkers will soon tire.

The Hhroxhi are battling back-to-back, lashing frantically at their enemies. Mabatan recognizes the taller one—Mhyzah. One of the Clerics arcs his sword in preparation to strike off Mhyzah's head. Raising her blowgun, Mabatan aims carefully, for fear the dart might miss its target and hit her friend. But as she takes her breath, an arrow pierces the neck of the attacker. Mabatan redirects her aim, and as one after another of the unknown champion's arrows hit their marks, the remaining Clerics become confused, easy prey for the blades of the two Hhroxhi.

Mabatan rushes toward her friend. To her surprise, the other Hhroxhi turns on her, weapon raised: Qrixxis, one of the most rabid of the human-haters. Mhyzah moves herself between them and placing her open palm on Mabatan's chest, hisses her thanks. Seeing Qrixxis back away into shadow, the friends turn and watch the approach of a dark-skinned man carrying a long bow.

After acknowledging Mhyzah's thanks, the man inclines

his head toward Mabatan. "I am Brother Stinger. Friend to the Hhroxhi—at least those who will have human friends," he says, casting a sidelong glance at the hostile Qrixxis. He holds up his wrist, showing the same mark Mabatan bears— the blood oath that summoned them both to this battle. "I was out on patrol and heard the call. You must be Mabatan."

Placing her palms together, Mabatan bows in formal greeting. "Your name is spoken with reverence throughout the Farlands and the mastery of your sand painting is renowned."

Stinger bows in response, murmuring, "You honor me." Moving past Mhyzah to one of the fallen Hhroxhi, he picks up a silver shard and sniffs it. Turning back to her, he asks, "What happened here?"

Mhyzah explains how she and her small hunting party were ambushed. The Clerics had a new weapon that killed instantly, invisibly. Her summons for help had brought a wave of Hhroxhi warriors but many were taken by the weapon before it was destroyed.

Stinger moves among the fallen, searching for the cause of their deaths. But Mhyzah shakes her head, saying to Mabatan that the Brother will find nothing. It was as if the life force of the warriors fled willingly before the weapon. They have never before experienced so great a loss against so few.

As Mabatan stares mournfully at the scores of dead, a stone rolls behind her and one after another Hhroxhi rise up from an underground passage. As each steps onto the frozen earth, they keen to the skies for their fallen sons and daughters, fathers and mothers.

When Qrixxis steps forward, face pinched, fangs jutting from his thick jaws, Stinger rises to stand beside Mabatan.

"Your human war kills our people," Qrixxis hisses at them threateningly.

"We stand against this enemy with you," Mabatan clicks.

"The Wazya do not join in battle. Why stand now?"

"We stand at the end of time and join hands to cross the abyss—"

"Prophecy nonsense!" Qrixxis spits on the crackling ice between them.

"The prophecies are coming to pass whether you will or no, and those who do not stand will fall."

"Nothing you can say will sway me, Wazya witch!"

Feeling a stirring against her skin, Mabatan extends her arm. Qrixxis backs away as her white cricket emerges from the cocoon of her cloak to climb out upon it. Other crickets fly out from the rock face. Mabatan watches as they settle on a paralyzed Qrixxis. Its pale aspect a mirror to their own, the white cricket is sacred to the Hhroxhi, central to their spiritual experience. And though Mabatan cannot hear their communication with Qrixxis, when his pink eyes roll back to look at her, she knows that they have commanded his attention in a way she could not.

"The crickets say I must meet Roan, guardian of the Novakin, and his sister, whose cry is death, tomorrow at moonset on the slope of the Brothers' valley. But I doubt that they will sway me any more than you have."

Turning away from Qrixxis, Mabatan places her open palm on her friend's chest. "Mhyzah, we will tell Roan of this weapon and the toll it has taken on your people."

Shoulders stooped with grief and weariness, Mhyzah covers Mabatan's hand with her own. "I must begin the rituals for our dead."

"May they walk freely in a better world." Mabatan and Stinger intone the Hhroxhi words together, as Mhyzah draws her knife and strides over to lead the prayer for her fallen friends. At her cry, the attending warriors raise their knives and slice their open palms.

"We must go," says Stinger, gently touching Mabatan's shoulder. "We have much to report to Roan before the gathering tomorrow."

As they walk silently over the frozen earth to retrieve their mounts, Mabatan wonders how a Brother of the Friend came to acquire the mark of the Hhroxhi. She knows that Stinger is a spiritual leader but still the Brothers are not renowned for acts of compassion. As she strokes her horse's flank in greeting, she sneaks a glace at the mysterious Brother only to find him staring back at her.

"You're wondering how I came to be a friend to the Hhroxhi?"

"Yes," Mabatan admits.

"I was a child, barely eleven, hiding from Clerics patrolling the river in their motorized boats. One of their boats had children in it, and the Clerics began tossing some of them out. The children flailed helplessly and, when they began to sink, the Clerics motored off laughing. I'd always been a strong swimmer; I knew what to do. But I could see that these children were different, so I hesitated. Only for a moment, but it was enough. I saved four but the fifth could not be revived. The four sat on the beach with me until a Hhroxhi elder came and pried the dead girl from me. Then she took me to a chamber deep in their tunnels. Several Hhroxhi drew their blades. I thought they were going to kill me but they gave me this instead," he says, pointing at the mark on his wrist. "My blood was made one with the four Hhroxhi I saved. Over the years, they taught me their language and we remain friends to this day. I was grateful not to find them among the fallen."

"Did you see anything on the bodies that might help us understand the weapon?"

"If I had I would have told Mhyzah. You heard the explosion?"

"I heard."

"It appeared to have happened when the weapon was somehow toppled, which means that if one gets close enough, it can be destroyed. The metal shards had no special qualities—they were just debris from the destroyed weapon and not what killed the warriors. I was unable to determine what caused the Hhroxhi to die. Many had no wounds at all, Mabatan. Nothing. But..."

"You sensed something?"

"I cannot explain it. It was nothing more than a feeling. I was overcome with the sensation that the Hhroxhi had been devoured by a monstrous emptiness, which had spat out their bodies whole but devoid of any life, the way we would spit out bones." Stinger looks away sharply. "But it matters not what I felt. It was a weapon fashioned by Darius that killed those warriors. Darius is the monster we must fight."

Mabatan waits for a moment but Stinger does not turn back to her. A tremor of dread courses up her spine. What has the Keeper of the City unleashed?

Mabatan and Stinger arrive the next day to find the encampment bustling with new arrivals. The Brothers look harried and tensions are high.

"Roan of Longlight has given us a great challenge. We are not used to visitors and have no skills at hospitality or diplomacy." Stinger nods at a distinguished gentleman in black velvet robes and whispers, "There stands a perfect example. Governor Selig. He arrived with his entourage yesterday. It was the reason I was so far away from camp—I had to ensure his safe passage."

"Excuse me." The Governor's tone is imperious. The group of Brothers busily erecting a large tent is forced to stop in order to hear him. "My wife and attendants require hot water for bathing."

The Brothers peer up at Selig as if he's speaking a foreign language and Mabatan raises her hand to conceal a laugh.

"Hot water," he repeats. "For our baths."

Seeing Stinger, the Brothers sigh with relief, obviously hoping he will take care of the demanding governor. But their leader only shrugs, leaving the men to their own devices.

Shifting to follow Stinger as he continues into the camp, Mabatan notices a tall, sharp-eyed woman behind the Governor. His wife. She feigns a diminutive air, but Mabatan can see her for what she really is: Apsara.

"I'll have to ask someone else, darling," Governor Selig calls out to his wife. "I don't believe these ruffians have the slightest idea of what I'm talking about."

The Governor's wife looks blithely at Mabatan and, almost imperceptibly, winks. Clearly, she's identified Mabatan, just as Mabatan recognized her, perhaps even because of it. Mabatan will have to take greater care to conceal what she knows.

"Come," says Stinger. "Before we speak with Roan, I'd like to show you something."

He leads her to a canopy where five Brothers are bent

over a large flat stone, bringing a portrait of the Friend to life. Each holds a small tube-like funnel from which they pour, with unwavering concentration, different colors of sand. The process is mesmerizing, and Mabatan finds herself drawn in, so much so that she can see each grain falling, becoming part of a greater whole. But her meditation is interrupted by the sound of familiar voices.

Roan stops just beyond the canopy, Kamyar, Lumpy, and Kira laughing round him, and Brother Wolf scowling at his side.

"My grandmother should be here within the hour," Kira says, but Mabatan can see Roan already knows. That must mean everything's gone according to plan and Willum and Stowe are with her.

"How many in Ende's party?" Wolf asks irritably. He must find it annoying—all these unworthy visitors in the Brothers' camp.

"At least twelve," says Kira, nonchalantly.

Wolf stiffens, his patience clearly nearing its end, but Lumpy gently intervenes.

"Why don't we set up some tents on the east side of the camp for the new arrivals, Brother Wolf? Then they'd be guaranteed the necessary privacy." Mabatan watches as Lumpy studies Wolf's grim expression before adding cautiously, "Wouldn't they?"

Everyone's holding their breath as Wolf stares curiously at Lumpy. Apparently not detecting any slight, Wolf visibly relaxes and turns back to Roan. "I'll see to it," he says, and bowing politely to Kira, he strides purposefully into the center of the camp.

"Well done, Master Lump!" says Kamyar. "A diplomatic

triumph! Well, it's to be expected—you're a born actor, and therefore devilishly politic. Bravo!"

Mabatan rises as Kamyar congratulates Lumpy. But just as she's about to call out a greeting to her friends, Roan's attention is suddenly drawn away to the edge of the camp. Mabatan sighs, hand poised in midair.

"Mabatan!" Lumpy reaches forward to grab her hand, a wide grin cracking across his scarred face. "We didn't know you'd arrived."

Roan turns, relief spilling over his careworn features. "I was worried you wouldn't make it."

"I had an escort," Mabatan says, indicating the Brother at her side.

Leaning forward, Roan whispers, "Mabatan, Stowe's almost here. I can feel her."

The hope radiating off Roan makes her pause, hesitant to take this moment from him; the last meeting he'd had with his sister had been brief and spoiled by violence. Still, her news cannot wait. "Roan, Brother Stinger and I must speak to you before the Apsara arrive. The shadow cast by Darius may be deeper than we thought."

BROTHER AND SISTER

THE UNBROKEN PRAYER VIGIL FOR OUR STOWE'S SAFE
RETURN CONTINUES AT THE PYRAMID. ANY CITIZEN HAVING
INFORMATION ON HER WHEREABOUTS IS TO REPORT TO THE
MASTER OF INCULCATION DIRECTLY. LET IT BE KNOWN THAT
WE WILL NOT REST UNTIL SHE IS RETURNED TO US AND
THOSE RESPONSIBLE FOR HER ABDUCTION ARE EXECUTED.
—PROCLAMATION OF MASTER QUERIN

WILLUM RIDES AT THE REAR OF THE APSARA COMPANY,
some of the best and the brightest Ende has. Three
talented young men, brought to continue training with Wolf,
are positioned in a semi-circle around her. No more than
fifteen years old, all showed potential far above what Willum
had expected—younger versions of himself, all eager to take
part in what is to come. A few weeks with them and he might
have made a difference, increased their chances of survival.
They do not deserve to die in this war.

The six young women of varying ages, hand-picked by
Ende to conceal but also to protect Stowe, are bursting with
pride; it makes him smile to feel it. Stowe, he knows, must
feel it too. It has been years since she's been with girls of
her own age. It was hard for her to leave the security of her
parents' love and return to the world; perhaps they will help
ease the way.

Last night, just as he was leaving his meeting with Ende,
news had come that Stowe was awake and in distress. The

instant the words escaped Petra's lips, he had known that the healing was not complete.

He had found Stowe curled into herself like an infant, shaking and sobbing, and though she allowed him to take her into his arms, he had known his care alone would not be enough to mend her sorrow. The Apsara would be leaving at dawn to see Roan, he had whispered, wiping her tears, knowing that her brother might provide her with some relief. But if she wanted to leave with them, she would need to eat and meditate.

It had taken her only moments to regain her composure—at what cost, though, Willum could only guess. It would have been better for her to empty herself of grief, but Darius was walking an unforeseen path and Willum knew they could not delay their return any longer.

Though his instincts cried out against being far from Stowe's side, it was imperative to remain invisible to any spies Darius might have along the road. And so he had donned an Apsara cloak and positioned himself between Dai, Petra, and Veet at the rear of the company. These three women were Kira's most trusted lieutenants. Warriors alone, they had refused to be paired with men of power and would not be induced into political intrigue of any kind. All three glow with strength. Confident in their abilities, they carry themselves with dignity and poise, and adopting the language of their bodies is a balm. It harnesses a little of the turmoil he himself is submerged in.

Letting his horse drift easily amongst his Apsara camouflage, he turns onto the trail into the Brothers' camp. He blends perfectly with the horsewomen, and observes from the rear as Roan formally greets Ende, flanked by an honor guard of Brethren.

"Welcome, Ende of the Apsara. We are honored to share our home with you."

"It is our pleasure to visit the Brothers of the Friend. We have brought three of our sons to train with Brother Wolf should he find them worthy."

Willum searches Wolf's face as he steps forward and says, "I am, as always, your student, and am honored to be chosen as their teacher." There is only awe and respect in the man's voice. Whatever else he may be, he owes a great deal of his skill as a warrior to Ende, and it is admirable that he does not try to hide this debt. But the man has a great weight on him; doubt and loyalty are at war inside that powerful frame. "The council convenes at sunset. Come, we will show you to your quarters."

Willum's gaze shifts to Roan. But the young man is preoccupied with something other than the Brothers' commander. He's sensed Stowe, and Willum can hear the current of their silent conversation.

I was so worried about you.

Yes, I know. I nearly died.

You should have stayed with the Apsara. You'd be safer—

I am with the Apsara. And you are here. What could be safer?

Stowe—

Roan. We stand together against Darius or we run. There is no middle ground.

Willum can see the twinge over Roan's eyebrow; the distress he feels for his sister is an anxiety they both share. Ende nods to her people and they begin to dismount. And as Willum passes Roan, he opens his mind to him, offering what small comfort he can. *She is alive, Roan, but wounded. She needs you.*

The Apsara are guided to a group of long, low tents that have been erected on the east side of the camp. Without consultation, the Apsara leave the tent beside Stowe's for Willum. He enters and sits, waiting for her to send for him. He empties himself of all thought and allows his mind the freedom of nothingness. He knows that this is the last time he will be able to do so for a long while.

After spending a frustrating few hours seeing to the final arrangements for that evening's Council, Roan puts the old map of the Dreamfield under his arm and sets off briskly across the frosted ground to the opposite side of the camp. He does not need to be told which tent his sister is in; her presence is like a beacon, shining in his inner eye.

The several Apsara lounging around her tent smile at him in greeting. Roan knows that their casual stance is all show, masking their role—anyone attempting to force his way through to the secret visitors would find himself very quickly compromised and, if he fought back, very likely dead.

The tent's small and unassuming, but standing before it, Willum, even concealed beneath an Apsara cloak, is an imposing presence. "She is waiting for you," he whispers.

"Thank you for finding her," Roan says, grasping Willum's arm.

"That, Roan of Longlight, is my purpose. I can do nothing else," replies Willum, echoing Roan's gesture.

"We found this in the Foresight Academy," Roan says, handing him the cylinder with the map.

"You've secured the Academy?" asks Willum, elated.

"We're making it our base of operations. That's a map of the Dreamfield."

"If you found it there, it will need updating."

"I was hoping—"

"I will start at once," says Willum, and true to his word he turns and slips silently into the adjacent tent.

Sensing his sister's impatience, Roan pushes through the fabric threshold. Seeing her, he breathes deeply, trying to steady his racing heart. She's such a little girl—no more than twelve, and yet the power she radiates seems ancient and dangerous.

I was raised to be a sophisticated aristocrat, Brother. By my adopted father, the Archbishop of the Conurbation.

The sadness welling up in Stowe's chest almost brings tears to Roan's eyes. She'd been happy once, a girl who played hide-and-go-seek and climbed trees. But no more.

"I was with our parents," she says softly. "They gave me my life back. I would have stayed forever if they'd let me."

"I saw them too, not so long ago, in that place," Roan says. "But I had so little time, and so many questions. I wanted to ask—"

"Why they sacrificed themselves?" Stowe finishes.

Roan nods. "Did they tell you?"

"No, of course not." Roan can hear the anger and frustration curling dangerously beneath the statement. "They're very sorry about it all, but not sorry enough to answer questions. I've decided to give up on that front and concentrate on the next. Willum and I will return to the City immediately. There's work to do."

Darius will kill you.

Mother says no. They knew I'd have to go back. They accepted it. You should too.

Why are you being this way?

"This is the way I am."

Her voice is so devoid of warmth, her eyes so cold. If only he had gripped her hand tighter, she'd never have left his side. Two years with the Turned and her ordeal with Ferrell have made her hard. Very hard. "You want revenge."

"Shouldn't I?" Her smile is almost cruel. "Don't you?"

Seeing her fierce passion reminds him all too clearly of his own rage. But it barely offsets the slyness of her question. "Once," he says, carefully, "but vengeance is a dull knife."

"Well spoken, Brother," Stowe smiles, her cheeks dimpling with sweet, little girl innocence. "But I take care to tend the sharpness of my blade."

Please, Stowe. We've just found each other again.

Partings are our fate, Roan. "It's in the prophecies, The Book of Longlight: 'Though the destiny of the son and daughter of Longlight be joined, it shall never be shared.'"

There is no escaping her resolve. In the end he knows she's right; he's the one whose motives are questionable. He'd failed to protect her once and doesn't want to make that mistake again. But maybe she doesn't need his protection. If she wants to go back and play Our Stowe, win Darius's trust and help destroy him, who is he to deny her? She suffered more at Darius's hands than he and she's earned the right to play the part she chooses. Still, he knows she's hiding something. He sees his sister but also…something else, something he's not sure he can trust. *Who are you?*

"Do you think you haven't changed too?" she asks impatiently.

Whatever Roan had hoped to recover in this meeting is lost forever. He should have known. History cannot be reversed. He hears her mind call out, *Willum*, and in a moment her guardian joins them.

"I have marked the locations of the more recent constructions. Shall I...?" says Willum, looking curiously from one to the other.

Roan nods, smiling weakly. "Please."

Arranging the map on the floor, Willum begins, "This is the Whorl, it sits atop the Well of Oblivion."

"I've been through it," adds Stowe. "Spirits are trapped inside. They try to tempt you to stay in there with them."

"The Spiracal," continues Willum. "Darius uses it for executions."

"But it's in the Dreamfield. Who...?" Roan looks quizzically at Willum.

"The Masters who do not agree with him," Willum states matter-of-factly.

"What is this thing with the tentacles?" Roan asks.

"The Antlia. Its purpose is kept secret to all but the Masters of the Inner Circle. The Gyre, here, is a mystery as well. I suspect these constructions feed the Masters' powers and help sustain them, though I am not sure how it is done. That is the Ocellus. It is made up of disks that can be used to fold space in the Dreamfield, so that long distances can be traveled with the speed of thought."

"But isn't that—"

"—what we can do, Brother, without any help," says Stowe. "But not so the Masters. They have many limitations."

"This is intriguing," Willum says as if the thought has just occurred to him. "All the Constructions seem to radiate around a central point."

Roan joins Stowe as they both try to view the three-dimensional map from Willum's perspective.

Stowe gasps. "The Spiracal!" Then she points at a

conspicuously undeveloped area. "Look down here, there's nothing."

"Where's Darius's Throne?" asks Roan.

Stowe and Willum exchange glances. "Throne," she says, musing. "He was talking about a new Construction, maybe that's where he's building it."

"The summation of his architecture," Willum concludes.

Turning back to Roan, Stowe asks, "What do you know about it?"

"It looks like a giant hand. The base of its arm sits in a pool, a silver pool. Darius told Saint that Stowe and I and the Novakin were meant to fuel it. But it wasn't just us. In the hand there were shapes flowing up from the pool. Hundreds of them."

"Willum, remember when we went to Cooperation Unlimited? There was something Fortin said about enablers that got me thinking. I could sense he knew something, something secret. Later, it occurred to me that it might have something to do with Darius's new Construction."

"Yes. Fortin spoke of their tremendous potential..." Willum pauses for a moment then, turning to Roan, asks, "Kira told you of the new enablers those Clerics were equipped with?"

"Yes. But what do you think they have to do with Darius's Throne?"

"You've seen the enabled?"

"Clerics. Yes. And people in the City."

"How did they seem to you?"

"Listless...soulless. Do you mean...those shapes I saw floating into the hand. Are you saying Darius is using enablers to steal people's life force so that he can power his Throne?"

"It is certainly a possibility."

"Mabatan said his new weapon—the Apogee—took the lives of the Hhroxhi without wounding them. Do you think—"

"We'll have to go back to the factory, Willum," Stowe says purposefully, "and find out."

"Yes," agrees Willum. "It would at least partially explain how Darius continues to advance despite the loss of both the Novakin and the son and daughter of Longlight."

"Pardon me for interrupting," Kira says, slipping into the tent, "but everyone is gathering for Council."

As Stowe rises to follow Roan, Kira stands between them. "You'll have to wear the cloak. Grandmother's conferred with Wolf. It seems he's a little jumpy about the possibility of spies in our midst and so she's decided that it is unsafe for you to stand openly in Council."

Though Kira towers over Stowe, it is clear that his sister does not fear her. She listens not out of obligation but respect and picks up her cloak without hesitation.

"Ende requests that we join her after Council. She would like to share some thoughts with us."

They all nod their assent and Stowe lifts her hood. *I don't think I'll be able to wait till after to share my thoughts with you, Brother. I hope you don't mind.*

I could use your help, actually. I've never done anything like this before.

You asked for it, she says mischievously as she follows Kira through the open canvas flap.

As the three "Apsara" go to join Ende, Roan starts walking back to Saint's tent and the dreaded council. There were so many things he'd wanted to discuss with Stowe and Willum to prepare for the meeting and he'd only scratched the surface. Maybe there'll be time when they met with Ende tonight. Would Stowe agree to meet with the Hhroxhi? There'd been moments in the tent when he almost felt he had his sister back again, but mostly she'd seemed distant, so much a stranger that he wondered if she still cared for him at all.

"Sorry to barge in on what is obviously some deep thinking, Roan, but I have an important proposition."

As Roan slows for the Storyteller, Kamyar blusters, "No need to slacken your pace. I've no trouble conversing on the move. After all, we don't want to be the last to arrive," he continues, hurrying Roan along. "You may have noticed, Roan of Longlight, that though you are on somewhat friendly terms with most of the people who are convening tonight, the rest of us are not all so well disposed to each other. Now my idea is this: how about we fire up this little gathering with a prophecy? It might be the very thing to remind us why we've come together. Get us off on the right foot."

"Sounds great," Roan says enthusiastically. "Got any ideas for the middle and the end?"

Laughing heartily, Kamyar strides past Roan and through the entryway to Saint's tent.

The evening mist is already rising. Roan stops for a moment, reminded of a night two years ago when four Brethren returning with news of the Farlands interrupted his first session with Saint. He had felt nervous that night too. Nervous but also excited. It was that night he'd accepted Saint's offer to teach him how to fight. He'd believed then that no harm could come of it. But he wouldn't be here tonight starting a war if he'd made a different choice.

the two councils

after the bull watches the moon's shadow ride
the earth, the sun will be set free and the future
decided.

—the book of Longlight

STOWE IS IMPRESSED WITH THE AUSTERE GRANDEUR of the central tent. Only six oil lamps, evenly distributed to surround the gathering, supplement the muted glow of the central fire. She notices a rainbow of colors shimmering around the participants. When did she first see something like this? It was right after her attack on Raven and Brack, after Ferrell had almost killed her. That Hhroxhi, Mhyzah, she'd emanated a bright red...and then, in the Dreamfield's Longlight, Roan had been blue. The light around him now is layered and it tendrils out to the others in the circle. It meets Ende's warm golden glow and blends beautifully with the wisps of orange that dance over Kira's heart. Stowe can sense the power of each individual from the quality of the air around them. This new ability could be useful, she thinks, noticing that the Governor's nimbus wavers, fine jagged bolts, like tiny twisting cracks, riving its surface—he's edgy, not at all comfortable to be here.

The guards are less interesting, though there are more of them than participants. Examining the Brothers closely, Stowe can see why Ende and Wolf are concerned. Some of them are no older than Roan—easy prey for any interested party to manipulate. One catches her eye. He has a scar that runs from eyebrow to chin and the air around him is the murky brown of dried blood—that can't be good. He's looking curiously in her direction, and though she knows she could easily kill him, Stowe's happy to be concealed within her broad hood.

The meeting had begun quite well, she thought, with a prophecy rousingly delivered by that Storyteller friend of Willum's. He had ended with: "And the son and the daughter of Longlight shall stand and be recognized. People shall gather behind them and the fall of the City will be won."

Then Roan had stood to say that he had called this meeting to discuss how they might, together, bring about this "fall." And everyone in the room has been shouting ever since.

"The Fandor are one thing, the Clerics another."

"No matter how many you kill, they'll still keep coming."

"There can't be an endless supply. I thought this was war!"

"War?"

"You can't fight the City head on."

"We could infiltrate."

"How? They have spies everywhere. It's better to fight."

"The City's impenetrable. You can't get close enough to launch an attack."

These are all powerful, opinionated people, most of them leaders. Roan's the youngest person in the circle, and it's obvious that he hasn't got a clue how to control them.

You're not handling them.

Roan cringes. *I don't know how to run a meeting. It's a disaster. Relax. Smile. Look as though you expected this.*

Are you sure?

When it comes to manipulating people, believe me, Roan, I was trained by the very best.

Stowe's happy to see Roan take a deep breath, cross his arms, and smile knowingly, just as she suggested. On that carpet of twisting snakes, his eyes flashing in the blazing fire, Stowe has to admit that, despite his age, Roan cuts quite an imposing figure.

Mabatan, the only one to remain silent amidst all the arguing, lifts her head, acknowledging Roan. Within moments, the Governor notices him as well. He's familiar with the cue, obviously. Soon Kamyar, Ende, Kira, Mejan, Stinger, and Wolf, one by one, all stop and turn to him, waiting on his next words.

Say nothing. Keep smiling. Let them stew.

Roan is silent.

Wait until they're all shifting uncomfortably. There. Now. Slowly. Softly.

"I have been to the City. I have seen its power. Darius has a large army equipped with advanced technology. We cannot match it. So what do we do?"

The room is silent, all eyes fixed on Roan. Good.

You have them, Brother.

"We approach the City and Darius the way we would any more powerful and better-armed assailant—with as accurate an assessment of our enemy as we can get. Yes, the City has a larger army, but the Clerics are all enabled—they follow orders blindly and so lack initiative. If we can control the engagements, we'll have the advantage. Yes, they're more heavily armed, but the City's dependence on technology makes it vulnerable to sabotage. Access and contacts will get us the information we need. Mejan, you've just come from the City. Ideas?"

"I'm afraid I'm the bearer of bad news. Since Our Stowe disappeared, the prisons have been filled to bursting. Executions are common. People are running scared. The Gunthers have been our contacts there for many years, but they are also the most reviled segment of the population and unfortunately are easily targeted as scapegoats. One or two are being arrested daily. They can't even find out where their people are being held. They're afraid they've been singled out by Darius for extermination. Roan, Number Seventy-Nine is missing."

You know Gunthers?

They're friends, we can't do this without them.

"Getting into the City right now is impossible. I only made it out because I'd gone in as one of a group of traders and had the good luck to be present when they were handed their expulsion papers. The City's in lockdown. No one goes in; no one comes out. Not until Our Stowe's returned. The one bit of good news is I have it from a reliable source that Stowe is heading back."

I don't want you to go back—

But I must, Brother.

Stowe, it's worse than we thought.

You heard that woman. They'll pick off those Gunthers, one by one, till I return. Do you want that on your head, Roan?

"Kira," says Roan. "How long can we afford to wait?"

"Not long. Darius may have locked down the City but he's sending his Clerics deeper into the Farlands than he ever has before, and in force. I had an encounter with a few of them. Their enablers were noticeably different but as to exactly how improved they are—your guess is as good as mine. Darius also has a new weapon. The Apogee. It's deadly. Mabatan?"

"The Clerics used it in an attack on the Hhroxhi."

"Excuse me. Who are these...Haroshi?"

The Governor is the City's major supplier of foodstuffs. He could hurt Darius. You need him.

I'm aware of that.

"You may know them as Blood Drinkers," Mabatan says patiently.

"Well then, good riddance, isn't it?"

Mabatan, Stinger, Ende, and Kira stand.

If you don't do something quick, there'll be a fight.

Tell me something I don't already know.

Well, look at that! At least someone is doing something about it.

Roan's friend, the Mor-Tick survivor, has also risen. She'd hardly noticed him before; there seemed to be no color wrapped around him at all. But now that he's standing, she can see silvery sheets, like floating water, pouring off him and wrapping around the others, dampening their emotions.

"Appearances can be deceptive, Governor Selig," he says. "The Hhroxhi are frightening to look upon. They keep themselves separate. I, like most people, once shared your feelings about them. Then, in a time of need, I was helped by them. I learned their language, saw how they care for their children and old people. I know that if we can win their trust, they will be invaluable allies."

The Governor's mouth drops open. "That is all very nice, Lieutenant, but it doesn't sound like much of a guarantee. How are they to earn *my* trust, I wonder."

"I understand how difficult your decision to be here with us must have been. I'm ugly, an eyesore of a thing who has nothing to lose by being here. But you've come here at great personal risk. You could lose everything. That takes courage, a lot of it."

The color slowly returns to the Governor's cheeks. "So you're saying, what's another risk among the many others I'm taking, is that it?"

"More or less." Lumpy smiles. "Besides, the Hhroxhi have tunnels throughout the Farlands. They quite literally can pop up anywhere. It's in everyone's best interest to be on their good side."

As the Governor digests this last bit of information, Mabatan, Stinger, Kira, and Ende relax back onto their pillows.

Brother, your friend has hidden talents. He pitched his voice to catch his victim just so. You should learn his technique.

I don't think it's something he learned. It just comes naturally to him.

Does it? Hmm. I think you should keep a close eye on your Mor-Tick Lieutenant. With a power like that, he just might turn and bite his owner.

He is my best friend!

Roan's words hit her like a punch in the stomach and Stowe's feelings catch in her throat. She wants to snap back at him, but she knows she was wrong to say what she did. She has so little time to share with her brother and now she's gone and offended him. Why can't she cast her petty viciousness aside? But before she can find it in herself to apologize, Roan proceeds with the meeting.

"Mabatan, you were about to describe the attack on the Hhroxhi."

"The Apogee kills instantly," Mabatan reports. "The Hhroxhi are great warriors but even they could not stand against it. Brother Stinger examined the dead; perhaps he should continue," she says, looking in the Brother's direction.

"The weapon left no apparent wounds on its victims." Brother Stinger lets this statement hang in the room a moment. He has Willum's calm about him and Stowe likes him instantly. "So it is impossible to assess how the Apogee stole their lives. The Hhroxhi did eventually manage to topple the weapon. It exploded, leaving only metallic shards behind. But getting close enough to destroy it cost them dearly—over forty Hhroxhi lives were lost. If Darius has many of these weapons, we need to develop strategies of approach. As you mentioned, Roan, controlling the location of the engagements will be key."

Kira's shifting on her cushion; Roan sees it as soon as Stowe does. "Kira?"

"Like you said, Roan, we can't prepare for things we know nothing about. I agree, we should wait for Stowe's return and hope things cool down enough for the Gunthers to spare a guide. But if that falls through, we need alternatives. Come next new moon we need to be on the move. We need answers. Whether we have the Gunthers' help or not. No later."

A slight shift to the left of Kira catches Stowe's eye. She notices the sleeve on the Governor's wife's robe swing once before the woman steadies it. Her eyes appear soft and expressionless but Stowe knows that look and she can see the steely decisiveness lying beneath it.

Roan. That woman. She's the power behind the man.

The Governor, emboldened by his mate, clears his throat.

See the way his eyes slide back to her? She's counseled him on his stand and she's here to see he sticks to her plan.

"In my humble opinion..." he says.

Oh yes. Very humble!

Stowe! Stop it!

"...we need to cut the City off. The question is how? My fellow Governors have never been more anxious, particularly now with the rumors that Governor Brack has been assassinated..."

The disruption is immediate. Stowe's dismayed to see that everyone's speaking at once. Again. But Roan's a fast learner and waits out the eruption of frenzied conversation. Lucky that he'd just pushed her back or he might have sensed her part in the crime.

"Does anyone know who's responsible?" That's Wolf, leader of the Brothers. Was it he, she wonders, who drew his sword across her mother's throat? How can Roan stand to have him at his side?

"Raven was seen leaving the scene of the crime, so he's the prime suspect. But no one knows where he is."

Stowe feels suddenly dizzy. Leaving the scene? It can't be. Willum told her Raven was dead. For the first time since council began she feels Willum's presence gently press at the edge of her awareness.

I wore the bird costume to smuggle you out of Fairview.

Stowe laughs silently. *What an idea! Raven being resurrected as a notorious assassin. More than the sniveling windbag deserves.*

"The general feeling," the Governor continues, "is that Raven was under Darius's orders. Who else could have facilitated his disappearance? Brack was the only one of us with a personal army of raiders at his beck and call. Presumably that was seen as a threat, and Darius is doing his utmost to ensure we don't follow suit. Rather than relying on marauders, the City is sending Clerics out to ensure the safe delivery of goods. Still, they seem to disappear as soon as they are promised. At your hands, I presume, but fingers are being pointed in our direction. Accusations of treachery are made daily against the Governors. No one is happy."

As the Governor stops, seemingly lost, his wife reaches out and gently puts a hand on his shoulder in what looks like a show of support, though Stowe knows it's a subtle reminder to return to the original subject of cutting off the City. After all, even the Masters can't live without food. "I believe it is in everyone's best interests to stop the delivery of our goods and starve the City," Selig boldly announces, back in control. "But if we deny the Masters our produce, Darius is likely to send even more armies of Clerics. With these new weapons…how is an embargo to succeed?"

"You're right, Governor, any attempt to deny the City would be instantly crushed," says Roan. He pauses. "That's why we will attack your caravans."

Stowe giggles as poor Selig nearly swallows his tongue.

"But I'm proclaiming loyalty to you."

"And we are most certainly in your debt. That's precisely why it's important to *stage*," Roan says, looking gravely at Wolf before returning his full attention to the Governor, "a series of raids, so that in the City's eyes, at least, you'll appear to oppose us."

"And we Storytellers would be delighted to help with the staging. It's theater at its best—thrills, spills, and fake kills!" Kamyar seems almost gleeful at the prospect.

"I don't suppose the Storytellers would like to help with some real raids," Wolf growls dangerously, his eyes glued to Kamyar's.

"In truth, our skills are better used to change minds, rather than dismember bodies." Kamyar smiles winningly and engages Wolf in a silent face-off. That Storyteller's not as soft as he seems.

But Selig's sputtering again. "But my...what about...? I can't just have..."

"All stolen goods will be promptly returned to you," Roan assures the indignant Governor. "But when it comes to the territories that are still loyal to Darius, the supply caravans sent to the City will be attacked in earnest. Can we rely on you to find out their routes? Times of travel?"

The Governor twists the rings on his fingers; clearly he's uneasy about the prospect of spying on his peers. His wife grips his shoulder just a little tighter and the Governor gives Roan a quick nod. "Of course."

Who is she? Stowe asks Roan.

Apsara.

You knew?

Maybe I know a little more than you think I do.

Maybe you don't know what I think.

Looking to Roan, the Storyteller inquires, "If I may? Have you considered what you're going to do about the Dirt Eaters?"

Governor Selig lurches from his seat. "The Dirt Eaters? Are you implying that they really exist?"

"Let me assure you, my good Governor, they most certainly do," says Kamyar.

"Well, then," says Selig, brightening. "Perhaps they too could be our allies."

"They're just as much our enemies as the Masters," says Roan, putting a quick damper on Selig's enthusiasm. "And there is only one way to break the power of both—we must destroy the Dirt."

"I couldn't agree more," says Kamyar.

The Governor shakes his head. "Dirt?" The Governor's wife bends to whisper in his ear. Realizing the council members are waiting on him, he nods, "Ah, yes. The Dirt. Of course. It is vital that it be destroyed. A key purpose of infiltrating the City. I understand."

Kamyar's face brightens. "That's a fabulous word, isn't it? Infiltration. That's what we Storytellers are about to do: infiltrate the hearts and minds of every living soul in the Farlands. Hope of an insurrection against the City has all but disappeared. The people are desperate. But we Storytellers are about to remind them of a lost dream.

"It was foretold that the light of hope would be preserved in a hidden village called Longlight. We will rekindle that light in the form of a whisper. A whisper: Roan is alive. He has been working in secret and is making this promise— Darius *will* fall and the legacy of Longlight *will* be fulfilled.

"That light will grow, my friends, it will grow into a blaze that will unite the Farlands and bring them all under the banner of one struggle. Our struggle. To put our destinies back into our own hands!"

No one speaks, they hardly breathe. Then Brother Stinger puts his hands together and starts to applaud. Soon everyone joins him, even Roan. Even Stowe herself.

She would have liked to have sat in on this council, voiced her support, but for now she must be silent. Which is as it must be if she is to be successful. Perhaps after, if they survive, she might figure in the tale. She might even live to hear it.

The moon's crescent is still high in the sky, at least three hours to moonset. Roan would dearly like to spend them sleeping. He knows he'll need to be at his most alert for the meeting with the Hhroxhi—Mabatan had been clear that the negotiations would be difficult. Well, at least he won't have to lead *this* meeting; Ende's called it and so presumably she'll be at the helm.

Stinger had given Roan sand-painting furs, but nothing could shield him from the windstorm battering the encampment. Weaving his way quickly through the tents on this chill night, he finds himself nervously looking over his shoulder—the noise from the buffeted trees combined with the snapping of canvas is so loud he cannot rely on his senses. As he arrives at Ende's tent, he breathes a sigh of relief, happy to place all thoughts of security in the Apsara's competent hands.

As the tent flap closes behind him, he joins Ende, Kira, Mabatan, Willum, and Stowe. It feels odd not having Lumpy at his side but Ende had insisted: "We have every trust in your Lieutenant, Roan, but tonight, it will be only the six of us."

Ende waits for him to be comfortably seated and then she begins. "This meeting was meant to include only the six surviving descendents of Roan of the Parting. But because of his injury, Khutumi is unable to be here tonight and cannot take active part in the struggle ahead. I have agreed to stand in his place as one of the Six and speak now in his name.

"We are the Six, as was seen in the river of time by Roan of the Parting. Six sides of two interlocking triangles forming a star, we join the world of the Dreamfield and the world of earth and fire. Like the six faces of a cube, we will surround Darius and the Masters of the City and defeat them. We are the Six that time has chosen to conclude Roan of the Parting's plan and return to an era of renewal.

"In the depth of his despair over Darius's betrayal, Roan of the Parting sought out in the world of earth and fire the rat he had encountered in the Dreamfield. That rat, then named Aithuna, shared Roan's vision of the future and agreed to join with him. They had two children. Roan of the Parting took their daughter to Longlight and Aithuna kept their son, Zoun, with the Wazya. Years later, when I met Zoun, he aided me in my misery and fathered my daughter and this is how her two children, Willum and Kira, come to claim Roan of the Parting blood."

Roan glances excitedly from one to the other. "That means we're cousins!"

With a wide grin, Kira nods. "You have no idea how long I've been waiting to tell you that!"

"The prophecy is specific. 'Only when the Six are gathered together will the children of Longlight recover their remaining family.'"

"And Mabatan?" asks Roan, searching his friend's elfish features.

"Zoun is also my grandfather, but *my* grandmother was Wazya."

"Of course," says Roan. "They were all rats—Aithuna, Zoun, and now Khutumi. You're next, aren't you?"

"Yes. If I survive, I will carry the Way of the Wazya."

"This common ancestry," resumes Ende, "has served to bring you together tonight and will no doubt come to play some part in the days ahead."

"Cousins," Stowe states, raising an eyebrow at Willum.

He smiles, opening his gaze to include Roan. "Cousins."

Ende raises a hand to command their attention. "I had hoped we would be able to take this time to celebrate our family reunion—but Mabatan brings disturbing news."

Mabatan pauses for a moment, then looks apologetically at Roan. "I would have spoken of this sooner, but I wanted first to confirm that my fears were justified." At Roan's nod, she continues. "When Brother Stinger examined the bodies of the Hhroxhi who had been killed by the Apogee, he experienced something. He said he felt as if the fallen had been 'devoured by a monstrous emptiness.' I recognized what he described, though he did not. We Wazya call it the Overshadower, but it has been known by many names. Only a human can call it into existence. A human with access to the Dreamfield and the means to feed the monster continually. I heard the horrible whispers of the Hhroxhi as they died. They were not the sounds of spirits expiring naturally; they were being…pulled, extricated painfully from their bodies."

A sudden gust of wind shakes the tent violently, echoing everyone's emotions as they absorb this new information.

Roan is the first to speak. "So Darius is feeding an Overshadower?"

"Presumably."

"And what does he get out of the arrangement?" Stowe asks, her tone a little skeptical.

Mabatan shakes her head, but Stowe's question sparks a memory in Roan. "Saint said he thought Darius was trying to take the Friend's place…the very place of god."

Willum focuses his attention on Roan. "Using the Throne you spoke of?"

"I think that's what Saint was implying."

"It might be, then, that this Throne is a mechanism designed to merge his essence with something much more powerful," muses Willum.

"And since he doesn't have the Novakin or Stowe or me—"

"He may try to use the Overshadower."

A pit of dread is expanding in Roan's gut. "Killing Darius, destroying the Throne, that's hard enough, how are we supposed to deal with this shadow thing?"

"Roan," Ende begins, her voice calm and reasoning, "if we fight Darius, we fight the thing he feeds. Bending our intentions toward that goal and having faith we can accomplish it are key. Willum and Stowe must find out where the Keeper is hiding the Overshadower and must ascertain whether his Apogee and enablers are in fact being used to nourish it. Then, we will seek a way to destroy them and the thing they feed." Looking meaningfully at Roan, Ende adds, "The Brothers' faith in their god has led them to fight beside you. They believe they will be victorious. You would be wise to share in that belief."

The Apsara leader slowly shifts her gaze from one to the other, until she has taken each of them in. Something in her manner keeps them all silent, and when she finally speaks the timbre of her voice reveals a fierce resolution. "This is the last time I will speak as a commander." Kira rises to protest but Ende gently places a hand on her granddaughter's shoulder. "Kira will act in my stead. I will make myself available where I am most needed. Now I am tired and require my rest."

The five cousins rise respectfully and leave the shelter

of the Apsara eldest. Wrapping themselves tightly in their cloaks, they shuffle indecisively, not yet ready to go each their own way, and gaze at the storm clouds rushing across the firmament.

ties that BIND

mabatan interview 4.0.
the parched earth brought forth the crickets
and the crickets opened the way and a covenant
was made. but understand that these crickets,
like nature itself, can be both nurturing and
destructive.

—gwendolen's cricket file

U NDER THE SETTING CRESCENT MOON, on the rise below
the Brothers' camp, Wolf edgily grips his hook-sword.

"They will not approach unannounced," says Stinger.

"I am surrounded by secrets and treachery. Do not expect
me to lower my guard," Wolf mutters angrily.

Stinger shrugs, maintaining an almost serene calm, but
Roan can see he holds his weight forward, battle ready.
Mabatan told Roan she believed Mhyzah could keep
Qrixxis in line, but there's no question they are vulnerable in this clearing, and so they remain poised in anticipation of an attack. Much rides on the success of this
encounter. Cooperation from the Hhroxhi means access
to the thrusalls—a way of traveling unseen across the
Farlands—an enormous advantage in their struggle against
the City.

Wolf freezes. A Hhroxhi has just risen from the ground.
As Gyoxhip, Lumpy steps forward. After a brief exchange,
the warrior goes back to the mouth of the hidden tunnel and

clicks twice. Another dozen Blood Drinkers appear, led by Mhyzah, who lets out a high-pitched hiss.

Mabatan and Stinger have been coaching Lumpy in Hhroxhi etiquette, which begins with introductions. As Lumpy announces each member of Roan's group, they step forward and are joined by two of the Hhroxhi. Names are exchanged—that of the individual and that of their homes. Soon only Roan and his sister remain.

The Hhroxhi gasp when Stowe drops her cloak to step forward. Dozens of crickets cling to her robe, their white carapaces ghostly in the sliver of moonlight. "I am Stowe. I am from the City."

Her words catch Roan by surprise. All of a sudden, he's unsure what he should say. He'd imagined they'd both claim Longlight, but that home is no more. Stepping into Stowe's place to face Qrixxis, he says, "I am Roan. I stand between two worlds." Qrixxis snarls and raises his weapon.

Lumpy's earnestly clicking and hissing at him, but the Blood Drinker's expression doesn't change as he hisses back. With a frustrated grunt, Lumpy turns his back on Qrixxis. And though he's addressing Roan, he raises his voice so that everyone can hear him. "He's challenging you. Fight to the death to settle the issue. He says, if you are the Guardian the prophecies speak of, then you will easily defeat him."

As half the Hhroxhi draw their knives, Roan feels his company move into defensive positions around him.

Stowe twirls and all of her crickets fly off her, encircling the two camps of warriors in a steadily rising hum.

Roan can see some of the Blood Drinkers are wavering. "Lumpy, tell them to drop their weapons."

As Lumpy hisses and clicks the directive, the humming

turns into a buzz. Ende and Mabatan are the first to lay down their blades. Xxisos and Mhyzah mirror their action. When Stinger flips his double-headed spear onto the ground before him, four other Blood Drinkers slide their weapons alongside his. Two of Qrixxis's cronies come forward when Willum does. Almost there. But as Roan lays down his weapon, Qrixxis rushes forward, his blade thrusting at Roan's neck.

An ear-piercing scream joins the crickets' pulsing drone. *Not my brother!*

Reaching for his hook-sword, Roan pivots to counter the attack and sees Willum grab his sister by the shoulders. Roan feels her fear—for him, for his life. As he twists to avoid the assailant, fire erupts from Qrixxis's eyes and mouth. Before Roan can even reach out, Qrixxis's entire body is engulfed in flame. By the time Roan's taken a step forward, the struggling Hhroxhi warrior is nothing but a pile of dust.

In the eerie stillness that follows, the crickets descend on Qrixxis's ashes and consume them.

Xxisos hisses to Lumpy and then stares piercingly at Roan as Lumpy translates. "Xxisos says the crickets' message is clear. The Hhroxhi will not raise a weapon in our service but they will stand with us in our struggle. After he has shared this experience and consulted with the elders, we will be informed of exactly how they will aid us."

In the waning darkness before sunrise, Roan stands at the foot of the road leading up to the Brothers' camp, watching two cloaked figures disappear into the horizon. He wanted time to stand still so that they could all stay together, but Willum and Stowe's hearts were not in the world of the encampment, his world. They belonged to the City. Darius was an imminent threat and they could not delay their departure any longer.

But at least now Roan is sure the bond between he and his sister had survived her years in the City; he'd known it the instant he'd felt her scream, *Not my brother!* It had been a cry of desperation in the face of an unbearable loss. A voicing of an unassailable love, for him.

Before she slipped away, Stowe had stopped, her face wet with tears. He can still feel her tiny hand gripping his. So white, so smooth. She's never toiled in the open air, never touched a shovel or sword; her skin is the skin of an aristocrat.

So perfect on the outside. Her scars are all contained within.

Travel well, my sister.

And you, my brother. Perhaps luck will bring us together again.

At that moment she'd squeezed his hand more tightly. Their bodies had begun to shake and, though they tried, they could not release their grip on each other. Then, with a loud snap, Roan's badger ring had split in two.

Willum had bent to retrieve both halves from the frozen ground. And rolling each half carefully in his fingers, he'd spoken in a hushed voice tinged with awe. "This ring contains a life-force, an energy that did not disperse when the ring was broken. It suggests that our great-grandfather must have intended you both share it." Giving Roan and Stowe each half of the ring, he'd wrapped their palms around the mystery, saying, "Guard it well."

Stowe came closer and, standing on tiptoe, she drew Roan's forehead to hers. *Goodbye again, Brother.* They'd stood like this until the longing was almost unbearable and then she walked out of his life, yet again. Hopefully not forever.

"Come on, I'll walk you up."

"Kira!" He'd been so deep in thought he hadn't heard her come down the path. "I can't seem to stop thinking that Stowe's only twelve."

"She's young, but she has Willum, that gives her a bit of an edge," Kira says, slipping her arm through Roan's. "He will guard her with his life. Willum carries deep, impenetrable secrets. And to be honest, most of them, I don't want to know. But they've made him very powerful. Sometimes I wish I'd gone to the Wazya, learned the Way from Khutumi, as Willum did; but it was swordplay I loved. I was never happy unless I was breaking a sweat." Kira's face is open, her manner freewheeling. But Roan knows she and Stowe share a deep, explosive rage. Kira's older, more mature, so it's more effectively buried—but because of that, maybe it's more dangerous.

As they approach the encampment, they walk in silence. Had it been only a few hours ago that he'd discovered they were related? Cousin. Roan is surprised at how comforting that is. When they reach the path into the center of camp, Kira squeezes Roan's arm tightly. "Petra and Veet ride out with me in the next hour. I'll see that the barracks at Foresight are well organized by the time you arrive. And yes, I promise I'll keep a close eye on our smuggler." With a wave, she disappears into the green haze of daybreak.

Roan sighs, and taking a quick look around, decides he's got a few minutes to make himself scarce. If they can't find him, they can't expect him to raise the sun again. But he only gets three steps toward the trees when the bell rings.

"Will you accompany me, Roan of Longlight?" Ende says, striding up behind him.

Roan nods, realizing the futility of escape.

"I am curious to see you raise the sun." The amused look on Ende's face makes it clear that she did not miss his botched attempt to flee. "It is a powerful affirmation of the Brothers' belief in the Friend, don't you think?"

Roan glances sidelong at Ende but she doesn't meet his gaze. "As far as rituals go, I suppose it's pretty effective."

But Ende's not even listening. Her arm extended in greeting, she calls out, "Mabatan, come, join us!"

Roan glowers at the new arrival. "Don't tell me you're coming to watch my performance too?"

Mabatan grins. "No. I come to greet the sun."

Roan laughs. "Finally somebody who doesn't believe in the Friend."

"I didn't say that," she replies, then whispers so the Brethren who are making their way up the trail do not overhear, "but *he* is not great enough to lift the sun."

After the ceremony and the morning meal are finished, Roan heads back to Saint's tent. He's hoping for a few moments' respite to think on yesterday's events while the visitors to the Brothers' encampment are all preparing to leave. But Wolf is waiting for him at the entrance, obviously upset.

Gesturing for the Brothers' leader to follow him in, he braces himself for what is to come. Entering the central tent, he crosses quickly to the serpent rug and sits, knowing that this is the most powerful position in the room. "What troubles you, Brother Wolf?"

Wolf's rage blazes across his face. "Everything I have

done, I have done in the name of the Prophet. He was touched by the Friend and bore the burn that proved it. I trusted him and I trusted the ones he chose for his lieutenants. Now I find Raven is Darius's minion, Asp a Dirt Eater spy, and Stinger... Stinger has some unearthly ties to those maggot Blood Drinkers. All that is left to me is a boy. A boy who walks with ghosts and a Mor-Tick. A boy whose sister can set a man aflame with a scream."

"She did not mean to hurt—"

"And what would have happened if she had?"

"It is true, Brother Wolf, that my sister can kill with her cry, but last night she screamed in fear for my life. That scream, combined somehow with the sound of the crickets—"

"Bugs!"

"They are more—"

"Yes, Roan of Longlight, tell me how bugs are greater than the Friend. Why Blood Drinker maggots who will not even agree to fight beside us should be tolerated. Why we must consort with Governors and Storytellers and coddle spies. Why I should believe in your vision to the exclusion of my senses and send my men to die beside unbelievers."

Steaming, Brother Wolf stands breathless, awaiting Roan's answer.

Roan holds back his panic with an iron will. "I will consider all your questions, Brother Wolf. I admit that I have sometimes been disrespectful, but my anger was justified. As yours is now. You have bent both to your Prophet's demands and to mine with little or no explanation. Give me until the end of the next full moon. If by that time your questions remain unanswered, I will set you free of the promise

Saint exacted from you. I know that is what has kept you at my side."

"With respect, Roan of Longlight, you do not know why I do what I do. But I will agree to wait. Until the last day of the full moon. No longer." An odd discomfort pinches Wolf's brow as if he is unsure of the wisdom of his ultimatum. But it passes quickly and, determined, he strides out of the tent.

As Roan sits frozen in the wake of Wolf's explosion, Lumpy steps in from behind the canvas wall. "Wow. So. How are you planning to handle that?"

Roan looks over at his friend in despair. "I don't have the faintest idea."

"Well," says Lumpy, without a hint of sympathy, "you'd better get one quick. We can't win this war without him."

By noon all visitors are on their way and Roan is bidding Governor Selig and his entourage farewell.

"I'll send word as soon as I have any information," the Governor promises. "I'm putting a lot of trust in you, Roan of Longlight. Brother Wolf is a good man but, well, since Saint's died, I don't understand exactly what has been going on. And those Apsara…it's not very proper, women fighting, is it? Storytellers and smugglers, and that young—was it a girl? My wife says she was. Who was she? And…" The Governor's wife takes his arm, smiling sweetly, and Selig clears his throat. "Well, time to be off. May the Prophet ride with you. And help you control that unruly mob you've got on your hands."

Mounting his gray mare, he squints at Roan. For the first time, Roan can see a shrewdness there. This is a man who, despite the odds, has weighed in on Roan's side...with some persuasion from his wife. As he watches the woman daintily perch herself on a white mare, Roan leans over to Ende. "She is paired to a governor, Kira was matched with a prophet—who else do the Apsara watch so closely?"

"I think it's best if those secrets stay with me."

Judging by the Governor's statement about her warriors, Ende has a point. How would Selig feel if he found out he was partnered with someone who owed her first allegiance not to him, but to her own people? On the other hand, what about him? Would the Governor's first loyalty be to his wife before all others?

What we expect from people, we're not always willing to give, Roan realizes. He'd wanted Stowe to be his little sister again, but she'd become much more than that: wise enough not to ask the same of him, to know he'd never again be the big brother who'd helped her carve her name in a tree. She is certain of her goals and with Willum at her side, she has the means to accomplish them.

Roan wishes he could be as sure of his own objectives. Wolf is set to launch attacks on the caravans to the City as soon as word comes from the Governor—but only until the last day of the full moon, then Roan has to somehow regain his trust. There's hope that maybe they'll find some clue on how to deal with the Overshadower or the enablers or the Apogee at the library—but what if there's nothing? When Ende had looked at him in her tent and said he would be wise to share in the Brothers' belief, what had she meant exactly?

The fact is, everyone seems much more sure of what they have to accomplish than he is. Kamyar'd been so fired up about spreading the word of Roan's return, he'd left immediately after the meeting. Even Lumpy has initiated a project with Stinger to transport Saint's collection of books to the safer locale of the library.

But as Roan makes his way back into the heart of the Brothers' camp, he notices that last night's windstorm has swept away the clouds. The sky is clear and the sun is blazing. If the weather holds, they can be at the Academy in three or four days. There, hopefully he'll find the answers he needs.

What Stowe had wanted to do on the way back to the City was...nothing. She'd wanted to mourn the brother she'd lost, the one she dropped the apple on, the one who'd helped her carve her name in the Big Empty. Roan had looked so old, she couldn't bear it. So careworn. He'd lived out in the open while she'd lived inside, and every heartbreak, every burden, seemed engraved in his face, his hands. She worries her half of the ring constantly because when she's not touching it, she feels as if she's lost Roan for good.

"The bond is not so easily broken" is what Willum had said, as if that were the end of that. And then he'd launched in. Every last possibility and complication of their return to the City had to be examined, and alternate responses gone over in detail. She was more of an improviser herself, but Willum would have none of it, too many lives at stake. Maybe he could think of all the deaths he might cause by doing *this* instead of *that* and remain calm in the moment, but she didn't know if she could.

Well, it didn't hurt to be prepared. The fact that she hasn't heard the last ten things he's said doesn't make her even a little nervous. He'll ask her questions and when she can't answer them, he'll scowl, but he'll go over them again.

"You haven't been listening," he says, reigning in his mount.

"Sure, I was: placate Darius," she replies indignantly.

"Those were my last two words, Stowe."

"I know, Cousin."

"Do not get into the habit of calling me that. It could mean death for both of us."

Stowe laughs, sharply. "Don't worry, Cousin, I know how to hold my tongue."

"Now…"

She would have to listen this time. Cousin.

Was that their bond? All descended from the man who betrayed Darius, all living out their great-grandfather's legacy, still attempting to do what he could not—destroy his adversary. Was her hatred for Darius more in her blood than from her experience?

She notices that Willum is silent. He's waiting for her to give him her attention. That is different. Less a teacher, more of a co-conspirator.

Co-conspirator. Stowe smiles. She likes the sound of that.

the apogee

volume xi, article 3.2.

number 126 has been listed missing and irretrievable. all tasks allotted to him are reassigned, effective immediately: number 139 to head enabler research team. number 87 to oversee filo product development. number 111 to manage microprocessor configuration. number 94 to translate the...

—gunther log

THE MORNING OF THE THIRD DAY ON THEIR WAY TO THE ACADEMY, a dark bank of storm clouds rises in the west, threatening snow. Roan had insisted on hugging the tree line—keeping the location of the Academy secret was a top priority, and his small company would be pretty conspicuous otherwise—even though he knew it might add a day or more to their journey. But they haven't had even one encounter and now, riding into the fast-approaching weather, he's questioning the wisdom of his decision.

Ende, Mejan the Storyteller, and a dozen Brothers and Apsara are not the easy targets Othard and Imin were—he probably should have put more trust in their powers of observation and taken the shorter route across the plain. But Roan hasn't relaxed his vigilance once the entire trip. Since the Council, he's felt responsible for everyone and everything, and he fears the strain of it's starting to show. He'd gone without sleep the night before they'd left, and had never recouped it. Mejan had kept him up both nights of the journey, regaling him with stories, both useful and fanciful, and now his eyes are heavy. He draws closer to his friends and their whispered conversation, hoping their banter will keep him awake.

Lumpy and Mabatan are comparing notes on the Governor's wife. Lumpy, it seems, is the only person who actually managed to speak with her. "I've never heard someone talk so much and say absolutely nothing so well before. I mean, when I was with her, it seemed like she was telling me her entire life story but after I left, I realized I knew nothing at all about her."

Mabatan laughs. Roan smiles at the sound, like the sun glimmering on still water. "Are you sure she said nothing important?" she asks.

Lumpy's face wrinkles up so comically that Mabatan laughs again and Roan begins to feel at ease for the first time in weeks. "Now that you mention it, she did say something strange. I don't know how important it is, though."

"And...?" Mabatan asks impatiently.

"It was something about dreams. First she asked me if I had dreams. I said yes, and then asked about her. And it seems she still had them, but she knew of a lot of people whose dreams had stopped. She said they shrugged it off but that they seemed 'profoundly unhappy' about it. Think it's important?"

"I'm still dreaming," Mabatan says, noncommittally. "Roan?"

"Sometimes I wish my dreams would stop." And as if the very statement invokes it, a vision of bombs dropping over the Brothers' camp, the entire mountain a raging pyre of poisonous green flame, flashes before Roan's eyes.

"Roan?"

Hearing the concern in Lumpy's voice, Roan motions his friends closer. "Over the next few weeks, all of the Brothers will have to be relocated to the Academy."

"Why? What did you see?" groans Lumpy.

"The moment Darius realizes the Brothers are part of a full-blown rebellion, he'll do the same to their camp that he did to the original rebels."

"You mean drop bombs like the ones that made the Devastation?"

Mabatan pales. "Revenge consumes the world." Roan's father had spoken the same words. It would seem Roan and Mabatan had more in common than just a bloodline.

"I guess I'll have to escalate my plan to move Saint's books," says Lumpy. "And maybe we should target the Governor of the western territory—what was his name? Pollard. To make sure no oil gets to the City. Darius needs a lot of it to fly his bombers, right?"

"Right. And...umm...Kira said she'd see to setting up some barracks, but I don't think she has these kind of numbers in mind, so...I'd like you to make sure everyone pitches in. It'll take a group effort to get the Academy habitable for everyone."

Lumpy looks around at the group they're traveling with. "You want me to wrangle them into *housekeeping*?"

"Why not? The Apsara like you and you have the Brothers' respect."

"Oh, no. The Brothers don't respect me, they're just terrified of getting close to me."

Leaning into Lumpy, Roan whispers, "When it comes to the Brothers, it's pretty much the same thing."

"And what will *you* be doing?" Mabatan asks, a mischievous glint in her eye.

"Looking for answers," Roan says, evasively. The hooksword slung across his back is a constant reminder of the vision he had at the Caldera. His weapon melded into his flesh. The blood. And the bull. The Friend.

Mabatan's mood changes suddenly. "Roan of Longlight... I must speak to you now," she says somberly, and Roan can see she's troubled.

"I thought we were speaking," Roan jokes, hoping to recover the lighter mood. His effort is not successful.

"I have news," she says, then after a brief pause, adds, "about Alandra."

Roan's stomach lurches. Alandra! He'd been so consumed with the events of the last few weeks that he'd not stopped to think about her. Mabatan's been with Alandra?

"She lives. She has eschewed the Dirt and rejected the Dirt Eaters."

"But that's good news!" Roan says. Alandra was a close friend until things went wrong. This could mean starting over, renewing their bond. The possibility lightens his heart.

"So she's alright?" prods Lumpy. Roan, too, is aware Mabatan's feelings don't seem to match her news.

"She is content," she says hesitantly. "For the first time in many months."

"You didn't quite answer the question," chides Lumpy.

"Her body is protected by the Apsara in Kira's village. But the rest of her is with the Novakin. She has been chosen to be their curatrix, their healer."

"It's what Alandra said she wanted," Roan says hopefully. "To protect the children."

"And that's bad—how?" asks Lumpy, not giving up on having his question answered.

"She has been given a very powerful form," says Mabatan. "A hydra."

"Bigger and stronger sounds good," says Lumpy. "How many heads do those things have again?"

Mabatan frowns. "Nine. A form of that magnitude can overwhelm the spirit. If...when...the Novakin are freed, Alandra may not have will enough to separate from it."

"You mean she'll be trapped in a monster?" Roan asks, distressed. Mabatan averts her gaze. Had she known? Was this part of some Wazya plan he had no knowledge of? "It should have been me. I'm supposed to be the protector of the Novakin. You should have done this to me. At the very least, I should have been asked."

"Roan, this was not planned. Alandra was there when we found Stowe. We got as far as Kira's village together but Willum had to get Stowe to the Caldera. Alandra had the sickness and couldn't travel so I was asked to stay behind with her. To assist her withdrawal from the Dirt. That in itself could have killed her. But then, we were preparing for a meditation when—"

A sharp bird's cry from Ende commands their attention. Barreling across the plain are two small motorized vehicles, each manned by a pair of Clerics, with a half-dozen Fandor riding alongside. Not much of a force against a dozen Brothers and Apsara.

Riding to Ende, Roan points to the vehicles. "They could have Apogees!"

"Then they must be destroyed. Flank formation!" orders Ende.

Breaking their cover, Brothers and Apsara split as they race toward the outmatched Fandor. The Clerics scoot between and around their cohorts, as if the Fandor were some kind of diversion. Then Roan gets his first good look at the long, silver objects, one mounted on each vehicle.

Rotating it on its stand, the Cleric aims his device at Ende. Taking out the commander, thinks Roan. There's a barely audible whistle. One of the Apsara rides in front of Ende just as a shimmer disturbs the air. The Apsara is frozen for an instant, then convulses as if she were somehow being pulled inside out. A moment later, when she collapses over the neck of her horse, Roan hears the whisper of an anguished moan, desperate and pleading. The look of terror on the dead warrior's face leaves little doubt in his mind that she has just come face to face with the monstrous emptiness Mabatan spoke of.

"This ends now!" Ende cries out as she gallops toward the vehicle.

The Cleric trains his weapon on three Apsara ahead of her and they all fall instantly. But they've gotten Ende close enough and she leaps, landing beside the Clerics. With two quick slashes she finishes them both. Seeing the weapon in the second transport swivel in her direction, she jumps out, pulling the driver of the vehicle with her. The truck careens into a tree and the weapon explodes.

While Ende rolls to safety, Roan rides to intercept the remaining truck. As the Clerics fire at the Brothers covering him, Roan leans alongside the vehicle and with one swoop of his hook-sword, he slices the front wheel. The vehicle flips over and the Clerics go flying. The weapon too sails up in the air, and then, smashing into the hard ground, it explodes, spraying debris everywhere.

Roan sees Lumpy collapse, holding his stomach. Frightened, he rushes to his friend's side. "Did you get hit?"

Looking pale, Lumpy smiles faintly.

"Let me see," says Roan.

Lumpy moves his hands. A shard of silver metal is embedded in his abdomen.

Mabatan nudges Roan aside. "I will look after him. Ende waits for you."

Roan, shaking, stares at Lumpy.

"I'm alright," Lumpy smiles. "Get out of here."

As Mabatan helps Lumpy off his mount, Roan reluctantly joins Ende, who's standing by the two Clerics that Roan sent flying. One is still breathing. The other is not. "Look," Ende says, pointing at the green crater in the dead Cleric's neck. "As soon as he died, it whined and then...this. Exactly as Willum and Kira described."

"Same for the others?"

"Same."

Roan stares at the unconscious Cleric. "Will he survive?"

"No more than a day."

"We need to examine it."

"And who will accomplish that task?" Ende asks.

"The physicians I told you about. At the Academy. We need to get this Cleric to them."

Ende considers the situation. "Go on ahead. Put him on the horse with you. The ride won't do him any good, but with some luck, you'll make it before he dies. Take two riders. You want to move fast. From what Stinger described, I doubt there's much left here that will be of use, but we'll search the area anyway."

Roan hurries back to Lumpy. Mabatan has removed the fragment and is cleaning the wound.

"He will recover," she says. Her voice is warm to comfort him, but her eyes never leave Lumpy. "He cannot move quickly. Go do what you must and leave his well-being to me."

"You heard her," Lumpy says, then gasps in pain.

"I warned you not to talk right now," Mabatan chides, wagging her finger.

"See you at the Academy," Lumpy mouths, before letting his head collapse back in exhaustion.

The Cleric secured against the pommel of his saddle, Roan climbs onto his horse. Lumpy's wounded. Alandra may be lost. Four Apsara and two Brothers were killed today. Nodding goodbye to Ende, Roan murmurs, "I'm sorry for your losses," though he knows full well the inadequacy of his words.

Ende's eyes betray her sadness. "You heard the whispers as they perished?"

"Yes, I heard."

"Death is the fate all warriors accept, yet to have one's spirit claimed in such a way…"

"Next time we encounter the Apogee, we'll be better prepared," says Roan, but the assurance sounds strangely hollow; he might as well be promising to destroy the City single-handed.

But his doubts do not escape Ende's notice. "If you bend your attention to the goal, Roan of Longlight, you will accomplish it."

These were the same words she'd spoken to him that stormy night at the encampment. He knows she shouldn't have had to repeat them. So he bears the reprimand without comment and with Mejan and a Brother beside him, gallops off, keeping his goal firmly in mind.

By the time night sets upon them, they've reached the five hills. When they come to the Academy's hidden entrance, they lead their horses inside the threshold, out of view. Laying the still-breathing Cleric on a blanket, Mejan and the Brother take one end, Roan the other. The narrow corridor makes the going awkward and slow, but moving steadily they soon arrive at the secret door of the library. Roan expertly opens the door and shouts, "Othard! Imin! Help!"

They are barely down the steps when the two doctors appear. "Put him down," Imin says with astonishing calm.

Setting the Cleric on the floor, they all step back to watch the two physicians as they palpate and prod the injured man.

"Ruptured kidney," says Othard.

"And spleen," adds Imin.

"Punctured lung."

"Liver's lacerated."

"Will he make it?" asks Roan.

They both shake their heads.

"Even if we had a proper operating room…"

"…and the correct instruments…"

"…we wouldn't be able to help him."

"These Clerics we fought had new enablers. When they died, the enablers… imploded." Uneasy, Roan pauses. Othard and Imin look at him expectantly. With a sigh, Roan asks, "Do you think there might be a way to remove his enabler before that happens?"

Imin examines the throbbing device, appallingly visible beneath the Cleric's skin, obviously reluctant. "Hmm..."

"Hmm..." Othard echoes.

As the physicians puzzle over the challenge of extricating the enabler, Algie pushes past Roan to hover over them. "My, my, my!" he exclaims, nudging Othard aside. "The technology really has zipped along!"

"Are you familiar with these?" asks Imin.

"Well, it was a long time ago," the old man says, tapping his nose. "And this one is definitely a different kettle of fish." He pulls out a magnifying glass and gently probes the area around the subcutaneous device. "Look at this...it's a masterpiece. A horrid one, of course, but nevertheless..."

Roan eyes the old Gunther with renewed hope. "Do you know how to get it out?"

"Well, I...it's possible, of course, but..."

Algie bends forward to look at the Cleric's wounds and then at the two doctors huddled beside him. Imin and Othard solemnly shake their heads. "Ah. Since there is no hope for the fellow. Yes. Yes. I think there might be a way."

DAUGHTER of the CITY

FOURTEEN WILL KEEP WATCH AND BLESS THE LAND WHERE
THEY LAY WITH THEIR INNOCENCE. FOURTEEN TO BE BORNE
BY A DRAGON UNTIL SHE WHO WAS LOST IS FOUND AND
WHAT HAS BEEN BROKEN IS MADE WHOLE AGAIN.

—STEPPE,
VISION #78, YEAR 5 A.C.
DREAMFIELD JOURNALS OF THE
FIRST INNER CIRCLE

WILLUM TELLS STOWE STORIES. All the happy stories
he remembers about his childhood escapades with
Torin, Resa, and of course, Kira. And Stowe is laughing. He
glimpses in her wide grin and crinkled, sparkling eyes the girl
she would have been in other circumstances. He wishes he
could keep her laughing and joyful forever, but with a sinking heart he sees that they've arrived at the ancient road that
leads into the City.

"What's wrong, Willum?" Stowe asks, her smile gone, her
brow furrowed.

"It will not be long now," he replies, reining in his
mount.

Stopping alongside him, Stowe looks at him wistfully.
They have grown familiar, the warmth between them a
comfort. They will have to abandon that now.

"I'm afraid, Willum."

"You must make your fear serve you, Stowe."

"I know, it's just..." She trails off, staring down the road ahead, her mind closed to him.

"You have doubts."

"Questions. Questions I'm not sure you can answer, or will want to answer."

Willum waits, his silence the only encouragement he can offer.

Stowe sighs, frustrated. "I hate it when you do that."

Willum smiles.

"And that," she says pointedly. "Why did our great-grandfather take on this responsibility? Why did he feel it was his fault? I know he discovered the Dirt and what it could do, but Darius was the one who abused it. He was the one who built the Constructions that are destroying the Dreamfield. Him and the Dirt Eaters."

"He accepted responsibility because the other Masters would not."

"That's it?" Stowe exclaims in disbelief.

"Roan of the Parting discovered the Dirt and how to use it. He found an opening into the world that is the source of all life, then invited in a group of plunderers. He allowed himself to overuse the Dirt and realized too late that his obsession had impaired his judgment."

"So we have to pay, possibly with our lives, for our great-grandfather's addiction?"

Willum sighs. "Stowe, you know it is not that simple."

"Oh? You certainly make it sound that way."

Willum breathes deeply.

"You're doing it again," Stowe snips. Willum waits for her mounting frustration to turn in on itself. Like a powerful undertow, it scrapes his surface but ultimately it withdraws.

"And what about our great-grandmother—what was her name again?"

"Aithuna."

"Why did she help? The Wazya weren't responsible. Why take that on? You and Kira, I understand. Your people were decimated by Darius. Your parents killed by Clerics. You have reasons."

"The Wazya view themselves as guardians, Stowe. If they see a hurt child, they do not wait for the person responsible to be brought to justice. They help the child. If they see a forest destroyed, they do not wait to petition those who destroyed it. They go out themselves and work to purify the soil. They collect and plant the seeds."

"What do hurt children and planting seeds have to do with us?"

"Stowe. The Novakin represent all the hurt children. And we are the seeds...the seeds of Darius's destruction."

Willum watches Stowe determine the implications of what he's said, the key events of their histories flashing across the curtain of her memory: the plague unleashed on the Apsara, the killing of his parents, and then hers, the destruction of her home, her corruption by Darius, her brother's weathered face, the warm glow that radiates from his heart despite all that has happened. Willum sees her eyes shift in the desperate struggle between the fragility of her love and the power of her hate. It is not long before she does as she must and the petulant, angry child is gone as surely as the joyful one. It is almost as if her skin has changed and she's become hard, an infanta of steel. When her gaze shifts to meet his, its watery veil reflects only light and it too seems armored.

"It's all very clear to me now. Thank you, my Primary."
Spurring her horse forward, she rides with her back straight,
the way she's seen Ende ride. Regally. Like a queen. Like...
Our Stowe.

Stowe can finally see the towers of the City in the distance.
Dust rises from the ruins littering the landscape. The City
once stretched this far in the time before the meteor fell and
the great wars destroyed the land. Now all that is left is the
core, much of it rebuilt by her adopted father, the Keeper of
the City.

On this exposed road, it hadn't taken long for her nose
and hands to become so chilled that she had to disappear
into her cloak. It was irrational, she knew, but she also felt
more comfortable physically hidden from Willum. He'd
respected her silence, of course; she was glad of that—and
angry at the same time. But if he'd spoken, she might—just
might—have started to cry. And that was a luxury she could
not allow herself. Not now. Not ever. This seed had blos-
somed into a Nethervine flower and she wanted Darius to
come and smell her. Oh, yes. Close. Very close. And then he'd
feel her thorns.

Pulling up alongside her, Willum can't help but add one
last piece of advice. "Whatever happens, Stowe, never doubt
the power of the people's faith in you. And in the prophecies.
Remember: we must slide very carefully on the edge of that
blade until it settles against our enemy's throat."

She looks into her teacher's guarded face and dispenses
with all her regrets. *Cousin*, she says, reaching into his mind.
Cousin, goodbye.

Goodbye, cousin—the words melt over her like a father's

hug, and she buries them deep so that even she might never find them again.

"Do you see?" Willum points. A cloud of dust is rapidly approaching. As it draws closer, Stowe identifies the vehicles and shiny weapons. Clerics—perimeter guards, a touchy lot.

Remember our plan, Stowe.

I will not forget, my Primary. The thoughts she sends him are confident. She knows it is possible Darius will see through the alibi she and Willum have concocted—the Eldest has eyes behind his eyes. But she has knowledge, secrets, powerful ones that have put Darius in perspective. He's still scary, all right, but more for the damage he can do than the person that he is—that person has weaknesses, many weaknesses, and she will exploit them all.

As the Clerics screech to a halt, Willum places a hand on his horse's neck to calm it. He looks on blithely as the perimeter guards point their weapons, anxious for any excuse to fire.

Their captain scowls. "Who are you, and where do you think you're going?"

"I have been away, but now I have returned," says Stowe, her voice warm and reaching none too subtly for the man's heart.

"Have you...papers?" the captain says haltingly.

Lowering her hood, Stowe reveals her face.

The Clerics can only stare, stunned. Then they gasp, falling to their knees. "Our Stowe!"

Stowe allows herself a smile, a benevolent one, as she directs her horse to move past them.

With Willum riding close on her left, they slip inconspicuously through the City gates. Instantly confronted by a gigantic billboard of herself shrouded in black cloth, Stowe whispers, "They're making quite a show of my absence."

"Master Querin has always had a genius for the telling image."

"Master Querin makes my hair stand on end." Stowe shivers dramatically, turning to smile at Willum. But he is looking ahead, unresponsive.

Giddy to be back, for a moment she forgot to be careful. Not good. Everything she says, every gesture, every expression will be scrutinized by Darius. She must not let down her guard.

As they approach the Pyramid, more and more people rush into the streets. Hundreds, thousands of citizens pour out of their offices and homes, desperate for a glimpse of Our Stowe. People rush up to touch her feet and press their tear-stained faces against her cloak, but they never push or pressure her in any way. Willum's surrounded her with a shimmering golden light. Gold is the strongest of all colors, so strong most people cannot tolerate it, even though they cannot see it. She notices the faces of the crowd when they touch it. Awe. Coupled with fear. They reach, but not for long and not too close. She's learnt a lot from Willum on the journey here, about the light, its different colors and their meanings. With practice, she too will be able to control it like he can.

A feverish chant begins: "Our Stowe! Our Stowe! Our Stowe!"

Inching closer to their destination, she feels bathed in an icy stare. There, on the landing, framed by the grand entrance of the Pyramid, is Darius. At his side stands Master Querin. What Darius does not see, Querin will. Willum's teachings echo through these thoughts, dispelling her fears: Listen to the people. Use them.

Stowe and Willum dismount at the foot of the Pyramid. A path has been forged through the frantic crowd that leads straight up to the Keeper of the City. She ascends the stairs, head held high, counting each step to maintain her calm. One…two…by the fiftieth step, she can see that Darius's face is frozen, his eyes cold. Querin is more skilled at deception; the smile on his face seems genuine. Perhaps it is—he's no doubt already translating her arrival into grist for his propaganda mill.

When Stowe finally glides onto the landing, Darius holds open his arms and without hesitation, Stowe runs into them. The screams of the citizens are deafening. Then, keeping one of his withered arms around her waist, he turns to the crowd and holds up a hand. Silence.

This entire level is an amplification platform and Darius needs only to whisper for his voice to boom over invisible speakers, giving him the illusion of omnipotence. "Did I not promise? Has she not been delivered? Yes! Our angel of mercy has returned! Back into the loving arms of the Conurbation. She has come to care for her people. We stand on the threshold of a new age. Our Stowe will lead us across it!"

"Our Stowe, Our Stowe, Our Stowe!"

She looks down at the masses who eagerly await a word from her, any word. For a moment she stands silently, projecting vulnerability and sweetness and unconditional love. Then, just as the crowd's muted anticipation has been pushed to its limit, her voice reaches out to each and every individual, as if her words were meant for each one alone. "I left the City hoping to discover the future promised by the prophecies.

I walked long in the wilderness. I searched the Devastation. Listened in the towns. But always the City called to me. The City is my home. It is my destiny. I am back and I will never leave you again."

"Our Stowe! Our Stowe!" Arms flail in the air as the people shriek out her name. They push against the Clerics who line up, forcing them back. It is not long before the throng breaks through the cordon, people trampling each other in their desperation to get closer to Our Stowe. Quickly opening the doors behind them, Master Querin gently guides Stowe and the others safely into the Pyramid.

"Go to your rooms and rest," Darius coolly commands. "I will summon you shortly."

With her sweetest smile and most open look, and allowing a quiet tearfulness to color her words, Stowe says, "How I've missed you, Father."

There is the slightest twitch in the corner of Darius's left eye as she keeps her gaze locked on his. Only a detail, she will not allow herself to make too much of it. Then she uses Willum's most effective tool and waits. She allows a polite amount of yearning to address her features. As if she were longing for him to say the same, call her Daughter, as if she has come back only for this. She knows she's won when he turns on his heel, Querin trailing behind him.

Darius has just been dismissed.

Stowe barely had time to change before the Cleric came knocking. Now, as he escorts her down the corridor, she takes in the marble floors, the glass hallways, even the claws on the shining doorknob that grants entrance to Darius's quarters. All the same. The only change she noticed during the interminable walk down the corridor is in her. Now she stands balanced, not trembling in fear. She and Willum determined her best hope would be to open herself completely to Darius, to speak only the truth, but to parcel it out, as if recalling it by accident. He must have no reason to suspect her—if he probes into the recesses of her mind where the whole truth lies hidden, all will be lost.

"Enter." Darius's voice is gentle, a ploy, she knows, to put her off her guard. Stepping into the room, Stowe bows to Master Querin. He stands in a dark corner, the better to intimidate her. The Eldest, however, sits apparently relaxed behind his chrome and crystal desk, positioned below two portraits: one of himself in his most splendid robes, and another of Stowe at her most beatific, the way he likes her. In the dim light, she can see the glimmer around both men.

Stowe lowers her head in shame and deference to Darius.

"So. You were not abducted?" Querin's amused tone strikes her as irritably condescending. Luckily she is past being affected by such simplistic gambits.

"Forgive me," she says penitently. "I was in error to abandon my responsibilities, to depart in secret. And I must apologize for all the worry and trouble my misguided actions have caused."

"The Gunthers were not involved in any way?" It is clear from Querin's inflection that he has known this all along and requires only her confirmation.

"None whatsoever," she acknowledges. "I acted completely on my own."

"Why did you run away from us, my darling?" Darius asks, his voice rasping and repellent and slithering.

Keeping her head bowed, she confesses humbly, "I had a vision. I wanted to tell you, Father, but I knew I had lost your confidence. I wanted to prove myself to you, offer you something that would make you believe in me again."

Darius snorts, dismissively. "You followed a *vision*."

Stowe breathes. He knows...something. How long before he has her on the ground, writhing? Breathe. Breathe.

"Please, Keeper, it would be useful to hear the nature of Our Stowe's vision," says Master Querin, stepping out from the shadows.

Ah. Now that's interesting. Darius stiffened. Just for an instant. But still. These are the small advantages Willum has urged her to press. So she responds as if Darius himself had commanded her to do so. "I saw the children you've been searching for. I'm certain they're alive, Father, somewhere in the Devastation, asleep, guarded by my brother. Or perhaps in the Dreamfield, somewhere I have never been. A huge crevice. They are stretched across it. They bind it together. Do the Eaters have them, Father? Is that where they are?"

The only sound is the whirr of a ventilator as the glimmer around both men is disrupted. A vibrant red spike tears through Darius's chest. Anger or fear? She reaches with her mind and detects fluctuations in his pulse. He's definitely unsettled. Querin on the other hand flickers orange: excitement. The information's excited him. Why?

"Tell me more," demands Darius, with a snarl that makes her knees feel strangely drawn to the floor.

"The children...they looked as if they were made of iron."

"How many?" says Querin, not bothering to hide his exhilaration.

"Fourteen."

"…Fourteen." Querin whispers the word. "'Fourteen will keep watch and bless the land where they lay with their innocence.'"

There's an odd sense of self-satisfaction in Querin's voice, but if there was any blood in Darius's face, it has flushed away completely. The air around him is tinged a fetid mustard color, mottled and sulfurous. The Novakin, Willum had called them. They terrify Darius—if not for her brother, they would have been dead by now, fed to Darius's new Construction. Willum explained they were keeping the Dreamfield from collapsing. You would think Darius would be grateful for that.

"I searched everywhere for them, Father. The vision was so clear, I was sure I would find them. Since I stopped taking the Dirt, I am cut off from the Dreamfield, but when I sleep I am taken to Roan and I am given glimpses of the children. Try as I might, though, I could not find any of them."

"No signs of Roan?" The Keeper's eyes are sharp, the raptor's gaze she remembers.

"There are many rumors, but I saw no *signs*. The visions must lie…or perhaps I do not understand them."

Darius stares at his desk as if waiting for her to say more, but she resists, remembering Willum's instructions not to embellish.

Finally the old man's skull-like face looks up, his mouth grim, his eyes intensely determined. "You do not really believe your visions lie and I think you are right not to abandon hope."

Stowe breathes more easily. Had he guessed that she'd actually seen Roan, their enterprise would have ended here.

"Your quest must be continued, I think...but under safer conditions."

What Darius has in mind for her Stowe can only guess, but the color seems to be returning to his cheeks.

"A quest? A quest. Of course," agrees Querin, bowing to Darius. "Ah, Keeper, I see it now. It was you who sent Our Stowe on her admirable journey. An attempt to fulfill the prophecies. I understand why you have trusted no one with this secret. Your wisdom is absolute."

Did Querin really believe what he'd just said, or was he simply flattering Darius, helping him save face? Either way, it seems to placate the Keeper. "You may provide the citizenry with a Proclamation."

"Thank you, Archbishop. I shall begin it with a prophecy: 'For a Daughter shall have the sight...' I think." Querin looks to Darius for approval, but the Eldest's thoughts already seem far away. "After which, something brief about Our Stowe's infinite love for her citizens, followed by an expression of her bravery on their account." With obvious excitement, Querin starts composing on the spot: "With no regard for her personal safety, Our Stowe wandered the Devastation on a spiritual quest, seeking a vision of the City's future. Our Archbishop, knowing the importance of this quest, kept her true plans secret. Thus shielded by the mystery of her disappearance, she wandered freely and was blessed with a revelation: a world—healthy, prosperous and unified, a world embracing Farland and City alike, Master and child. All praise Our Stowe, beneficent shepherd of the new age." Querin, finishing his speech with a flourish, turns to receive Darius's appraisal.

How could these words fail to incite Darius against her?

She feels a bit like a fiery ball Querin is passing from hand to hand, now saving, now damning her. But Darius is staring off into some unknown gloom, curiously unresponsive. If she didn't know better, she'd have thought he hadn't heard a word Querin had said.

As if by rote, Darius mutters, "You may begin circulation of this official account."

"The only matter remaining to resolve then, Keeper, is that of the Gunthers," Querin says, trying to re-engage Darius's attention with official business. "While their condemnation has placated the populace, it has caused disruptions in the efficiency of our infrastructure. Swiftly reinstated, the Gunthers could rectify these failures."

"The people have been promised an execution, Master Querin, and they must not be denied their justice," Darius snaps testily.

"Farseeing words." Praise slips from Querin's lips as easily as breath. Years of practice, Stowe thinks. Still, he seems so sincere. No mean feat, that. "The absence of evidence does not equal the absence of guilt. The Gunthers separate themselves from the Conurbation's grace, and this contempt alienates our citizens and demands retribution."

"Four would be sufficient," says Darius, plucking an errant hair from his eyebrow. "Arrange for the executions to take place in Conurbation Park."

Stowe reigns in her emotions. Any empathy on her part would only serve to betray the Gunthers.

"And the rest discreetly released over the coming weeks?" suggests Querin.

"As always, Master Querin, I trust the details to you."

"Keeper," Querin murmurs. He inclines his head, not

so far as to indicate acquiescence, but not so little that any insult could be inferred.

Stowe's fascinated by the shift in the light around him, like a pale blue flame licking an oily surface. Before she can divert her attention, Querin's gaze locks ferociously onto hers.

Following it, Darius turns to her, his eyes stroking her face. "My darling, do you not approve? Are the deaths of four not enough payment for the agony the City's residents have suffered on your behalf?"

A year ago, she might have happily been held culpable for the murder of a few Gunthers. But now, she is appalled at the idea. Still, she cannot see any alternative but to agree. "It will suffice," she says, forcing a glitter of satisfaction to sparkle in her eyes.

"I think it will be much more effective if you preside over the executions, my darling." Darius's lips stretch into what she is sure he intends to be a smile.

"Perfect," Master Querin declares, his gaze remaining implacably circumspect. "Don't you agree, Our Stowe?"

Pushing down the sickness she feels deep in her belly, Stowe looks at Darius with all the admiration she can muster. "My father's wisdom is, as always, peerless." For an instant she fears her repulsion will reveal all and struggles valiantly with the panic rising within her. But like a predator who suddenly smells larger prey, Darius's glance slides back to the dark corners that seem to have occupied his thoughts throughout her interrogation.

She notices Querin motioning her to the door. As she gratefully glides past him, his hand rests on her back for the briefest moment, as if he were discreetly directing her toward her exit. Though she fears him more than Darius, the touch does not make her cringe or even flinch—the thing is, it feels oddly protective.

She must be tired. He's probably even more dangerous than she thinks.

the burden

the brethren feared the shunned one. but time
dulled their fear and soon, awe replaced it, for it
was he who set roan of longlight on the path to
illumination.

—orin's history of the friend

ROAN QUIETLY STEPS INTO one OF THE SMALLER ROOMS of
the Academy. Mabatan chose well. Lumpy's new quarters are spare but practical, with a desk and room for books, one of which he's poring over now.

Looking up at Roan guiltily, Lumpy sighs. "Lying here's nice but there's a ton of things I should be helping with."

"Nothing that can't wait a couple of days," says Roan, wagging a cautionary finger. "You got off lucky. Imin told me that if that fragment had hit you a thumb's width to the left, you'd have died."

"Funny how luck can feel like a big pain in your gut. Umm...speaking of pain, how's Ende?"

"Very quiet."

"Do you know how the Apogee killed them? Could you see?" Lumpy shifts in his bed, wincing at the movement.

Roan steps forward awkwardly, not quite knowing how to offer his friend assistance, but Lumpy waves him back. "It's okay—I didn't rip anything. Go on: Apogee. What do you know?"

"I couldn't see much. The air rippled like it was a piece of cloth and when it reached the Apsara it seemed to suck the life out of them. Devour them, like Stinger said. And when they collapsed, there were whispers…horrible…"

"Mabatan heard them too."

"I wish I'd just disabled the thing, not destroyed it. Then at least we might have a better idea of how it works."

Lumpy smiles reassuringly at his friend. "Don't waste your time feeling bad about that. A world with a couple less Apogees is a better place no matter what."

Roan sits down carefully on the edge of Lumpy's bed. "We finally got the enabler out. If I'm understanding Othard, which is not always easy, they fooled it into thinking it was still inside that Cleric."

"Find anything out?"

"I piggybacked the energy straight to the Dreamfield. Territory of the Turned. But I didn't dare follow it to its final destination."

Lumpy nods casually, as if that were obviously the right choice. "What about the Cleric?"

Roan shakes his head. "Didn't make it. Imin was amazed he lasted as long as he did…Lumpy?"

"You're not feeling like this was all your fault, are you?"

"No. No. It's just I don't know where to go from here."

"You remember what I said about finding the Friend?"

"Believe it or not, yes. And I've given it a lot of thought. I just don't know how I'm supposed to go about doing it."

Lumpy taps the ancient book in his hands. "That's where being bedridden helps. You get time to read. This book, for instance. It says you have to…walk."

"Walk?"

"Yeah. You fast. And walk."

"For how long?"

"Till you find what you're looking for."

"Uh huh. In what direction? Where do I go?"

"Ever heard of *ley lines*?"

"Sort of...no, not really."

"Read this—I've marked the page."

"Uh huh. And who's going to run things while I'm gone?"

"How about Ende?"

"I don't think she'll go for it. She's given up leadership to Kira."

"Kira, then."

"Wolf wouldn't like that. It needs to be someone neutral, who's not going to take one side over another...hey! Someone like you."

"Wait a minute, hold on!" yells Lumpy.

"Calm down," Roan says, one hand gently keeping his friend stationary.

But Lumpy obviously does not want to calm down. "Calling me your Lieutenant, okay, I admit I like it—but I never agreed to actually *do* anything!"

"You'll be fine."

"No. I won't. I won't do it. I'm not qualified. Anyway, look at me. I'm injured."

"I know it's risky..."

"Risky? It's insane. Me, trying to wrangle everybody, while you go wandering half—or totally—starved, around the Farlands, a sitting duck for every roving gang of marauders, Clerics, or Fandor. Not to mention wild dogs and Nethervines. On second thought, it's a really terrible idea."

"No, it's not. You're just jealous."

Lumpy takes three fast gulps of air and rubs his mottled face with his hand. "That's brilliant, that's perfect."

"Everyone knows what their responsibilities are, and I'll inform them that in my absence, they're to answer to you," Roan says firmly.

"...Oh, great. Great. But what...what if...you don't come back?" There's a quaver in Lumpy's voice that Roan has only ever heard when Lumpy's talked about Lelbit.

Roan looks encouragingly at his friend. "I think I will, Lumpy. I wouldn't leave if I didn't. But if for some reason I'm wrong, then you've got to find a way. You and Mabatan and Kira. To keep going. If I'm not back before the next full moon, contact Willum. You're not alone in this."

"When are you leaving?"

"Right now. If I'm going to do this, it can't wait." It's been a long time since Roan's traveled anywhere without Lumpy and it's not easy standing up to go. "Get some rest. You've got a big day tomorrow."

"You're asking a lot."

Roan smiles. "Too much. I know."

"Now I know why Darius burned all those books," Lumpy grumbles.

Roan strides through a beehive of activity, passing both Brothers and Apsara fixing broken furniture, cleaning, setting up an infirmary. But as he nears the entranceway of the former school, he hears shouting. The clamor grows louder as a slew of bloody Apsara, led by Ende, burst in with four bound and blindfolded Clerics in tow.

Seeing Roan, Ende approaches him and reports. "We encountered them on patrol, a group of ten on horseback."

"And the other six?" asks Roan.

"Casualties," Ende says bluntly.

Imin and Othard rush breathlessly up to Roan, the two men dwarfed by the huge Apsara. "Shall we disengage them?" asks Imin.

"He means dis-enable them," explains Othard.

Roan's taken aback by the physicians' enthusiasm. "Can you do it without killing them?"

"...Oh, yes..."

"...Once you've seen how they're connected..."

"...And of course, the more specimens we have, the better the chance of unlocking their secrets..."

"...And finding new uses for them," says Imin.

"New uses? Like what?" asks Roan.

"Not uses, really, it's an untested theory..." corrects Othard.

"...Algernon's helped us with the principles of it."

"In certain cases..."

"...we might be able to use these enablers..."

"...as a form of...ah..."

"...communication device."

"But it's just a theory, you know," adds Othard. "We..."

"...still need to test it," concludes Imin.

Looking askance at the two doctors, Roan demands, "What certain cases? Testing on whom?"

"Well...umm..." The doctors shift uncomfortably, trading sheepish glances.

"...it involves Mabatan..."

"...and Kira..."

"...with their full consent, of course..."

Furious, Roan turns abruptly from the physicians and

strides out of the Academy and into the great library. Quickly determining where his two cousins can be found, he heads for the small room where he first discovered Algie.

Mabatan and Kira are sitting cross-legged on the floor, facing each other, eyes closed. Roan clears his throat, loudly. "What are you doing?"

"We are trying to touch each other's minds," explains Mabatan. "To find the places where they meet."

"This wouldn't have anything to do with Imin and Othard and their little experiment?"

Kira sighs heavily as she stands. "I don't have the gift, Roan. I can't travel in the Dreamfield or do any of the fancy mind-talking the four of you can. But I do know how to meditate, and I can clear a place in my mind for Mab. Algie and the doctors figure that with the help of an enabler, Mab might be able to see what I'm seeing. Roan, when I'm doing reconnaissance in the City, you'd have the information I'm gathering instantly, instead of having to wait for me to get back. It might give us a crucial advantage. This could be a life-saver."

"Or taker." Trying to keep a reasoning tone, Roan continues, "We don't know anything about these enablers."

"Yeah. But they won't be *those* enablers. They'll be *our* enablers," says Kira. "The old guy, Algie, says they can be rewired, 'reconfigured.' Come on, Roan, he helped invent the things."

"That was over forty years ago!"

"The principles are the same," Mabatan interjects calmly, attempting to divert the volatile path of the conversation.

Roan urgently searches Mabatan's dark, unblinking eyes. "I'm surprised you agreed to this. You know the dangers."

"I know what it is to share someone's mind," Mabatan respectfully replies. "You are right, it is not easy. But there is no danger here of one taking over the other. With Kira, I am only a listener. Roan, the advantages outweigh the deterrents."

"It isn't safe. I don't want the two of you taking this kind of risk."

Planting her hands firmly on her hips, Kira smiles defiantly. "So, Roan, tell me how can we hope to win this war without laying our lives on the line?"

Roan stares long and hard at his cousins. Their strength relaxes his apprehensions. They all face the same peril; each has taken on a share. Besides, Mabatan and Kira probably feel surer of where they're headed than he is. Roan smiles. "You're right...and in that spirit, I'm here to tell you I'll be leaving for maybe a week or two."

"Not without adequate protection," Kira says, feigning shock.

"Ah...in fact, I go alone and take nothing. That's the way it has to be done."

"Seems a little long to be away," she chides.

"We're in a holding pattern. I do it now or never."

Mabatan takes Roan's hand. "You go to find the Friend?"

Roan nods.

"Whoa! Meeting a god! That is pretty risky. If I were you, I'd bring a change of pants," chuckles Kira.

Ignoring Kira's smart remark, Roan pulls Mabatan up. "Mabatan, you wouldn't happen to know anything about ley lines, would you?"

Roan finds the Storytellers in a reading room, huddled around huge piles of books.

"Dew drops—how better wash away the world's dust?" reads Dobbs.

"Basho, the great Japanese poet," cries Mejan, obviously excited.

"Right again," sighs Dobbs.

Holding a thick volume behind her towering column, Mejan recites, "The dream was marvelous, but the terror was great: we must treasure the dream, whatever the terror, for the dream has shown that the end of life is sorrow."

Scrunching up their faces, Dobbs and Talia look grumpily at each other.

"She's got us again," Dobbs mutters, irritated.

"No doubt about it," Talia says, resigned.

But Roan knows this story. His father read it to him when he was a boy. It had been one of his favorites. "The Epic of Gilgamesh. Enkidu says it to his friend, Gilgamesh, when he realizes he's about to die."

"Roan! Are you joining the game?" Mejan asks eagerly.

"I'd like to, but I can't. Sorry," says Roan. "Actually, I was hoping you'd help me with a disguise."

The Storytellers' faces brighten with devilish glee.

After an hour playing mannequin to the threesome's creative flurry, Roan sits in the kitchen, blissfully alone, stuffing down the last meal he'll have for a while. But his moment of solitude is quickly disrupted by the appearance of Algernon.

"Thank goodness. Lumpy said I might find you here."

Roan smiles at the old man. "Got some exciting news for me, Algie?"

"Enabler this, enabler that—if those blasted physicians hadn't been pestering me every five seconds, I would have had this deciphered sooner. But then, oh, see where this has all ended up!"

"Another section of the book?" Roan asks hopefully.

Algie takes a roll of paper from his pocket and unfurls it. Then, holding the sheet between both hands like a town crier, he peers closely at the words he's written. "Blast!" he utters unhappily. "Can't read my own writing!"

After a moment of squinting at the page, Algernon clears his throat and reads: *"My optimism was unbounded as I reveled in the potency of my discoveries in the Dreamfield. I had found evidence for what I had previously only surmised: that it was the awesome power of every farmer, manufacturer, student, teacher, child, and adult alike to manifest visions and dreams. If a device could be made to harness that ability, there would be no limit to what we could do. I did not stop to think before revealing all this to Darius. My trust in our friendship had not yet been betrayed. But I often wonder, if only I had waited and given my idea the weight of thought it deserved, I might have foreseen how my concept for an enabler would lead directly to Darius's desire to make himself a god."*

Roan can't believe what he's hearing. His great-grandfather not only discovered the Dirt but thought up enablers as well. Algie gives him a sympathetic look. "It's quite possible I've made a mistake. It seems to be what the word is. Enabler. Hmm. Enabler. Darius. God. Linked somehow. Unpleasant idea."

"Not just an idea, Algie. It's exactly what Darius is up to—we just don't know how he's doing it. But we're going to find out, right?"

"Yes. Yes, of course."

"How could my great-grandfather be so...so stupid?"

"He was excited, Roan. Of course he was. The way he speaks of the concept…is the exact opposite of how Darius utilizes it."

"What do you mean?"

"Umm, let's see…hmm…here, he mentions dreams. Everyone dreams. And when we do we must somehow become part of the Dreamfield. Of course. Visions, obviously, are more rare but similar. I think your great-grandfather was saying that if enough people have the same dream, or believe in the same vision, then it becomes real—it *manifests*. I think he hoped to boost people's ability to…share their dreams…make them come true. What Darius does is the opposite. His enablers sap life-force, they drain a person's biofield. I'm sure you've noticed that. The lifelessness. It was one of the reasons I left the City, as you know. That monster's motives were quite apparent. Control. Domination. Hrumph! Had to take a stand. Oh, but I suppose none of this is of any help where you're going."

"You never know. Have you told Lumpy about this? He'll be overseeing everything while I'm away. The part about dreams will interest him too."

"I shall do that then. Immediately. And dreams, eh? Why?"

"Seems some people have lost the ability to dream. I can't help feeling it's related in some way." Smiling at the old Gunther, Roan slips on the ragged cloak of a poor farmer. "Thanks, Algie. For everything."

Nodding shyly, the old Gunther backs away. "Good luck on your journey, Roan of Longlight."

As Roan makes his way out of the Academy, his father's voice resounds in his mind: *Treasure the dream, whatever the terror.*

Maybe that's what Ende meant when she spoke of faith and belief. Treasure the dream, whatever the terror. He finds the words oddly encouraging, something to bolster his resolve in the days ahead. Although he hates to admit it, this search for the Friend *is* terrifying—and not just because of his lack of ideas should it fail. The whole notion of coming face to face with something he finds difficult to believe in, something that, if it exists, must be unimaginably powerful, is...chilling.

His father couldn't have known when he read Gilgamesh to Roan how a few of its words might one day carry such meaning for his son. Or could he? Maybe nothing his parents did was spontaneous, maybe it was all preparing him for this. He doesn't suppose he'll ever know but, right now, he's quite glad to have their wisdom accompany him as he becomes an old farmer in search of an ancient god.

the execution

> Let it be known: our glorious stowe has returned
> to us and justice shall at last be served. she will
> appear at conurbation park tomorrow afternoon
> to oversee the execution of four gunthers found
> guilty of sins against the conurbation.
> —proclamation of master querin

Willum's journey down into the lower levels of the Pyramid has proved uneventful. Darius's gratitude to him for having brought Our Stowe safely home has been widely proclaimed and his freedom to roam the inner sanctums of power, at least for the moment, remains unquestioned.

Moving soundlessly down the narrow passage, Willum touches the east wall. He senses two life forms just beyond the sealed entrance that leads to the cellblock. Now he must wait for the Gunthers to do their part.

Breathing slowly, he calms his body and mind until, with a sound like an exhalation, the door beside him slides open and the lights are extinguished. Amid the pandemonium of panicking Clerics, Willum easily slips through the receiving area unnoticed.

Striding down the long corridor of cells, he's overwhelmed by a barrage of sadness and confusion. This wing holds dozens and dozens of political prisoners. All declared criminals by virtue of Master Querin's Proclamations, they are here for no better reason than that they failed to conform to the City's dictates.

After screening out the random emotions of despair, Willum is drawn to an oasis of hope. The imprisoned Gunthers know there can be only one reason for this blackout and their anticipation is like a lantern lighting his way. Feeling for the small slit in the polished door of their cell, Willum slips in an envelope. He hears all four Gunthers move simultaneously to the package. Good. Once they open it, they will understand.

Quickly retracing his steps, he has only to avoid one pool of muted candlelight to be through the exit. Within five breaths the door slides shut and Willum is free to ascend the staircase in darkness. Putting his palm on the steel banister, he is jolted by a powerful consciousness. Someone touching this same banister, just a floor above. Querin.

Questions about the Master have been nagging at Willum since Stowe recounted her meeting with Darius. She'd said that Querin seemed genuinely excited to hear about the Novakin—but in the prophecies the rise of the Novakin foretells the Keeper's fall. The logical explanation is that Querin must have designs to set himself in Darius's place. Even more troubling is the prophecy he quoted: Fourteen will keep watch and bless the land where they lay with their innocence. Where does it come from? It is not one Willum has ever heard.

Mulling over his suspicions, Willum glides up flight after flight, following the mysterious Master. By the time he arrives at the seventh floor, the lights have flickered back on. He was supposed to be out of the building by now. As the Blue Robes scan the ceiling chattering excitedly, he places his palm on a keypad. Detecting the pattern that has been pressed there innumerable times, he enters the code. The maintenance closets are accessed only by the Gunthers; he should be safe here. Locking the door behind him, Willum sits on the floor and with one quick inhalation parts from his body.

High above the activity in the main room, his ether self spots Querin watching a trainer instruct a score of Clerics on their sword technique. They're clumsy, obviously new recruits. The look on Querin's face is inscrutable, though Willum can sense he is not pleased. Abruptly leaving the scene, the Master pushes through a set of ornate doors into a small chapel where several dozen Clerics kneel, offering reverential prayers to a glowing portrait of Our Stowe. Querin bows to the image, then slips behind the dais. Entering another corridor, he stops at a bare wall, and taps it in six different places. The wall separates, and as he sweeps through, the panels realign, making the entrance again imperceptible.

Passing through the wall, Willum pulls up short, startled by the sight before him. Images of Stowe, hundreds of them, large and small, cover every inch of the tiny room into which the Master steps. Photographs of her giving speeches, standing on the steps of the Pyramid, smiling and waving to the crowds. As the man responsible for shaping her public image, Querin would have a large collection of photos—but why here? Spread all over the walls like this? Over in one corner, at standing height, are six sketches. Composite drawings, as if an artist was trying to identify a person based on a verbal description, no doubt Raven's. Although inaccurate in many small ways, they are unquestionably of Roan. The most complete of the drawings shows his intense eyes. His palm is extended and on it sits a white cricket. Below this picture, on a small table, is a series of books. Querin kneels before the table and opens one. Handwriting. Journals, then? On the cover of one of the books Willum can see a name. Steppe.

Could it be? One by one, he examines the spines. Haron. Roan. Darius. Yana. The fabled lost journals of the First Inner Circle. How did they come into Querin's possession? And more: Barthold, Valeria, and Krispin—the three known as the Mad Masters. Willum searches his memory. What had he heard of them? Killed or imprisoned by Darius. Imprisoned. Could they still be alive? Where would Darius be keeping them?

Before Willum can shift closer to see what Querin's reading, he's abruptly snapped back. His ether self jets through walls and doorways to fall battle-ready into his body. Gunther Number Six is peering questioningly at him through the crack of the open door. Relieved, Willum puts a finger to his lips. The Gunther nods and points to a metal box at Willum's right. Willum slides the box over and Number Six tips its contents onto the floor. He winks at Willum and wailing, "Oh, oh, oh!" chases the ball bearings as they skitter across the tile floors and under the feet of suddenly careening Clerics.

Surreptitiously sliding out of the closet and down the stairs, Willum puzzles over what he's observed. One thing is certain: Querin is not at all what he seems.

Stifling in fila-armor again! True, it succeeds in keeping assassins' sharp objects out, but unfortunately, it also keeps perspiration in, and right now Stowe's swimming in it. She chose this miserable dress to please Darius; still, it offers no consolation whatsoever when he turns to smile approvingly at her.

"It is good to have you back," Darius purrs, patting her hand, positioned ever so delicately on the leather armrest between them. It is a little like being licked by a poisonous snake.

"I missed you terribly, Father." Turning her palm up to join his, Stowe squeezes his ice-cold hand. His circulation is failing again. Must be time for another vein replacement.

"No more than the people have missed you, my pet. The thought of Our Stowe presiding over an execution has proven impossible for the citizenry to resist. I'm told they began to gather in Conurbation Park at dawn."

Willum's in the front seat, next to the driver. He stares ahead, never turning, never letting a stray thought reach her. They've made a plan, of course, but still, she is on her own with this task.

The limousine turns down a vile, untended street that is all too familiar. "What is this place, Father?" she asks ingenuously.

"I have avoided showing you this before, my dear," he says, scanning the slum with self-satisfaction. "But I think you're ready to see it now."

He's brought her to the underbelly of the City, the same decaying ghetto she hid in when she ran away. She remembers the stench of stale urine and rotting garbage, the people wandering like zombies under her image or praying at shrines they'd created for Our Stowe. As hollow eyes shift lazily over their passing vehicle, she realizes that here things only ever get worse.

"This is the home of the Absent," says Darius. "Master

Querin came up with that appellation." Turning his ravenous eyes on Stowe, he continues, "A very dangerous man. But you know that, don't you? Lucky for us he prefers to serve rather than rule. Still…"

Darius looks vaguely out the window.

Adopting her most worried tone, Stowe whispers, "Father?" She's astonished at how quickly his head snaps back. She would not have been surprised if he had bared his teeth.

But the effect is dissipated the instant he flashes his most fatherly smile. "Ah, yes, what was I saying? The Absent. They abandoned their productive labors in the Farlands and migrated to the City hoping to find an easier life. We cannot reward their choice. If we did, who would tend our fields and work our mines?"

Stowe knows that most of these vacant-eyed women and defeated men came as refugees when their villages were destroyed by marauders. They believed they'd find succor here, salvation. They never would have imagined this.

"We have no plans for reconstruction in this part of the City, so it costs us nothing to let them squat here. They pay their way by contributing their offspring to our recycling laboratories."

"Cattle," Stowe says in dawning awareness. "Do you breed them, Father?"

A deep, dry chuckle rises from Darius's sunken chest. "Good question!" The sound, like a death rattle, sends chills up her spine. "For all their self-inflicted deprivation, we still have compassion for them, which we mete out through you, Our Stowe. It is you who brings meaning and value to their lamentable lives."

Stowe does not fail to notice that he has studiously

avoided answering her question. Unable to repress a shudder, she covers by saying, "I don't like it. It feels dirty, having those vermin worship me."

"Adulation has its uses."

"How shall I use it?" she asks, allowing a tiny amount of genuine excitement to creep into her voice.

"Consider the park a learning opportunity. Feel the crowd, play with them, allow them to bask in your divine presence again. We should very much like to put the problem of the Gunthers to bed. Whatever else they are, my dear, the Gunthers are efficient. We like our City to run smoothly. A repulsive appearance is a small price to pay for that. So, when you address your devotees, be sure they know that Our Stowe is satisfied with the sentence we have passed on these four chosen ones."

"And if the crowd is not happy?" she asks with a mischievous grin.

"You have my permission to improvise."

"I won't disappoint you, Father." There. She's accomplished her objective. Since Darius has so kindly granted her secret wish, Stowe offers him her most gracious smile. "Oh, Father, it's so good to be back."

Conurbation Park. The last time she was here it was strewn with banners, alive with music. Of course, that was before the riot she had precipitated with her scream. The mood today is somber but there is also a current of anticipation.

Stowe waits behind a veiled grandstand at the south end of the square. On the gleaming platform sit four ebony gallows surrounded by a phalanx of well-armed Clerics—Querin flexing his muscles.

"How many are in attendance?" Darius asks, with only a hint of boredom.

The Master of Inculcation radiates satisfaction. "Approximately fifty thousand. Speakers positioned throughout the City will reach every citizen. All shall be blessed with the sound of Our Stowe's voice."

Angry shouts from the throng announce the arrival of the four prisoners. Protected by Clerics on all sides, the Gunthers are assaulted by jeers and taunts that quickly escalate to a fevered pitch. They're all wearing glasses, just as Willum said. One of them is a young girl, not much older than Stowe. Though she's trying to appear unaffected, Stowe can see her flinch again and again. It is not difficult to imagine the insults thrown at her as knives; the scars they leave will be as permanent.

Wrists bound behind their backs, the Gunthers are roughly pushed onto the platform. The veil parts enough to reveal the prisoners as they are positioned over the trap doors. When the nooses are fitted around their necks, they do not quake with fear or beg for mercy; instead they stare at the inside of their lenses, oblivious to their surroundings.

Master Querin steps out to announce her. "Our Stowe," is all he says, raising an arm toward her.

Willum signals Querin to wait as he adjusts Stowe's filo-armor collar. "Listen," he whispers.

"Yes, my Primary," she says. And the veil opens wide to reveal Stowe gliding regally down the stairs. As she sweeps onto the grandstand's amplification platform, the crowd's chant rises to greet her, "Our Stowe! Our Stowe!"

But Stowe stands silently before them. She does as Willum ordered, and listens to their cries of "Monsters!"

"Scum!" "Eviscerate them!" "Make them bleed!" And worse. Much, much worse. These people are so cruel, so rabid in their hatred, she can't help doubting Willum's crazy plan. But with a sweep of her hand all are silenced.

"Before you stand criminals." Stowe extends an arm, indicating the four Gunther prisoners behind her. "But what is the nature of their crime? They did not spirit me away as the Conurbation suspected. No one could do that. I go where I will and always where I can be of service to my people. To you.

"No. They did not commit this offense against my person, but they deserve to be treated as criminals. And I will tell you why.

"Look at them. Are they like us? Can one of you call a Gunther *friend*? Or even *neighbor*? Do they walk in your streets? Shop where you shop? Work where you work? No. They hold themselves apart. They think they are above participating in our Conurbation. But are they?"

"No! No! No!" The crowd shouts.

"No!" Stowe cries. Allowing the amplified hum of her breath to work its magic, she waits until the mob breathes with her. "No." This time her voice barely rises above a whisper. "Death is an end. It is quick. It will not open their eyes to our compassion, to our love." Stowe raises her voice, letting the crowd know she will tolerate no protest. "Yes. I love them. As I love all my citizens. As I love all of you."

"Our Stowe! Our Stowe! Our Stowe!"

Stowe allows the crowd to bask for a moment in her love; then, turning toward the Clerics, Stowe issues her command. "Remove their glasses! Blind them!" She rather enjoys the stunned silence of her audience.

"No! Please!" the Gunthers beg, in a state of panic. They fight against their ropes and snap their heads away from the guards, bobbing frantically—all to no avail.

Stowe points dramatically to the floor before her, and the four pairs of glasses are laid at her feet. "Perhaps the Gunthers have become too fond of their difference. If they wish to live apart from the Conurbation—so be it." Stowe places her foot on the pile of spectacles and bears down again and again, pulverizing them. "They shall know what it is like to live without our compassion and love. They shall be exiled and abandoned to wander blind in the Devastation."

The gasp is instantaneous, almost creating a vacuum in the plaza. She has sentenced them to the one thing worse than death. The crowd is in an uproar but Stowe shouts over them: "Let this be a warning to all Gunthers! Those who wish to remain shall report to the offices of the Master of Inculcation. We will see that they contribute to our Conurbation and thus be returned to our good graces. Those who do not will be banished forever."

As the Gunthers are marched away, Stowe watches the crowd taunt, spit, and throw garbage at the innocent offenders. She sees Willum slip into the crowd behind them. The shouting continues, but as if deterred by an unbearable stench, a wider berth is given to the prisoners. She hopes the four make it out of the City unharmed.

Querin takes her arm and draws her back to the Eldest, who places his hands on her shoulders. "You surprised even me, my daughter," he says, his newly implanted teeth sparkling. "Yes. It might work."

"With a few encouraging proclamations," Querin agrees. "And, I think, new uniforms. By the end of the week, every Gunther in the City will be visibly taking part in our Conurbation."

Darius laughs and so Stowe laughs too, relieved to have saved the Gunthers' lives but even more at the Masters' apparent lack of suspicion. It is clear they're happy that the Gunthers have become one less thing to worry about. They've other pressing concerns, that much is obvious. With any luck, it will be enough to keep them distracted while she and Willum get on with a little snooping.

a friend in need

there will be great rips in the fabric of the
dreamfield and I will be the one to close them.
But one day, I will recognize their source and its
power will become my destiny.

—Darius,

vision #831, year 21 a.c.
Dreamfield journals of the
first inner circle

Winter has most definitely arrived, and ice coats the
flat barrens. For the first few days of his trek Roan
felt exposed, a solitary traveler over their vast emptiness. In
keeping with his disguise, he's had to move more slowly than
he would have liked, and sleeping on open ground, he's had
to maintain a level of alertness that's kept him from getting proper rest. That combined with the cold nights and his
growing hunger is compromising his ability to think clearly.

Roan stops for a moment, looking in every direction for
some clue as to where he should proceed. He laughs, painfully aware of the irony of his journey—the last trip he took
by himself he was running from the god of the Brothers, now
here he is trying to find him, and he is most definitely lost.

Mabatan's explanation of ley lines has been all he's had
to go on. The world, she said, was not unlike the body, and
it was possible for him to use his senses to find its lines of
power, just as needles are used by healers to tap into the

body's energy flow. Along these lines there were places where the earth's potency pooled and if he followed their path he would find what he sought. As good a theory as any, but he's beginning to despair of such places even existing, never mind his ability to find them.

Looking up at the hazy outline of the sun, Roan realizes he's lost all sense of direction, so he takes out his recorder, and sitting on the frozen ground, he empties his mind and plays. The notes fall like embers igniting invisible waves that weave a subtle magic around him. His music has never sounded so beautiful, and it is unmistakably tugging one way, urging him forward.

As he resumes his journey, Roan of the Parting's words return to him. "...*it was the awesome power of every farmer, manufacturer, student, teacher, child, and adult alike to manifest visions and dreams.*" Whatever his ancestor's culpability was regarding enablers—something Roan found really unpleasant to think about—if the Friend existed because people believed in him, then *how* they believed could change him. Maybe. Or maybe that was where the muddle-headedness that hunger and lack of sleep brought on could lead you.

Roan wakes, suddenly realizing he'd dozed off. Not knowing how long he's been walking in a stupor, he stops bleary-eyed at a dense thicket, overgrown with a forbidding mass of black woody vines and tangled bramble. Sitting down to rest, he hears the whisper of a rivulet of water. With great difficulty, he cuts a narrow swath at the base of the thicket and exposes a clear running stream. As he eagerly dips his face to the frigid water for a drink, he glimpses an opening. In an instant his cricket has leapt from his shoulder and is scrambling through it. Without a thought, Roan follows.

The sharp brambles tear at his skin but his hands can feel a strong pulse beneath them, as if he were above the very heart of the earth. Following the cricket, Roan inches painfully forward until the thicket opens up at last.

As the white cricket hops back onto his shoulder, Roan rises and feels his heartbeat synchronize with the pulse beneath his feet. The trickle of water winds through what he now recognizes is a labyrinth. To free his mind of fear and expectation, he begins a walking meditation. Proceeding this way, he loses all track of time, but eventually he reaches the labyrinth's heart—a perfect circle about fifteen strides in circumference, mysteriously clear of all roots and bramble.

The cricket leaps into its center and Roan sits beside it. No longer aware of any hunger or thirst or weariness, his senses attune to the scent of the bramble, the fluttering of the cricket's antennae, the cold hardness of the clay. The crackling sound of dead leaves shifting on the ground makes him start. He feels no wind, yet he can see the leaves are being blown this way and that. Then, as suddenly as they began, they stop.

Directly in front of him, a thin mist rises from the ground, a wispy thread ribboning out in Roan's direction. Like a viper striking, it hurtles toward him and wraps around his throat, his arms, his face. He rolls on the ground as it blocks his nose and mouth, suffocating him. Realizing the futility of struggle, Roan retreats into himself, consciously slowing his heart rate.

What are you?

The response comes instantly. The vapor squeezes around his chest, pulsating with a red glow. At first the sensation is pleasantly warm, but in moments he is on fire. Screaming in pain, he watches his torso bubble and blister until all the water has exploded from his chest and nothing remains but his organs aflame within his charred ribcage. Through the blinding agony, Roan realizes the damage must be an illusion. How else could he still be conscious? The fog makes every inch of his skin a blazing inferno, but to survive he must ignore the sensation. Though it takes all his willpower, he is able to endure by submerging himself in the impenetrable essence of his etherbody.

As Roan's pain subsides, the mist swirls and swells until it towers over him, a huge undulating mass that, twisting in on itself, evolves into a pair of horns. White eyes streaked with blood appear and around them a gigantic head takes shape. The head of a bull. The loose skin of its neck falls and folds into flesh. Then a human torso appears. Rippling with muscle, its thick blue veins threaten to burst the confines of its skin. The being exudes a strength far beyond anything Roan has ever encountered. It smells of the earth, its breath a gust of wind.

Sweat steams off the newly formed being like dew rising in a spring dawn. As its elevated spine curves down into the hips and hind legs of a bull, the creature's nostrils flare.

Taking care to be still, Roan reaches with his mind. *Are you the Friend?*

The minotaur's jowl does not move, but a strange melodious voice resonates in Roan's skull. *Do you doubt it?*

The red streaks in the Friend's white eyes look like gouges, jagged and chaotic, as if something or someone had slashed them. *No. It's just that. . .I thought you were a man. The man who slew the bull.*

The Slayer and the Slain are one.

I killed a bull. In a vision.

The veins in the Friend's muzzle pulsate with emotion. *Yes, and my blood healed the Novakin. But for that to happen, you will have to fulfill my request.*

Every fiber of Roan's being is charged with explosive rage. This is the god who inspired the brutal rituals that culminated in the massacre of Longlight. Still, it is Roan who has sought the monster out. Pushing back his anger, he confronts the god with as much reason as he can muster. *I won't agree to anything without knowing what it is.*

A buoyant laughter echoes painfully in Roan's head. *You are brave. I will make my request, and you will choose. If you refuse, never seek me again. I do not ask for much. Just one life. . .one life that you alone can take.*

Roan remains silent. It seems ridiculous that he has come all this way for this. It just can't be. It can't.

Do this thing for me, and you will gain much of what you seek.

And who is it you want me to kill?

The Friend shakes his head in fury. Blood sprays from his lacerated eyes in beaded wisps that slash across Roan's chest, burning holes into his cloak. *Me. You must kill me.*

It's impossible. How could I—

You will understand when the time comes.

Why do you want me to do this?

The minotaur stands so still that, for a moment, Roan wonders if he's staring at a statue. But as the beast's warm breath blasts over Roan like heat off a smelting fire, he knows the Friend is deliberating.

I will show you. The air between them vibrates and Roan gasps as the energy hits him like a skillfully delivered punch. With both hands, the Friend digs deep into his own chest, and rips it open. Cracking his ribs apart, he pulls the two sides of his torso wide, exposing a giant beating heart, lungs swelling with air, arteries pulsating. Roan's ether body is pulled from him and drawn through the Friend's gaping wound, and into the Dreamfield.

ROAN STARES AWESTRUCK AS AN OPAQUE VERSION OF THE ENTIRE DREAMFIELD SPREADS OUT BEFORE HIM. LINES LIKE VEINS CRACKLE BACK AND FORTH ACROSS IT, A GRID OF PULSING AMORPHOUS FORMS ALL HEADING FOR ONE PLACE—THE AREA CONTAINING DARIUS'S CONSTRUCTIONS. HELD FIRMLY IN THE FRIEND'S MIGHTY GRIP, ROAN CAREFULLY FOLLOWS THE PATH OF THE SHADES PAST THE TOWERING RAMPARTS, THE GIGANTIC SPIRALING GYRE, THE OCELLUS'S GLEAMING DISKS AND THE EERILY PHOSPHORESCENT UNDULATIONS OF THE TENTACLED ANTLIA. BUT AS SOON AS THE GHOSTLIKE FORMS CONVERGE ON THE IMMENSE, WHIRLING CLOUD THAT IS THE SPIRACAL, THEY VANISH.

"THE OVERSHADOWER LIES IN THE PIT BENEATH THAT DARKNESS. AS YOUR DESTINY WILL BE DETERMINED IN YOUR STRUGGLE WITH DARIUS, MINE FALLS TO THE ENEMY CONCEALED THERE." THE FRIEND TURNS HIS LACERATED EYES TOWARD ROAN. "SINCE THE BEGINNING OF TIME THE GODS HAVE DISCOVERED THEIR PURPOSE AT THE WELL OF OBLIVION. YOUR GREAT-GRANDFATHER STOOD IN THE WATER THAT ONCE RAN INTO IT AND UNDERSTOOD THAT THE ESSENCE OF ALL LIFE IS CARRIED TO THIS ONE GREAT HEART. BUT DARIUS SAW IT ONLY AS A RESOURCE TO BE BENT TO HIS WILL, DIVERTING ALL OF ITS WATERS INTO THE WHORL. ONE AFTER ANOTHER HE SUBVERTED THE PLACES OF POWER. AND AS HE DID SO, THE FABRIC OF THE DREAMFIELD WAS RIPPED AND THE OVERSHADOWER EXPOSED. IT WAS NOT LONG BEFORE HE FELL UNDER ITS THRALL. NOW ALL THE DREAMS AND MEMORIES OF PEOPLE BOTH ALIVE AND DEAD ARE NOTHING MORE THAN

FODDER FOR THE HUNGER OF THIS BEAST." THE MINOTAUR WHIS-
PERS, "DARIUS HAS ROBBED US OF OUR VISION AND OUR PUR-
POSE. WE MEAN TO GET IT BACK. SINCE HE PLAYED A LARGE PART
IN MY RESURGENCE, THE TASK IS MADE MINE."

THE FRIEND BLINKS AND THEY ARE TRANSPORTED TO A
GIGANTIC OPEN PALM IDENTICAL TO THE ONE SAINT SHOWED
ROAN. WRITHING SHAPES APPEAR OUT OF NOWHERE TO TOPPLE
INTO IT. THE SHADES DIM SLIGHTLY AS THE THRONE ABSORBS
THEM, THEN SLIDE THROUGH A NARROW VEIN THAT DRAWS THEM
INEXORABLY TOWARD THE SPIRACAL.

"WE WILL MEET AGAIN WHEN YOU COME TO DESTROY
DARIUS. AT THAT TIME, ROAN OF LONGLIGHT, YOU WILL FIND
ME AND OBEY MY REQUEST." THE BASE OF A TORCH APPEARS IN
THE MINOTAUR'S HAND. "TAKE THIS AND SWEAR."

ROAN GRASPS IT AND THE BASE BURSTS INTO FLAME.

"GOOD," SAYS THE FRIEND. "WE ARE AGREED."

The darkness is more overwhelming than any he's ever
experienced. But gradually, as he's wreathed by pinpoints
of light, Roan realizes that he's in the earth's atmosphere,
floating over clouds, surrounded by the night sky's countless
shimmering stars.

Do you see the bull?

Roan gazes at the brightest star, Aldebaran, shining
orange. *There is its face, made by the Hyades. The stars Elnath and Zeta
Tauri mark its horns. They form the constellation Taurus.*

*I survive because I am written in the stars in the shape of a bull. Every
generation that sets its eye upon me names me anew, and gives me life.*

But if humanity dies, so will you.

And what gives life to humanity?

Roan thinks of Stowe, Alandra, Lumpy, Mabatan, of the
Novakin, of everyone he has ever known, has ever loved. He

thinks of the scent of one flower, of his cricket's song. *That's a difficult question to answer.*

Difficult enough for an eternity. If we are lucky.

Roan wakes to find himself back in the center of the Friend's labyrinth. Parched and famished, he reaches into his bag. His encounter with the Friend had not been what he'd expected. Instead of answers, he has even more questions. What does it mean to kill a god? What has he agreed to? Why did he agree? Maybe somewhere deep down he just didn't believe it was possible. Or maybe he thought a world without the Friend was a safer place.

Still, he feels bound to the god somehow and though much of what the Friend said to him is a mystery, he knows it's vital for him to unravel it.

Roan winces as he puts some jerky to his mouth; his lips are swollen and hot to the touch. As he chews, he places a cooling hand over them and thinks on the Friend's final words.

My offer is a gift, Roan of Longlight, though you may not guess now what it is.

tHe LieuteNaNt's DiLemmas

eyes ON tHe sky
feet firm ON tHe gROUND
HeaRt waRm as tHe suN
His suRvivaL ReNowNeD

LoyaL to tHe eND
tHe best of aLL fRieNDs
tHat is tHe tRUtH
of ouR LieuteNaNt.

—LoRe of tHe stoRyteLLeRs

"I S IT WORKING?"

The insertion of the enablers, which finally took place yesterday after two weeks of testing, seems to be a success. Ende, Lumpy, and the doctors are all excited, clearly impressed; and Algernon's face is so hopeful that, despite all her apprehensions, Mabatan smiles. "Yes. Kira is looking at a book. It has a picture on it."

"What is the picture, Mabatan?" asks Ende.

"A girl with long blonde hair and a rabbit holding a clock."

Rushing to the door, Imin calls out, "Othard! Bring the book!"

After a moment, Othard appears, breathlessly holding it up. "You see? It's called *Alice's Adventures in Wonderland*."

Mabatan feels the Gunther's dry papery hand pat hers.

"Is it tolerable, my dear? Seeing through two sets of eyes, hearing through two sets of ears, I know it must be difficult."

The wound in her neck is throbbing, and her discomfort doubled, because she's experiencing Kira's pain as well as her own, but it is tolerable, a small price to pay.

"Yes. It is difficult but it will get easier, I think." Mabatan gently squeezes the Gunther's long fingers. "Thank you."

"That completes the visual and aural testing," says Imin.

"Pity that the communication's only one way," says Othard. "A few more weeks and we might've been able to sort something out."

As if it has nothing to do with your natural talents as compared to mine. By the way, can you hear all my thoughts?

Feeling Kira's smirk, Mabatan grins.

I wish I could hear your answer.

"You can come in now," Imin calls out.

Kira strides past the bookshelves and stands near the door, looking directly at Lumpy. "In some ways it's better that it's one-way. If I'm captured, the last thing we need is for them to be able to hook into Mabatan. If it's alright with you, Lumpy, I'll make my arrangements to go."

"We still have more tests—" says Othard, but Kira cuts him off with a glare.

"There will always be more tests, my good doctors," she says, softening the blow, "but who says you need me for them?" Not pausing to wait for an answer, she turns to Mabatan. "As long as you're sure it's alright?"

Mabatan nods, but as she looks into Kira's eyes, she simultaneously experiences Kira seeing her. The image doubles and triples until there are more Kiras than she can count, all sandwiched between images of herself, seen through Kira's eyes. The room starts to spin and she jerks back, falling to the floor.

"Mabatan!" Lumpy cries out, rushing to her.

In a moment, she's surrounded. The doctors take her pulses, while Ende puts a hand to her forehead.

"What happened?" the Apsara matriarch asks.

"When...I looked into Kira's eyes...there were so many of us..."

"She was caught in a feedback loop," Algernon explains. "Like the effect of looking into two angled mirrors, and seeing a multiplicity of images of yourself."

"I see," Imin says, stroking his chin.

"Only much more intense..." surmises Othard.

"Is this safe?" Lumpy asks, clearly disturbed.

"As safe as we could make it," Algernon says, patting Lumpy on the back, "given the time at hand and the equipment available."

But Mabatan can see that her friend is not going to be easy to comfort. "I know the risks, Lumpy. It only happened when I looked into Kira's eyes. She is leaving and it will cease to be a problem."

"What if there are other complications?" asks Ende. "Something life-threatening."

Othard gasps, indignant. "But that's highly unlikely!"

"An exceedingly low probability!" Imin adds.

"Still, it *is* possible," snaps Ende. "Lumpy, as Roan's Lieutenant, you must bear responsibility for the decision."

Lumpy takes in all the expectant faces around him. But in the end, his gaze falls on Mabatan. "Are you sure you want to continue?"

I don't feel any ill effects at all, Mabatan, but I'll understand if you want to back out.

Mabatan, resisting the urge to turn and look at Kira, keeps her eyes on Lumpy. She can read in his face the hope that she'll give him a reason to stop what they are doing, so she states her decision as definitely as she can: "Yes. I am sure."

Seeing that her lips are firmly sealed, Lumpy reluctantly pulls himself away. "Go ahead, Kira. That smuggler's been nothing but a nuisance since he was brought here; I'll be glad to see his back. Just don't show him yours; he'll do business with whoever fattens his purse."

"I won't hesitate to squash the bug if I have to," Kira assures Lumpy. Then, eyes shut tight, she turns and opens her arms. "Take care, Mabatan."

Mabatan walks into the embrace, the feeling of warmth pleasantly amplified. With a whispered goodbye, Kira strides to the doorway, where Ende waits.

Ende's forehead grazes her granddaughter's. "I will always hear you with my heart." The emotion that wells up in Kira brings tears to Mabatan's eyes. But Kira, always the warrior, shows nothing outwardly. She grips her grandmother's shoulders, hugs her quickly, and leaves the world of the library behind.

Over the next few days, Mabatan's efforts to balance Kira's consciousness with her own are not entirely successful. Any powerful emotion or physical experience brings Kira to the forefront of her awareness, momentarily blinding Mabatan to her own surroundings. She's had a few painful collisions and is covered in bruises. After she'd crashed into Kamyar, she ended up in the infirmary.

He'd arrived yesterday with four Gunthers from the City, none too happy, and it appears to Mabatan, as she sits in the library's vast atrium, that things are going from bad to worse.

Gunther Number Fifty-One, the tallest of the four Gunthers, is on his tiptoes squinting at Kamyar, so outraged his entire body is quaking. "We are Gunthers, not warmongers!"

"You know, those contact lenses Willum provided you with are making you a little touchy. After all the trouble I went to rescuing you, one would think you'd give me the benefit of the doubt." Kamyar's tongue is in his cheek, but Mabatan can tell he is not completely insincere.

"You did not rescue us!" Fifty-One snorts. "We would have survived quite well without you." His three companions crowd behind him, heads bobbing.

Kamyar laughs. "Really. I seem to remember that when I found you in the Devastation you were all face-down on the ground."

"We were resting."

"Don't try to pretend you aren't ecstatic to be here. The least you can do is help research some battle strategies."

"That is not within our moral parameters," Fifty-One states flatly.

"Oh? And designing enablers is?" Kamyar's face is almost purple with frustration.

Lumpy steps out from the shadows and, with a wink at Mabatan, rushes over to the angry Gunthers. "Hello! Are you feeling any better?"

"This Storyteller," says Fifty-One, pointing an accusing finger at Kamyar's chest, "this Storyteller is insisting we turn into warmongers."

Lumpy glowers, quite impressively, at Kamyar. "Is this possible? You've asked them to carry weapons? Kill Clerics? Fandor? Marauders?"

"Hmm, that's an idea!" Kamyar turns dramatically to face the irate Gunther. "How are you with a crossbow?"

"Kamyar, I'm surprised! A stray arrow might puncture one of these books."

Seventy-Nine puts a hand to her mouth, but Mabatan can see her eyes twinkling. She has a great curiosity, Mabatan recalls, in the ways of the world—outside the boundaries set by her people. And, obviously, an uncharacteristic sense of humor.

"You are right, Fifty-One. Our friend should never have asked you to take up arms. He will apologize."

Lumpy lifts an eyebrow at Kamyar. Kamyar inhales grandly and bows to them. "Profound apologies for my miscreant behavior. May my eyebrows be plucked and my tongue flogged."

"Your apology is accepted," says Fifty-One.

Seventy-Nine vigorously shakes her finger in her ear. "But he never offered us weapons."

"No one asked your opinion, Seventy-Nine."

"But—"

"The discussion has been agreeably terminated. Do not interrupt again."

"But—"

"Have you been taken through the library?" Lumpy jumps in before the argument can distract them any further. "And the laboratory may be of interest to you as well. Algie said he mentioned—"

"Excuse me, you mean Gunther Number One Hundred

and Twenty-Six. Please use the correct appellation when referring to him."

"Come, come," says Kamyar. "The fellow was alone for *forty* years, surely he's entitled to a name."

Gunther Number Thirty-Three is clearly mortified by this thought. "His absence may have deteriorated his memory, but this does not excuse a lapse in Gunther tradition."

Kamyar guffaws. "I'm sure helping him regain a sense of propriety will keep you quite busy."

"Perhaps my friend is right," interjects Lumpy. Sighing wistfully, he looks at each Gunther in turn. "Though I have to confess I was hoping…well…No. Never mind, I don't want to burden you. I'll just borrow Kamyar. I'm sure he'll be of assistance with these puzzles."

All of the Gunthers immediately crowd Lumpy. "Puzzles? What kind of puzzles?"

"Well, for one, Number One Hundred and Twenty-Six, due to his lapse, no doubt, is struggling with the encryption in the journal he's deciphering."

Number Thirty-Three shoots an accusing glance at Kamyar. "It's in code? You didn't mention a code."

Kamyar throws his arms up in mock apology.

"It's excruciatingly difficult," Lumpy sighs. "I don't suppose you'd be interested."

"I would!" yells Seventy-Nine. The other Gunthers glare at her, and she quickly shifts her attention to the floor.

"You know, I suppose, that the Clerics have a new weapon," continues Lumpy, "I think it's called…the Apogee."

"Yes," says Fifty-One. "We unwittingly created some of its components. Extremely complex and deadly. We will not be fooled into such complicity again."

"Of course not," Lumpy concedes. "And I would never ask it of you. I was thinking more along the lines of a device I remember from when we visited you in the City. It disabled a Cleric's stun stick."

"Oh, yes," Fifty-One sniffs, bobbing his head proudly. "The Allayer. It's a simple device. In fact, Number Thirty-Three here invented it."

"I suppose it would be useless against an Apogee."

"Completely useless," agrees Thirty-Three. "To create a device to allay the Apogee would be extremely challenging."

"You'd have to reverse the magnetic field," says Fifty-One.

"Then amplify it," Thirty-Three adds.

After conferring excitedly with his fellow Gunthers, Number Fifty-One addresses Lumpy with an air of great importance. "An Allayer to counteract the Apogee's effects would be an appropriate project. We will begin work immediately."

Utterly shocking the Gunther, Lumpy takes his hand and shakes it heartily. "Kamyar, will you show our friends the way to the laboratory?"

Mabatan struggles not to laugh as the Storyteller, his nose in the air, sighs deeply. "Very well, if you insist. Come this way."

Only Gunther Number Seventy-Nine stays behind. Smiling shyly at Lumpy, she asks, "May I work on the decryption?"

"Number One Hundred Twenty-Six—"

"You can use his chosen name with me if you would like," she says quietly. "I do not mind."

"Alright," Lumpy replies with a grin. "Algie would be really grateful for the help. Do you know where to find him?"

"Oh, yes. I've been there already." Seventy-Nine pauses when she sees Mabatan. "Mabatan of the Wazya, greetings. As you know, I conducted tests on the cricket belonging to Roan of Longlight when I saw you last. With your cricket's permission, might I add its measurements to my data…and perhaps ask you some questions? Not right now, of course…"

Sensing no objection from the white cricket on her shoulder, Mabatan smiles. "I believe that will be acceptable."

As the beaming Seventy-Nine rushes away to Algie, Lumpy collapses beside Mabatan. "I wish Roan would get back. It's been a couple of weeks now, and I'm starting to get worried."

"I worry about him too, but—" Mabatan breathes deeply, trying to still her heart.

"What's wrong?"

"Clerics."

"Kira? Is she safe?"

"For the moment, yes."

"Good. Then how come…you look so…"

"When Kira gets agitated, her experiences overwhelm me. I'm not used to it yet, that's all."

Lumpy places his hands on Mabatan's shoulders, turning her toward him. "Mabatan. You'll tell me, won't you, if it gets worse? It's not worth harming yourself. We'll find another way."

"I promise."

Lumpy grimaces, still troubled. "Has Kira had any problems with that smuggler?"

"Not yet. Have you—"

"Yeah, I've contacted Mhyzah. The Hhroxhi have agreed

to let us use the thrusalls. I just hope Mhyzah will get to Kira before that thug pulls something."

"Kira does not trust him either. She is always on her guard."

Lumpy nods but Mabatan can feel the weight of his concern. She hates to add to his load but right now he's the only one she feels comfortable enough with to share her burden. "There is something I must speak with you about, Lumpy," she says, keeping her voice level and firm.

"What is it?"

"If something should happen—" Lumpy tenses, but Mabatan grips his hands as she meets his eyes. "Do not misunderstand me. I believe this connection with Kira is the right thing to do. The need is great and the sacrifice very small. Still, I would not do it if I felt that I would come to great harm. I am to be the Carrier of the stories of my people; and you must trust that I do not take unnecessary risks. But...*if* something should happen..."

"Mabatan." Tears pool in the corners of Lumpy's eyes.

"You must not bury me. You must not burn me. Take my body to my father. To Khutumi."

"How do I find him?"

"If I die, he will know. He will send you a vision. You will find him. Make me this promise," she says, taking his hand. "And tell no one. It is a secret only we must share."

Gripping her hand tightly, he clutches it to his heart. "I promise."

Mabatan leans forward so that her cheek touches his. "Thank you," she murmurs, and lifting his hand to her lips, she kisses it.

A piercing cry echoes through the library. "Lieutenant!"

As Wolf charges down the steps, Lumpy stands to meet him. "Five Brothers have fallen. There is no blood, but they are clearly dead." Wolf is shouting in Lumpy's face. "Those caravans are all defended with Apogees! We have no defense against that weapon! We cannot fight it. Four clerics took five of my best warriors! For what? I will not watch my people slaughtered like cattle!"

Lumpy holds his ground before the infuriated warrior. "I grieve for your men, Brother Wolf."

"I don't want your grief, Lieutenant!"

"We are working on a solution."

Wolf's hook-sword is twisting menacingly in his hand. "How many more will die before you find one?"

"You will not fight again until we do, Brother Wolf." Every face in the atrium lifts at the sound of the voice. Roan is standing at the library entrance. Half his face is burned a deep red, as if he had walked, one side masked, in the summer's sun.

Pushing everyone in his way aside, Wolf stumbles to the foot of the stairs. He gapes up at Roan as if he were seeing an apparition. Then, trembling, he cries out, "Prophet! You have met the Friend!"

the vapor

we knew we would be buried alive. but we wouldn't
stay buried forever.

—krispin,
vision #787, year 38 a.c.
dreamfield journals of the
first inner circle

STOWE HAD MERELY TO EXPRESS CURIOSITY IN COOPERATION
Unlimited to excite Master Querin's interest. Certain
that the physical presence of Our Stowe among the
workers of the City would accelerate its restabilization, he
had quickly arranged a grueling tour of all the Conurbation's
factories and communication centers. So for the past two
weeks, her beatific presence has graced a better part of the
City's industrial complexes and now, at last, Stowe and
Willum have arrived at their goal.

The prospect of spying at Cooperation Unlimited is
quite exhilarating and Stowe grins widely back at Master
Fortin as he flashes his small white teeth in greeting.

"Our Stowe," the manager warbles, trying to maintain a
stately pose beneath the entranceway. "We are truly blessed.
Two visits to our lowly facility in less than a year. The
workers are ecstatic."

"It is my pleasure, Master Fortin, to return here to honor
your tremendous achievement," replies Stowe with perfect
grace. "Your factory is the apple of the Eldest's eye."

Speaking of eyes, Stowe notices that the manager's acquired a new pair—scintillating green, they are far too lovely for his toadlike countenance. They might have been Lem's eyes. But she mustn't allow these thoughts to affect her, not now.

"You flatter me," he smiles. "We work hard, it is true, production increasing daily, but it is a calling, Our Stowe, a sacred duty we perform. It inspires us, imbues us with a religious fervor that feeds and enhances our labor."

Oh! How the man goes on! "Of course it does. Well. I suppose we shouldn't keep our workers waiting."

"Forgive me, I'm prattling!" Fortin exclaims. Extending an arm, he leads her and Willum into the main hall.

How many speeches has she given in the past two weeks—thirty? forty? She used to find them such a chore, but now they have acquired the patina of a challenge. By subtly altering a phrase here, or intonation there, she and Willum seek to place a suggestion in the minds of the workers that the prophecies might deliver on their promises, not in some vaguely prescribed future but soon, very soon. With a bit of luck, maybe she can make Darius sweat enough to do something stupid—well, better not be too optimistic. That road leads to overconfidence and carelessness.

She watches Willum quickly change into the sterile overalls, mittens, and overshoes required to enter the factory. Due to her elevated status, Our Stowe is exempt, but she'd gladly trade. The outfit looks much more comfortable than the one she's decked out in. Being in the Farlands hadn't been pleasant, but she has fond memories of never having to be trussed in and weighted down by her clothes.

Fortin, now conscientiously germ-free, escorts her up a

metal stairway that leads to a balcony. Below, hundreds of workers are busy at their conveyor belts, but the moment Fortin steps onto the amplification platform, every worker stops to look up. No one so much as breathes.

Raising his hand, Fortin declares, "Our Stowe has returned!" And as he welcomes her onto the platform, the murmuring chant begins. "Our Stowe, Our Stowe, Our Stowe!"

She regards the workers' adoring faces, the longing in their eyes. Willum is right. There is more there than an enabled obsession with an inaccessible icon. They believe she will play an integral part in fulfilling the prophecies. She must ensure that her presence here, today, bolsters that faith.

"When I left you, I sought the vision of the prophecy," Stowe says softly.

Every voice rises together. "The Daughter shall have the Sight."

"Yes. I have seen, and what I have seen has brought me home. To you. Because you are the future. The prophecy has declared that when my father passes on his scepter, our love will blossom with unity and purpose. Do not be impatient. Labor in the knowledge that a light, suppressed for so long, shall soon be released into the world. That light will benefit you all. I swear this to you!"

"Our Stowe...Our Stowe..." they whisper, every hand raised, palms facing her, fingers wide, in surrender to their goddess.

As she backs off the platform, Stowe does not miss the troubled look that darkens Master Fortin's face. If he has a problem, Willum will have to sort it out. Right now, she has to stick to the script they've devised.

"That was magnificent, Our Stowe. Inspiring." How quickly the manager masks his misgivings.

Her voice piteously weak, Stowe sighs. "You are too generous, Master Fortin." She wobbles precariously and grips Willum's arm.

"Our Stowe?" Willum whispers, reaching out to hold her.

"Is there a problem? Is she not well?" Fortin's voice is shaking.

"Her schedule has been very demanding," Willum explains. "She insists on making two or three appearances every day, but it is a terrible strain."

Stowe stumbles, collapsing into Willum's arms.

"I see, I see," says Fortin, wringing his hands. The possibility of the Archbishop's daughter becoming ill under his roof is making him squirm. "There's a couch in my office, Our Stowe. If you would overlook its inadequacies, perhaps you could rest there."

"You are too kind," murmurs Stowe. Then with a sigh, she promptly pretends to faint.

Her head leans into Willum's shoulder, and through the curtain of her hair she is able to catch a covert look at her surroundings. The corridor Fortin leads them down is clearly the administrative wing of the factory. In office after office bookkeepers and data processors punch figures into machines. Coming to a parquet door, Fortin pauses to look back at Stowe. A piteous groan seems to be just the right key to open it.

Stowe has to exert a lot of control not to smirk at the elegant interior. The room is far more opulent than the Archbishop's: the floors are marble, the carved desk ancient oak, and the walls hand-painted tiles. It's a flagrant exhibition of a status far above a manager's position.

Fortin hastily dismisses the decor, distinctly embarrassed to be so exposed. "The previous manager is responsible for this extravagant interior," he sputters. "Rather than waste more precious resources having it removed, I bear with it."

Shaking her head, Stowe makes a show of opening her eyes a fraction to vaguely scan her surroundings. "A prudent choice," she says with a generous smile. Spotting a velvet chaise, she signals to Willum to lay her down. "If you don't mind," she says to Fortin, as she splays herself across its entire frame.

Clearly embarrassed, the manager coughs nervously. "We'll leave you alone then."

But he remains there, waiting. Stowe knows he'd like her to stop him—doesn't much care for the thought of her in his room unsupervised. Resting her head on a feather pillow, she studiously ignores him. And as soon as he realizes a reprieve is not coming, he leads Willum out.

As much as she'd like to snoop around and see what he's hiding, time is limited and she must constrain herself to the task at hand. Her etherself rises and floats past Fortin and Willum. For a moment she hovers invisibly before them. *On my way, then.*

Willum brushes his hair back in surreptitious greeting. *Go carefully, Stowe.*

Sinking through the floor, she notes the very different quality of this corridor. The floors are polished concrete, the walls burnished steel. Heavily armed guards closely examine every worker entering or exiting. Drifting through the fortified portal, she's drawn to three technicians hunched over a translucent globe no larger than an eyeball, with two finger-length appendages dangling from it. A faint lumines-cence is darting through veins in the globe, shifting in color from blood red to turquoise to marigold. An enabler. The technicians place it on a tray, and as one of them walks with it, Stowe follows.

At another set of steel doors, the technician's retina is scanned and he's waved through. This laboratory is larger, bustling with workers in sterile garb. The technician takes the enabler to a huge bell jar, at least twenty feet tall. Plum-col-ored gases swirl inside it under the watchful gaze of a group of scientists. Behind them lies a comatose man, head shaved, the stitches still bleeding behind his ear. As she approaches the jar, Stowe can see what they're observing. A humanoid shape, perhaps the size of her thumbnail, is skimming the swirling mist, rising until it arrives at what looks like an out-stretched hand...Darius's Throne, just as Roan described it.

On the other side of the jar, another patient's neck has been incised; the enabler she followed here is about to be connected. As the second appendage wraps around his spinal cord, the patient's body spasms. Then a vapor rolls off him, like a second skin being pulled away and toward the enabler. Without hesitation, she slides alongside.

THE VAPOR SOARS THROUGH BILLOWING CLOUDS, THEN SUD-DENLY PLUMMETS INTO OPEN SKY, ACCELERATING TO TREMEN-DOUS SPEEDS. SEPARATING HERSELF FROM THE FORM, STOWE BANKS HARD TO HER LEFT. AN OLD ACQUAINTANCE OF HERS IS LANGUIDLY GLIDING BELOW HER, A VULTURE WITH A HUGE SCAR DISFIGURING ITS HEAD. KORDAN. ONE LOOK AT HER WITH HIS GOOD EYE, AND HE'LL GO STRAIGHT TO DARIUS.

BUT THE VULTURE DOES NOT SEE HER. HIS EYES ARE ON THE VAPOR.

Catapulting into the gigantic outstretched hand, the form lands on the open palm, twitching horribly. Kordan soars over it as if preventing any possibility of escape. The living shape abruptly dims and then is sucked, writhing, into Darius's Throne.

The Throne is clearly collecting the life essence drawn out by these new enablers. Will it be enough—without Roan or Stowe or the Novakin—to join Darius to the Overshadower? To make him omnipotent, immortal, a god beyond the gods?

As she inches closer, a surge of energy reaches up to meet her, drawing her toward the Throne—better back up.

Nothing happens. This can't be right...

She's in her etherform! She stole into the Dreamfield on someone else's steam and now she doesn't have enough substance to draw herself away. She expends every bit of will she has, but it only seems to propel her even more speedily toward the ravenous palm.

Stowe did not deviate much from Querin's proclamation, but still...it made Fortin anxious and he is sure to report it to Darius. The situation must be handled with perfect delicacy; the Keeper will seek to interrogate either him or Stowe and one misstep could mean their destruction.

"Our Stowe's speech," proclaims Fortin, as they walk down the corridor, "was most provocative."

"Provocative—how so?"

"That business about the prophecy."

"You find Master Querin's proclamation provocative?" asks Willum, carefully choosing each word.

"No. No. Of course not," Fortin twitters nervously. "It's just…is Darius planning to retire? To hand over the Conurbation to that *girl*?"

Striking a pose of surprise, Willum gasps, incredulous, "You were not aware of the prophecy?"

"Well, of course I am," Fortin's irritation is palpable. "We are all aware of the prophecies. Master Querin makes sure of that! But…well…" Fortin glances up and down the hallway, then whispers in Willum's ear, "I mean they're prophecies. Nobody really expects them to come true. She's a child. How could the Archbishop cede his power to her? It's impossible!"

"Our Stowe is his daughter," says Willum, stating the obvious.

"She's only been here two years. She's…unproven. Some of us have served the Conurbation for three-quarters of a century."

"Yes, but we are, none of us, indispensable." Willum goes over these words again and again to himself, indelibly embedding them in his memory.

"No, none are indispensable," mutters Fortin, his bitterness rising. "And you—who are nothing more than a nursemaid—you will end up with everything, won't you?"

"I serve as Our Stowe's Primary. Her well-being is ample enough reward."

Something dangerous flutters behind Fortin's new eyes. But before he can shape it into words he is stopped short by the loud thrumming of an alarm. The manager's face suddenly drains of color. "If you'll excuse me," he says curtly, an unmistakable note of panic in his voice. And with a bow, the manager makes a hasty retreat.

NOTHING SEEMS TO BE HELPING HER OUT OF THIS MESS! AS SHE DESPERATELY TRIES EVERY TRICK SHE KNOWS TO SLOW DOWN, STOWE FEELS THE HALF-RING TIGHTEN ROUND HER FINGER. MAYBE IT COULD HELP—IF ONLY SHE KNEW HOW. THE INSTANT SHE THINKS THIS, A PHOSPHORESCENCE ENVELOPS HER WHOLE BODY AND LIFTS HER WITH GREAT SPEED FURTHER AND FURTHER FROM DARIUS'S VORACIOUS HAND.

OF COURSE. THE SHOCK BOTH SHE AND ROAN FELT WHEN THE RING SPLIT IN TWO. IT MUST HAVE BEEN THE RING LINKING TO THEIR LIFE-FORCE AND NOW IT RESPONDS REGARDLESS OF THE FORM THEY TAKE. SHE SIGHS, GRATEFUL FOR ONCE TO HER GREAT-GRANDFATHER AND HIS FORESIGHT. AN ALARM SHRILLS AND KORDAN'S MANGLED HEAD LOOKS UP. HA! TOO LATE. SHE IS ALREADY GONE.

Stowe has barely come to before Willum flings open the Manager's office door.

"Are you alright?" he asks, but his eyes lock on hers. *Was it you who set off the alarm?*

"Yes," she replies. "I feel better now." *I'm sorry. I followed a vapor-like form from an enabler straight to Darius's Throne—it's just as Roan described—and it gobbled the vapor up. But. . .*

"Are you well enough to leave?" Willum asks, helping her up. "You are expected back at the Pyramid." *Did anyone see you?*

No. But. . . "Should we say goodbye to Master Fortin?" *Just before it was absorbed, the form dimmed.*

"He may be busy. Perhaps we'll see him on the way out." *Darius must be siphoning off some of its energy before he feeds it to the Overshadower. The enablers' new design might serve that purpose. Perhaps even the Apogee as well.*

Stowe stands, locking her arm into Willum's.

It's why he's after more and more victims. Feed the dark god greater quantity and he might not notice the poor quality. Think Darius'll get away with it?

It's our job to see he doesn't.

a pain in the head

I am badger. this ring was forged in my image,
imbued with my life-force. all I have to offer is
now yours.

—journal of roan of the parting

Roan's worried about Mabatan. She's terribly pale, a ghost of herself. Every once in a while her hand gestures in a way distinctly not her own, serving some unseen purpose. She scowls inappropriately, and swaggers. If he didn't know she was carrying around Kira's consciousness, he'd think she'd lost her mind. Watching her sit distracted, in front of her untouched lunch, so oblivious to her surroundings, moves him in an unexpected way. He reaches out to take her hand in his.

Looking up, she lifts her other hand to trace a finger down the center of his face.

"Your mark is already fading," she says softly. Then, her brown eyes returning to this world, their world, she smiles, happy to see him.

But the bulge on her neck is frighteningly disconcerting and he's barely able to return her smile. "How are you doing?"

"Kira is in a barren wood. It is a place my people have twice attempted to restore and failed." The sadness in her voice, combined with a sense of futility he has never heard before, makes Roan grip her hand even harder. "She does not like the fact that they are exposed close to Fandor territory. But she's calm, relaxed."

The cost of this incessant doubling of experience on Mabatan is making him doubt its worth. "What happens when she isn't?"

Mabatan sighs wearily, responding to his look. "You've been talking to Lumpy."

"So. Is he wrong?"

"Sometimes, Kira has an unpleasant memory...or a nightmare. Jumbled faces and thoughts...death...violent death...and I can offer her no comfort. Her breath becomes my breath. My heart beats fast, too fast, with hers. There is nothing I can do to help." Mabatan lifts a fork and pokes at her untouched salad. "Those are the bad times. I know I appear...distracted but it is not always unpleasant." She takes a deep breath, then smiles. "It is good to talk with you, Roan of Longlight. Will you tell me of your encounter with the Friend?"

Roan feels the weight of her hand in his. He wants to tell her about his promise to the Friend, ask her if she knows how you go about killing a god, report on what he discovered about Darius and the Overshadower, but he can't. Whenever he even thinks about the experience, the fire, the stars, the astonishing nature of the Friend's request, it all catches in his throat and he finds himself holding back.

"It's hard to put into words. I'm just happy it's made a difference to Wolf and—Mabatan?" Leaping over the table, Roan catches her as she crumples.

"Clerics on patrol," she gasps, crunching into a tight ball at his side. "They've got a sword to a woman's throat, and to her child's. The smuggler is holding me back. Oh no!"

"What is it?"

"Kira's…remembering. Her mother…dying on a Cleric's sword. Aiee!" Mabatan lurches up from her crouch and darts forward, her arms and legs slashing the empty air. When Roan rushes to stop her, she steps confidently on her left leg and kicks him smartly in the chest with her right.

Leaping out of the brush, Kira slices off the Cleric's arm before he even sees her. His sword clatters to the ground and she finishes him, hissing at the mother and child, "Flee!"

The innocents scramble down the road and Kira attacks the other three Clerics but they're ready for her, encircling her and warding off her blows. Kira aims low at the closest one, hitting the Cleric behind the leg. As he goes down, she whirls, taking out the second. That leaves one, the biggest of the group. She bears down hard, testing his strength, and he easily repels the blow. This one's good, but not good enough. She pivots, kicking him in the chest and takes him out with a perfect sword thrust.

Something hits her hard on the head, flashing light behind her eyes. Blood pours down her face and she staggers, turning to ward off the next blow. It's the smuggler, a bloody rock in his hand, grinning. "Sorry, but you have no idea how high a price I can get for you."

He's flickering in and out of view; she's losing consciousness. But as he raises the rock for another blow, she sinks her blade into his stomach. His scream rings in her ears, then all is silent.

Mabatan feels the soft pillow below her head, the scent of aromatic herbs. She opens her eyes to find Ende blowing on the herb burner.

"Ende. Kira lives."

Lips drawn tight, Ende nods once in acknowledgment of Mabatan's news. "You need rest, Mabatan. Sleep."

Too weak to protest, Mabatan sinks into her pillow just

as Lumpy appears. "I was out helping build the stables."

"I am fine."

"Yeah. I can see that." Sitting at her bedside, Lumpy takes her hand. "You sure knocked the wind out of Roan." He glances over at Ende, no doubt trying to determine the severity of what's happened.

Squeezing his hand, Mabatan answers his unasked question. "Kira was betrayed by the smuggler."

"I knew it," Lumpy moans.

"He was just waiting for his moment. I think she killed him. She killed them all—" Mabatan stiffens. "Where am I?" She gasps. Her eyes narrow and she speaks menacingly with Kira's voice. "Stay back or die."

Kira's sitting at the side of the road. Her head throbs. She's surrounded by Hhroxhi warriors, fangs bared. She can hear hoofbeats in the distance, moving quickly toward them.

One of the warriors reaches for her, and Kira pushes herself back, grasping her sword and trying to focus her vision. "You want it? Come and get it."

The Hhroxhi's face strains, and curling its lips around its sharp fangs, it struggles to make a sound. "Frehhhnnnd."

"What?" Kira asks, doubting what she's hearing. "Friend? Did you say, friend?"

The thundering horses are almost upon them. With red eyes riveted on Kira, the Hhroxhi tries again. "Llllummpeee. Frehhhnd."

"Lumpy's your friend?"

The girl nods. "Lllumpee."

"Mhyzah?"

Mhyzah anxiously motions for Kira to follow her companions down through a hidden hole.

Extending a hand to Mhyzah, Kira rolls her eyes. "Why does it have to be tunnels?" *Putting her feet down the hole, she slides into pitch darkness, hoping for the best.*

Roan's at her bedside now as well, one hand on Lumpy's shoulder, both their faces so filled with concern it's nearly enough to make Mabatan smile. Still, she looks beyond them to Ende. "Mhyzah found Kira and has taken her into the thrusalls."

The Apsara matriarch sighs with relief.

Mabatan turns back to Lumpy, and lifting an eyebrow, asks, "When did you teach Mhyzah our language?"

Roan raises an eyebrow. "You gave Mhyzah *English lessons?*"

Lumpy stares at his feet. "Just a couple of words."

"Yes. Friend and Lumpy," Mabatan grins as Roan gives Lumpy a teasing poke.

"I thought they might come in handy."

"Lumpy." Ende turns from her balms and ointments. "Your work as Gyoxhip has saved Kira's life. Thank you."

It's almost worth the ache in Mabatan's head to see Lumpy beam.

Cries of "Time, time, time!" greet Roan and Lumpy as they round the corner to the laboratory.

"Time is vastly overrated."

"Overemphasized."

Roan steps into the converted day room, already chaotic with dozens of books strewn amongst beakers and suspended enablers that shimmer with fluctuating light. "Greetings, doctors. What's the breakthrough?"

The physicians twitter nervously. "Oh. Well. We *have* made progress."

"Inroads," says Imin.

"Advances," adds Othard. Then looking uneasily at Imin, he mutters, "However…"

"…that is not why…"

"…we sent for you."

"Last night…" says Imin.

"…we were visited…"

"…in our dreams…"

"…by the mountain lion…"

"…Sari."

Even the sound of her name makes Roan uneasy. "What did she want?"

"We're to meet in the Dreamfield safe place at the next new moon."

"It was a command…"

"…sent to all Dirt Eaters."

"A summoning."

"And how…" says Roan, scrutinizing every eye movement, every twitch, every flick of their faces, "…did you reply?"

"We couldn't."

"No Dirt in our bodies anymore, you see…"

"…no way to respond…"

"She can't even know if she's reached us…"

"…but we heard her and she…"

"…she said…"

"The time has come for action!" they blurt out together.

Roan's silent, trying to understand exactly what that means.

"So," Lumpy frowns. "What do you think the Dirt Eaters are up to?"

"We don't know…"

"…but it can't be good."

"They haven't got much of an army, but it's well trained—like Lelbit was. They could be a pretty big thorn in our side… if it's us they're after."

The doctors and Lumpy turn to Roan, obviously seeking his opinion. The doctors, however, soon stare discomfited at their feet and Roan knows his dismay must be written all over his face.

"We can't be trusted anymore," says Imin.

"We understand," adds Othard dejectedly.

"No! I trust *you*. It's the Dirt Eaters I don't trust. I just wish…well, that Sari'd been clearer, that we knew more. If you dream anything else, you'll be sure to tell us?"

"Absolutely!"

"Without question!"

"We will honor your trust, Roan of Longlight."

Nodding, Roan turns to go, but Lumpy holds his ground, catching the attention of the physicians.

"Yes?" Imin asks, eyes flitting nervously from Lumpy to Roan.

"Have you found anything that can help Mabatan filter Kira's experiences?"

Shaking their heads, the physicians let out a frustrated sigh. "Not yet."

"It's going to be a bit slower now that Algie's with the Gunthers," explains Imin.

"Working on that Allayer," adds Othard. "Not that what he's doing isn't important, but…"

"…when he can be spared…"

"…we could use his help…"

"…we're just doctors…"

"…and the technology is…"

"…sophisticated…"

"…if we knew more…"

"…but we don't."

"Sorry," Imin says, looking sadly at Lumpy.

Lumpy pats both doctors on the back. "It's alright, I know you're working hard. Thank you."

Feeling a little sheepish at not having asked about Mabatan himself, Roan follows his friend out of the laboratory. Despite Mabatan's assurances, Roan can see that the connection with Kira isn't getting any easier for her. Not only is she having trouble meeting the simple demands of her own life, like eating and walking from one place to another without getting hurt, but Lumpy's said her headaches are getting worse. Whether that's from the enabler itself or having to share Kira's experiences—the smuggler's blow to the head couldn't have helped—it's impossible to tell. And Roan feels as least partially responsible. "…Lumpy…it was me who asked Algie to work with the Gunthers."

"I know. I've talked to them. You were right. We're paralyzed until we find something to repel the Apogee. That's the priority. It's just…a year ago things were a lot clearer. We'd be helping our friend, not feeling horrible that other things are more important than…"

Roan knows the look on Lumpy's face. It comes with the knowledge that no matter what you choose, somebody's going to get hurt. "I wish it didn't have to be this way either."

By the time they arrive at the library and its door shuts behind them, Roan has a sense they've left a part of themselves behind. A part they might never recover.

As they walk down the stairs, Gunther Number Seventy-

Nine runs up to Roan, waving a piece of paper. "Roan of Longlight, Algernon left me with this section of the journal to decipher and I—"

"Read it to me!" says Roan, eagerly.

She brings the paper close to her eyes and reads. *"Now it is time to tell you of the ring. I have burdened you and your sister with a great responsibility; the ring is my one gift. I have left it with Steppe. She will pass it on to her daughter, who will see that you receive it."*

Roan rubs his half of the badger ring with the tip of his thumb. "Go on," he urges.

"The badger is known for its tenacity and ability to survive. It can be helpful to you in many ways. By now, you and your sister should be linked to the ring and through it to each other. You see, despite its being broken, it retains the desire to make itself whole and that can be very useful indeed. To explain..."

the primary's interrogation

use what your enemy seeks as your shield, and
withdraw all else to the core. an enemy will
rarely look past what you appear to value if they
desire it as well.

— the way of the wazya

STOWE IS BEING ESCORTED TO A FITTING BY TWO CLERICS when her body begins to shake uncontrollably. *Willum!* The call is sent before she has time to censor it.

What is it?

I don't know. The Clerics walking on either side of her do not appear to notice the convulsions that are tearing her apart. She glances anxiously around, trying to think of a way to stall them without arousing any suspicion, but waves of nausea are preventing her from connecting one thought with another. Willum appears before her just as she feels her knees give way.

"Our Stowe has been summoned," he says, and without any explanation whatsoever, his arm glides under hers. Supporting almost all her weight, he whisks her down the corridor out of the Clerics' sight.

"I need to go to my room," she whispers, barely able to shape the words.

Indicating that Willum should join her, she shuts the door behind them. Holding up her hand, she shows Willum the half-ring. It's glowing: she can see the path of its energy as it surges through her bones, down her spine, pulling her, pulling her.

Willum lifts her into his arms. *It's alright. I'll watch over you.* And slipping from her skin, Stowe is drawn away.

A DELUGE OF FLAMING STONES PLUMMETS TOWARD HER AND SHE DUCKS. INCHES FROM HER FACE, THEY EXPLODE, SOMEHOW LEAVING HER UNSCATHED. ONE COLLISION AFTER ANOTHER DEFINES THE INVISIBLE BUBBLE THAT SURROUNDS HER. THE SLATE FLOOR SHE'S STANDING ON TREMBLES. THE AIR IN FRONT OF HER SHIMMERS AND ROAN APPEARS. HE FLINCHES AT THE ONSLAUGHT OF FIERY ROCK, THEN, SEEMINGLY UNPERTURBED, HE TURNS TO FACE HER.

"YOU KNOW WHERE WE ARE?" STOWE ASKS, CONFUSED. "IT FEELS FAMILIAR, BUT I DON'T REMEMBER EVER BEING HERE."

"I HAVE. WITH RAT. IT'S A SAFE PLACE."

"AND WHY EXACTLY ARE WE HERE NOW?"

"A NEW SECTION OF OUR GREAT-GRANDFATHER'S JOURNAL'S BEEN DECIPHERED. IT'S ABOUT THE RING, THE THINGS IT CAN DO."

"WHAT? LIKE UNPLEASANT TRAVEL TO EQUALLY UNPLEASANT PLACES?" STOWE GRUMBLES.

"DON'T YOU SEE? WE CAN CALL ON EACH OTHER. MEET SAFELY HERE. EXCHANGE INFORMATION. YOU HAVE TO ADMIT IT'S USEFUL."

"AND DANGEROUS. I ALMOST COLLAPSED IN THE CORRIDORS OF POWER. IT WAS LUCKY WILLUM WAS CLOSE BY. WE ARE TRYING NOT TO ATTRACT TOO MUCH ATTENTION TO OURSELVES."

"TRUE. OUR GREAT-GRANDFATHER SUSPECTED THESE MEETINGS MIGHT HAVE TO BE QUICK. SO, NOT ONLY CAN THE RING BRING US TOGETHER, HE SAYS IT CAN ALLOW US TO SHARE OUR MEMORIES INSTANTLY. WANT TO TRY?"

"Do I have a choice!" Stowe says dramatically, oddly pleased when her brother smiles back.

Holding up his hand, Roan exposes his half of the ring to her. "Put yours against mine."

Touching her half-ring to his, she cries out. It is as if she is catapulting through a minotaur's open chest, Roan's memories becoming her own as they pass through his half-ring into hers. It takes all her concentration to simultaneously access her experiences at Co-operation Unlimited and offer them to Roan, but once there she feels the force of what she remembers—the vapor being drawn out by the enabler and then fed somehow to Darius's Throne, her own struggle to escape destruction—being drawn from her in a flash.

The exchange completed, she drops her hand, looking wryly at her ever earnest brother.

"So. You get to kill a god. Any idea why?"

"None. Well...maybe...a month or so ago, I had this vision..."

"Do you see the future? Willum sees the future. He doesn't like it much. I haven't had a real vision yet. What's it—"

"Stowe!"

"Sorry. It's exciting, is all. Please. Tell me your vision."

"I sacrificed a bull and its blood healed the Novakin. So now I can't help thinking killing the Friend is somehow related to saving the children. But how I'm supposed to do it, I don't know. Any ideas?"

"Afraid not. If it makes you feel any better, we don't know how we're going to stop Darius either."

"I suppose trying to contact the Overshadower to let him know he's being cheated is out of the question."

"Willum and I haven't ruled that out. We're planning to go and explore. There might be a way to expose Darius in the real world too. We're thinking maybe Master Querin is planning a coup. He's twice as clever as Darius, just as terrifying, and he is hiding something."

"Stowe...I..." Roan stares at her. She knows he's about to tell her to be careful and she gets more than enough of that from Willum.

"If I find out anything about killing a god along the way, I'll let you know. But...about the next time you want to talk...can we find a way to warn each other? It'll look suspicious if I go around fainting every two minutes."

"Sorry," Roan says, and the worry in his voice is almost more than she can bear. "In the journal it says our life-force is connected through the ring. We should be able to let each other know if there's something important to share, thinking about something familiar, that we both feel strongly about. Something from home... what about the Big Empty? The day we carved our names in the top."

"Maybe I think about that too often already," Stowe says.

Her brother reaches out to her. "Stowe, the Dirt Eaters are planning something. We don't know what..."

But she's already dissolving back into her world. Away from the past. And a brother who always makes her want to cry. And she can't cry. Not now. Maybe not ever.

Willum is sitting on the chair close to her. The sight of him fills her with a comforting warmth. She is about to speak when he puts his finger to her lips. *Careful.*

The ring took me to Roan. We were able to share what we've learnt.
Good.

The Friend wants Roan to kill him.

She has barely time to enjoy the look of shock on Willum's face when a sharp rap demands their attention.

"Yes?" Stowe brusquely shouts.

The Cleric's reedy voice whistles on the other side of the door. "The Archbishop requests the presence of Our Stowe and her Primary."

Stowe gives Willum a frightened look. *Could he know? Sense my absence? Did the Clerics—*

Assume nothing. Keep your mind clear and ready. Do not reveal yourself.

Willum rises slowly, his demeanor solemn. He holds out his hand. Stowe takes it and he draws her up. Just as they reach the door, she stops, pocketing the half-ring. Willum places a reassuring hand on the small of her back as the door slides open. Repressing her anxieties, Stowe nods benignly and the two clerics lead the way.

Darius is alone. A bag of fluid suspended over his head slowly drips into his carotid artery, an attempt to replenish the cells in his withered body.

Hiding behind a daughter's empathy, Stowe allows a bit of her own despair to color her words. "Oh, Father, what are they doing to you now?"

But Darius's smile is dangerous and razor sharp. "You know these doctors, Daughter, always finding work for themselves." He motions her and Willum to sit on the high-backed chairs across from him. "I had the most interesting visit today with Master Fortin. Bit of a toad, don't you think?"

Stowe laughs. "You are wicked, Father," she says, attempting to cajole, "but he does seem to be doing an excellent job."

"He was most impressed with your speech, my love. He found it terribly... provocative." His eyes flit across her face.

"How so, Father?" she asks ingenuously.

But his gaze shifts away from her. Onto Willum.

"Fortin's concerns, though, seem mostly to center around your Primary."

Willum looks back at him guilelessly. "How might I best respond to them, Eldest?"

"I'm not sure, Willum. Fortin seemed to wonder whether you might not be abusing your position."

"I have always been your servant, Archbishop."

"Have you really?" Darius's eyes narrow and Stowe is almost blinded by the stream of smalt green light that slices from them directly into Willum's chest.

Willum's knees buckle and he falls to the floor. Stowe wants to cry out, hurl a scream at the ancient man, but she feels pressure around her, holding her back. Who is stopping her, Willum or Darius? She concentrates on the barrier. Willum. It's Willum. Keeping her from exposing herself. Dutifully she relaxes, and attempts to watch with appropriate detachment.

Stowe's amazed that Willum is doing nothing to defend himself. His body convulses again and again as Darius scythes through his mind. Unable to sit back and watch, she rides the intense beam of light, following Darius on his search into Willum's memory.

Master Fortin's agitated face comes into view. *Is Darius planning to retire? To hand over the Conurbation to that girl?*

Our Stowe is his daughter.

Some of us have served the Conurbation for three-quarters of a century.

Yes, but we are, none of us, indispensable.

Darius abruptly releases Willum, leaving him an unconscious heap on the floor.

"He is lucky his mind is weak. Had he the skill to resist me, there would be nothing left of him." Darius sneers. Rising to place his withered hand on Stowe's shoulder, he laughs. "Come, come, Darling, don't pout. He's a mere Primary, easily replaced. Besides, you're becoming too old and too strong to be attached to playthings."

Stowe has to tighten every muscle in her chest and abdomen to keep from throwing herself on Willum. She wants to listen to his pulse, cry out to whatever life may remain inside him. "You are the only person in my world who truly matters, Father. Still, he was a useful toy. So helpful. I was hoping he'd facilitate my search for Roan and the children."

Darius's pale eyes look dully at the crumpled man lying at his feet. "A point, my love. But, I promise you, should he not survive, we'll find you another able companion." Smiling venomously, he cups his skeletal hand under her chin. "Would that satisfy you?"

"Yes, Father," she says, forcing her eyes to smile, the corners of her lips to curl upward. "That will do."

"Come!" Darius calls out and a Cleric promptly opens the door and awaits his command. "Take Stowe's Primary to the hospital. See if he can be resuscitated. If not, instruct them to salvage every part. He's an excellent specimen." The Eldest pulls the intravenous drip closer. "I suppose I shouldn't have exerted myself. I must rest now, Daughter, but I'd like you to dine with me four days hence. I'll see to it your favorites are on the menu. After dessert we will receive a visit from Governor Pollard. I'm interested in what you might think of him."

"Me? I haven't any experience with Farlands politicians," Stowe says humbly.

"Exactly my point. It's time you took an interest in matters of state, my sweet. I need you to accept more responsibility in these areas."

Anxious to leave, Stowe stands up and bows. "Of course. I am always delighted to have the opportunity to share time with you, Father."

No sooner has she closed the door than she rushes down the corridor, doing her utmost not to stumble, not to betray herself. She has to stay with Willum's body, stop the doctors from jumping to conclusions, until she's had time to think. How could he let this happen? How? It seems so impossible. If Willum dies, she will kill Darius. Kill him. And then she will kill herself.

masks

IN THE aftermath of THE PLAGUE ENDE VOWED THAT THE
APSARA WOULD NEVER AGAIN BE TAKEN BY SURPRISE. AND
SO SHE BEGAN THE PRACTICE of STRATEGIC MARRIAGES.
NONE WERE FORCED BUT few REFUSED THE CALL AND BY
THE TIME of HER DEATH, THE APSARA HAD BECOME a
GREAT, IF SECRET, POWER.

—ORIN'S HISTORY of THE APSARA

"LAY HER BACK DOWN!" orders Ende, putting one hand under Mabatan's head and another on her forehead.

Mabatan gasps, "Can't breathe….tunnels!"

"Mabatan. The fear is Kira's. Kira's mother saved her by hiding her in a crawlspace under the floor. She has a fear of enclosed spaces. That is Kira. You are Mabatan. You have no such fear. Smell the earth. Let your own blood speak to you. Mabatan. The fear is Kira's…"

Roan watches Mabatan breathe deeply, steadying her pounding heart. For the whole day he's drifted in and out of this room, waiting for her ordeal to end. Lumpy's guess is that Mhyzah is taking Kira right into the City. Roan's sure the physical demands of pulling herself along the thrusalls of the Hhroxhi are helping Kira manage her fear. Mabatan, on the other hand, is blinded by Kira's nightmarish memories and has no option but to wait the experience out.

As sweat pours down Mabatan's face, a weight settles behind Roan's eyes. The Roan who'd traveled with Mabatan through a jungle of Skree would've ordered her enabler removed in a second, but the Roan who's seeking a way to defeat the City can't. All day long he's stood at a distance despairing over her pain and hating himself for not stopping it.

He forces himself to step forward and as he does, his cricket leaps from the edge of his pocket onto Mabatan's cot, almost as if it's been waiting for Roan to take that step. He stares in amazement as, one after another, crickets appear until they blanket his endangered friend, singing.

Ende reaches up, touching his arm. "Look to what we can change. You listen well, Roan of Longlight." She motions for Roan to take her place at Mabatan's side.

Mabatan draws him so close he can feel the warmth of her breath. "It's over. We've arrived."

Kira raises her arms over her head and stretches. They seem to be in some kind of massive ventilation system, and it's good to feel the wind and the space. Mhyzah's placed her earhole against a metal circle in the wall. Slipping her hands through a pair of handles, she rotates the disk and pushes it open. As a bright light spills into the chamber she signals Kira to pass through.

A dozen Gunthers, all dressed in bright orange work clothes, are standing behind a wall of glass. There is an egg-shaped object on the floor in front of Kira. A tall, scrawny Gunther, one arm in a sling, is pointing something at the egg.

Kira smiles disarmingly at him. "I am Kira of the Apsara. I know you weren't expecting me to come this way, but there were complications."

For a moment, the Gunther appears to relax, and lowers his hand. "According to the message, you were to be brought by a smuggler to the safe house, not to the air purification facility."

"I was attacked. The smuggler...died. The Hhroxhi brought me here instead."

"Hhroxhi?" The Gunther quickly raises his hand again as Mhyzah appears.

"Wait, wait!" Kira shouts. "Don't do anything rash."

The Gunther peers at Mhyzah through his thick lenses. "How do you know about this place? How did you get in?"

Mhyzah clicks and hisses. The Gunther's eyes flick back and forth rapidly behind his lenses. "Her name is...Mm...Mzaza. I think. She says, that the Hhroxhi...are offering help...with... the war? Is there going to be a war? Now?"

The Gunthers behind the wall of glass tap anxiously on its surface, then bend their heads together in agitated conversation. A few moments later the youngest of the Gunthers approaches them. "I am Gunther Number Eleven. Due to the alteration in your plan, I have been appointed your liaison."

Following closely behind him, the Hhroxhi interpreter makes some tentative clicks. Mhyzah replies, and he announces, "She has agreed."

The Gunthers behind the glass chatter excitedly: "A new lexicon." "Such a complex grammatical structure." "Greater comprehension might illuminate some of the histories."

Clearing his throat to get their attention, the Hhroxhi interpreter adds, "At some future date."

Kira suppresses a smile as the Gunthers grumble. Standing beside her, Mhyzah says, "Friend." Holding up four fingers, she hisses something further to the Gunther.

"She says she'll come back to this spot for you in four days."

Kira smiles at the Hhroxhi. "Thank you for saving my life."

Mhyzah puts her open palm on Kira's sternum. "Friend," she says, and vanishes into the hole.

The Gunthers quickly seal it and Number Eleven turns to Kira. "Have you ever worn glasses?"

When Roan and Lumpy burst into Algernon's office, Number Seventy-Nine and Dobbs look up blearily from the blueprints they've been working on.

"Are they ready?" Roan asks.

"Kira is almost at the munitions factory," Lumpy adds urgently.

As he rolls up the schematics in front of him, Dobbs takes a sidelong glance at Number Seventy-Nine, who's nodding vigorously. "Ah...is it alright if Gwendolen—"

Number Seventy-Nine turns bright red.

"Oh, sorry, I'm an idiot!" Dobbs sputters, smacking himself on the head.

Algernon walks over to the young girl and puts an arm around her shoulder. "Her delightful new name is a secret. Please don't let the other Gunthers know."

Smiling broadly, Roan and Lumpy nod in agreement.

Still blushing, Number Seventy-Nine pats awkwardly at the Storyteller's large back. "Do not worry, Dobbs. I think Roan of Longlight and his Lieutenant can be trusted."

"If you say so, Seventy-Nine," Dobbs says, looking at her shyly. Then turning to Roan, he continues, "Anyway, as I was about to ask...can Gwendolen join us? These blueprints are still a little confusing to me."

Lumpy looks at Seventy-Nine, concerned. "Gwendolen, are you sure? I don't want to get you in trouble with the other Gunthers. If they see you there, they might be angry that you're helping us."

"There, there, not to fret," Algernon places a folded-up piece of paper in Gwendolen's hands. "Take this—if you're caught by surprise in there, just say you're carrying a message from me."

"Alright?" asks Roan anxiously. "Come on, we'd better hurry."

Kira pushes a cart down a busy walkway, Number Eleven beside her. Her orange overalls are comfortable, if a little bright. The glasses, though, obscure her vision and make her feel irrationally vulnerable. As they move down the street, people give them a wide berth and Kira does not miss the sneers of the passersby. "I thought Stowe ordered your acceptance."

"Things have improved greatly," Number Eleven replies congenially. "We have all been released from prison, hardly anyone drops heavy objects on us from windows, and I have not been spat upon in over two days."

"Terrific."

"And we have been given these practical uniforms to wear so that our ongoing contribution to the Conurbation is better recognized."

"We do stand out," Kira acknowledges wryly.

"Stare at the back of your glasses. Let me answer the questions."

They hold up their security passes, and once they're scanned, the gate opens. But when Kira pushes her cart through, one of the Clerics stops her.

"I haven't seen you before."

Kira stares at the back of her glasses as instructed.

"Gunther Number Forty-Eight has been reassigned from Sewage."

"Well, that's a step up," says the Cleric, leering. "I've never seen a Gunther grow so... large."

Kira bites her tongue, determined to be well behaved. There are, she supposes, certain advantages to knowing Mabatan is reporting on her every action.

"We have great variation in height, weight, color——" Number Eleven seems all too eager to expound on Gunther statistics.

"Yes. Yes. Move along," orders one of the less interested Clerics, shoving Kira's interrogator aside.

But Kira can feel him eyeing her from behind. He makes no attempt to hide his sniggering. She grips the handles of her cart more tightly. She'd like to teach that bottom feeder a thing or two, but she has bigger fish to fry and silently scuffles forward.

"Fourth floor," Mabatan reports. "Two guards: enabled. Workers: enabled. Twelve guards watching from a catwalk. Apogee. Situation much like Stowe described at the enabler factory. Lots of men and women in laboratory coats. Kira thinks this disguise would be the best way to gain access."

"Where's the power source?" Ende asks, scanning the blueprints.

"Here," says Seventy-Nine, tracing the path for Ende.

"Eleven is taking her to a utility room. Accompanied by two Clerics."

"Clerics armed with deadly weapons, accompanying you everywhere. How do we overcome that kind of obstacle?" asks Lumpy glumly.

"I know a few who would jump at the chance." Ende sounds almost gleeful.

"Kira thinks seven Apsara will be enough."

Roan edges alongside Ende to look at the blueprint. "It would be nice to minimize the risk, though."

"Of course, Roan of Longlight," Ende says with a smile. "If only your Lieutenant would speed along that Allayer."

"We're almost there," Lumpy says, shaking off his gloom. "In fact, we should be getting a report any—"

As if on cue, Gunther Number Fifty-One rushes in, making way for Sixty-Seven and Thirty-Three. "We have a prototype," he announces proudly as Number Thirty-Three arranges what appears to be a large shoe on the table and starts fiddling with the wires inside it. "The Allayer!"

"It looks like a shoe," says Lumpy.

"It was a shoe," says Thirty-Three, as it begins to hum.

Fifty-One glares at Gwendolen. "What are you doing here, Number Seventy-Nine?"

Gwendolen flashes the piece of paper Algie gave her. "Making a delivery."

"Well, deliver it then, and return to your work." Having dismissed her, Fifty-One signals Thirty-Three to continue.

"The Allayer emits a limbic frequency that will disrupt the Apogee's transmission with a range of—"

Mabatan gasps.

"What's wrong?" asks Roan, rushing to her.

Shaking her head, Mabatan shrugs. "I don't know. I've lost contact with Kira."

"Turn it off!" orders Roan.

Thirty-Three quickly obeys, and Mabatan smiles. "I am with her once more."

The Gunthers crowd around Mabatan, closely examining the enabler behind her ear. "It would seem," says Fifty-One, "that we may have discovered an ancillary use for our device."

After gently shooing them away from Mabatan, Ende takes a closer look at the Allayer. "You mean this thing can also disrupt enablers?"

Thirty-Three, already scratching notes on the edges of one of Dobbs's blueprints, mutters excitedly, "Hypothetically. Of course, Mabatan's enabler has been modified. But we might be able to design something to specifically target Conurbation enablers."

Joining the crowd behind the Gunther, Roan examines Thirty-Three's diagram and equations. The potential of the device is evident—the question is how to use it.

Roan shares an optimistic silence with Lumpy and Ende

as the Gunthers chatter away all at once: "An interesting problem." "We will have to pursue it." "We doubt the effect would be permanent." "But for a short duration." "During which they could be modified." "We think maybe, yes."

Eager to set to work on this new possibility, the Gunthers carefully gather up their Allayer as Thirty-Three and Lumpy try to separate the Gunther's newly made diagram and equations from Dobbs's grid with the least amount of damage to both.

Roan turns, thinking to sit by Mabatan. But Dobbs is already there, taking notes on Kira's path with one hand, while his other wraps encouragingly around both of Mabatan's.

Roan's spent the last couple of days with Wolf and Ende, devising strategies that would use the Allayer—presuming it would work in all the ways the Gunthers have promised— and it's getting harder and harder to keep his mind from wandering. Kamyar, true to his word, has been drumming up support throughout the Farlands and Roan is desperate to get out and see all the new recruits Stinger's training. He'd settle for a workout with the Apsara...even shoveling horse dung in the stables would be a welcome break.

As if sitting cooped up for two days in a stuffy chamber having to do nothing but talk isn't frustrating enough, Wolf has taken to calling him Prophet. As Roan listens to his Captain's plan for the final assault on the City, he's wondering if there's a polite way to get Wolf to stop being so... reverent.

"Prophet, our greatest obstacle is synchronizing our actions with the Apsara's sabotages in the City."

Catching a glint of the warrior's hook-sword, Roan

suddenly recalls the vision he had of Wolf, as a young man, watching his father fashion their crescent moon blades. Just that morning, Dobbs announced that an eclipse of the sun was coming. In an eclipse, the moon would diminish the sun until all that was left before darkness would be a...crescent. That was it.

"A crescent, Brother Wolf, that will be the signal. The Friend will pull the sun behind the moon until all that is left is a crescent of light. When even that disappears, we move under the cover of the Friend's darkness."

Wolf hangs his head awestruck. "Blessed be the hand of the Friend."

Roan bows his head as well, hoping the warrior will not ask when the Friend imparted this information. Just as Wolf's about to speak, Lumpy sticks his head round the doorway. "It works."

"The one for the enablers as well?"

"That's so small it'll fit in your hand. And they're finishing your Allayer as we speak."

"So," Roan says eagerly. "We ride out at dawn tomorrow. And put them both to the test."

"Yes," Wolf agrees. "And pray for all our sakes that the Gunthers are as clever as your Lieutenant believes them to be."

The cold winter air biting his face, Roan heads into the rising sun, a small group of Brothers led by Wolf at his side.

A series of whistles from the Brother riding point puts them instantly on guard.

"One vehicle, one Apogee, nine Clerics—six on horseback," says Wolf. "Perfect."

Roan signals the Brother with the Allayer while Wolf

directs a three-point assault. Coming up over the rise, the Brothers gallop straight for the approaching vehicle. Confident in their weapon, the Clerics don't even bother to counter the approaching warriors. Two Blue Robes aim the Apogee. Not only does their instrument of death have no effect, but the men controlling it are looking confused and disoriented. The remaining Clerics charge at the Brothers, but too late. The Brothers are already upon them, taking them captive.

Wolf had asked "the Prophet" to stay back, but when one of the Clerics manages to escape the fray, Roan feels compelled to act. If news of the Allayer were to reach Darius, they could lose their advantage. Driving his mount alongside his opponent's, he slides his body to one side of his saddle and kicks the man off his horse. To his surprise, the Cleric does not turn to face him but runs. Riding behind, Roan leaps on top of him and pins him to the ground. Taking the cloth Ende gave him, Roan presses it over the squirming Cleric's mouth and nose.

Dragging his captive over to the others, Roan ignores Wolf's disapproving frown and activates his device. The hand-sized box has two purposes: to erase all memory of the Brothers' attack and to stop the Clerics' enablers at a pre-arranged time—Dobbs's eclipse.

The confusion suffered by the Clerics within the Allayer's range confirms that if they can modify enough enablers, they might be able to incapacitate the Clerics long enough to even up the odds. It had been difficult to convince Wolf that they should not kill all the Clerics that fell into their hands, but Roan did not hesitate to press his advantage as "Prophet."

Finished with the final Cleric, Roan heads over to the

Apogee. Within moments of making the adjustments taught to him by Fifty-one, the weapon starts to smoke, then bursts into flames.

Wolf shakes his head. "A weapon of that power would greatly help our cause."

"We've stopped it, that's enough."

For a moment, the look on Wolf's face is not so reverent, but the Brothers' Captain soon recovers. "I'll send someone back to let your Lieutenant and Ende know of the Allayer's success and that they can proceed as planned. Then..." Wolf pauses. He hasn't been enthusiastic about this part of the plan, but traveling across the Farlands quickly and invisibly is difficult to argue against. "...through the Hhroxhi tunnels to Governor Selig."

And his mysterious wife, thinks Roan, as Wolf strides away with a grunt. He hopes she's able to accomplish all that Ende promised. Though, remembering the woman's firm grip on the Governor's shoulder, he doesn't know why he has any doubts.

By sunset, they are looking out at Armstrong, capital of the southern territory. Surrounded by high rock walls with towers crenellated like the fortresses of long ago, it is impressive indeed. Governor Selig is much more powerful than he appeared at the Council. No army of raiders to protect him, but by Ende's account, a number of his courtiers are well trained in arms—many unknowingly wed to Apsara warriors—all ready to act if necessary.

As the Governor had expected, as soon as the Brothers started raiding the caravans, Darius had sent out Clerics—armies of them. Selig had arranged for a gathering of them here tonight, in honor of the Archbishop's generosity and the return of our Stowe.

The Brothers, disguised as a modest contingent of her acolytes, draw up their hoods and make their way through the fortress's front gates. Welcomed in, they glide, heads bowed, in slow procession, surreptitiously counting the numerous Clerics stalking the streets. Roan knocks twice at the scullery door of the Governor's palace and it soon opens. After bowing reverentially, a maid whisks them inside where preparations for a huge banquet are taking place. Seated in a far recess of the enormous kitchen, the "monks" are fed and in exchange, pictures of Our Stowe are doled out to the kitchen staff.

When the Governor's wife comes down to check on the chef's progress, she is accompanied by a Cleric who observes carefully as each dish is smelled and tasted. After one of the cooks directs her mistress's attention to the monks, the incognito Apsara sweeps over gracefully to greet the acolytes, Cleric in tow.

Placing a hand on Roan's shoulder, she takes her measure of the table. "How fortunate we are to be graced with your presence at such an opportune time."

"All times are opportune for the celebration of Our Stowe."

"Of course. We are always prepared to be guided by her love. Perhaps tonight? Might I convince you to lead our guests in prayer?"

"We live in the service of Our Stowe."

Just then, an elderly man, clearly pushed to the limit, struggles through the bustling kitchen to bow before the Governor's wife. "Your Excellency, I have received word that another fifty of the Archbishop's men are arriving from the northern territory."

"Wonderful! In time for our celebration?"

"I believe so."

"Dona! Patino!" she calls out to the cooks. "Make preparations for an extra fifty guests!" Obviously impatient to continue her supervision of the banquet room, she addresses the Cleric at her side. "Father Mathias, shall we? There is still much to—"

But Father Mathias, having somehow managed to single out Wolf, interrupts her. "Why do these monks hide their faces even in your kitchens?"

Roan's eyes dart to the Governor's wife but she appears devoid of any trace of unease. "Why, Father Mathias, I do not concern myself with the devotions of monks."

"Perhaps this one might cough me up an answer," the Cleric snarls, both hands coming down heavily on Wolf's shoulders.

Roan is about to intervene when Wolf reaches up—and slips off his hood. Eyes lowered to the Cleric, he answers. "We hide nothing, Father. The clamor of the kitchen distracts us from prayer."

"What? Are all of you so poorly trained that a little noise distracts you?" The Cleric scrutinizes Wolf's dark eyes, bald pate and grizzled face. "You seem awfully robust for a holy man."

"I was a farmer. Then Our Stowe cast her light upon me."

The Cleric smiles. "As she has done to us all. All love to Our Stowe."

"All love," the monks humbly reply.

"Farlands converts. We should have sent to the City,

Excellency, for a more elevated group. I doubt that these have great skill with prayers. Their voices——"

"Father Mathias," the Governor's wife says, leading the Cleric out the door, "we are all inglorious before Our Stowe. I am sure the humility of these monks will prove illuminating."

Roan can see Wolf release his grip on his hook-sword. "Thanks be to Our Stowe," he growls.

"She watches over us all," Roan agrees with a relieved smile.

When they finally find themselves at a small table in a corner of the banquet room, Roan is startled by what Governor Selig has achieved. The hall is packed with Clerics—by Roan's count, two hundred and fourteen.

As the servers bring platters of meat and vegetables to the tables, the Governor rises to make a toast. "As you all well know, these are perilous times. Attacks from those despicable renegades, the Brothers, have decimated three of my most heavily laden caravans. We are indebted to you all for coming so quickly to our aid. This disruption in trade threatens the City itself and it must be stopped. Provinces come and go but the City must always stand!"

"To the City! To the Archbishop! To Our Stowe!" thunder the Clerics.

The Governor raises his glass and drinks. As do all of his guests—apart from the monks, who are sworn to abstinence.

"Your courage and devotion will secure the trade routes and keep the scourge in check. Our caravans will run again, thanks to your watchful presence and," he pauses with twinkling eyes, "that fabulous new weapon of yours. The Brothers bow before it—literally!" He snorts, and the Clerics erupt in laughter. But just as quickly they fall silent, every Cleric looking forward, a blank expression on each face.

The Governor's wife tilts her head slightly. "Will the monks come forward for the blessing?"

As she rises to escort the monks, the old man at her side directs the reluctant staff. Roan can hear him whispering, "Won't be the first blessing you've missed. They'll have this polished off in no time. And who's to answer if the dessert's not ready and waiting? Me. So out! Out!"

"I suggest you work quickly," the Apsara whispers as she reaches Roan. "The hypnotic I administered will last a half hour, no more."

"Secure the doors," Wolf orders as Roan and four other Brothers throw back their hoods and begin methodically modifying the Clerics' enablers.

Halfway into the room, Roan comes to the Cleric who questioned them in the kitchen. Roan can't help but smile as he presses the box against Father Mathias's neck. His wrist, however, is almost wrenched out of its socket when the Cleric bolts up and puts a knife to his throat.

Wolf reaches for his blade, but the Cleric presses the knife hard into Roan's skin, drawing blood, and the Brothers all stand back.

"One move and he's dead. What is this machine?"

"Let me go and I'll show you," Roan says calmly.

But Father Mathias is not about to loosen his grip. "Darius shall be pleased to find his suspicions of the Governor justified, Excellencies. You, in particular, my lady, he will enjoy to make suffer."

The Governor's wife, a picture of grace and calm, sips

from her glass of wine. "You are very arrogant, Father Mathias. You are alone, and these monks are many."

"They value this one, though. Didn't you see them cringe when I made this little nick in his pretty neck?"

Father Mathias directs his attention to the knife at Roan's throat and the Governor's wife, with lightning speed, throws her glass of wine in the Cleric's face. Roan quickly shifts his weight and, twisting his captor's hand, leans forward and flips him over his back. The Cleric crashes hard onto the floor but is quickly up again, knife poised as Roan charges toward him. But just as Roan is about to deliver a kick to the chest, the Cleric crumples, a steak knife neatly planted just below his enabler.

The Governor's wife takes a linen napkin and wipes her hands. "Roan of Longlight, forgive the interruption. When you have finished, my man will lead you to the stables. Mounts and weapons have been arranged for you all. We will make a suitable excuse for the good Father's absence when the others awake. Please, continue. This interruption has wasted too much of our time."

Turning away from Roan, she rings a bell and the old man slips in again. After a few hushed words from her, he leaves quickly. When he returns, it is with three women Roan recognizes at once as Apsara. Within moments, they've whisked the body away, leaving no trace of a confrontation.

His labor finally completed, Roan looks back in the direction of the head table. The Governor's wife is kneeling before her husband, head bowed, her body shaking with sobs. Even more surprising is the fact that Selig is reaching down, drawing her toward him, stroking her hair. Roan remembers the strength of Saint's feelings for Kira. She was the last thing he spoke of before he died. How much of that love did the women return? Would the Governor ever know the truth about his wife? Maybe it's enough that she makes him more than he might have been otherwise.

Roan had asked Ende for the Governor's wife's name before he left. *Isodel.* He will always remember the woman who'd killed for him this night.

In their time away from the Academy, they have adjusted a total of three hundred and forty-seven enablers and destroyed three Apogees without sustaining any casualties. Spirits are high. Roan will be happy if the other two teams have done half as well.

For the first time since he watched the Brothers emerge over the lip of the Caldera, Roan feels genuinely optimistic. But as they reach the plain that takes them to the Academy, his eyes narrow—a thin plume of smoke is rising from the hidden entrance of the cave. Without a word, the troop gallops straight for the hideaway, all hoping, Roan is sure, that they are not too late to make a difference.

Arriving at the entrance, Roan sees several Brothers and Apsara, coughing. Soot-covered Gunthers drift around, confused, in shock. But alive. Alive. With a sigh of relief, Roan leaps from his horse and greets Lumpy. "What happened?

"Sabotage."

"Where's Mabatan? Ende?"

"The explosion was in the barracks…the others are…in the library…with the wounded."

"Losses?" asks Wolf.

Lumpy, trembling, takes a deep breath, his eyes welling. "Two. They were making tea in…in the kitchen, they…"

Lumpy stares at Roan. "Gunther Number Seventy-Nine..."

Gwendolen? Roan shakes his head, not wanting to believe it. Of all the Gunthers, she was the most curious, the gentlest; she even let herself smile. His breath stops when Mejan and Talia walk toward him, holding each other, weeping.

"...and Dobbs," says Lumpy. "Dobbs..."

the overshadower

every consciousness collectively creates this
world and the next. but every consciousness
carries a shadow and if those shadows gather,
they can spawn a great darkness. a darkness
capable of snuffing out all light.

—the journal of roan of the parting

As if dinner had not been interminable enough, Darius has been toying with this groveling Governor Pollard for an hour, like a bored cat with a squeaking mouse. The Governor apparently has felt her brother's sting, assaults on his supply caravans a daily event, or so it would seem from the way he whines on. The Keeper, naturally, parries every complaint with an accusation. The City requires oil to run smoothly. Oil is a necessity. To withhold it is treachery. Stowe's attempting to concentrate, for Roan's sake, sure something of value is being said. But the sniveler's numerous justifications and proofs are no competition for her worry about Willum.

Those greedy little butchers had hovered over his body like flies over a corpse. She'd had to confront them in her most imperious tone for them not to begin gutting him on the spot. Eyes flitting constantly in her direction for approval, the doctors had tentatively begun attaching electrodes to Willum's head when she'd seen it: a blue tendril of iridescent flame curling around the pad and up the wire. Claiming a headache, she'd demanded that the lights be lowered, so that she might see more clearly. A haze of firelike light covered him like a second skin, like...armor. She'd reached out in as supercilious a manner as possible—it would not do to have any of them think she really cared—and penetrated the shield.

Her hand had instantly been bathed in blue flame; it had prickled her skin, but almost instantly receded, one of Willum's fingers twitching under her own. She'd felt a warmth she'd not realized was absent return to her. He was in there, somewhere deep, had descended into an unreachable place even Darius could not probe, for protection. This halo of light had to be a warning system, a protective layer that, if breached by something it recognized as life-threatening, would wake him.

Was she right? How could she be sure? Those doctors could not be trusted; she'd seen the hunger in their eyes. But the iridescent flame had curled over her finger, like a ring binding her to him. A ring. She'd reached into her pocket to stealthily withdraw her half of the badger ring and slip it over the curl of flame. A thread had raced from her forehead through her throat, and piercing her heart, had traveled down her arm to join the now glowing ring. Its rich crimson had floated through Willum's opalescent flame like blood. Blending into a deep purple, it had hovered for an instant over the badger's eye before being pulled into it. She could feel their combined power contained in the ring, throbbing like a pulse. And, for the past four days, she's clutched it, sensitive to any alteration in its steady beat.

"Are we boring you, my sweet?"

Startled, Stowe adopts her most daringly disaffected

persona. Tilting her face so only Darius can see it, she says sweetly, "Of course not, Father. I was only wondering what on earth we need Governors for?"

Darius cackles and a burst of smalt green energy shoots from his mouth in a jagged bolt of light. The wretched Governor twitches. Blood spurts over the man's brow. His eyes dart back and forth as he feels a drip rolling down his nose. Touching it, he sees the blood. He's so terrified, it's difficult not to feel sorry for him. But Stowe's heard enough to know this one is no innocent. He's cut from the same cloth as Brack, the Governor that she'd—"Didn't you send Raven to kill one of them awhile ago?" she asks, mischievously.

"Where did you hear that, Daughter?"

"Is it only a rumor, then?"

"Rumors always have some basis in fact." Darius stands, the full weight of his presence bearing down on the Governor. "Betrayals demand justice, do they not, Pollard?"

"Yes, Archbishop. Yes. Of course," Pollard stammers, dabbing his handkerchief to his nose. Stowe could see he was concentrating on getting out of the room alive. Still, the man's mouth was opening and closing like a fish choking on air.

"Have you something to add, Governor?" Darius demands impatiently.

"I have been asked to deliver a prayer to Our Stowe."

"Oh?" Stowe feigns an excited interest and offering her most condescending smile, she waits.

Pollard looks nervously from Darius to Stowe. "May I...?"

Stowe turns to Darius. Ah. It is he who is bored now, his mind has moved onto more interesting intrigues. Just as well.

"Please, Governor," she says, her voice encouraging.

"Our Stowe. Your children awake screaming. A demon comes in the night to swallow our dreams. We sleep but are not rested. We eat but are not made strong. Our thoughts scatter on the wind and our work lies undone. Our Stowe, daughter of light, turn your merciful eye upon us that we may be blessed again under your protection."

Stowe thinks about the memory Roan had shared with her. Throughout the entire Dreamfield, pulsing amorphous forms moved through a veinlike grid, all headed for the Spiracal. Most of them coming from areas far beyond the Masters' control. Was Darius's Throne leaving the Overshadower so hungry that it was reaching out to some other power source? Could it steal people's dreams? It might be that the Governor's demon was one and the same as their own.

"You are dismissed, Governor." Darius's voice sends an icy chill up Stowe's spine. Had he been listening after all? She casts her eyes down.

As soon as Pollard is gone, she turns back to the monster at her side and asks as if nothing had happened in between, "But Father, why *do* we have Governors? Why not just send a Master to manage the Farlands?"

Darius blinks. She's actually taken him off guard. At least for an instant. Then his eyes narrow.

"Smart girl like you and you haven't guessed," he hisses.

"But Father, why should I have given it any thought?"

"Precisely the question I'm asking myself."

Stowe giggles girlishly. There it is again, only a flicker this time, but he's genuinely surprised. "The man was such an idiot, Father. Unworthy to be in your presence. And so I was struck by how unnecessary he was, really. Am I wrong to think that? Was there more to him than I saw?"

Darius seems suddenly exhausted. He believes her and is maybe...disappointed. It is very difficult to keep her glee at bay. As if warning her against overconfidence, the ring begins to throb in her palm. Something's changed. Not in a good way, she's sure of it.

"No, Daughter, you are not wrong. If I could send Masters to control the Farlands, I would, but we are tied to the City in more ways than I am willing to explain right at the moment. I am weary and have yet to give myself over to deliberation on tomorrow's challenges. What about you? What will you do with the rest of this evening, Daughter?"

"Whatever I do, Father, I shall do it with you in mind," Stowe says, gently caressing the thickly veined hands. His skin has a sickeningly unnatural smell that makes her want to retch. The ring has become hot, a burning heat that she can only identify as a threat. It is all she can do not to bolt from the room, but that wouldn't be wise, not at all. Power has a laziness to it, an inertia; it's important never to be the first one to make a move. So she waits for Darius to wave her away, then smiling sweetly, she turns and sweeps out of the room as if he were not capable of throwing a knife into her back and piercing her heart.

Rushing down the corridor, Stowe sees an empty wheel-chair. With a flick of her wrist, she twirls it so that it rushes ahead of her. She can see the light from Willum's room spilling into the dim corridor. Bursting in, she cannot believe her eyes. Chest bared, Willum is thrashing on the bed. Metal cuffs have been snapped around his wrists and ankles, and metal bars cross his shoulders and hips. His head is completely contained within a metal cylinder. One doctor is poised, scalpel in hand, but all heads are now twisted toward Stowe.

"Our Stowe," they mumble, all bowing their heads but not moving. Not yet.

"Why, Doctors, you have revived my Primary!" She grants them each a benevolent smile, then fixes on Willum, trying to ascertain the damage. There is a line drawn from his collarbone all the way down his torso...the proposed path of the scalpel still poised to slice. "Could you remove the restraints now?" She's happy to see the doctors recognize a command when they hear one.

Behind her veneer of twittering pleasure, she's wondering if Darius ordered this, and prays her attempt at guilelessness is convincing.

As they remove the helmet, Willum smiles at her weakly. "Oh, look! He's smiling. Isn't that sweet?" she says as if speaking of a favorite pet. "I was so hoping he'd be well enough for a ride."

Waving the remaining doctors aside, she holds Willum's arm and helps him into the wheelchair. She catches his eye without speaking, without thought. She knows exactly where she must take him, and grinning a gracious goodbye to the doctors, whisks him from the room, down the long corridors, and through a transparent passage into the adjacent building. Negotiating a maze of halls, she finally arrives at one of the smaller, less conspicuous Travel Rooms.

"I fear I lack the strength, Stowe," Willum whispers.

"Believe me, Willum, it is just what you need."

Securing the door behind her, she helps Willum onto one of the glass recliners. Cautiously, she touches a pinpoint of blood seeping through his hastily thrown-on shirt.

"I'll recover. But I am weak."

"The Dirt Eaters' Wall helped me, Willum. I know it will do the same for you. Will you need Dirt?"

Willum laughs. "No. If you give me your hand, that will be enough." He lays his head back. He's so tired. They'd drawn him out of wherever he was too soon.

Grasping his hand, Stowe reaches for his mind. *Willum.*

I am here, Stowe. And in an instant, they are gone.

WHEN STOWE HEARS THE FAMILIAR THRUM OF THE WALL, SHE DRAWS THE HAWK CLOSER TO HER CHEST. WILLUM'S FEATHERS ARE DULL AND HIS TALON'S GRIP ON HER WRIST DISTURBINGLY WEAK. PLUNGING INTO THE GREAT SHIMMERING CURTAIN, THEY ARE BOMBARDED BY A CASCADE OF EFFERVESCENT COLOR. CAREFULLY EXTENDING THE HAWK AT ARM'S LENGTH, SHE WATCHES AS HE IS BATHED IN THE FULL SPECTRUM OF THE WALL'S LIGHT. ARCING BACK, SHE MARVELS AT HOW BEAUTIFUL HE LOOKS, RE-ENERGIZED, THE SHEEN RETURNING TO HIS FEATHERS, HIS EYES BECOMING KEEN AND BRIGHT.

"WE HAVE GOTTEN WHAT WE HAVE COME FOR," HE SAYS. "I'D RATHER NOT ENCOUNTER THE DIRT EATERS TODAY."

"WE SHOULD GO CHECK UNDER THE SPIRACAL. SEE THE OVERSHADOWER FOR OURSELVES. I COULD SAY THAT MY SEARCH FOR ROAN AND THE CHILDREN DREW ME THERE."

WILLUM HESITATES, BUT ONLY FOR A MOMENT. "ALRIGHT. ENVISION THE SPIRACAL."

AND WITH A THOUGHT THEY ARE AT THE CONSTRUCTION'S RAPIDLY CHURNING CLOUD. THE PROBLEM IS THEY HAVE TO KEEP THEIR DISTANCE. GET TOO CLOSE AND YOUR DREAMFORM IS ABSORBED IN A BURST OF FLAME; DARIUS HAS EXECUTED MANY A MASTER HERE.

Stowe shudders. "I sense...hunger. The Over-shadower?"

"Yes." Willum's hawk eye glints red.

"So...how do we get to it?"

"We must send something down." The hawk turns his head, and digging his beak into his breast, pulls out a feather. "Endow it with your being. I shall do the same. Then crystallize it so it will not burst into flame. It will be our eyes."

The crystalline feather floats for an instant before being sucked into the Spiracal. It spins in a steadily decreasing spiral until it is hurled into the muck of a huge black pit. Clinging to its slimy walls are vapors, human-shaped like the one she saw drawn from the enabler, their faces clenched in torment. Long scabrous arms swipe at them with clawed hands, until tumbling helpless, they are inhaled by a monstrous mouth that spans the base of the pit. Two unblinking green eyes swim in the pools of gore around it and shift asymmetrically, scanning their dank empire.

It's like my dream, Willum. The nightmare I had in Kira's village.

Yes. I recognize it too, the feel of it.

One of the demon's claws strikes the feather and Stowe's mouth fills with mud. Choking, she tries to cough and spit the muck out as the beast's warted lips cup together, sucking the quill closer.

As if from a great distance, she hears Willum cry out urgently, "Pull your essence from it, Stowe! Now!"

Her body oozing mud from every pore, Stowe feels her essence slip along with the other wailing spirits

INTO THE OVERSHADOWER'S CAVERNOUS MAW. FIRE LICKS HER SLIME-COVERED SURFACE AND IT TIGHTENS, THE HEAT AND THE PRESSURE THREATENING TO SUFFOCATE HER.

THE HAWK'S TALONS DIG INTO HER SHOULDER. HIS VOICE SCREAMS IN HER MIND. AS SHE LIFTS HER HAND TO PULL HIM IN A PROTECTIVE EMBRACE, HER HALF-RING BEGINS TO GLOW. A PEARL-LIKE RADIANCE ENCOMPASSES THE FEATHER AND THE OVERSHADOWER INSTANTLY BELCHES IT OUT. RIDING THE WAKE OF THE THWARTED DEMON'S INFURIATED SCREECH, THE QUILL ERUPTS OUT OF THE SPIRACAL AND CRACKS THE SUFFOCATING SHELL ENCASING STOWE.

THINKING ONLY OF DISTANCING HERSELF FROM THE DEMON, SHE IS SLOW TO SEE THE SHADOW CAST ON THEM FROM ABOVE.

"WHAT ARE YOU DOING HERE?" CRIES THE ONE-EYED VULTURE AS IT CIRCLES MENACINGLY TO MEET THEM.

"MASTER KORDAN, WHAT A SURPRISE!"

"OUR STOWE. YOU...YOUR FORM..."

"YES. ISN'T IT WONDERFUL? YOU CAN IMAGINE HOW SHOCKED AND PLEASED I WAS TO FIND MYSELF FREE OF THE CLAY. MY PRIMARY SAYS IT IS BECAUSE I AM ABOUT TO REACH THE FULL POTENCY OF MY POWERS. BUT YOU ASKED A QUESTION," STOWE LOOKS TRIUMPHANTLY INTO THE VULTURE'S TWITCHING EYE. "I'M HERE ON MY FATHER'S COMMAND. I AM ON A QUEST TO SEEK OUT MY BROTHER AND THE FOURTEEN DARIUS SO DESIRES."

KORDAN'S MANGLED HEAD REDDENS. HE WOULD HAVE TO BE VERY SURE OF HIMSELF BEFORE HE WOULD RISK LOSING HIS REMAINING EYE TO THE ARCHBISHOP. INSTEAD, HE GLARES AT WILLUM. "YOU STARTLE ME, PRIMARY, OUR STOWE IN THIS FORM IS UNDEFENDED. TO EXPOSE HER IN THIS VULNERABLE STATE TO SOMETHING AS DANGEROUS AS THE SPIRACAL IS UNCONSCIONABLE."

"In future I will remember to be more cautious," says Willum respectfully.

"You're lucky I have more important work to attend to. But you can be sure I will file a report on this incident." Kordan sniffs importantly, and then swoops away.

Still watchful of her old enemy steadily dwindling in the distance, Stowe whispers, "I think we can eliminate talking to the Overshadower as an option."

The hawk tilts its head. "Yes. It seemed fairly intent on a single endeavor."

"So how do we find a way to kill it?"

"Stowe...in Querin's sanctuary, among the Dreamfield Journals of the First Inner Circle, I noticed the names Valeria, Krispin, and Barthold. The Mad Masters. Have you heard of them?"

"Cautionary tales, mostly. They were involved in an accident, weren't they?"

"Building the Spiracal. It is said that afterward they possessed some kind of deadly power and had to be destroyed or imprisoned, no one knows."

"You think they saw the Overshadower?"

"It seems more than mere coincidence. When we get back, Kordan is sure to have us watched. I must find a way to leave the Pyramid without his knowledge. I have to see Gunther Number Six."

"Why?"

"If the Mad Masters are imprisoned, the Gunthers will know of it."

"You want to talk to them?"

"Stowe. If they fought the Overshadower and survived, we need to know how they did it."

saboteurs

technology binds the masters to the city, the dirt
eaters' hidden caverns keep them underground.
thus both require servants. some live in fear of
their lords, others have ideas of their own, and
some serve gladly.

—the way of the wazya

GRIEF-STRICKEN AND FURIOUS, Roan scans the wreckage.
"So much for hiding from Darius here," growls
Wolf.

Lumpy turns to Roan questioningly. "You think this was
Darius's work?"

"If it was Darius, you'd all be dead."

"Who then?" demands Wolf, barely able to contain his
frustration and rage.

Roan looks at the Brothers' commander with a certain amount of empathy. The senselessness of the attack is
making his blood boil too. "Find the perpetrator and we'll
have our answer."

Apsara and Brother labor together, bracing the destroyed
walls, removing rubble and damaged furniture. Roan drifts
over to them, saying nothing, not even looking into their
eyes. He simply focuses on each one as he passes, sensing
their being.

"The explosion destroyed the kitchen and blew through
these two barrack walls," says Lumpy, following behind.

Amongst the workers in the most interior portion of the damage, Roan senses an emotion different from the rest, annoyance laced with bitter triumph. In an instant, Roan throws the Brother to the floor, his hands collaring the traitor's throat.

"Naj!" cries Wolf.

As the Brother smirks, his livid scar twists across his face. "Nothing personal, Brother Wolf."

"You killed two innocents. Why?" Roan's thumbs rest under the man's Adam's apple. He could end his life so easily. "Why?" Roan squeezes Naj's neck a little tighter.

"Accident. Pity really. I quite liked them both. The timer buggered up. It was meant for you."

"Who gave you your orders?" Roan's never heard Lumpy's voice so filled with rage.

Naj snorts. Roan can see the image of the mountain lion as clear as if it were reflected in his eyes.

"He takes his orders from the Dirt Eaters," Roan answers. "Why do they want me dead?"

"You declare an intention to destroy the Dirt and then think they will sit idly by waiting for you to do it?"

Roan casts his mind back to that night at the Council... the Brothers in the tent...he remembers this Brother's scarred face. Yes. Naj had been there.

The traitor laughs. "Fool."

Stepping in front of Lumpy, Wolf glowers down at the Brother, then lifts his gaze sharply to Roan. "Are you going to interrogate him?"

"He doesn't know anything."

"Then...Prophet..." Wolf murmurs, eyeing Roan's undignified position over his prisoner.

Roan slowly picks himself up, wary of the slightest movement from Naj. Out of the corner of his eye, he sees Wolf lift his hook-sword. Roan cries out, but too late to stop the downward arc that cleaves the treacherous Brother in two.

Though Lumpy is shaking, he doesn't turn away. He'd helped gather what was left of Dobbs and Seventy-Nine, and Roan can only guess at the emotions boiling beneath his surface.

Wolf stands solemnly before Lumpy. "It is our way, Lieutenant. He confessed his crime and received the Friend's justice. His body will not be burned, but left in the open air for carrion."

"We are not executioners," Roan says, stepping between them.

Turning abruptly back to Roan, Wolf speaks through gritted teeth. "Might I ask, Prophet, what you intend to do with Darius when you have him in your grasp?"

His face on fire, Roan stands his ground. "That, Brother Wolf, is between me and the Friend."

Wolf's eyes narrow but he acquiesces. Then, looking past Roan, he addresses Lumpy. "I will see to the removal of the traitor."

Roan stares at his hands. He's spattered with Naj's blood. He had so wanted to squeeze the life from the man. Seventy-Nine's curious face, Dobbs's laugh. Everything crowds in on him like a long agonized scream.

"Roan." Lumpy's voice is heavy with grief. A grief Roan's not ready to succumb to.

"I'm going to talk to the Dirt Eaters."

Almost blinded by his rage, Roan whirls to move around his friend, but Lumpy blocks his path.

"Roan, stop, think. That's exactly what they want you to do. In the Dreamfield, you'll be exposed. And outnumbered."

"Lumpy, I have to face them. Then I'll know what to do."

MULTICOLORED FISH FLIT OUT OF HIS WAY AS HE JETS UNDERWATER THROUGH AN IMMENSE CORAL JUNGLE. BUT HE PAYS LITTLE REGARD TO THE EXTRAORDINARY SUBMARINE LANDSCAPE, HIS MIND SET ON ONE SOLITARY GOAL THAT CONSUMES HIS ATTENTION THROUGH THE COUNTLESS LEAGUES IN THIS ABUNDANT SEA.

FINALLY, AT THE LUMINESCENT CURTAIN BARRICADING THE WATER, HE BREAKS THE SURFACE. NONE COULD TOUCH THE SPEED AT WHICH HE HURTLES INTO FERRELL'S GREAT WALL. LIGHT FLARES AND COLOR DANCES AROUND HIM, AND HIS WHOLE BEING SCINTILLATES WITH ITS ENERGY AS HE BLASTS INTO THE DIRT EATER TERRITORY ON THE OTHER SIDE.

THE SEA BEGINS TO BOIL AND A MOUNTAIN LION, A WOLVERINE, AND A JACKAL RISE OUT OF THE FROTH TO CONFRONT HIM.

"WHAT ARROGANCE!" SNARLS THE MOUNTAIN LION. "TO HAVE COME HERE, ALONE."

"SARI. I HAVE COME IN PEACE TO SPEAK WITH YOU. YOU ONCE BEFRIENDED ME AT OASIS."

"YOU DESERTED US, ROAN. NO PEACE OR FRIENDSHIP REMAINS BETWEEN US."

"YOU ORDERED AN ATTEMPT ON MY LIFE. TWO OF MY FRIENDS HAVE DIED BECAUSE OF IT."

"HOW UNFORTUNATE."

"WHAT DO YOU STAND TO GAIN FROM MY DEATH?"

SARI'S COLD BLACK EYES LOCK ON HIS. "ARE YOU TRULY SO NAÏVE? WE WAITED NEARLY A CENTURY FOR YOUR COMING. ALL OF OUR HOPE WAS INVESTED IN YOU. YOU WERE TO TOPPLE

Darius, use the Novakin to secure the Dreamfield, and stabilize the supply of Dirt. But instead you have turned our own people against us and, we are told, are intent on destroying the Dirt. You are no better than your namesake and much, much more dangerous. We should have killed him. We won't make the same mistake twice."

"You are destroying the Dreamfield."

"Nonsense. The Dreamfield cannot be destroyed."

"I've seen it."

"You lie. And it is an old lie. Your great-grandfather said the same and here we are a hundred years later, more powerful than ever."

"The Dirt is a poison. It is affecting your judgment."

The lion's muscles tense, its teeth bare. "Be warned, Roan of Longlight. What happened at the Academy is just a taste of what we can do." Padding closer to Roan, she says gently, "Understand, we will not allow Darius to defeat us."

"I will stop you," says Roan unequivocally.

The three creatures look at each other grimly. The jackal's sharp teeth click together, "Then we are at war." As she snaps at Roan's hand, the mountain lion leaps, but Roan evades them and, still raging, he disappears into the foaming sea.

Lumpy's waiting at his side, looking at him expectantly. His face falls at the sight of Roan's expression. "I guess it didn't go so well."

"They've declared war on us."

An Apsara appears at their door. "Ende requests your presence. Kira is in the Quarry."

As she reports to Roan, Ende mops the sweat from Mabatan's brow. "The Gunther has taken Kira to the main storage area. She's fully described all the entryways and security bypasses. They've just gone down a long elevator shaft and opened some kind of steel wall."

"There's glass," Mabatan mumbles. "Behind it...Dirt. Mountains of Dirt. Eleven is looking into his glasses. Cleric! Not supposed to be here."

"Get out, Kira, get out!" Ende pleads under her breath.

We must hurry." Number Eleven leads Kira through a narrow hallway. But before he can push the button that will close the steel doors, the elevator opens and the Cleric steps out, weapon aimed.

"What are you doing here?"

"Checking the integrity of the filo-armor."

"I didn't see a work order on file."

"I am sure it is attributable to an oversight."

"We'll see about that. Let's go."

With lightning speed, Kira smashes the Cleric's jaw. He reels backward into the wall, his weapon firing accidentally. A siren wails. Before he can fire again, Kira finishes him with a blow to the neck. As his enabler implodes, she strips off her clothes before the startled Gunther, and exchanges her overalls for the Cleric's blue robes.

She puts her glasses on the Cleric, then, draping his shirt to conceal his enabler, she lifts him up and hauls him into the elevator. "Let's go."

Seeing the Gunther's panicked expression, Kira rests a reassuring hand on his shoulder. "Follow my lead. When you see an opportunity to leave, go."

"What about you?"

"Don't worry about me."

When the elevator doors open, a crowd of Clerics awaits them, weapons ready. Kira makes a gesture of appeasement. "My fault. This Gunther insulted Our Stowe and I lost my temper. I fired and triggered the alarm. I think he's hurt." She drops the dead man on the floor. "Am I under arrest?"

The other Clerics smile. Then one of them turns to Eleven. "Did you see this terrible accident?"

Number Eleven shakes his head warily.

"Good. Take your friend and get lost."

Eleven hesitates for a moment. Kira walks over and gives him a motivating kick. Turning back to the Clerics, she makes a face mocking the trembling Gunther. "A little slow, aren't they?"

Eleven drags the body face-down and with some difficulty manages to lift it into his cart. The Clerics chuckle as he wheels it away.

But their laughter quickly dies at the sight of a ranking member of their order, clearly their supervisor. "Who's she?" he asks, stepping into the room.

"I just arrived this morning from—"

"Papers," he says tonelessly.

"Right here." Aiming the dead Cleric's stun stick, she fires again and again, felling a half dozen Clerics. But as the last standing Blue Robe charges, the trigger on her weapon jams. Using the butt of the stun stick, she takes him down and runs.

Sirens wail. Sprinting to the main gate, the whine of stun shots from the guard towers surrounds Kira. She plows into a half-dozen gate guards, her fists and feet ablaze, each blow making its mark. Just down the road is a stand of trees, and in that stand is a large rock, and beneath that rock—

Her leg goes numb and she topples over. Another stun blast hits her in the back. She can barely breathe. Three Clerics put their swords to her throat. Kira spits at them. They kick. And kick. And kick.

Ende stares at the wall. Her face is gray, the grim reality of what is happening to her granddaughter all too clear as Mabatan jerks and twists in attempts to avoid blow after blow after blow. No one speaks. Emotion caught in his throat, Roan is silent. But even if he could speak, what could he possibly say?

Suddenly, Mabatan is very still. All color drains out of Ende's face as she reaches out and places two fingers on Mabatan's neck. After a moment, she whispers, "Alive. She's alive. The sleep is very deep but she's alive." Without looking up, she asks, "Roan, will you sit with her a bit? I won't be long." And before Roan can reply, she rises and with quiet dignity, slips silently from the room.

Settling himself beside Mabatan, Roan sees dark bruises forming on her arms and her chest and the sides of her face. She shivers, then her whole body begins to tremble. Roan anxiously pulls a blanket over her, but she cries out and he quickly draws away. She's so hurt, so fragile, his slightest touch has brought her pain.

Her hand, stone white, slips out from the covers. As Roan reaches ever so carefully to tuck it back in, Mabatan's fingers wrap around his. Startled, heartsick, his eyes glaze over with tears—and through them he sees a brown, speckled rat hovering above her.

"I feared the worst," Rat sighs, his sharp features inclined toward his injured daughter.

"Kira's been captured," Roan says quietly. "We don't know what will happen if she's killed. We want to sever Mabatan's connection to her but Mabatan refuses, so I don't feel we can. But with your permission—"

"Her will is strong. She follows the path. If she says she wishes to pursue this thing, we would be wrong to stop her. Worse still would be to allow Mabatan's choice to distract you from the goals you must pursue."

"Two of my people died today, victims of Dirt Eater sabotage."

"You are sure of this?"

"The Dirt Eaters have declared war on us."

"Then it is time to act, Roan of Longlight."

"What can I do? Even if I knew how to defeat them, to take the fight to the Dreamfield now would reveal my hand to Darius."

Rat's tail twitches dangerously. "No need for that yet. You know where they live."

"What do you mean?"

"Why take the fight to the Dreamfield, Roan of Longlight, when you know where the Dirt Eaters live?"

Licking his paw, the rat slowly disappears.

If you are able, tell Mabatan she is in my thoughts. Always.

There is a soft knock at the door. Kamyar. His eyes are red, his face weary and somber. "Sorry if this is a bad time. But we're going to bury our friends now."

the mad masters

WE WILL KNOW THAT ROAN OF THE PARTING'S PLAN IS
REACHING ITS CULMINATION THE DAY WE ARE OFFERED
OUR CHANCE FOR REDEMPTION.
—VALERIA,

VISION #543, YEAR 32 A.C.
DREAMFIELD JOURNALS OF THE
FIRST INNER CIRCLE

THE ADMINISTRATIVE LEVELS OF THE PYRAMID have meandering hallways that never seem to end. Stowe slips around one corner, only to see the ominous shadow appear again. After pausing a moment, she picks up her pace. Dashing down a utility stairwell, she turns into a cluttered corridor and ducks behind some crates.

Still there. Kordan's anticipated her move. No time to waste. Up the main staircase two flights. Which way? Assimilation or Records? Kordan's approach is silent, it's his robes swishing over the concrete that she hears as she crosses the landing into Records. A receptionist. Stowe smiles warmly but the young woman at the desk fumbles and dozens of sheets go flying.

Placing a hand on the receptionist's wrist, Stowe whispers, "I have come to thank you for your work." The girl can't be much older than her and Stowe quite easily guides her down behind the desk. The stunned receptionist is about to protest when Stowe places a silencing finger to her lips. In the grip of religious ecstasy, the girl doesn't notice the door open or hear Kordan's rasping breath or the door sliding shut again. Sweeping the fallen papers back into the young woman's arms, Stowe smiles her most beatific smile and makes a quick exit.

A door's opening on the next level. Kordan's continued up. So back down it is. Three levels below, she waits for the sound of a door opening, then closing. A few steps and she lets her door close with a thump. That should attract his attention. How long has this been going on? More than an hour? She hates to admit it, but she's having…fun. Kordan's following her every move, completely oblivious to the fact that it's she playing cat to his mouse. She just hopes it's buying Willum the time he needs.

On the lowest level of the Pyramid, tier upon tier of file shelves extend in every direction, each heavily coated with dust. The room is a vast labyrinth of bureaucratic records dating back to the earliest days of the Conurbation. "Is this the only entrance?"

"There are seven others equidistantly spaced around the perimeter." Willum's Gunther guide, Number Eighty-Two, stops stock-still, raises a hand, and then shakes his head. "Mice. Not to worry, though. We've copied everything."

"The dust would indicate the books have not been touched in years."

"Oh, we put it there. We like to cover our tracks."

Willum smiles to himself. The Gunthers' fastidiousness is legendary, if a little compulsive. "But if no one comes here…?"

"Master Querin still comes."

The journals Willum saw in Querin's secret room instantly come to mind. "Is this where he got the journals of the first Nine?"

"He got the copies. We have the originals."

To think the Gunthers have had the journals all this time without Willum knowing it! Curse them and their parsimonious approach to communication. "Might I read them?"

"I will inform Number Six of your request."

Turning a corner into another row of stacks brings the Pyramid's central pylon into view. Number Eighty-Two signals Willum to stop. "Number Six has asked that I apprise you once again of the risks of establishing contact with the Mad Masters. I believe he explained that when Darius entombed them here at the bottom of this pylon, a series of earthquakes localized at the Masters' would-be tomb quickly followed—an indication of the level of power at their command."

"Yes. He was quite clear on that point."

"Do you also know that when Darius ordered us to transform the catacomb into a prison—no doubt hoping to appease the Mad Masters—twelve Gunthers were lost."

"The Masters attacked you?"

"No. They reach out to no one but we learned too late the extent of their…disability. To touch them is lethal. They never speak, yet in their presence one hears screams so terrifying and penetrating that it can take weeks to recover from the experience, if you recover at all. We had to develop a series of pipelines to supply nourishment, eliminate waste, and respond to the Masters' basic needs. But no shield we have devised can dull the cries. Willum, it defies all logic. The continued use of the pipelines proves that, without any medical enhancement whatsoever, the Mad Masters are still alive. Perhaps they have grown even stronger. Every year we are required to provide Darius with a report and it is obvious even he feels helpless before them."

"Thank you, Number Eighty-Two. I'll keep all that in mind."

The Gunther pauses before tapping the code into the last of three massive lead-lined portals. "The slightest deviation in these codes will make it difficult for these doors to be opened again."

"I understand."

"Your decision remains unchanged?"

Willum nods.

"Number Six has a great deal of faith in your abilities."

"And you do not?"

"You are unique. I do not understand why such a risk is necessary."

"I cannot say that I do either. I only know it must be so."

Willum directs his vital energy into creating a barrier to protect him from the Mad Masters' psychic onslaught, then signals the Gunther.

Tapping in the code, Eighty-Two swiftly steps aside. Scrunching up his face, he mutters an uncharacteristic "Good luck," and before the whisper of air that accompanies the unlocking of the gateway is ended, the Gunther has disappeared.

Seventy years entombed in the base of the Pyramid has taken a significant toll on the Mad Masters. What hair remains on their heads is transparent, and in the amber light of their prison it makes a fiery halo over faces and bodies so wrinkled and dry they appear to be nothing but crumpled masses of stained paper ready to burst into flame. Except for the eyes. Their eyes are pale blue and focus straight ahead. They are blind. But there is no mistaking that they have vision of a different nature as they steer their sightless eyes unerringly in his direction.

One by one the Mad Masters reach out their fingers, their nails bony spirals the length of Willum's forearm. They speak as one: a wavering soprano weaves around a tenor while the third's voice, no doubt once deep and sonorous, punctuates the duo's eerie harmony with an ostinato of sighs and gasps. "We know you, Willum. You are one of Roan's. One of Roan's many powerful branches. Yes. We knew he'd find the rat. He was so clever. Always...considering the long term. Yes. Not like Darius. No. Not like Darius at all."

They have walked in the River of Time, and they have seen...what? Willum wishes he had known of the journals before. Then he would have a better idea where he stood.

"Oh, yes. We knew you would come to us. Yes. And we know what you have in store. Trapped. You will be trapped. It is so unfair."

Do they sense what he is thinking? Or is it just that they have "seen" this meeting? Know what he is about to ask?

"Don't be weak, Willum. Speak. Speak." The Mad Masters sigh, the sound so chilling it makes Willum shiver. Still, it is only a pale shadow of what they are truly projecting.

"So you know why I have come?"

"Darius. What lies beneath the Spiracal. You want what we know. What we have seen. What we can do."

"Yes."

"We were the Master Builders. Roan said: Stop eating the Dirt. Share the River of Time. But no one wanted to do that. Darius said: Use the Well of Oblivion. It will make you stronger. Haaa. We chose the wrong side. We capped the Well and the river that ran into it dried up. Darius said: Eat more Dirt. Drown in it. It will provide what the river cannot. So we did. And in our Dirt-addled haze, we built and we built. But one after another, great crevices opened up. Ohh, we sealed them all, but it was only a matter of time before one opened up right under our feet and we fell. We fell and at the bottom of that crevice we found a monster. You know the one. It lies now, ever hungry, beneath the Spiracal.

"We had 'seen' our fall, and so we had planned for it. We were able to fight. Able to escape. But we did not defeat it. And Willum, we know no way of defeating it. But we can help with Darius."

The three Masters shudder, their bodies tense. "You will release us. Yes. We know you will. We know what you have in your pocket."

Willum's hand touches the Dirt hidden in his robe. From this decision there will be no return.

"You have much to fear, Willum. But not from us. No. We are alive—do you know why?"

"No."

"Can you not guess?"

"You fear death."

"Not quite. We fear *it*. The monster—you know its name. We do not wish to be consumed in its gaping nothingness. We want to walk into the Well of Oblivion and join with the Dreamfield. So we will do this last thing. Give us what is in your pocket and we will help destroy what we created. We will stand by Roan's namesake—yes, we know the prophecy—in the hope that he will accomplish what his great-grandfather could not."

Willum takes out the Dirt and as the Mad Masters turn their hands over to accept it, their voices thread a haunting path around the boundaries of his defensive barrier.

"We know you, Willum. Yes. We have had visions of the hawk. The hawk that is you. Trying to fly. But he can't get away. His wings are clipped. Clipped by the one he cherishes most. He cannot fly. No. He screams and cries out, begs and pleads, but she prefers his cries to the vast emptiness she carries without him. We understand her well. Oh, yes. We do."

Careful not to touch them, Willum places a small mound of Dirt in each of the Mad Masters' palms, then turns and walks to the exit. But he cannot walk away from the voices echoing painfully at the borders of his awareness.

"Wants to run, doesn't he? Yes. But time will run faster."

Stowe pauses in the foyer of the Induction Offices. Kordan's looking stranded at the end of the hallway. Completely bewildered. Well. She's bored now. Willum *must* have accomplished all he needed. Just as Kordan's about to continue his search in the opposite direction, she steps in front of an oncoming Cleric. Startled, the man clasps his hands together in supplication, and bows to her. "Our Stowe."

She smiles beneficently at her supplicant, touches his forehead with her index finger and he stumbles away, directly past Kordan.

"Master Kordan?" Stowe calls out in greeting. "Why, I did not know you haunted administrative corridors."

"Of course not. And neither do you. First I find you exploring the most dangerous site in the Dreamfield, and then I notice you skulking around here. Whatever can she be up to, I ask myself."

"You are no longer my mentor. What possible concern is it of yours?"

Kordan's one functioning eye gives him an anxious, rabid look. "It's only that I am concerned you have lost your direction. Willum's fear of Dirt will waste your potential. Do not let his prejudices limit you."

Stowe widens her eyes, pretending to be intrigued. "But Master Kordan, I want nothing more than to be all that I can be."

Half of Kordan's face is animated with excitement. And although the paralyzed half is horrifying, Stowe thinks she prefers it. Watching his lips twist in preparation for his next words, she's quite relieved when a Cleric rushes between them.

"Not now, fool, can't you see who I'm talking to?"

"Master, you asked that—"

"Yes. Yes. Alright. Excuse me, Our Stowe." He offers the Cleric his ear, and as the underling whispers, Kordan's eye gleams with delight. Waving off the messenger, he turns back to Stowe. "Forgive me, Our Stowe, but I am called away on urgent business."

"And what could be more urgent than me?"

"Spies." Kordan's mouth writhes like a slithering worm. "Enemies of the Conurbation."

"Really? May I come along?"

Kordan's eye shifts anxiously in confusion, wondering no doubt if he has the authority to refuse her. "Our Stowe's presence might preclude...your compassionate nature might be wounded by..."

"Surely not." This was worrisome. For a moment Stowe fears Willum has been discovered. But no. She would feel it;

they are still linked through the ring and there's been nothing but a steady pulse.

"It may be dangerous. Over the years, we've heard intermittent reports that some of the rebels we thought exterminated long ago by the Keeper may have survived. Their descendants are said to be ferocious female warriors. It is believed this spy may be one." Kordan beams at Stowe, bursting with anticipation.

Kira must have made it to the City only to be captured. "Well, I couldn't possibly attend such a glorious event in pale yellow. I must change—do you think it will last long?"

"No doubt, Our Stowe," Kordan says, turning on his heels.

Stowe waits till he is out of sight before she runs. If they can't do something to save her, Willum's sister will suffer a slow and excruciating death.

the fall of oasis

volume xxxvi, article 22.0
roan of Longlight has requested oasis be assessed
as a possible open center for education, research,
and development. we have agreed to inventory
the Library, access hydroponics, and determine
whether the energy grid can support manufacture
of our filo-membrane flying device. hhroxhi have
assured transit.

—gunther Log

HERE ON THE FAR SIDE OF THE HILL, and masked by an overhang of rock, Roan can taste the chill in the air. The night is utterly still. Not even a breeze.

It was only three days since the explosion. Knowing where the Dirt Eaters live had been key. Mejan had helped Lumpy chart the three secret entrances into Oasis. Kamyar had taught the Apsara and Brothers how to open the stone doors and navigate the labyrinth into the underground community. And Talia had explained the workings of the ventilation system to Roan.

One day to strategize. Two nights and a day to travel. And now, they are here waiting for sunrise in the frozen gardens of Oasis.

Lumpy's at Roan's side worrying frost into ice with one foot. As they both eye the pale glow of approaching daybreak, Roan draws an arrow and notches it in his bow.

"You sure we're doing the right thing?" Lumpy asks Roan nervously.

"Ask Seventy-Nine. And Dobbs," Kamyar snarls, no trace of the light-hearted Storyteller in his manner.

"For us He raises the sun, for us He brings the dawn," Roan intones as a Brother lights his arrow. Drawing back the string, he fires it into the sky. At Roan's signal, the pyres are lit. To the east and the south, smoke soon rises. Torches are kindled and runners from all three pyres move to ignite sodden grasses set to collapse into Oasis's ventilation system.

The day has begun and the declaration of war answered.

Wolf, hook-sword in hand, is positioned by the steep rock face that overlooks the field. He points to the bottom edge of the stone—smoke—then quickly recedes, concealing himself.

The rock shudders, then opens smoothly. Dozens of goats rush from the cave, bleating. Almost screened by billowing asphyxiating clouds, a handful of archers, arrows poised to fire, warily scan the shadowed landscape. Roan can see they are listening as much as looking, hoping for some clue of the threat's origin. Clearly uneasy, they have no choice but to let the coughing residents of Oasis spill out of the cave onto the ledges that form a path along the precipice. Among the crowd, four stand out: Haron, the elder of the community; Orin, the librarian; Sari, their leader; and the withered shell of a man she's supporting—Ferrell.

Making their slow descent into the field, the people whisper anxiously among themselves as the archers attempt to take a defensive posture around them.

As soon as they are all in the center of the first of the gardens, Roan calls out, "Lay down your weapons. We will accept nothing but complete surrender. Surrender and no harm will come to you."

Roan hears the arrow before he sees it. He bends slightly, allowing it so close that the disturbance it creates in the air makes him blink. But before the archer can ready another, one of Kamyar's knitting needles finds its way to her shoulder.

"Old friends," Kamyar shouts, "I heartily recommend that you accept Roan's offer." And sixty battle-ready Brothers and Apsara slide out from behind the trees, fingers on the triggers of their crossbows.

With a sweep of his hand, Haron angrily motions his archers to put down their weapons; but when Roan steps from the shadows of the overhang, his eyes blaze with defiance.

Staring steadily at the old man, Roan speaks quietly into the tense silence. "You will be escorted to a remote village where you can threaten no one and you will be kept there in custody until the struggle with Darius has been concluded."

"That is a death sentence, Roan. Outside the caves, we'll age and die. It's genocide." Sari's voice is strong and clear, filled with righteous indignation. Roan remembers the response she had for him when he'd complained of his friends' deaths. "How unfortunate," she'd said, dripping with condescension. The words echo in his mind, fueling his anger, and for a moment he's rendered speechless.

"That's a rather liberal usage of the term, Sari." Roan's thankful that Kamyar, at least, hasn't lost his tongue. "Everybody dies and your lease on life has already been over-long. Fair's fair. You should consider yourselves lucky Roan of Longlight does not subscribe to the ancient rule of an eye for an eye. If it was up to me, you'd find a needle in your chest for killing Dobbs."

The Storytellers take careful note of the community's reaction to Kamyar's news. They are aware that not everyone in Oasis is culpable for the crimes of the Dirt Eaters. If not for that, Kamyar's needle would have surely found the archer's heart.

With a glance, Sari silences the outraged murmurs of the Oasis residents, and ignoring Kamyar's accusation, she continues in her attempt to engage Roan's attention. "You will be hard pressed to defeat Darius without our help. Let us make a truce and fight the Masters together."

Wolf's already in the field collecting the archers' weapons and Roan waves in some Apsara to help him. "That would require trust, Sari," he says, walking down to her, the circle of captives parting before him, "something that no longer exists between us."

"All we have done, we have done in order to defeat Darius." Her voice has taken on a pleading tone, playing to her audience, but it doesn't fool Roan.

He can see Sari's edging closer to Haron, many of the elders of the community gathering around them. He stops, trying to ascertain what form the attack will take, all the while answering her with apparent unconcern, "You and Darius are cut of the same cloth. He builds a Spiracal; you build a Wall. He seeks the Novakin; you feed them Dirt. He kidnaps Stowe; Ferrell invades her. You both share the same ambition, control of the Dreamfield."

The crowd doesn't like what it's hearing and now the grumbling is not so easily silenced. Sari snaps back to Roan, no longer caring to hide her malevolent intent. The air around her and the elders shimmers. Everything is suddenly tinged with blue. The intensity of the color steadily increases. Not knowing what else to do before the onslaught, Roan concentrates on his half-ring. Each hair on his body rises as he's enveloped in a pearl-like radiance. He tries not to stagger when the blast reaches him. His insides feel as if they're being turned out, but the blue light shatters against his newly formed shield, its tiny shards exploding pinpoints of blood before his eyes. Still, whatever it was the ring drew from him has left him weak.

Hoping to buy time before the next assault, he uses the only weapon he's sure of against them—words. "My great-grandfather told you to stop eating Dirt, to stop defiling the Dreamfield. But you, like Darius, ignored him."

"If we'd listened to Roan of the Parting, we'd all be dead by now," hisses Sari, "like your family and friends, like all the inhabitants of Longlight."

As Wolf thrusts his way to Roan's side, the atmosphere around the Dirt Eaters darkens menacingly.

"Get everyone back!" Roan orders. But Wolf doesn't need to do anything, the crowd's already pulling away. Only one person stumbles into the ever widening circle—Ferrell the architect, his vacant eyes lost in the past. "Roan, Roan, you are so wrong. Without Dirt, how can I build towers to touch heaven, walls to kiss eternity. Do not part from us, Roan, join us, help us fulfill our dreams."

"Get out of the way!" Sari screams, but too late.

Reaching for Roan's hand, the architect embraces him and the lethal blast of energy aimed at Roan strikes Ferrell, his body sagging limply in Roan's arms. Clutching the architect's corpse, Roan falters, exhausted. Why is he doing this? Wouldn't it be better to set it all aside? He's only a boy, a boy shouldering a man's burden. He should put the burden down. Put the burden down. Put—

You must prevail, Roan of Longlight.

A wash of radiant light pours over him as Orin the librarian steps forward to stand at his side. One by one, Dirt Eaters emerge from the crowd of onlookers to join him, channeling their life force in Roan's defense.

No one moves. No one speaks. Sari raises a hand and the attack is terminated. But Roan can see she does not believe herself defeated. She is merely recognizing a stalemate, reserving her life and death assault to confront him another day. He knows with a certainty that she believes this possible. It is part of the madness the Dirt brings to those who use it: they forget that without it, they are only human; their powers, both real and imagined, gone.

As he steps close to Sari, Roan almost reels from the smell of Dirt on her. "Good luck with your cleansing, Mountain Lion. I know it will not be easy."

At Roan's nod, Apsara head over to separate Sari and her companions, and divest them of their Dirt. But before Roan walks away, Haron catches his eye. He'd been the first to talk to Roan about his great-grandfather; he claimed Roan of the Parting as friend. Roan knows now that it had all been lies.

Looking into the old man's steely gray eyes, Roan whispers, "I consider this our first victory against Darius, an old betrayal finally answered."

Two years ago the bitterness in Haron's eyes would have crushed Roan; now it's not even disappointing—there are some minds Roan knows he cannot change. So he turns his back on the old man and smiles at Orin—best to concentrate on the ones he can.

PRISONS

ONE OF THE WAZYA, THREE SINGERS ON EACH PALM,
SHALL GUIDE THEM TO THE EASTERN EDGE OF THE EARTH'S
DISGRACE. THERE, BENEATH THE CRATERS OF THE MOON'S
two faces, to a CHOIR OF EARTH'S SONG, the APSARA
WILL BE FREED BY THE SON OF LONGLIGHT.

—THE BOOK OF LONGLIGHT

FOR THE LAST FOUR DAYS, Mabatan has lain curled up on her bed. Though she drinks water and eats food, her mouth feels dry, her stomach empty. Ende keeps reminding her that she is not Kira, but how does that knowledge help when Kira's suffering is her own?

Kira's in a box. She cannot stand—Mabatan, are you there? Are you listening? —She cannot stretch. She curls, knees to her chest, swollen lips pressed over the pinholes that provide air, but it is not enough. Never enough. Her lungs ache. Her heart races. Races—Mab? Mab? —Time floats. Weeks pass. No. Not that long. She can tell because of the bruises. The bruises and the cuts are still fresh. The smell of her own blood nauseates her. If only she had air but there isn't enough. —Help me breathe, Mab. Help. —She practices swordplay in her head. Lunge and thrust. Recover. Twist. Stab. Slide. Jab. Lunge. Recover. If only she could breathe. —Mabatan, you'll teach me. When I get out. How to follow the path. The Way of the Wazya. I'll get out. Willum will come. Maybe not. Mab, are you listening? Are you there? —Her tongue is fat. Thick. The smell of blood overwhelming. Her heart races. But time. Time moves slowly. Very slowly.

The crickets hum. Mabatan wants to tell them to take it

out, take the enabler out. She wants to scream it. But then who will Kira have to talk to? There would be no witness to her suffering. It's hard to breathe—Kira. Kira. I am here, Kira. I am listening. You will come back—Time floats. Her lungs ache—Willum will find a way and he will come. I will take you into the new forest and you will teach me the ways of the sword. Kira. Breathe. Breathe! I *am* here. I *am* here.

Ende is squeezing water over Mabatan's swollen lips. Roan can't make out anything she's saying. "Is she alright?"

"What does it look like?" snaps Ende.

Roan and Lumpy had come here the instant they'd returned from Oasis, hoping desperately for good news. But things have obviously only gotten worse. Lumpy clutches Mabatan's hand. Her sleeve slides back and he gasps. Her skin is livid with welts and bruises.

"Her body is covered in them," Ende's voice is tight with frustration. "It reacts to the trauma as if it were real. We need to use that Allayer." Roan and Lumpy exchange an uncomfortable glance. The eruption from Ende is instantaneous. "What is wrong with you! It's only a matter of time before they find Kira's enabler. Do you want to lose them both?"

Mabatan begins to gasp, greedily gulping air. "I can breathe. I can breathe. But can't stand. Oh. My knees. Can't feel my legs. Falling. That hurt. But I can breathe." Mabatan's eyes open wide. "Hold my arms, Lumpy. Hold them!"

Roan rushes forward to help, but still they are hard pressed to hold her down, her screams so piercing Roan almost doesn't hear Lumpy's anguished refrain, "They're breaking Kira's arms, Roan. Roan, they're…"

Water. It's good. Maybe drugged. She'd know soon enough. Her eyes. She can barely open. A man. An ugly, ugly man with a half-smile. Well, I'm not smiling back.—Mab? I'm not smiling back. If my mouth wasn't so dry, I'd spit in his face. Mab? Mab? I'm scared now. Blue needle claws on his fingers. They're making me scared.

Watching Mabatan's face swell while she howled in agony had made the decision easy. This had to be stopped. Now.

An acknowledgment passes between Roan, Lumpy, and Ende. But just as the Allayer is about to be activated, Mabatan grabs Roan, drawing him close.

"No," she gasps in his ear. "Not yet. Please. I must not leave Kira. Must not. Please."

"It will kill you, Mabatan."

"No. Not yet. There is something…I've seen…I'm not sure…something important…please."

Roan looks up at Ende and Lumpy.

"She's delirious." Ende's furious, but Roan knows her anger is fueled by her fear for Kira and the weight of having to choose between her loyalty to her granddaughter and the life of a friend.

So Roan keeps his voice as calm as possible. "What if she's right? She says there's something she needs to hear. Am I not supposed to believe her?"

Ende's glare is an indictment, accusing him of being numb to Mabatan's pain, though Roan would like nothing more than to free her.

Lumpy frowns. "It's Roan's choice." The bitter edge in his voice makes it clear what he'd do if the choice was his.

Mabatan tenses. Roan knows she's suppressing a scream. One and then another and another. "Mabatan."

"Not...yet..."

Mab. I can't hear anymore. I can't hear. Can you? Mab. Someone's trying to get in my head. Is it you? I'm so tired. That can't be you. Mab? Stop him, Mab. He's in my head. Stop him. Stop him. He's taking my mind, Mab. Mab! Please, Mab. Please. Stop him. Get out, Mab. Get out. Get out! Get out!!

"Now!" Mabatan wails and Lumpy initiates the Allayer. Her hand still clenching Roan's shirt, Mabatan shakes violently, her wide eyes vacant. But when she slowly shifts her gaze to his face, Roan realizes she's sobbing and gently takes her into his arms.

"Someone very powerful...took everything...she could not stop him. He took it all from her mind...Kira's village...Ende...the Caldera...Willum. She could not stop him. Roan. She could not. He was too strong."

Ende, ashen-faced, whispers, "Did he kill her?"

"I don't know. I don't know."

As Mabatan's body convulses with grief, Roan holds her tighter, trying to absorb some of her pain. His own head is about to explode. What do they do? What do they do now?

Willum and Stowe have been training for hours. Every once in a while he staggers and she retreats. Then he insists that they go on. Days. It's been days since she'd run in exhausted, demanding that they break Kira out, but Willum's reaction had dampened her fury. It was obvious he'd considered this eventuality—how could she have imagined that he hadn't? But he, who always had a dozen possible responses to every problem, had only one now: wait. They had no way of knowing what Kordan had discovered. He already has them under surveillance. To act might not only jeopardize Kira's chances of survival, but the success of their entire enterprise.

Willum's fist is plowing toward Stowe's face and she watches it come, then at the last moment she jerks back, her chin nicked by his knuckles. Too slow. Find the rhythm of the attacker's mind. Then dance with him.

Without warning, he twirls with a cross-kick. This time she gives full focus to the movement, echoes his body, and meets his twirl and kick with the same. He strikes again with his fist, and this time she matches him, blow for blow, drawing him closer and closer, till he's almost in position. Her hand is perched above his face when he falls abruptly to his knees. He is perfectly still except for a solitary tear that traces a slow path down his cheek. Has Kira died? She dares not ask. But when she tries to retreat, unsure of what comfort she can offer, he holds onto her and his dry sobs shake her, until the dim winter light fades and darkness surrounds them.

A knock on the door thunders into their silence. Willum stands, composing himself.

Master Querin enters and light floods the room. Stowe's blood freezes. Assuming her most irritated air, she snarls, "Yes?"

Taking a small box from his pocket, he places it in the center of the floor and flicks it on. "Spies, as you know, are everywhere. This will allow us to speak privately—at least for the moment." With a terrifying smile, his gaze locks on Willum. "I've had the most interesting encounter with...your sister."

Willum remains expressionless. Stowe works hard to harness her fear, her rage. She suppresses her desire to act, to scream, to kill. Extending her awareness beyond the room, she senses no Clerics outside. He's come alone. Why? Though she desperately wants to catch Willum's eye, she stares ahead, looking as surprised as possible.

"She is very strong, your sister. Her resistance was extraordinary."

When will Willum speak? They are two to Querin's one. He came alone!

"I have proclaimed her guilty as charged. We follow the inspired guidance of Our Stowe in meting out our punishment: your sister's expulsion to the Devastation has been initiated."

"What do you want?" Stowe can hear the murder in Willum's voice. She is ready.

Querin squints inquisitively at Willum. "Apsara. Enemy of Darius. You are treacherous, of that I have no doubt. But I must determine the nature of your treachery. To that end, I shall test the prophecy."

"What prophecy?"

Querin's dark eyes glaze over. "Beneath the craters of the moon's two faces, to a choir of earth's song, the Apsara will be freed by the son of Longlight." Querin pauses, his gaze shifting from Stowe to Willum and back again. "I have never doubted you, Our Stowe. But now I find you are under the sway of a man who may be dangerous. Very dangerous. Let the events unfold as they may. I will pray, for your sake, Our Stowe, that your brother does save my captive. Otherwise Willum is not the friend you think he is and we will have to eliminate him...and perhaps even...you."

the prophecy

IN THE CITY, WHERE YOU LEAST EXPECT IT, YOU WILL FIND A
TRUE DEFENDER OF THE FAITH.

—JOURNAL OF ROAN OF THE PARTING

"PROPHET, WHAT IS YOUR WILL? Shall we evacuate?" Wolf's voice is urgent but respectful.

"Mabatan says nothing came up about this location," Roan replies. "At least not before she was separated from Kira…Exercise caution. Double the patrols. We should be ready to move if we have to. We'll need some alternate locations."

"It will be done."

Roan's happy to be having the meeting. Addressing the obvious necessary details is all there is between him and despair. If Willum is exposed, then what of Stowe? He'd wanted to contact her through the ring but didn't dare—what if he distracted her at a crucial moment?

"Ende?"

"The eclipse is in ten days. Not enough time to move my people from the Caldera. At this time of year, the journey is too dangerous for the elderly and the children. So we prepare for siege. Alandra's being taken there—it is the only place we can guarantee her safety…at least for the time being."

Earlier, Ende had conferred with him about Alandra's situation. She'd needed final confirmation that the healer was not to be awakened. The Apsara were keeping his friend alive, but only just, and she felt she had to warn him that even if Alandra were able to withdraw from the Hydra and return to her body, she might never be able to regain her previous strength and control. He'll have to take what comfort he can in the fact that all that can be, is being done for her. Trying to shake off his worries, he thanks Ende and returns to the matters at hand.

"Kamyar?"

But before Kamyar can respond, Wolf rounds on him. "Yes, Storyteller. Stinger expected new recruits yesterday but they never arrived."

Surprisingly, Kamyar does not reply with his usual glib retort. Instead, he shakes his head and sighs heavily. "There is a strange lethargy in the villages. The people are aimless and exhausted. They say a demon is stealing their dreams. These people are not enabled, Roan. How is Darius doing it?"

Roan, unsure of how to express what he knows, looks at Ende.

"Darius has sought to control an Overshadower," she says, training her gaze first on Kamyar, then on Wolf.

Kamyar blanches, but Wolf leaps up. "Enemy to the Friend! The great darkness which casts his shadow over the sun. But Prophet, you said the Friend will pull the sun from the shadow."

Roan looks at the warrior in amazement. The Overshadower is the Friend's enemy? Why not join together, then, to fight their common foe? The god had told Roan they would meet when Roan returned to the Dreamfield to destroy Darius's Throne. And Ende had said if they fought Darius, they would fight the thing he feeds. So, what possible purpose could it serve to kill the Friend? Why—

Roan starts when Kamyar touches his arm. Realizing he must have been staring off into space, he looks at the others sheepishly. "Sorry, I—"

"No need to explain." Kamyar pushes away from the table and gestures at Mejan, who's waiting impatiently in the doorway. "But the Storytellers are making their way to the City, Roan. I have to say goodbye."

"Be careful, old friend." Roan rises, extending a hand, and Kamyar envelops him in a walloping bear hug.

"Be strong, Roan of Longlight, and ride with the wind at your back."

But Roan's head begins to spin. He's spiraling up the Big Empty and then, through a haze of exploding rock, he sees a puzzled frown.

"Kamyar?" he whispers and collapses.

Roan is barely present before Stowe has clasped his hand, her conversation with Querin flooding his awareness.

"Kira's alive?"

"If Querin is to be believed. But for how long, we can't be sure."

"But beneath the craters of the moon's two faces— where's that?"

"We don't know. Presumably that's part of the test: can you find her and will you enact her rescue according to whatever's in the prophecy that Querin hasn't told us."

They stand for a moment, silent.

"This could be a trap."

"I know that, Brother. Querin has us under guard, so Willum can't contact the Gunthers. We're hoping

YOU CAN DECIPHER THE PROPHECY HE'S REFERRING TO IN TIME."
PLACING HER HAND OVER HER BROTHER'S HEART, SHE SMILES. "I
KNOW YOU'LL DO IT, ROAN. I KNOW. THE PROPHECIES NEVER LIE,
DO THEY?"

Kamyar's shaking him. "Roan! Roan! What's wrong with you? What is it?"

Reaching up to assure the worried Storyteller, Roan says urgently, "Kamyar, 'Beneath the craters of the moon's two faces...' Do you know that prophecy?"

But it is Ende who responds. "One of the Wazya, three singers on each palm, shall guide them."

Nodding, Kamyar interjects, "And on and on it goes. Roan! It's one of the most debated of the prophecies. Since I met our friend, Lump, I've developed my own personal theory."

"I need to hear it. Kira's been released and the prophecy's supposed to tell us where to find her. Our lives depend on it."

Lumpy's furious. "Ende says the ride alone could kill her. Mabatan's so weak, Roan. And since she's heard, well—she insists. But every time we shut off the Allayer...it's as if she's dying. Roan. If Kira dies and Mabatan..."

"Do you believe in the prophecies?"

"What?"

"Do you?"

Lumpy looks at his friend, confused.

"Do you believe in the Dreamfield? The crickets? That Darius must be destroyed? His presence in the Dreamfield eradicated? That I was chosen to do this? That you were destined to be my friend? Do you believe in the prophecies, Lumpy? Do you?"

Lumpy's eyes are red, but he does not blink or try to avoid Roan's gaze. "Yes."

Roan sighs. "Then we go."

The three riders gallop across the Farlands bordering the wasted fields of the Devastation.

"Any change?" Roan yells.

Mabatan's slumped against Lumpy, and as he bends to hear her, his arms squeeze even more protectively around her. Having them ride together has slowed their progress, but given her condition there simply wasn't any other way.

"She says we're getting closer. It's a scarred place, just beyond that ridge."

"Should we dismount?"

Lumpy leans forward again, his ear brushing Mabatan's cheek. "She says no. There's a vehicle. But she doesn't think anyone's inside. And only one Cleric with Kira. He's carrying a cage with two birds in it—one white, one black."

As they crest the ridge, streaks of red slash the sky like claw marks over a festering wound. The Cleric is patiently waiting, his cage on the ground beside him. On a wide smooth stone, her hands and feet bound, lies Kira.

Roan's heart is in his throat. The sight of the broken Apsara warrior unbearable, he turns to the moon, hanging behind him on the eastern horizon, and dismounts.

Lumpy carefully slides Mabatan into Roan's arms. She presses her head into his shoulder and breathes compulsively, stifling sobs. When she's finally calmed herself, Roan whispers, "As soon as the moonlight touches Kira."

The three stand silently together, watching the moonbeams slowly trace their way across the plain. Finally they reach the stone.

Mabatan holds out her palms and three white crickets leap onto each one. Staring at the ground, she moves with excruciating care. He knows the effort it is taking for her to stand tall, to walk steadily. Seeing the damage to Kira has brought home the extent of their suffering and he flushes with rage. Though he tries to quiet his pulse, the anger will not leave him.

Mabatan passes the Cleric and steps toward Kira, making sure their eyes do not meet. When she's close enough, the crickets begin to sing.

Placing a hand on Lumpy's shoulder, Roan whispers, "Go."

Without hesitation, Lumpy walks straight to Kira. Standing beside her, he faces the moon. Its glow is reflected on Lumpy's face, his ravaged skin an ethereal echo of the moon's surface.

Hook-sword in hand, Roan strides over to his companions. His own white cricket crawls out of his pocket and sits on his shoulder, joining the song. Then, with his blade, Roan cuts Kira's bonds, and intones the words Kamyar taught him. "We walk in the shadow of greatness. But when the shadow passes, we will be blessed with the sun." Lifting Kira's fragile body, he turns, Mabatan and Lumpy at his side.

The Cleric opens the cage. Before they pass over the rise, Roan looks back and as the Blue Robe raises his arm, a white bird flies away.

Waiting is not something Stowe does well. She wanted to come up with a plan, try to kill Darius now before it's too late. Willum's great idea was that they trust in Roan. So here they are again. Waiting.

"Kira's still alive?"

"Still."

That's about the hundredth time she's asked. Willum had said she'd know too if something happened to Roan. "Would it be the same if something happened to you?" she'd wanted to know. "Those who are bound by blood and love," he'd said. "So only you can answer that question." And what about him, would he feel it if she died? She knew the question wasn't worthy of an answer, but he'd smiled and whispered, "Yes. I would know."

It's the first evening of the full moon, and as its light spills into the chamber Willum gasps. "It's done. Roan's got her."

He covers his face with his hands. Stowe can read the exhaustion in his body. He hasn't slept or eaten since Kira was captured. She wants to comfort him, but instead she lifts the bowl of fruit from the table and brings it to him.

"Eat. You must eat."

When Querin steps in, Willum is almost himself again. The Master carefully locks the door, and leaves the lights dim. Then, stepping into the center of the room, he activates his small box. His expression is almost feverish, eyes swimming, his head a whirl of purple streaks of light. At a speed that takes Stowe's breath away, he's beside them withdrawing a long, sharp stiletto. Stowe is about to scream, but Willum places a hand firmly on her arm.

Opening his robe, Querin draws the knife across his chest, raising a thin line of blood. He places the knife down in front of them and kneels. "Stowe of Longlight, Willum of the Apsara, the prophecies are at last coming to pass. I mark myself as your servant. Forgive my doubts."

Stowe stares openmouthed.

"You are forgiven," Willum says calmly.

"For decades I have prayed in secret for this day. Now it begins."

"But you are the Archbishop's most trusted advisor," Stowe blurts out. Willum sighs. Had he covered this one of those times she hadn't been listening?

"I serve only the prophecies."

"How much time do we have before Darius activates the Throne?" Willum is taking Querin at his word. Querin. Master of Inculcation. Second only to Darius in power. Are they really supposed to trust him? Darius had been afraid of him...but maybe for the wrong reasons.

"He has announced the Throne's unveiling. The Masters are to assemble before it in eight days' time."

"Master Querin." Willum motions the man to rise. "I suspect you and your colleagues are about to be sacrificed."

preparations for the eclipse

> you are told you're not forgotten
> but that monument smells rotten
> yes, it's shiny but remember:
> all that glitters is not gold.
>
> —Lore of the storytellers

BOTH STOWE AND ROAN ARE OBLIVIOUS TO THE ROCK RAINING DOWN ON THEM. THEY ARE EXHILARATED AND THE ATMOSPHERE AROUND THEM SEEMS ELECTRIC.

ROAN SHAKES HIS HEAD IN DISBELIEF. "I ALWAYS HATED THE PROPHECIES. I FELT LIKE THEY WERE FORCING ME INTO A CORNER I DIDN'T WANT TO BE IN."

"I NEVER PAID ATTENTION TO ANY OF IT. PROBABLY SHOULD HAVE. BUT WE WEREN'T BROUGHT UP WITH THEM, ROAN. QUERIN WAS. I KNEW HIM ONLY AS THE MASTER OF INCULCATION, BUT HE TOOK HIS SECRET TITLE MUCH MORE SERIOUSLY."

"DEFENDER OF THE FAITH." ROAN CAN'T KEEP THE SLIGHTLY MOCKING TONE FROM HIS VOICE.

"HE SAVED KIRA."

"BARELY. SHE WAS HURT, STOWE, IN WAYS I DON'T LIKE TO THINK ABOUT. THAT HE WOULD LET IT GET THAT FAR——"

"WE DON'T KNOW EXACTLY WHAT HAPPENED, ROAN. I KNOW HE'S DANGEROUS BUT WILLUM SAYS WE CAN TRUST HIM. FOR NOW. THE CLERICS WILL GO WHEREVER HE ORDERS——EXCEPT FOR DARIUS'S PERSONAL GUARD. THEY STICK CLOSE TO THE

Keeper. We're only suggesting it because Willum thought it would help."

"Don't get me wrong, it's a great plan. The fewer Clerics Wolf has to deal with at the City gates, the better. It's just hard not to be suspicious."

"Willum says it looks like a good site for an ambush, but if you get there and it feels wrong, get out. Then let me know. Our plans will have to change too if we're being double-crossed." Stowe grabs Roan's hand. "Something's wrong. I have to go. Is it a yes?"

"Yes. Stowe—"

"I'll be very careful, Roan. It seems certain Darius is planning something at the top of the Pyramid. You just have to find a way there."

"What if—"

"No matter what, I'll get him there. I promise. Don't worry about me!"

How can he help it? Roan thinks as he watches his sister fade away. Once Darius had needed her; now she is expendable. The next week will be more dangerous than any Stowe has ever experienced—and he never even said goodbye.

The Academy is thrumming with anticipation. Although the Brothers have already been deployed to the gorge, the Apsara are still honing weapons and checking supplies in preparation for their departure to the City. Roan too is anxious to be on his way, but there's still one last meeting and, before that, he has to attend to the summons he's just received from Algie.

He finds the old Gunther bent over Roan of the Parting's

journal, muttering. He sits opposite him and slides his hand onto the desk where Algie can see it.

Sighing irritably, the old man slowly props up his head, but upon seeing Roan he flashes a gap-toothed grin. "Oh, there you are, at last! Everything seems to take too long since Gwendolen…"

"I know."

"There was a passage she was working on that she was most excited about. I've just finished and thought you should hear it before you go." The old man bends his head as close to the paper as he can without touching it: "*To defeat Darius, Roan of Longlight, you must not stand alone against a darkening sky. Alone, you are nothing. You must travel with a friend.*" Algie shakes his head. "Do you know who that might be?"

Roan smiles. "Could that 'a' be a 'the,' do you think?"

"Humph. You know, Roan of Longlight, you might be right. My mistake, my mistake." The old Gunther shakes his head unhappily.

"Algie, I was teasing. 'A' or 'the' doesn't matter. You've done so much. More than I could ever thank you for."

"No, no, Roan of Longlight, really you mustn't," Algie stands and pats Roan awkwardly. "Just come back. Please. Come back."

Kira, her arms in heavy casts, is arguing with Ende, much to the bemusement of the many warriors who surround them.

"It's not your place!"

"Oh? And are you planning on clobbering your foes to death with those?" Ende scowls, pointing to the casts.

"Let Dai, Petra, or Veet—any of them is well able—"

"I will lead the Apsara into the City. You will not deny me this."

"You ceded leadership to me and I say no!" As Kira gestures emphatically to make her point, she crumples in pain.

Othard runs to her, looking pleadingly at Lumpy and Roan. "These are multiple fractures."

"She risks infection and amputation," adds Imin, joining him at her side.

Kira grimaces, her face pinched, pleading with Ende. "Grandmother, please. Don't go."

"You know I must." Ende kneels before her grand-daughter. "They are not ready, and I will not see life wasted. Kira." Lifting a hand, Ende lays it gently on Kira's cheek. "Kira, they are all my daughters. I must keep them as safe as I may. I will not return, Kira. Shush. I know this. But I go at peace knowing you will be here to lead the Apsara when this is over. My time, Kira, is now. Please, give me your leave."

It is obvious Kira wants to fight but her outburst exhausted her last reserves of energy and she simply inclines her head and sighs, unable to look her grandmother in the face.

"Everyone's waiting, Ende," Roan says gently.

The Apsara matriarch acknowledges him curtly, all emotion tautly reined in. As she leaves, Roan crouches at his cousin's side. "I'd like for you to be there as well."

But Kira does not look up. She lets her head drop even farther and her red hair parts to reveal a livid wound at her neck—where the enabler was removed.

When she notices Roan staring, Kira abruptly twists away. "I'm not...ah...very portable."

Roan signals to Imin. "Imin's brought you a present. It's not much use on stairs, though."

"Not like the ones they have in the City," Othard demurs as Imin rolls a wheelchair over to Kira. "Still, it works."

"Thank you." But as Kira leans forward, she cries out in pain.

Roan tries to catch her eyes but she avoids his gaze. "May I?" he asks cautiously.

The Apsara warrior hesitates and for a moment he worries he's insulted her irreparably. But then she murmurs, almost beneath her breath, "Please."

Arms circled round her waist, he slides her into the makeshift chair. She's lost so much weight since her imprisonment that she feels wraithlike in his grasp. Before he can let her go, she whispers, "Roan. Roan. I'm sorry. I'm sorry."

Roan sighs, gently wiping the tears from her cheeks. "Kira. Nothing I can say will repay your sacrifice. But you are here and you are alive and in this fight your contribution has been great and I thank you. We all do."

Raising her head to look him in the eye, Kira smiles. "Go. I'll be right there." But when he stands, Kira stops him. "Saint was right about you, Roan of Longlight. You will be a great leader."

"You honor me, Kira of the Apsara." And with a bow, he stops up his grief and strides away.

Roan's eyes cast about the room. "The beginning of the eclipse will be the signal for all to act. The Hhroxhi have offered us safe passage. The Storytellers, as you know, have already taken advantage of this and should be plying their trade in the City as we speak. Lumpy."

"Mhyzah's sending an escort; they should be here within the hour. Ende has designated groups of Apsara for each target and will coordinate methods of sabotage with the Gunthers." Lumpy pauses for a moment, then looks intently at Roan. "We need to discuss what we do if the worst happens. If our plan fails. If you don't make it to the City."

Before Roan can protest, Ende concurs. "Your Lieutenant is right. To plan an attack without addressing the threat of the Masters is foolhardy."

"If Darius is killed," says Roan, "it won't be a problem."

"The *if* is exactly what is being discussed."

"You need a failsafe," Kira says, so quietly she is almost not heard, yet everyone stops at the sound of her voice and listens. "Something that will ensure the destruction of the Masters."

Number Fifty-One gapes open-mouthed at Kira. "But... to do that, you would have to destroy the Pyramid."

Eyeing him coolly, Kira simply asks, "How?"

Everyone waits. The Gunther looks down at his hands. Roan understands his dilemma—the Gunthers have steadfastly refused to become directly involved in any violence, but that didn't prevent their persecution in the City or Gwendolen's death. Fifty-One takes out a small cloth and carefully polishes his glasses. "That I cannot say. The Pyramid was built to endure. Its central pylon goes deep into the earth, providing support for the entire structure." Then, putting on his glasses, he says, "Now. If you'll excuse me, I still have some work I need to complete on the Allayer before the Hhroxhi arrive."

The moment the Gunther's left, Lumpy says, "So we have to destroy the central pylon."

"Explosives laid from top to bottom," Kira agrees. "But it

would have to be manually detonated, by someone strategically placed, able to tell if and when it has to be done."

"I'll do it," Lumpy says emphatically. And before Roan can object, he cuts him off. "I'm your Lieutenant. I'm the one who should do it."

"I will go with Lumpy."

Roan gasps, stunned, but Mabatan speaks with a cool clarity, as if what she is saying were the most reasonable thing in the world. "If all else fails, there should be someone with him in case he is attacked. Someone to give him the time he needs to ensure the Pyramid's destruction."

Ende reaches for the Wazya's hand, "Mabatan, I will send one of my warriors. They would be better suited to such a—"

"It's her decision." Kira doesn't look at Ende, but keeps her eyes locked on Mabatan. "The least you can do is respect it."

In the awkward silence that follows, Roan's gaze drifts anxiously between his two friends, terrified at the prospect of losing them both.

As if reading his thoughts, Mabatan speaks quietly into the stillness. "If we reach the point where this must be done, the future we have reaped is one I can no longer be part of."

Roan doesn't want to understand what she's saying. The bruises on her face are fading, the swelling gone down. There's no hint of accusation or even sadness in her eyes or voice. But there's a cold hardness, like what he's seen in Stowe, that speaks to something permanently broken, something that can never be given back.

"Prophet, we must return to the business at hand."

As Roan's gaze falls away from Mabatan, he nods. It takes

a great effort, though, to thrust his emotions to the side and look Wolf in the eye. "Querin is set to reveal our decoy location. My sister says we can expect a full division of Clerics."

The Brothers' commander pauses, scrutinizing Roan, and to his surprise, in the empty space Wolf provides, Roan finds the anticipation he felt an hour ago returning, his energy flooding back to focus on the battle ahead.

Having seen what he's been waiting for, Wolf continues. "The physicians have made the drug, the Gunthers constructed blowguns—both to Mabatan's specifications. Brother Stinger and a contingent of brethren are readying the site. But," Wolf scowls, "if I may, Prophet—Our Stowe is certain of her information?"

"Believe it or not, Brother Wolf, faith is a powerful force in the City as well." Roan looks around the table for further questions but there are none. The next few days will decide their future and it may very well be that this is the last time they will see each other. Still, they must all believe they will succeed.

And so he smiles warmly, and speaks with a heartfelt conviction, "We all meet again, then, when the sun returns to the sky."

The Keeper of the City's brow, normally so taut, is noticeably furrowed. Stowe has no idea why she's been summoned but whatever it is, it can't be good—the Eldest is tilting his head, almost coyly, an early warning of impending doom. "I am about to announce your Coronation," he says.

It's no effort being genuine—Stowe is honestly stunned.

"Did I not promise, my love? I am weary of this world, bored with ambition and appetite. You are young and beloved and ready to rule in my stead."

"Father," Stowe chuckles, but stops abruptly under Darius's suddenly angry stare. "You cannot be serious." She's oddly flustered—but that's appropriate, isn't it?

"Daughter, I know you too well for you to deny that you have dreamt of this moment. Do not weary me with polite protestations."

"But, Father, in the midst of all this turmoil?" *Is* this the moment she's been waiting for? Or did Querin slip somehow? Kordan spot something?

Darius's fury rolls over her like a hot iron. "Are you questioning my judgment?"

"No, Eldest, but your expertise is—"

Darius's eyelids have almost closed, but even so his eyes are locked on hers. "If you are not willing to embrace this privilege, perhaps I should choose another."

"Father—"

"Do you accept?" A scintillating smalt green smoke escapes from his eyes, reaching, reaching toward her.

"Of course, I accept, Father, since you desire it."

"A Coronation. In two days' time I shall unveil my Dreamfield Throne, and then you shall take your place at the center of the Pyramid."

"Who will I go to for help, Father? Who can I trust?" She hopes Willum has good news when he returns. If everything went as planned, the timing couldn't be better.

"You have always known the answer to that, Daughter: trust no one. Everywhere I turn, I hear them sharpening their knives. All clamoring for advancement. You must keep them occupied fighting each other; that way the fools will not see the true threat."

"And what is that, Father?"

Darius stares blankly beyond her.

"Father?"

His eyes glide with sickening slowness back to her. "Yes, my pet?"

"What is the true threat, Father?"

"My apologies, Daughter. My mind is restless with dreaming. You see why it is time for me to leave everything to you."

"Father—"

Darius rises and kisses Stowe on the forehead with his desiccated lips. "You will discern it soon enough, my love." Turning from her, he shouts to the unseen Cleric beyond the door. "Yes?"

The door opens and the Cleric bows. "It is done, Eldest."

Darius's lips pinch into a smile. "Oh, good. And it was well received?"

"The Absent pray before it as we speak, Archbishop, many hundreds, perhaps thousands."

"You may go." Darius waves the Cleric away. There is almost a jauntiness to his step. "We've created a new monument to you, my daughter, in honor of your Coronation. Pure silver with your image engraved upon on its surface."

"A monument?" Stowe asks, dumbfounded. What is Darius up to? "For the Absent?"

"Precisely. They're starving down there, poor souls, it should bolster their spirits. Now you must see to your wardrobe. I've taken the liberty—" Darius glowers suddenly, looking down at her feet. A white cricket rubs its wings together, beginning its song. "Vermin. Second one I've seen today," he hisses, then stepping so close that her cheek grazes his robe, he squashes it under his heel.

While Stowe is with the Keeper, Willum moves covertly toward the ghetto of the Absent. Querin's scheme to divert Clerics to a battle in the Farlands has had great effect. Their numbers are remarkably reduced; it will be much easier now for the Apsara to pass unnoticed into the City. He makes his way toward a massive gathering.

People are bowing in supplication to a great silver cylinder, twenty feet high. Etched upon its face is a portrait of Our Stowe, her fingers raised in blessing. This is no ordinary monument. Willum recognizes it at once as an Apogee. He would like to get closer—but it is not possible. Clerics hover around the perimeter, ready to act if things get out of control, and he needs to move unseen.

Gliding past the throng into an alley, he quickens his pace. It is not long before he's arrived at the decrepit stucco wall. Entering the courtyard, he steps over to the windowless concrete cube and touches it in an elaborate configuration. A small door slides open and Willum steps in.

Gunther Number Six is there to meet him. "Willum, your friends are about to arrive." The floor they are standing on descends.

"Your cooperation is much—"

"Did you know? The Dirt Eaters have taken Seventy-Nine's life."

"Seventy-Nine?" He remembers her face as he last saw her, proud but etched with tears, forever marked by the abuse she'd experienced in the square that day.

"I see you were not informed. So many disquieting events.

Seventeen of us have been lost, murdered by the Conurbation. It is clear now that many of those who were returned to us from prison are damaged beyond hope of repair."

"Perhaps we are wrong to involve you—"

"At first I was upset by the request. But it is our contribution, Willum, to this cause. Your sister put the life of Eleven before her own and we know the price she paid. We will not fight, but we do not have to sit quietly before this injustice."

"Thank you, Number Six."

"The devices are ready. And you were correct about the Hhroxhi. Their language and culture are fascinating."

Willum smiles. "They also share many of your aversions."

"Yes. And yet they stand with you as well."

The elevator passes the library and Number Six clears his throat. "The explosion that killed Seventy-Nine took our friend Dobbs too. I thought you...should know."

Number Six pushes his glasses against his nose and as the elevator shudders to a halt on the lowest floor, he scurries away.

"Well," a jocular voice calls out, "old friend. Close calls on all sides."

"I'm sorry, Kamyar, Number Six just told me—"

"Willum. There will be time enough for that after. Sorrow cannot ride at the warrior's side."

"You've begun?"

"Of course, we've been at it for days, telling tales of renewal and insurrection to whoever will listen. We've been trying to convince the Absent to stay in their homes, but that shiny eyesore Darius erected has attracted them like ants to honey."

"It's an Apogee. It must be destroyed, Kamyar."

"Final deployment's being discussed tonight. I'll add it to our agenda."

"Quickly, they are here!" announces Number Six, who is standing beside a large, open duct. One by one, they climb over its edge—Mabatan, Lumpy, Mhyzah, with dozens of Apsara behind.

Mabatan spots Willum instantly. The echo of Kira's suffering still marks her cheek and eye, and the loss he feels when she presses herself into his arms is almost beyond bearing.

"Much has happened since I saw you last," she says, pulling away from the embrace, her voice burdened but her old pragmatism shining through. She has survived the ordeal and will, in time, be stronger for it.

"And more is still to come," mutters Ende, emerging from behind her warriors.

The memory of his vision slams over the sight of her, blood flecking the air like the first heavy raindrops in a downpour. "What are you doing here, Grandmother?"

"I'm Kira's replacement." Ende pauses, squaring her jaw defiantly. "There was no other choice, Willum. I do only what I must."

Any frustration he may have had with the Apsara matriarch dissipates instantly. It is an obvious truth she speaks and he needs no special power to sense her personal anguish and the effort it is taking for her to conceal it. "I know," he whispers, and wraps her, one last time, in his arms. Looking over her shoulder he sees Petra, and her cocky smile of greeting is like a spear piercing his side.

With a sigh, he draws back and scans the faces of all the friends around him. "I cannot stay. I just needed to ensure you had all arrived safely. When the moon bites the sun, it will begin. May we survive these days."

The sounds around him muffled by his own heartbeat, he memorizes tiny details—Dai tossing her hair and laughing, Lumpy's concerned but confident nod, Mhyzah's fist tapping her heart—then he pries himself away, and strides quickly to the elevator.

Stretching an arm around his shoulder, Kamyar joins him for the ride. They stand silently together, deeply immersed in their own thoughts, until the floor settles with a jolt at the top.

"What say, Willum, after this is over," Kamyar says with a sidelong glance, his usual bluster muted, "we sit together in the open air of Conurbation Park, and share an ale or two or three and speak of old friends?" They had both long ago accepted the inevitability of this moment; now their faith must endure the ultimate test—and Kamyar was never one to acknowledge the possibility of failure.

"Agreed," Willum accepts with a smile, and with Kamyar's firm slap still stinging his back, he crouches through the door. His head has barely cleared the concrete wall when he spots them—three Clerics in the courtyard. Well-armed.

"So. What do we have here?" one of them crows arrogantly. "A strange place for Our Stowe's Primary to be lurking about."

"What business is it of yours?"

"Master Kordan's business is our business. And, it seems, his doubts about you were justified."

These three are so full of swagger and self-importance, they should be easy to take.

The Cleric smirks at Willum as he motions his cohorts to enter the concrete cube. "How kind of you to open this door. We've been at it since we saw you go in." Brandishing a flare, he continues, "Master Kordan says you're dangerous, so I'm not taking any—" Mouth gaping, the Cleric stares down at his chest. A knitting needle is protruding from his heart.

As the dead man falls into Willum's arms, Kamyar slips out from between the two Clerics at his feet and whispers, "Always glad to be of assistance."

the gorge

PRESUPPOSING THE KEEPER'S FORTIFIED BIOFIELD IS FED
BY THE THRONE CONSTRUCTION, I HAVE DETERMINED THAT
a TIMED CEASE-FUNCTION WILL WEAKEN HIM at a
CRITICAL JUNCTURE, *if* sufficient NUMBERS OF ENABLERS
ARE affected.

—ALGERNON'S ENABLER FILE REPORT 7.4

EVERYONE IS IN POSITION AND READY. Roan hopes they won't have to wait long. It's hard to keep focused in the cold and even he finds his attention wandering.

The Caldera is barely visible against the eastern horizon. Alandra must already be there. His falling out with her in Newlight seems a lifetime ago. And yet, that was where so much began. If he comes out of this battle alive, he'll go see her. Even if she's unable to hear him or even know that he's there.

Far in the distance, glints of silver reflect the sun. "They're coming," reports Stinger, peering through a spyglass. "Twenty-five troop carriers, all equipped with Apogees."

"Glad to see Querin went all-out," Wolf comments dryly. "How much fuel do they have stockpiled?"

The awe in Stinger's voice is echoed in Wolf's face, as he turns to Roan. "We're lucky the embargo was successful or he'd be sending air machines, like he did during the Consolidation."

The quickest way here had been through the Devastation. One hundred years hadn't lessened the reek of death, and visions of Darius's bombs exterminating rebel armies are fresh in everyone's minds.

"Still," Wolf mutters, shifting uneasily, "we'd better hope the Master of Inculcation hasn't cooked up any nasty surprises."

Roan can understand his reservations. He'd had his doubts as well. But when he arrived he knew they couldn't have found a better place for an ambush. The oncoming Clerics would see nothing but a forbidding cliff face running for miles on either side of the gorge. In reality, though, there were many avenues of descent, and numerous small corridors wide enough to hide horses and through which they could ride to attack their enemy.

"Don't worry. There won't be."

"Good. Because seventy-five against a thousand means we all die. And there's no guarantee the darts—"

"Mabatan can be trusted." Pulling away from the spyglass, Stinger stares sternly at his commander. Both he and Roan know why Wolf's being so difficult. A third of the army is untested, Roan's age and even younger. Eager, but if things went wrong, more of a liability than help. "The drug will work as planned."

"Brother Wolf," Roan says, drawing his attention away from Stinger. "When I saw the Friend, his eyes were gouged, his vision impaired. We choose this path to give Him back his sight. He will breathe fire into the hearts of us all this day."

Pulling himself up to his full height, Wolf smiles proudly. "You speak like a Brother, Roan of Longlight."

Only a few weeks ago he was ready to fight Wolf for saying much the same thing, but in that time Roan's come to realize that distinguishing between enemy and friend, whether god or human, was more of a challenge than he'd thought. So he lets the statement stand and returns Wolf's smile. Then, eyeing the approaching vehicles, he breathes deeply. "How long, Brother Stinger?"

"It is time."

In the long, narrow gorge sits a sprawling campsite, with scores of tents flapping in the wind and campfires blazing. Brother Wolf whistles long and loud, and the Brothers positioned there ready their weapons. Then he whistles again, this time short and sharp, and a dozen crossbowmen scramble to their positions along the ridges.

The trucks are almost upon them when Wolf gives the final signal. Arrows rain down from the ridge and along the ground, piercing the wheels of the vehicles. The trucks career wildly, smashing into each other, skidding across the plain. Secure in the effectiveness of their new weapon, hundreds of Clerics pour into the gorge, brandishing swords and stunners, like lemmings off a cliff, while others man the Apogees.

Wolf gives the signal to ready the Allayers. The archers on the ground sprint straight back through the camp, chased by hosts of Clerics. As the Brothers reach the back wall, ropes swing down and they are hoisted up. With a glance at Roan, Wolf and Stinger make their way down to the horses hidden below.

The Clerics suddenly realize that they're at a dead end—but too late. At the mouth of the gorge, thirty blowguns have already begun their work. The Blue Robes collapse from the drug, one after the other, obstructing the exit for those further in.

Alerted by the whirr of the Apogees powering up, Roan gives the command to initiate the Allayers. The reaction of the Clerics behind the weapons is at first confused, but within moments, calls for retreat fill the air. Roan looks down at the litter of unconscious bodies below him. At least two hundred Clerics are still struggling to get out. As soon as he's signaled the crossbowmen, Roan takes out his blowgun and sets to work.

Out of the corner of his eye, he sees that the first fusillade of fiery arrows has forced the remainder of the Clerics out of their trucks. Then, from either side of the perimeter of the gorge, he hears Wolf and Stinger emerge, leading the Brothers' cavalry attack. Only a handful of Clerics are still struggling in the gorge. Leaving two Brothers behind to finish the job, Roan motions the others forward. They're going down.

As they fan out to join the battle on the plain, Roan is swarmed by a phalanx of Clerics. Drawing out his hook-sword, he strikes again and again, hitting heads with the flat side of his blade, kicking hard to the chest or chin—careful not to land a mortal blow. Weaving through the scores of horses that lie wounded, their riders trapped beneath them, Roan circles and spins, his sword strokes a blur until a Cleric's hand cinches around his ankle.

Stumbling back, he's pinned by two Clerics against a fallen horse. As he fends off their swords, Stinger, moving with the stealth and focus of a sand painter, rives them one after another with his double-pointed spear. Throwing himself back into the melee, Roan plows through the Clerics until they are a sea of bloodied blue cloth.

Chest heaving, his ears ringing from the silence, Roan turns. In every direction, only Brothers are left standing.

Joining Roan at the center of the battlefield, Wolf's breath is short, his eyes overly bright, the veins on his bald head still pulsing with adrenaline. "They battled well and died with honor."

Stinger, arm bleeding, stares out at the grisly remains, shaking his head. "I'll keep fifteen Brothers with me," he mutters. "We'll set the pyre, separate the wounded." He does not wait for Roan to respond but turns instantly to choose his men.

The Hhroxhi are already on the field. They've agreed to tend the injured, but shelter in the tunnels for an army of a thousand was out of the question. Crowded together and protected by the gorge, the uninjured will survive the cold, but Roan is worried some of the wounded might not.

"Everyone else to the gorge," Wolf orders. "Begin the scan!"

Pulling out the hand-sized devices, the Brothers creep from Cleric to Cleric, modifying their enablers. The sight is disturbingly reminiscent of stories Roan's read about scavengers who scour the battlefields to rob the bodies of the dead. But these men are alive. Most of them. And they're being released from a prison they might not even know they were in.

Brother Wolf watches with a disgruntled look on his face. "And when they awaken. What then?"

"How would you react? If you woke up no longer in Darius's control."

"They will still have their faith."

"The prophecies shape their beliefs. You may find they are not so dissimilar to your own."

Wolf eyes Roan skeptically. "Soon the war will be over. What need will we have then for such an army? Killing them would have been easier." Before Roan can answer, Wolf looks back in the direction of the City and asks, "When do you leave, Roan of Longlight?"

"After the tribute to the Friend."

"Hhroxhi are readying Allayers for positioning outside the City gates as we speak. The moment the eclipse begins, we attack."

"Friend willing, in two days' time I will find you there."

"Friend willing," Wolf says, squinting at the horizon. And running a hand over his bald head, he sighs and turns to join his men in the gorge.

Roan had hoped their parting would be easier, but Wolf has never approved of this part of the plan. He'd wanted Roan to lead the Brothers to the gates of the City, and dismissed all of Roan's protestations with outraged sputterings. But in the end, he'd accepted it, in his fashion, because Roan had said that he knew it was what Wolf had dreamt of doing since he went to train with Ende as a child. The Friend had clearly singled him out for this task, and so Roan was sure Wolf would succeed.

As he watches his commander take charge of the field, Roan goes over the events of the day. Over a thousand Clerics demobilized with a minimum of blood spilled. Walking toward the pyre, Roan wishes he could find it in himself to look at the faces of the fallen so that he might remember the cost of this accomplishment. But he cannot.

the wrath of darius

when, by day, the moon's shadow is seen crossing the city, children will laugh, as if awakening from a bad dream.

—the book of Longlight

T HE FATES WERE WITH THEM, and the sky is clear. The wind's forbiddingly frigid, but here, near the top of the tallest building in the City, heat rises from the elevator shaft and keeps Mabatan and Lumpy warm.

This vantage point provides them with an unobstructed view of the battle about to unfold. Through the binoculars Number Six gave her, Mabatan scans the areas where the initial clashes will take place: the gates of the City, the square where the giant Apogee stands in the ghetto of the Absent, and, far in the distance the Quarry's great pit and the concrete bunker where the Dirt is refined and stored. Mines have been set, Allayers transported, troops positioned. Soon, at the top of this very building, Roan will confront Darius.

But if all fails, there is the detonator in Lumpy's hand.

Last night, disguised as Gunthers, she and Petra had entered the Pyramid. While they'd seemingly gone about maintenance work on the central elevator shaft, they'd covertly completed their mission. Swinging down from ropes attached to a pulley at the Pyramid's apex, they'd positioned the explosive gum along the entire length of the central pylon.

"Look, Mab, no hands!" Petra had whispered, flipping as

she let herself down another story, her harness bearing all her weight. Mabatan had followed, but slowly, hand over hand, carefully pressing the explosive into place.

"It's not good, being so serious before battle," Petra'd said, slipping alongside. "It's bad luck. Come on, Mab. Roan will be here. The Hhroxhi sent word the battle at the gorge went as planned. It will all turn out right."

"I am not worried about myself, Petra. But...hundreds of people dwell in this building. People who are not Masters—"

"Every war has a price," Petra'd said, her manner matter-of-fact. "They're killers, Mab."

"I know that. But if Roan fails, the Dreamfield will collapse...and it will only be a matter of time before—"

"Blast the prophecies, Mab! We fight till the bitter end, no matter what, because even if we lose the battle, even if we lose our lives, maybe someone else will win the war. That's who you fight for. The ones who come after."

Mabatan had managed a weary smile, and the young Apsara had grinned content, flicking her wrist and rappelling down to the next level.

Still, Mabatan had been unable to sleep, and the sun had been barely over the horizon when the Gunther had guided her and Lumpy onto this platform just beneath the top floor at the apex of the Pyramid. She has had all morning to inspect the site and determine where an attack might come. But Lumpy is still nervous, and she cannot blame him. Watching him inspect the detonator for the hundredth time, she hopes against hope that Petra is right. That there will be an after.

"Are you sure they can't see us?" Lumpy stares at the glass above and below them suspiciously.

"I believe Eighty-Four answered that question many times last night."

"Yeah. He said stuff about alignment of girders and light refraction and depth of field and I didn't understand a word of it."

"If they come, I'll be ready," Mabatan says, patting the quiver of Nethervine-dipped darts that's mounted to her blowgun. Then, lifting a hand to shield her eyes, she looks up at the sky. "The moon's disk has just touched the sun. Is Ende in position?"

"Nearly. See them? There, at the edge of the ghetto." Lumpy frowns. "It's a weak position, Mabatan. Once they're in the square, they'll be hemmed in—"

"There was no other choice."

Kamyar's news about the giant Apogee had altered their plans. Disguised as Absent, the Gunthers had ventured out for a closer look. Their news hadn't been good. The silver encasing the Apogee masked a shield that rendered their Allayers useless. The engravings of Stowe disguised doors set to open when and only if the Apogee was activated. The only way to destroy it would be to topple the monument before the weapon was put into use.

An Apogee surrounded by Clerics meant there would be a bit of a fight. So Ende had decided to take it on. With twelve of her best, the matter would be easily dispatched—they'd infiltrate the crowd, getting close enough to take down the Blue Robes quickly, without warning, then, together, topple and destroy Darius's disguised weapon. Kamyar had come forward to commit his Storytellers to replace Ende and her twelve at their appointed installations, sabotage and subterfuge being very closely linked, he'd said with a wink. Still, he'd spent most of the night sharpening his needles.

"If Ende'd seen it from here, she might have changed her mind." Lumpy lets the binoculars drop and looks helplessly at Mabatan.

"Ende can take care of herself."

"I'm aware of that."

Mabatan can see she's offended him, but she is so sick with worry herself that she feels incapable of offering any calming words.

"I hope they do it quickly," Lumpy mutters anxiously. "And get out fast."

A flash of light draws their attention from the square to the refinery. Over the percussive blast that follows, Mabatan cries out, "It begins."

The mines ignite one after another around the rim of the great pit, and within seconds, it collapses inside itself. The concrete bunker blasts apart, sending a black cloud into the sky. The ground around it caves in, and soon the entire site is one huge hollow, the Dirt within buried under thousands of tons of concrete and earth.

Mabatan allows herself a moment of quiet satisfaction and fixes an image of Khutumi firmly in her mind. *Father, today we see an end to the Dirt.*

Sirens blare from the east side of the Absents' ghetto. "How many do you see?" Lumpy shouts.

Her heart starts to pound as she tries to count the racing vehicles. "Seven—no nine, ten. Ten trucks, perhaps twenty Clerics in each. All headed for the Quarry. It is working! Only skeleton defenses at the gates, as we hoped. Look! The Brothers. Can you see them?"

With the Allayers positioned before them, Wolf and his

warriors are spilling out onto the plain by the dozens and there are virtually no Clerics left to stop their incursion.

Mabatan cannot help but feel hope bursting in her chest, filling her with purpose and pride. "Light the flare, Lumpy! Light it!" But when she turns to Lumpy, she sees a tear roll down his cheek. "What's wrong?"

Lumpy does not answer. He lights the flare and watches it explode over the ghetto. Then, setting his crossbow down, he leans in close and speaks quietly into her ear. "Over the last few weeks, those Apsara have become my friends, Mabatan. Up here, giving the signal...I feel like their executioner." Turning his face away, he stares down at the square below. "They're friends, Mabatan," he calls out. "Friends."

When Stowe enters the Grand Travel Room two steps behind the Archbishop, the Masters stand by their glass chairs in deference. Darius glides to the only Master still sitting, but Stowe can read his anxiety and rage in the tiny red sparks that fly from his shoulders. Willum had said the Mad Masters would destroy all they could, in the hopes of weakening Darius's defenses and clearing the way for Roan—how much they had managed to accomplish with Kordan and his cronies on their tail, she's about to find out.

As the Keeper touches his servant's sagging face, Kordan's eye opens and he bolts forward. "Archbishop, the Mad Masters are defeated."

"Yes, my dear Kordan? But at what cost?"

"The Ramparts, the Antlia, the Gyre and Ocellus...all destroyed."

"You said defeated. Are they dead, Kordan? I want them dead."

"We maneuvered them into the Spiracal's influence. They were swallowed up. They must be dead. They must be... Keeper—"

At that moment, the door bursts open and Querin enters, the Clerics behind him delivering the desiccated corpses of the three Mad Masters. "The code to their quarters had been altered." The Master of Inculcation seems to scrutinize every face in the room simultaneously. "Presumably by the same individual who provided them with Dirt."

The Masters all begin to talk at once, trying to make sense out of what's happened.

"Get them out of my sight," Darius hisses.

But Querin only moves closer to the Eldest, his voice rising above the clamor. "Theirs," he says, pointing to the bodies of the Mad Masters, "is not the only act of sabotage. The Quarry and its contents have been destroyed."

The room is deathly quiet, but the terror in the Masters' faces is fleeting and is rapidly replaced by doubt and disbelief.

A grin spreads across Darius's face. "It matters not. Dirt is obsolete! Not required!"

Terror's back now. And suspicion.

"Not required?" simpers Master Fortin. "How can that be, Eldest?"

"Come, my friends. I will show you. The Mad Ones did not succeed in harming my greatest achievement. Join me now and I will show you power beyond anything we had thought possible. Kordan, distribute the Dirt. It will be the last time you need to use it, my friends. The power of my Throne has made Dirt an anachronism."

But not one of the Masters accepts. Not one sits down.

"Do you dare to doubt me, Masters?"

Stowe wants to take a step back. Distance herself from him. But she must not. One wrong move and he'll try to kill her.

"Explain, Fortin."

Master Fortin opens his mouth but he cannot speak. He blubbers and drools.

She can feel Darius gripping Fortin's little mind. To Stowe, Fortin appears glazed in a slippery putrid green that squeezes him relentlessly. But she can also see what the other Masters witness. The manager's arms tightening against his body, his hands in fists, his face frozen, the gasps, the blood gushing from his eyes. Fortin convulses on his feet for minutes, a sickening recreation of the puppet he has always been, before he collapses in a motionless heap.

"I created you," snarls the Eldest, hand outstretched, searching for his next victim. "I redeemed your rotting flesh, rejuvenated you in the Gyre. If it were not for me, you would all be long in the grave. Masters! I have defeated death itself! Your last chance," he calls out. "Take your Dirt and immortality shall be yours."

Most of the Masters are old, decrepit. They are exhausted and habit has reduced their talents to the intrigue of maintaining their positions. Direct confrontation is foreign to them and they stand paralyzed, incapable of action. What now?

"Shall I kill you all?" *Sit.*

The command is felt, like a compulsion, and is obeyed instantaneously, the Masters' eyes glazing over.

Take the Dirt at your sides.

Stowe's heart sinks as she watches the Masters' fingers dipping into pots, sliding over lips. Darius pivots slowly to face her and Querin, the only two who remain standing. "Ah,

Master Querin. This is not a surprise, but tell me anyway, why you do not sit?" *Sit.* "You disappoint me."

"I serve the Conurbation as I have always."

"And when exactly did you stop serving me?"

Stowe gasps as wave after wave of serpentine green issues from Darius's mouth.

But Querin was obviously aware of the Keeper's destructive capabilities and has prepared a defense. A helix of purple filaments unfurls from his feet to the crown of his head. One layer after another, they protectively weave around him. Darius's furious assault loops harmlessly along these threads until the deadly energy is dissipated.

Undaunted, Darius grins at his betrayer. "Their deaths will be quick. Not so with you. You, I will roast over the fires of hell. You ignorant prophecy whore." But just as Stowe feels a lethal power building within Darius, he collapses, writhing, to the floor.

Querin looks coldly down at him. "Roan of Longlight found a way to simultaneously shut down a great number of the clergy's enablers. Without their support, you are nothing but a pathetic mad old fool."

"You dare! You dare!?"

Crawling to the closest seated master, Darius reaches for his Dirt. He smells it, then his head snaps back to Querin. "Orgeine powder to induce sleep."

"Archbishop, you issued the command. You forced them to take the Dirt. It was you who sealed their lips. Your servant, Kordan, surely would have warned you if he could have."

As Darius's head swivels in her direction, Stowe trembles, tears flowing down her cheeks. "Father," she whimpers.

Darius's gaze narrows. The bulge of his eyes beneath his

drooping lids rolls madly from her to Querin. But Stowe remains steadfast in her performance, Querin's promise helping her to overcome a rising panic: "He will expect me to protect you because of my faith. When I do not, he will assume it is because I believe you corrupted. He will see you as his only possible power source, an ally. He will not harm you." That was what Querin had said; Stowe hopes he was right.

Rallying his strength, Darius rises and reaches out a hand. "Come, Daughter. Help me. Hurry!"

The moon has halved the sun and its waning life drains across the eastern sky like blood in a pool of water. At its side, Mabatan can see the bull's horns clearly traced by the now visible stars. *We have until the bull rises in the east. After that comes the end of all possibility.* The prophecy spoke of *this* day. It was not just Darius rushing things forward—everything that had happened had moved them all toward this moment.

"The Hhroxhi are coming up behind the gates!" shouts Mabatan over the harsh, whistling wind. She and Lumpy have found a position on the edge of the platform where, leaning back to back, they can each easily follow their respective engagements; but even this close the relentless howl of winter makes it necessary to yell. She's surprised at the release shouting gives her, as if this was what she'd needed all along. "No opposition. The Brothers eliminated all the perimeter guards in the field. The Hhroxhi are opening the gates! The Brothers are pouring in!"

"Ende's almost made her way through the crowd," Lumpy calls out, his voice ragged with tension. Mabatan can feel it in the tightness of his back, in the strong thumping of his heart. And without warning, it takes her over, it takes her over and she's back in the box with Kira, with the smell of blood and the fear and the pain. The terrible pain. She longs to close her eyes, leave this place, this battle, ride the wind to her father. Not since she was a small child has she so longed to be encased in his arms, still and empty.

"The Apsara are throwing off their robes. One Cleric down. Two. Three. Almost there—" Lumpy jolts forward, throwing Mabatan off balance. Falling to his knees, he screams helplessly into the raging winds. "Look out!"

Mabatan edges closer, placing a hand on Lumpy's shoulder. He twists his head so she can hear him and shouts, "Four battalions. They're coming from all sides. Send up a red flare."

Mabatan follows the order. She does not say that no one can possibly make it in time to help the Apsara. They must do whatever they can. Fight to the bitter end. As she puts down the crossbow, she breathes deeply, even though she knows there is no preparing for what she is about to witness.

Training her binoculars on the square, she watches the crowd part for the Clerics. Just as Lumpy feared, they have the Apsara trapped. There are scores of them to Ende's twelve.

"How could we be so stupid," Lumpy cries out, furious. "It must be Darius's honor guard. We should have known a giant Apogee was too important—" Lumpy gasps. "Oh. Oh. No."

"Veet. Dai. Nim." She whispers their names as they fall.

Petra's collapsed into Ende's arms. To see the leader's scream is to feel it rattling your bones. As Petra slides down Ende's body, lifeless, the Apsara leader smears the blood of the slaughtered warrior across her face. Her blade, one with her rage, takes every life it touches. Clerics' blood cascades through the air like rain. But she cannot save them. Nira. Kai…one after the other they fall. One after the other. Lumpy is shaking beside her. Guin. Ilf. His friends.

Almost two hundred against their twelve and the last Cleric has fallen. But of the Apsara only Ende remains alive. She is at the Apogee struggling to bring it down. There is no one left to help. The monument is ten times her size and she has nothing but her sword. Though Mabatan cannot see her face, she knows Ende is weeping, howling with fury and frustration. She strikes again and again with her weapon—she might as well use her fists for all the good it will do. Soon there's a sea of hands clawing at her. The Absent. The very people she's trying to save tug and pull at her, trying to drag her from their goddess's monument.

And she and Lumpy are here. Out of reach. Unable to help. Only able to witness. Staring at the square, she memorizes every detail she has seen. In case there is an after. For you, Petra. For Ende…Dai…

There is a rush of warm air behind her. The elevator is on its way to the top of the Pyramid. Mabatan reaches for her quiver but then remembers—Darius's honor guard lie dead in the square. It is unlikely now that the battle will come to her. No. Now it is up to Willum and Stowe.

The elevator doors open to the staggering view of a crescent sun against an electric blue sky. Stowe can sense that Willum's near. But where? Here or on the floor just below. She can't see him. As Darius pushes her into the apex of the Pyramid, the doors whisper closed behind them and the elevator descends, providing them with an uninterrupted view of the entire City. Clouds of black smoke rise from the ruined Quarry. Dozens of buildings are already aflame and one explosion after another rocks the floor. Darius turns to take it all in, and extending both his arms, he cries, exultant, "Tear it all down! Nothing on this earth matters."

Digging his nails into her wrist, he stumbles to the east face of the pyramid with her in tow. The Keeper peers down at a shining obelisk, the monument he had dedicated to her. Thousands of Absent are rioting in the square around it. From here they look like ants crawling over each other for a chance to touch the garish object. Roan's people have failed to destroy it.

"Here's a lesson for you, Stowe." Darius is gloating. "I lost Roan and the Novakin, but did I give up? No. I enhanced the enablers. Querin says your brother has disabled them. That might have defeated me had I stopped there. I'd hoped the Masters might have provided me with enough of a boost, but I wasn't relying on them, oh no, I was prepared for Querin to make his move, and a good thing too. I created the Apogee and now the Absent shall return all the favors I have bestowed on them." Darius flicks open a panel on one of the girders. "I want to smell the death, Stowe. Breathe it in."

A cold blast of air forces them back as the entire eastern wall of the Pyramid opens outward and unfolds to form a platform. Stowe feels the panic rising inside her. Willum must not have made it to this floor. She can't wait any longer, or it might be too late. She has to act now.

Marshalling all her reserves, Stowe faces Darius and screams until he is thrown hard against the wall, his decrepit chest heaving. She screams until his face turns a bony white, his eyes bulge in their sockets and his ears bleed. He's clawing at something behind him and yanks it forward. Willum! NO!

He must have been holding Darius from behind without her seeing him. The veins stand out on Willum's face, a bright blue. Oh no. Nononononono. *Willum, I didn't mean to hit you, I didn't...*

Sliding back toward the platform, Darius scrambles to reach the open panel.

Stop Darius. Stop him, Stowe.

Turning from Willum, she rushes to grab Darius's feet, but he kicks like a struggling pig and she can't get hold. She shoves at him but it only moves him closer to the girder. Pulling himself to his feet, the Keeper begins to tap in a code. Willum stumbles toward Darius just as he finishes. The high-pitched whistle of the Apogee can be heard even from here. All hope is lost for the Absent. How many seconds before their life-force revitalizes Darius?

Willum swings Darius toward the edge of the platform, but the Keeper's ancient claws hook into Willum's robe. As they crash to the floor, Willum plunges his thumbs into Darius's eyes.

Reaching below her dress to the knife concealed there, Stowe advances on the struggling men. She feels as if she were pushing against a mountain of flame and ice. With a gasp of despair, she sees the air folding in shimmering waves over the ghetto. The Keeper is beginning to glow, glow like the edges of the moon. The Apogee is feeding his biofield, just as Willum explained, and in the growing darkness it is clear that soon he will be powerful enough to cast Willum aside.

She has to move. She will not be cheated of her prize. With all her will, she pushes herself forward. She cannot scream, Willum is too close, but Darius's chest is almost in reach. She raises the knife. Suddenly her feet slide out from underneath her. Darius grasps her wrist and squeezes. The knife. He's trying to get the knife. She rolls away but he wrenches her back and… she's caught. Caught in the stupid dress. Kicking, desperate to free herself from the fabric, she pushes her wrist as hard as she can against his thumb. Her wrist abruptly wrenches free, but her weapon is jarred from her fingers.

As she tries to slide away, she can see the knife, her knife, in Darius's hand. She can't move fast enough, it's plunging right for her. Willum throws himself on top of her and she feels his body stiffen. The knife moves straight through him. She feels it scratch against the filo-armor that covers her chest. It scratches back and forth and Willum slumps…his blood…his life…escaping…escaping.

Stowe. Stowe. Kill him. You must kill him.

Stifling sobs that thrash like a furious sea within her, she pushes Willum aside. Darius is taking out his small box of violet dust. He takes a pinch between his fingers and puts the Dirt to his lips. A white cricket lands on his hand. Shaking it off, he crushes it with his foot. One after another they land around him.

Push him. Push him now.

Bending toward her, Darius reaches for her face. But before the Dirt can touch her lips, a light flares. A white cloud passes over the hole that was the sun, moving straight toward them. Her brother. With wings. Wings and a cloud of millions of white crickets around him.

"Look, Darius. My brother comes to destroy you."

Darius turns and is swarmed by crickets. Roan lands beside her, quickly sliding out of the translucent wings. But she can't wait. She pushes. She pushes with all her might.

But even as Darius falls, she knows he has already left this world for his Dreamfield Throne and she has lost. Lost her chance for revenge. Lost everything. Far below them she can see the wisps of life-force streaming from every corner of the ghetto into the Apogee. She knows where it is heading: straight to Darius and his Throne.

She cries in rage and fury. She feels her brother's arms around her.

"Stowe, it's not too late. We can—"

"No. No. I can't go. Not now, Roan. Get him. Please. Please!"

She hears him whisper, "I'll be back, Stowe, I'll be back. After."

But what does that mean—After? Willum is dying. He's dying. *Willum. Willum. Don't go. Please come back.* She puts her face against Willum's chest. *Come back. Come back.* Filaments of the life remaining in his blood reach out to her fingers, her eyes, her heart. *Come back.*

Stowe, please, let me go.

She pulls the badger ring from where she'd hidden it and slips it on her finger. She can feel Willum on the edge of her consciousness, the hawk, trying to fly away. Fly away from her. *Noooo.*

Stowe, please, let me go.

I can't, Willum. I can't. You have to stay with me.

Stowe, no. Please. You don't know.

Willum, I can't. You have to stay. You have to.

ROAN STREAKS AFTER THE RED EAGLE. SPEED. SPEED. HE NEEDS MORE SPEED.

AS DARIUS BEGINS HIS DESCENT INTO THE IRIDESCENT OUT-

STRETCHED PALM, ROAN ROCKETS INTO HIM. THE COLLISION SENDS THEM BOTH CAREENING WILDLY THROUGH THE AIR. ROAN REACHES OUT, GRIPPING ONE OF THE EAGLE'S LEGS.

THE EAGLE RAKES ITS FREE TALONS ACROSS ROAN'S CHEST AND SINKS ITS BEAK INTO HIS HAND. OILY BLACK SMOKE CURLS OVER THE OPEN WOUNDS. REELING WITH PAIN, ROAN LOSES HIS GRIP AND DARIUS HURLS HIMSELF DESPERATELY AT THE THRONE.

CRICKETS POUR OUT OF THE SKY, SWELLING IN SIZE UNTIL THEY ARE GIANTS. BUZZING LIKE LOCUSTS, THE CRICKETS SURROUND DARIUS'S CONSTRUCTION. PERCHED PROTECTIVELY ON HIS THRONE, THE EAGLE SLASHES AT THEM, SHRIEKING.

SEEING AN OPENING, ROAN DIVES. THE HALF-RING QUIVERS AND ITS GLOW SURGES OVER ROAN, ENCASING HIS BODY FROM HEAD TO FOOT. BRISTLING HAIR SPROUTS FROM EVERY PORE. HIS ARMS SHORTEN. HIS JAW—HE'S TRANSFORMING INTO THE BADGER, JUST LIKE WHEN HE FOUGHT SAINT IN HELL. HOW CAN THIS HELP HIM NOW!

AS HE CRASHES INTO THE THRONE, DARIUS LURCHES BACKWARD. GRASPING THE OPPORTUNITY, ROAN SINKS HIS BADGER TEETH INTO THE EAGLE'S WING, THEN THRUSTS HIS POWERFUL JAW FROM SIDE TO SIDE, SNAPPING IT VIOLENTLY. DOZENS OF GHOSTLY SHAPES ESCAPE AS THE WING CRACKS AND TEARS, AND, FOR A MOMENT, THE EAGLE'S EYES DULL.

DARIUS PLUNGES HIS BEAK DEEP INTO THE THRONE'S SURFACE, DRINKING IN DOZENS OF AMORPHOUS FORMS. AS ROAN FIGHTS FURIOUSLY TO DISLODGE HIM, DARIUS, REVIVED, SLASHES, HIS CLAWS RAKING ONCE MORE INTO THE BADGER'S CHEST.

"DID YOU THINK SEEING A BADGER WOULD FRIGHTEN ME? HA! I SHOULD HAVE DONE THIS A CENTURY AGO!" HE SCREAMS IN TRIUMPH, AND WITH AN OPEN BEAK TAKES AIM AT ROAN'S JUGULAR.

THE BADGER TWISTS ITS MASSIVE FRONT LEGS AND THE TWO ENEMIES BEGIN TO SLIDE SLOWLY TOWARD THE THRONE'S EPICENTER. THE EAGLE CLAWS INTO THE THRONE BUT IT'S TOO LATE. THEY ARE BEING SUCKED ALONG A NARROW CHANNEL——ONE OF THE MANY VEINS ROAN SAW CRISSCROSSING THE DREAMFIELD—— AND CATAPULTED TO THE OVERSHADOWER.

AS ROAN AND THE EAGLE PLUMMET TOWARD THE DEMON'S PIT, A MINOTAUR'S POWERFUL ARMS SUDDENLY GRIP THE RAPTOR'S WINGS AND SPREAD THEM TO THE BREAKING POINT. ROAN CAN SEE THE TERROR IN DARIUS'S EYES AS PALE YELLOW FLAMES MELT INTO HIS GLOSSY FEATHERS.

OVER THE ARCHBISHOP'S SHRIEKS, THE BLIND GOD WHISPERS, "REMEMBER YOUR PROMISE."

"HOW——?"

"LOOK AT YOUR HAND, ROAN OF LONGLIGHT."

ROAN IS ABOUT TO PROTEST THAT HE HAS NO HANDS, WHEN HIS BADGER CLAWS TRANSFORM. IN AN INSTANT, HIS GREATGRANDFATHER'S DREAMFORM IS GONE. AND AS SOON AS HE IS HIMSELF AGAIN, HIS LEFT HAND BURSTS INTO FLAME.

"IT IS TIME FOR YOU TO FULFILL YOUR PROMISE."

AS IF FORGED FROM PURE FIRE, A BLADE BEGINS TO EMERGE. EMBEDDED IN THE FLESH OF HIS PALM, ITS CURVED CROSSING POINTS ARE THOSE OF HIS HOOK-SWORD.

"YOU KNEW YOU COULD NOT KILL A GOD WITH ANY ORDINARY BLADE." THE FRIEND'S VOICE IS GENTLE, ALMOST KIND, BUT AS THE OVERSHADOWER PULLS THEM EVER CLOSER, THE GOD BELLOWS, "CUT OFF MY HEAD, ROAN OF LONGLIGHT, CUT IT OFF NOW!"

ROAN REMEMBERS THE SACRIFICES DEMANDED BY THE FRIEND——THE LOSS OF HIS FAMILY, OF LONGLIGHT. HE ARCS BACK HIS ARM AND WITH ALL THE PENT-UP ANGER OF THE LAST

TWO YEARS, HE SWINGS. THE FRIEND'S HORNED HEAD TUMBLES STRAIGHT INTO THE OVERSHADOWER'S GAPING MOUTH. BUT THE GOD'S HOOVES SIMULTANEOUSLY TEAR DOWN THE FLESH-LIKE WALL OF THE DARK PIT, PINNING THE GREAT GULLET OF THE OVERSHADOWER OPEN. JAGGED CLAWS RISE UP AS THE MONSTER GAGS, CHOKING ON THE BULL'S HORNED HEAD. RIPPING FERO-CIOUSLY AT THE FRIEND'S HEADLESS TORSO, IT SNAPS BACK HIS ARMS, AND THE BLEEDING EAGLE IS RELEASED.

THE GREAT BIRD SQUAWKS AS IT STRUGGLES TO LATCH ONTO THE GRUESOME, GELATINOUS MASS COATING THE WALLS OF THE PIT. BUT AS SOON AS IT HAS HOLD, IT'S SURROUNDED BY THE THOUSANDS OF AMORPHOUS FORMS ACCUMULATING OVER THE OVERSHADOWER. THEY CURL AND SNAP AND CLUTCH AT THE DAMAGED, BLOODIED WINGS. FOR EVERY ONE THAT DARIUS BEATS AWAY, A HUNDRED MORE TAKE ITS PLACE.

THREE BIRDS OF PREY SCRAPE AND CLAW THEIR WAY ACROSS THE VISCOUS WALLS TO PERCH ABOVE THE KEEPER OF THE CITY. DARIUS TRIES TO MOVE AWAY BUT THEY FORM A TRIANGLE AROUND HIM, COOING, "YOU LEFT US TO DIE, CALLED US MAD, BUT WE KNEW. WE KNEW. WE'VE WAITED A LONG TIME FOR THIS, DARIUS. SEE HOW YOUR LIFE-FORCE DRAWS THEM. OH, YES. YOUR VICTIMS ARE VERY HUNGRY, ARCHBISHOP, VERY HUNGRY."

ALL ROAN HAS TO DO IS EXTEND HIS HAND. BUT HE DOES NOT. HE FORCES HIMSELF TO WATCH AS, STILL THRASHING AND SCREAMING, DARIUS, THE ELDEST, KEEPER OF THE CITY, ARCHBISHOP OF THE CONURBATION, THE GREAT SEER, IS EATEN ALIVE ONE TINY PIECE AT A TIME.

ROAN'S SO MESMERIZED THAT HE DOESN'T NOTICE HIS GRIP ON THE EDGE OF THE PIT SLIPPING UNTIL HE IS LASHED BY ONE OF THE OVERSHADOWER'S LONG CLAWS. TOSSED INTO THE CAVERNOUS MOUTH, HE STRADDLES THE DEAD GOD'S HORNS,

CUTTING ONE AFTER ANOTHER OF THE DEMON'S ENDLESS ARMS
UNTIL THERE ARE NO MORE.

BUT THE AIR CONTINUES TO BRISTLE WITH ANGUISH AS
VAPOROUS SHAPES SCREAM ALL AROUND HIM. DESPERATELY TRY-
ING TO CLAW THEIR WAY OUT, THEY ARE STILL BEING SUCKED
TOWARD THE BELLY OF THE BEAST BENEATH HIM. HOW?

"WHY AREN'T YOU DEAD?" ROAN CRIES OUT FURIOUSLY.
SLASHING OVER AND OVER AT THE MASS BENEATH HIS FEET, HE
WAILS, "WHAT DO I HAVE TO DO? WHAT?" BUT ALL HIS EFFORTS
ARE USELESS. HIS BODY QUIVERING WITH EXERTION, TEARS MIX
WITH THE GORE HE'S COVERED IN AS HE STARES HELPLESSLY AT
ALL THE LIVES STOLEN BY DARIUS ACCUMULATING AROUND HIM.
HOW CAN HE HELP THEM?

FEELING SOMETHING TUG AT HIS LEG, HE RAISES HIS ARM TO
STRIKE. BUT IT IS ONLY AN INFANT CHILD. ITS TINY LEGS WRAP
AROUND ONE OF ROAN'S AND IT LEANS FORWARD. IT PAUSES ONLY
A MOMENT BEFORE PLUNGING BOTH ITS CHUBBY ARMS TO THE
SHOULDER INTO ONE OF THE OVERSHADOWER'S ROLLING EYES.
SEEMINGLY WITHOUT EFFORT THE CHILD POPS THE EYE OUT.
DRAWING ITSELF BACK TO LEAN AGAINST ROAN'S LEG, IT SUCKS
OUT THE LIQUID UNTIL THERE IS NOTHING LEFT OF THE EYE BUT
A PALE SHEATH.

SLURPING THE FILMY REMAINS, THE CHILD SAYS INGENU-
OUSLY, "TO KILL IT YOU HAVE TO CONSUME ITS EYES. YOU SHOULD
EAT THE OTHER ONE."

ROAN STARES AT THE CHILD, PUZZLED. ITS FACE AND BODY
ARE YOUNG, BUT IT LOOKS AT HIM WITH EYES THAT ARE OLD,
VERY OLD. AS OLD AS AN ANCIENT GOD'S.

"FOREVER CHANGING, RESPONDING TO THE NEEDS OF A NEW
WORLD," THE CHILD SAYS WITH A MOURNFUL SMILE, CONFIRMING
ROAN'S SUSPICIONS. "THE OVERSHADOWER'S MEMORY IS IN ITS

EYES AND IT REMEMBERS EVERY SHADE IT HAS EVER SWALLOWED," THE FRIEND TELLS HIM. "YOU NEED TO KNOW WHO IT IS THAT YOU HAVE FOUGHT FOR."

LOOKING AT THE REMAINING EYE, ROAN HESITATES.

"DO YOU LEARN NOTHING FROM YOUR FRIENDS? IT IS NOT THE APPEARANCE OF A THING THAT MATTERS, BUT WHAT IT CONTAINS, WHAT LIES WITHIN."

ROAN THINKS OF LUMPY. HOW PEOPLE RUN FROM HIM WHEN THERE IS NOTHING TO FEAR. OF THE FIRST TERMITE JERKY HE MADE AND ATE AT HIS SIDE, HOW REPULSED HE'D BEEN, BUT HOW IT HAD NOURISHED HIM. HE REACHES DOWN DEEP INTO THE SOCKET AND PLUCKS THE EYE OUT.

THE MOMENT HE TOUCHES IT TO HIS LIPS, DREAMS AND NIGHTMARES FLOOD HIS CONSCIOUSNESS. EACH EXPERIENCE DEMANDING HIS ATTENTION, CALLING OUT TO BE HEARD. LIVES AT THE MOMENT THEY WERE LOST. ALONE, DESPERATE. AN INFANT TORN FROM ITS MOTHERS' ARMS. A FARMER CUT DOWN BY MARAUDERS. CHILDREN SCREAMING THEIR LAST BENEATH THE BLADES OF THE MASTER'S PHYSICIANS. ALL AT THE BRINK OF MADNESS FROM PAIN AND GRIEF AND TERROR. ROAN IS OVERCOME BY HELPLESSNESS, FUTILITY, BLINDING RAGE, AND SORROW. ENDLESS, ALL-CONSUMING SORROW. AND IT'S TOO LATE TO HELP ANY OF THEM. TOO LATE. FOR THESE ARE MEMORIES. THE MEMORIES OF A DYING DEMON.

THE PIT QUAKES VIOLENTLY. SHAKEN FROM ITS WALLS, THE VAPOROUS FORMS RISE AS THE SPIRACAL WHIPS APART AND THE GREAT PIT ONCE AGAIN LIES UNCOVERED.

THE MAD MASTERS SOAR, CIRCLING THE FALLEN CONSTRUCTION ONLY FOR A MOMENT BEFORE VANISHING INTO THE DISSOLVING FUMES. ANOTHER TREMOR REVERBERATES ALONG THE CHANNEL THAT FEEDS THE THRONE AND DARIUS'S FINAL CON-

STRUCTION EXPLODES IN A FLASH OF POISONOUS GREEN LIGHT.

Darius is dead, his Throne destroyed, and Roan's great-grandfather's dream realized. But Roan is reeling from exhaustion and anguish. So many. There were so many. Though he knows there was nothing he could have done earlier to change things, every moment he relaxed, every smile and careless laugh lurches into his mind.

Just as he feels himself collapsing, a brown speckled rat whispers at his side, "Take me in your hand."

Perching on the hook-sword embedded in Roan's palm, Rat blinks. And for a moment, Roan closes his eyes and sleeps.

When he wakes, he's at the Rift. The children are spread painfully across it, a massive nine-headed hydra hovering over them. Alandra—though he would never have known it if Mabatan hadn't told him. He can sense nothing of his friend in the beast, only a fierce devotion, a willingness to protect the children at all costs.

The people of Longlight are circled above the Rift, humming in unison, an ethereal, pulsating tone. Moving into the space between his mother and father, he looks down in horror at the bloodied blade extending out of his palm. But his mother reaches out, and together with his father, she places her hands over the blade. One by one the people of Longlight join them. They sing over the weapon that is his hand.

The dried blood on its surface becomes liquid once more and it falls into the abyss like tears. The rust breaks off the bodies of the Novakin and the Rift begins to move, one side joining the other until it closes completely.

Released, the children hug the hydra's many necks. "We promise we will find a way to bring you back." They smile, pointing to Roan. "With his help."

He feels their thanks, like a caress, touch him briefly and then they are gone.

The shades of Longlight take to the air and Roan follows through the orange sky. Below, the great desert that was once ruled by the Whorl is already changing color, bursting with life. Freed from its shadow, the Well of Oblivion's waters swirl hypnotically.

As the shades of Longlight descend one by one into its depths, he clutches his mother's small hand.

Her dark brown eyes smile knowingly into his. "We've long awaited this moment, Roan. Hoped beyond hope that it might come to pass. Now we must drink of these waters and forget, so that we may live again."

"I would like to forget, Mother."

"I know. But it is not your time. Not yet. It is for you to remember and to pass your memories on. That is the way of the living."

"But what do I tell Stowe? I still don't understand. Is that what you died for? Just to sing over my blade? What...What if...I hadn't?"

"We died for a hope, Roan. Tell her we died to bring hope to your future."

His father's embrace is not long enough. Could never be enough. "I am so proud of you," he whispers. He takes Roan firmly by the shoulders before he backs away. "Your life is your own, Son. Now you must live it."

As they turn hand in hand toward the waters of

THE WELL, ROAN FEELS HIS PARENTS' LOVE ENVELOP HIM FOR A MOMENT. AND THEN HE IS LEFT ALONE AS THEY SINK INTO OBLIVION'S GENTLE WAVES.

The last crescent of moon slices the sun, as across the City its shadow races from rooftop to rooftop, heralding the return of day.

Lumpy stands over Roan, his hand outstretched. "I knew I could depend on you," he says. But as he helps Roan up, he's not smiling. "Wolf and Stinger have secured the City. But we've lost twelve Apsara...Ende..."

Lumpy's eyes drift off to the east and Roan, following his gaze, sees the ghetto of the Absent. The total stillness. Hundreds, maybe thousands of people lying dead in the streets.

"Ende tried but they were hopelessly outnumbered...and then it was too late. It was..."

Roan wheels at the sound of an agonized moan. Stowe's kneeling over Willum, stroking his hair. She's covered in his blood. Moaning. Moaning.

Mabatan is standing over her, silent tears streaming down her face. "How is it, Roan of Longlight, that we have won our struggle only to end so lost?"

Just then, the apex of the Pyramid is flooded in the light of the newborn sun and they are all bathed in burnished gold.

κhutumι

DO NOT GRIEVE. ROAN OF LONGLIGHT HAS BEEN LIVING HIS
GREAT-GRANDFATHER'S STORY AND NOW HE MUST SEARCH
FOR A STORY OF HIS OWN. AND WHAT A TALE THAT WILL BE.
                    —LORE OF THE STORYTELLERS

ON A SEA-SWEPT ISLAND RICH WITH TOWERING FIR TREES
AND STONY CLIFFS, Roan stands before a mound of
rocks, a small, wiry man with pixyish eyes beside him.

Two weeks ago in the City, Roan had said his goodbyes.
The Council had been reconvened with the addition of
Master Querin, and a prophecy had been read: "Those who
were estranged shall be brought together. And though one of
the Shunned, the Lieutenant will stand in the Prophet's stead
and unite them."

Lumpy resisted, but everyone had been in agreement.
Roan's Lieutenant would become the new Keeper of the City.

The moment he was alone with Roan, though, the argu-
ments began. "But the City needs you, Roan. Everyone
wants—"

"Lumpy. Don't you believe in the prophecy?"

"Oh, no. You're not going to use that against me again."

"As a friend, then. Please."

Lumpy had followed his gaze into the deep double-cres-
cent welt that scarred most of Roan's hand and in the end,
he'd agreed …as long as a Council could be appointed to
govern with him. So Kamyar, Wolf, Xxisos, Stinger, Querin,

Gunther Number Six, Stowe, and Mabatan are, at least for the moment, united in their efforts to mend City and Farlands alike.

Kira, though, had been too devastated by her losses. Lumpy could think of no better way to help her than putting the Novakin in her care. Accompanied by a group of Apsara, she has left for Newlight, taking the sleeping Alandra to the children who will one day hopefully free them both. Isodel, the Governor's wife, had agreed to stand in Council until Kira is ready to return.

Roan shudders as he remembers the horror of trying to pry Stowe from Willum. The more he'd attempted to comfort her, though, the more distant she'd become. He'd wanted so much to be close, to mourn as a family the final passing of their parents and their newfound cousin, Willum. Roan knew how much Willum had meant to her. He wished she could have shared more of her pain...but perhaps that was untrue. Perhaps he'd welcomed her distance because he'd needed it as well. Perhaps that was the only way they would be able to heal.

After the final battle, he'd gone down into the City to walk through its streets. Over and around the numberless bodies. The smell of death in the square where the giant Apogee had been mounted was appalling. Rats darted amidst the corpses and flies...swarms of flies...

He wondered if the Dreamfield had been sealed soon enough for some of these people to find their place within it. It seemed a shallow hope. The loss was overwhelming, the senselessness of it...the stories of their lives crowded one after the other behind his eyes in an eternally changing kaleidoscope of despair until he could no longer remember who he was, what he had come for, why it had seemed so important.

"The Council is waiting. Decisions have to be made," Lumpy had said, putting his arm around Roan's shoulder. But Roan had refused to move. He was afraid to take a step. The future yawned before him empty, devoid of purpose. "Please, Roan."

Lumpy's face had been so full of sorrow, his eyes swollen, his voice swallowing back the pain.

Roan is aware of how selfish he seemed when he asked his friends and sister to let him go. It was the hardest thing he's ever done, deserting Lumpy and Mabatan and Stowe. But he needed to know the meaning of what had happened with the Friend and the Overshadower—what he had done, what he had felt, what he had become.

The journey over water to this island had been difficult, but paled beside what he'd been through. What he was going through now. Amongst the giant trees, lovingly preserved by the Wazya, he stood day after day, paralyzed at the grave of his great-grandfather, Roan of the Parting.

"Before he died, Roan told Aithuna his greatest hope was that one day you would stand in this spot, and offer him the prayer of Longlight. It was what he lived out his life for."

"I don't know. I don't know if I can."

"We have time," the Carrier of the Wazya had said lightly, much the way his daughter would, with no trace of disappointment.

And so Roan stood, one day folding into the next, wondering if he could find it in himself to forgive his great-grandfather's discovery of the Dirt and his trust of Darius and the destruction it had wrought. Each day, just as Roan found the thread, the possibility of forgiveness, it was snapped from him by a memory—his sister howling over Willum, or Mabatan's empty eyes, or the buzzing flies over the endless corpses, whose lives he knew better than his own.

Until one day, after he lost count of the days, the thread of forgiveness merged with the memories and he knew somehow that they were the same.

And lowering his head, Roan began the prayer of passing, striving to keep all of it alive in his heart.

That the love you bestowed might bear fruit
I stay behind.
That the spirit you shared be borne witness
I stay behind.
That your light burn bright in my heart
I stay behind.
I stay behind and imagine your flight.

Roan picks up a pebble and places it on one of the larger stones that mark his ancestor's grave. Then he breathes as if for the first time and inhales the fragrance of the giant firs.

Surrounded by a chorus of white crickets, he listens intently to their song. A song that, with Khutumi's help, Roan of Longlight hopes one day to understand.

acknowledgments

Thanks to Pamela Robertson, Barbara Pulling, Guillermo Verdecchia, Susan Madsen, Elina Levina, and Teri Snelgrove, for their wise words and support. Elizabeth Dancoes has been instrumental in the creation of this book, as she has with the entire Longlight Legacy. I am forever, and gratefully, in her debt.

about the author

Dennis Foon has written four other acclaimed novels for young adults: *Double or Nothing*, the award-winning *Skud*, and the first two books in *The Longlight Legacy*—*The Dirt Eaters* and *Freewalker*.

He has written over 20 stage plays that continue to be produced internationally in numerous languages and for which he has received the British Theatre Award, two Chalmers awards, and the International Arts for Young Audiences Award. He has received the Gemini Award, two WGC Top Ten Awards, and the Robert Wagner Award for his screenplays, which include *Little Criminals*, *White Lies*, *Torso*, and *Terry*.

Dennis lives with his family in Vancouver, BC.